TO THE
TENTH
GENERATION

ALSO BY RITA KASHNER

BED REST

TO THE TENTH GENERATION

RITA KASHNER

G. P. PUTNAM'S SONS

NEW YORK

Designed by Richard Oriolo

THE TEXT OF THIS BOOK IS SET IN ELECTRA

Library of Congress Cataloging in Publication Data

Kashner, Rita.
To the tenth generation.

I. Title.   II. Title: To the 10th generation.
PS3561.A6968T6   1984   813'.54   84-3267
ISBN 0-399-12996-0

Printed in the United States of America

ACKNOWLEDGMENTS

I am indebted to the YIVO Institute for Jewish Research and to the library of the Jewish Theological Seminary of America, whose unique resources and endlessly helpful staff members were invaluable. I sought information from the following people, whom I thank for sharing their expertise generously: in the United States, Stephen Cohen, Andrew Gilman, Elisabeth Kashner, Leonard Kashner, Gabriel Schonfeld; in Israel, Harriet Elazar, Alix and Chana Hadar, Sara Joffe, Dr. Pesach Schindler, and newsmen Ted Levite and Michael Huler. The hospitality and wisdom of Henya Kvashne during my stay in Israel were the *sine qua non* for all the rest. Yaakov Atsmon told me the story about Meshugenah Malkah.

Finally, the numbers that Anni and Chava bear on their arms, A50062 and A49488, were borne by two women who were murdered at Brzezinka, a part of Auschwitz. Their names were Elsa Jager and Stella Kunz. I hope that this book will be worthy of their memory.

for my parents,
Mildred and Ludwig Danziger,
with love

TO THE
TENTH
GENERATION

Dani. The name he was born with was Daniel Kovner, son of Dov, but he had that name for only seven days, until Rachael, his mother, snatched it from him on the day of his circumcision and replaced it with Daniel ben Rachael, meaning son of no man, meaning bastard.

When he was older he gave himself another name, Daniel ben Avraham, and that was the name he yielded to the Syrian who waylaid them in the darkness on October 18, 1973, and took them hostage, him and his men:

Daniel ben Avraham, age 22, serial number 2141053, Jew.

BOOK

ONE

You must plan on having at least three children: one for yourself, one for your husband, and one for the Jewish people.

FOLK SAYING

Tel Aviv, 1950

Everyone said that Rachaeli would never have declared him a bastard if it had not been for the pressures put upon her as a result of the mixup of her baby and another baby boy in Tel Aviv hospital, but that is not true. She had never intended for him to have a father. She'd decided that before he was conceived. *Mine*, she had said to herself when Yossi held up the obscene little sac, dangled it in the air before he flushed it away— deciding in that moment that she did not love him and that she was going to arrange for him to give her a baby.

They had been in his flat, the sunlight moving across their bodies in stripes as it filtered through the shutters. It caught his curls and played like a narrow moving spotlight over his face as he came down over her. It was the intensity in his face at these moments that had convinced her that he loved her. Looking at him then she would congratulate herself, He loves me. He would draw in a sharp breath and moan and she would triumph in silence as he came. He loves me.

But this time he stood by the bed and peeled off the rubber afterward, as they talked, and he said the thing that decided her. She lay with one arm bent behind her head, still feeling him on her skin and her mouth and, to hold him there, she said something provocative about an oboist they both knew, so instead of going into the bathroom as usual he stood there to answer her, absent-mindedly peeling off the rubber. If she had let him go, if he had walked silently into the bathroom and pulled the door almost shut behind him and come out a minute later as usual to flop back down beside her with his hands cold and still damp and the sound of the toilet roaring in the background, she might never have been provoked to have the bastard child.

But as it was, he stood striped with sunlight and held up the rubber by its rolled end, bouncing it a little and peering comically at it. "There's my son," he said and, grinning, ambled in to flush it away.

By the time he came back she had stopped loving him. The thought came flying with such force through her mind that she wasn't sure for a moment that she hadn't heard it or said it out loud herself—with such force that it left a vacuum behind it, cold and empty. Oh no, the thought said, not your son. Mine.

She had two sons already, by Dov Kovner, her husband, and they had decided that was enough. But now, with a mischief that for once matched Yossi's, she decided to have one for herself. Mine, she thought. And she thought only so far ahead as to how she would get it: she would tell them both, Dov and Yossi, that she was using a diaphragm, and then she would just wait for one of them to impregnate her. It doesn't matter which one fathers it, she figured then, but she was certain in her heart that it would be Yossi.

She thought only that far ahead, how to get it. And she thought with deep and gleeful satisfaction about having something, finally, to herself. The thought surprised a smile out of her and her smile unsettled Yossi because it came unbidden from some secret place in her and his being unsettled gave her, suddenly, a power. Being the one who smiled and owned the mystery that disturbed the other gave you power. After all, it was as easy as that. Even owning the idea of the fatherless child made her rich with power, needing nothing from him. As easy as that.

She turned the smile toward her spent lover and soothed him back to her, snaking a finger through his curls. If he had recognized it for the easy touch of ownership, if he had feared it and the unbidden smile, he might have spared himself and Dov. But ownership was no issue to Yossi and so he didn't recognize it in time.

She smiled and tightened the curl around her finger only a little, a sort of reminder to herself where to find this tool when she wanted it. Mine.

16

Kibbutz Degania, 1928

Everything on the kibbutz belonged to her and she, Rachaeli, was every-one's child. But except for some books and a toy tumbling clown on two sticks, nothing was really hers. Even her mother and father called all the children "my daughter," "my son." She called her parents Rivka and Avram.

When she was very little, she would make a stash of the things that pleased her—a toy, a green crayon, an undershirt that had her father's smell. They'd find the things under her pillow in the children's quarters or behind a chair in her parents' room. "She's a throwback," Rivka would laugh. "Rachaeli," she said once, "you remind me of Reb Meilech the Collector. Remember Reb Meilech, Avram?"

Startled out of his concentration, Avram turned absent blue eyes from his article on wheat strains to his wife and daughter. "Hm?"

"Reb Meilech. The Collector, how could you forget? Doesn't this one remind you of him?"

Now he smiled. "But Reb Meilech at least asked. Rachaeli appropri-ates."

"Who? What Meilech? Who are you talking about?" She was frantic with excitement; they were talking about her. "*Who?*"

He picked her up, swung her around onto the table, where she sat on his papers. "A man from our village in Poland, where we were born."

"Where my grandma and grandpa live?"

"Yes, from Plotsk. Reb Meilech was his name. He would come around—"

Rivka jumped up and stomped across the room, pushing out her stom-ach like a fat man's and swinging an imaginary bell sharply in an arc, back and forth in time to her words. "Give to the poor! Co-llecting for the poor! Co-llecting, co-llecting! Give to the poor!" She stopped, grinning at the two of them. "So we all gave, of course. Who didn't want to think of himself as rich enough to give to the poor? Besides, if you didn't go out to him with something, he'd come and bang on your door yelling, 'Nothing for the poor, missus? Nothing at all?'"

"What if you didn't have anything?"

"You hid! Or—once, *once*, my mother had nothing and she was so embarrassed, she grabbed my father's belt"—the grin split her face and she finished the sentence in spurts, between spasms of laughter—"and gave—it to him! Then she ran back—into the house, wailing, 'Gottenyu, Gottenyu, his only belt!'" Rivka was leaning against the door now, bent over and holding her stomach, whooping with laughter. "'How will he hold up his pants? His only belt!' And for months—what am I saying, *years*—my father went around hitching up his pants all the time." She lowered herself to the floor, laughing helplessly—it sounded like crying—and shaking her head. "Anyway," she said, sniffing and wiping tears off her cheeks, "that was Meilech. And you know what happened to all that stuff he collected for the poor? Tell her," she commanded.

"When he died," Avram told Rachaeli, "they went to clean out his place and it was crammed, loaded with everyone's donations. Everything anyone ever gave him. Where he sat, in that room, or how he lay down to sleep, I don't know, there was so much. Clothing, big shoes with holes, little shoes with holes, pans, cups, books—"

"Belts."

"—belts. Everything. You can't imagine. A treasure house of Plotskiana." He went to where Rivka sat on the floor and held his hands out to her. She reached for them and jumped up. His hands stayed on her. "So you think our Rachaeli is in training to be another Reb Meilech?"

She slid off the table, taking some of Avram's papers with her, and stamped loudly toward them so they couldn't talk, ringing the phantom bell too, like Rivka, and shouting "Co-llecting for the poor!" They took her into their circle that time, lifting their twined hands to let her in, letting down the gate, holding her between them and rocking her. That time they let her in.

And when they walked her back to the children's house at dusk she was still between them, swinging on their outstretched hands like her wooden acrobatic clown. But they let go of her hands to return her to Aviva, and they went off together. They never touched, of course, walking around the kibbutz, but Rivka was always telling Avram some story, pulling a face, stopping him in his tracks to make him look while she mimicked someone's gestures. And he was always bent over toward her, his blue eyes burning on her like stage lights. At solemn kibbutz occasions like the twentieth anniversary, when Rachaeli sat with her group of children, she would see Rivka, at one moment sitting proper and serious next to Avram and at the next leaning over with the light of mischief in her eyes to whisper something to him, and he would poke her with his elbow— *quiet. Be serious*—but he would bend toward her, caught. Lit. It was always like that between them. There was no room in it for anyone else. They didn't go around clasped, mooning, twined; no one did on the kibbutz. But they didn't have to be touching to be holding everyone out. You could be with them, but you couldn't get in.

Rachaeli always knew it. She was raised, of course, in the nursery with the other children of Degania. Maybe that accounts for the fact that she always knew: if she had spent her days immersed in their atmosphere like children in other kinds of homes, she might have been much older before the character of their relationship became clear to her, as other children are. But she didn't live in that room with them, she visited it late in the afternoons, and the scent and the heat of it assailed her senses fresh daily. Long before she knew how to put a name to it, she pictured in her mind that when she left their room, Avram and Rivka would fly together, tangled, laughing, an impenetrable unit. When they left her at the nursery in the evenings to go to dinner, when they walked away not touching, Rachaeli saw Avram bend to Rivka, saw her tease him in toward her. If the current between them had been etched in the air it couldn't have been clearer to the child.

Alas for Rachaeli, she simply assumed that all grownups loved and were loved like that.

She didn't want to wait to be a grownup; she wanted something to belong to her now, something to keep for herself as Rivka and Avram had each other. Everything on the kibbutz was hers, she knew that, but nothing belonged to her so that she could hide it away, for example, or break it if she wanted to. The things around her seemed lifeless, blurred, because anyone might use them at any time. She was always trying to possess something, and she was always being gently reprimanded for it. It was bad to be selfish; she knew it, but she couldn't seem to help it. She was just bad that way.

After a while she gave up her stashes. She didn't want everyone in the kibbutz to laugh at her the way Rivka laughed at Meilech the Collector, and anyway her stashes were always found and dispersed. Then she tried for a time to attract one child out of the group to be her special friend. "Do you like Dafna?" she would ask Tali, watching closely for an opening to pry Tali away from the others, closer to herself. "Do you really think Benjamin plays fair?" But she couldn't count on the bond to hold.

"Rachaeli thinks she owns you; she never wants to share you," someone would tell Tali, and that would be the end of it.

She acquired a secret once. It was about one of the teachers; she overheard him on the phone when she was supposed to be at swimming. She'd come in to find him, actually, to bring him a calendar she'd made for him. His name was Asher, and he was new. She wanted him to like her best, so she made things for him and did jobs for him. What she heard him saying on the phone was that he was leaving Degania. It wasn't working out.

She tiptoed as lightly as air out of the hallway and out of the building. She clamped her mouth shut so no sound would escape her. It was very important that he should never know she'd been coming to bring him a present. She hated him. She was running on the grass, breathing loudly, looking for someone to tell, and then she stopped. No one knew but her, she was the only one. She forgot about Asher and thought about the secret, beginning to smile. She could almost feel it in her head, a shining package. Hers. Absolutely only hers.

She meant to keep it, and for a couple of hours she did, but it was no good. No one knew she had it, and there was nothing she could do with it. Yes there was. She went over to Dafna. "I know something no one knows," she told her.

"Who cares?" Dafna retorted.

"You'll care if you hear it. Everyone will care."

"Yeah? What is it, then?"

"I don't know if I should tell you."

"Come on."

She waited.

"Come on, Rachaeli. Tell me."

"I should only tell one special friend."

"That's me."

"Better than anyone else?"

"Sure. Come on, tell."

She told, and for the rest of the day it was a sweet tie between them. They exchanged knowing smiles and notes, and twice at lunch they had fits of giggles until Aviva almost sent them out.

She came back to the children's house at dusk and didn't even watch Rivka and Avram leaving, because she wanted to find Dafna right away. She was the last one back and there was already a game forming up. Benjamin was game leader and he was picking two captains. Rachaeli came in just in time to hear Dafna wheedling Benjamin. "I'll tell you a secret," she offered. "A big one."

Rachaeli didn't even try to stop her. Let her tell it. Let her be anyone's best friend. She, Rachaeli, was never going to like Dafna again. Let Dafna be captain and let her team lose, let everyone make fun of her and let no one like her, ever again. Next time Rachaeli had a secret she would find someone a lot better to spend it on. A real special friend.

Nothing could be counted on to stay hers, only hers. Especially not Rivka. She was reminded of that every time Rivka came on one of her illegal visits to the children's house.

Rivka would sneak in when they were supposed to be resting in the afternoon or even after lights-out when Aviva was in looking after the infants. "Anybody awake?" she'd whisper stagily. "Anybody want to talk to a chicken?" Then she'd flap elbow wings and let out muted "puck-pucks" and twitch her head around to peck at her shoulder until they all slipped out of their beds and came to her. She had a whole repertoire of stories about a dim-witted chicken and her crafty eggs. "You'll never believe what I heard from the eggs today," she'd say and they'd all tumble out of their beds to listen.

Rachaeli would sit rigid with pleasure when her mother made one of her "chicken raids" on the children's quarters, even though Rivka, painfully fair, would choose all the other children before choosing Rachaeli to help act out the stories.

But then Rivka would leave, climbing out through the window ("You be good little eggs now. Back in your crates.") Rachaeli would trail her, waiting at the window, and Rivka would stick her head in the window and give her a kiss. But if other children demanded one, too, they'd get it and Rachaeli would be left feeling plundered. It was always like that: the fleeting pleasure of ownership gave way to the bewildering sense of loss.

The cello was different. It was really hers, all the time. She got it by pretending not to want it. There was a children's orchestra at Degania and in it there was one cello. When the music teacher, Chaim Josef, asked the children to try out the instruments and choose one to learn, Rachaeli watched carefully. A lot of children wanted the horns and the flutes, and there were three or four who wanted the violins, but no one spoke for the cello. "It's really very beautiful," Chaim Josef said, "and very important," but still no one raised a hand. "Oh, I'll take it," Rachaeli said then, carelessly. "It doesn't matter to me." She looked on as the others made squeaks, thin whistles, bleats on their violins and flutes and horns, but she didn't touch the bow, just sat with one hand on the cello, looking at the light gleaming on its belly.

It kept its secrets, the cello. You had to go in and find them. You couldn't just depress a lever or put your finger over a hole and come up with a note; every time you played you had to find the exact place the note was, hidden in the string, and pull it out. When you found the notes one after another, they hummed in the gleaming belly and in your legs and in the fingers of your left hand. When you moved the bow easy over the string, hard enough to pull out the note and make it sing, not so hard that it turned harsh, you teased out all its secrets and they hummed in you, too, all over you.

She was older then and she knew better than to hide it away or to claim it. "Won't someone else learn this stupid instrument?" she'd plead at rehearsals. "It's so *hard* and you never get to play the melody." So she was left alone with it and in time she had in one hand the hideouts of all the notes, their edges and their centers, and in the other the precise bowing that would make the strings yield up richness or thinness or any of the eerie qualities between. She was good enough that no one else even thought of learning the instrument. So it was hers. But she never took it to the living quarters to practice, although she could have. She played it in the music room and she left it there and never looked back.

Boys and girls lived together in Degania, in the children's quarters and even as older children and teenagers. Like their mothers and fathers they shared their tasks and all wore the same shorts and shirts and had, theoretically, open access to each other. As children they dressed and undressed and bathed together. But then the changes came and their bodies betrayed them to each other. It was imperative, suddenly, to hide to dress and undress; it became an event fraught with dangers and possibilities. The boldest of them giggled and shouted taunts and dares; the shyest were victimized. Rachaeli simply took cover. Boys and girls refused even to hold hands in line. They quarreled over everything. Later, in the silent darkness, Rachaeli cherished the insulting interchanges she'd had with the boys, turning them over for signs of desire: *he chose me.*

Eventually, though, the hysteria of their changing bodies burned out and they returned to an easy affection for each other. Boys dressed here, girls there; girls showered first, then boys, no big deal. They had lived together all their lives and they loved each other in the deprecatory way of siblings. They would have died for each other and some of them did, later. But they didn't pair off and they didn't touch each other. They didn't want to.

So when Rachaeli went into the army at eighteen and a boy singled her out, pursued her, arranged to be alone with her, she was at first hypnotized by his foreignness. She didn't know him; she had never known him, and it seemed impossible that she ever could encompass him. He seemed wondrous, like a creature of another species which had suddenly, magnetically pulled her up close to an impenetrable barrier and which cruelly urged her through it. Then he kissed her and held her up against him, and from the stirrings in her body she recognized what was possible between them. This was the way through the barrier. It was simple, and once through, they were going to be utterly known to each other. They'd be bound.

His name was Ezer. For several weeks he courted her intently, but now that she knew what was possible, she was cautious. She knew how it was supposed to be. You were supposed to be completely consumed by each other, bound only to each other, and then you were each other's to keep. So she was careful how she kissed him, holding back until she judged that he was serious about her. "I love you, Rachaeli," he gasped to her at last, and the rush went through her and she let the touching go a little further. Step by step she meted it out, watching.

But then one of the girls came up to her in the shower. "Did you and Ezer break up?" she asked. "I saw him with Miriam, so I figured . . ."

Rachaeli smiled at the girl and carefully rinsed off the rest of the soap. "You know how it is," she said. She dried off and dressed and walked out in the hot afternoon light. She found them leaning against a jeep. The girl had both hands in her hair, lifting it off her neck. Ezer wasn't touching her, but his eyes were caught in her hair. Rachaeli walked away, chilled in the sunlight. "You are dead," she told Ezer in her mind. "You died."

Then for a while there was no one. The army sent her to Tel Aviv to learn coding and she gave herself over, relieved, to the intricate task of uncovering the patterns that were the key to making the jumble of letters and numbers fall back into simple sense. Even better than that was the encoding—costuming a message in apparent chaos, hiding its secrets safely away but always knowing how to get them back out again.

She went home on leave, and she sat on the grass with Avram one evening before dinner, diagramming a letter code on a sheet of paper. "See this pair of letters here, that keeps reappearing?" she pointed out. "That's really the key. You—"

"Hello, Rachaeli! Hello, father of Rachaeli!"

It was one of the kids, walking back to the children's house with his parents. He'd been about five when she left. Must be six now. "Hello, David," she said. "Are you keeping Aviva running these days?" He giggled and pulled his parents away. "'Bye Rachaeli. 'Bye, father of Rachaeli."

She watched them go. "What's this 'father of Rachaeli' business?" she asked Avram.

"Something the kids have started saying. Everybody is father-of, mother-of."

"What if you have no kids?"

"They call you 'father-of-no-one.' What a thing to be called. Glad we've got you. Aren't you glad we've got her?" Rivka had come out and was standing squinting against the setting sun, a half-eaten apple in one hand and a book in the other.

Mother of everyone, Rachaeli thought, watching her. *And of no one.*

Avram got up to go to Rivka. Rachaeli watched them: there. There it still was. Rivka held up the apple and the book reverently in both hands. "Glad! Magnified and sanctified!" she said. She laid them at Rachaeli's feet. "Heir of all we possess," she intoned. She spotted the paper, took it, and held it up.

"What's this? Looks like Yehuda's idea of a budget."

"It's the key to the secrets of the universe," Rachaeli told her. "In code, of course."

"On one sheet of paper?" A new voice. She looked up. A man had come out of her parents' room. About twenty-one, twenty-two. Solid, tallish. Nice face. Wearing khakis but too pale to be a kibbutznik. "That I'd like to see. Airmail from God?"

She smiled.

"Hand delivered," Rivka put in. "A chubby little fellow in white. Said his name was Elijah." She held it out to him. "Unfortunately, it makes as much sense to me as His other messages in the last three thousand years or so. Maybe the pure of heart can read it."

He shook his head, smiling at Rachaeli. "I don't even want to look. The better a secret is, the closer it ought to be kept."

"Just like a banker," Rivka said. "Rachaeli, this is Dov Kovner. He's a banker. If you want, he'll lock your secret message up and keep it safe."

Rachaeli looked at him and was struck by the thought that he might do that, keep her secrets safe. The thought was electric in her face as she looked at him and she almost forgot to slide a smile over it.

She could have been wrong about it, of course. She'd been wrong before. But as it turned out later she was right; the one thing Dov Kovner was was safe. It wasn't his fault that she discovered thereafter that it wasn't safety she wanted but the fever of possession. It wasn't her fault either, really. She had no way then of knowing the distinction between owner-ship and possession.

That was later. They started out the way people do, carefully and hopefully. He was in fact a banker, a specialist in land development and agrarian loans, and he was visiting Degania for the purpose of considering their application for a loan. The kibbutz was expanding. Avram's new strain of wheat had taken wonderfully and there were plans for several additional vegetable crops and a new dairying enterprise. Dov spent two working days and Shabbat at Degania, evaluating the land proposals and Rachaeli.

She was tall and rangy like her father, and very pretty. She had blue eyes like Avram's, startling with her amber coloring, and black hair that she wore in braids when she was in uniform and when she swam. When she came out of the water, she'd undo the braids and shake out her hair and it would curl around her face with the water still glinting in the curls. She showed none of her mother's mischievous humor, but she had her own wry insights. The father, Avram, was serious and intense and the same intensity seemed to charge Rachaeli at times. For example, on the third day Dov was there she described the work she was doing.

"Look, the message is there, clear and complete, only it's hidden," she said. "You spot a pattern—or you think you do—and you try it out, and then sometimes it just all falls into place and you've got it. They've got all these new combination codes now, one linked to the next, two used in alternation—but eventually you find a way in. That's a great moment, when you've got the key and you haven't used it yet; you know in a moment it will all become clear but—well, after all, what's in the messages? Times, locations, types and amounts of armaments, names. That part's rather dull. The exciting part is before you decode it, just knowing it's all going to be yours whenever you want it to."

He looked into her blue eyes and he did that fatal thing that lovers sometimes do when emerging desire has pushed them, cruelly, beyond their actual limits. He became what he was not, romantic and seductive and poetic, deceiving her and ensnaring himself, creating a Dov he had no desire, no intention, and no ability to be. He brushed her cheek with gentle, slow knuckles and said very softly, "That's how I feel now. *The world was all before them, Where to choose . . .*"

So there it was; he was quoting Milton to her. She let it begin. She knew where and when he had been born and what he did, and that he could be brought to love her. And that he would be safely hers. He knew her parents, her dates and places, and that she listened intently to what he said. The rest they filled in with touching, kissing, and sighs.

But the touching, kissing, and sighs held messages they didn't know how to decode. They were nineteen and twenty-two. Everyone is driven by a certain amount of desire and curiosity at those ages. Few wait to see whether the condition will last, or whether they will want it to. Rachaeli and Dov didn't.

For Dov it was a matter of ripeness. He was ready, and Rachaeli simply happened to him. He wasn't ambitious in matters of emotion, and so when she appeared to respond to his initial approaches and then even to cling to him, he accepted her with pleasure as his fate.

And Rachaeli couldn't wait to complete the transaction. On another leave later that spring, in his room in Tel Aviv, she lay long and silky on his bed wearing only her khaki shorts while he reverently touched her nipples. Suddenly he buried his face in her neck. "I love you, Rachaeli," he said in a muffled voice. She waited. He drew in a long, ragged breath. "I want you to be the mother of my children," he whispered.

There.

She unzipped the shorts herself, spending it all, all at once. She was burning for him, he saw it in her blazing eyes. He hesitated, touching her but not moving to take her. She didn't take her eyes off him. "Now," she breathed. He obeyed.

Virgins are supposed to be slow. The first time is supposed to be painful and awkward, requiring lengthy preparation beforehand and loving reassurances afterward that the next time will be better. They both knew that. It was army gospel.

Rachaeli was clearly a virgin, but she was not slow. She was ready for him. The flight up from her groin through the center of her had begun before he touched her, increasing its surges unbearably when he said it— *I want you to be the mother of my children. I want you*—so that when she felt him probe the outside of her and she arched herself upward a little to meet him, she was already very wet and driven mad by the extraneous things he was doing with his hands to make her ready. He was careful and slow, moving in her, but she was beyond caring and she came fast and hard, arching up farther and crying out in wordless triumph as she tore him along with her. *Here, take it, take it. Now it's all connected forever.* She did cry then, finding him through prisms of tears and seeing fleetingly on his face not the match to her consuming fire but confusion, wariness, and—was it, for an instant, resentment?

But afterward she turned on her side to sleep and, nearly unconscious, felt him wrapping himself around her so that he surrounded her from behind, big and warm and dry. "You have the right name," she murmured. "Dov. My bear—Doobie." *Mine.* So there it was.

Why didn't she make sure of it then, after seeing that wary look fly across his face, make sure that he would burn for her?

Because it never occurred to her that he wouldn't.

It never occurred to her that he wouldn't. He was twenty-two and when she saw him on weekends he was always ready to make love, and she was nineteen and she thought that meant he burned for her. She thought her own constant state of desire meant that she burned for him.

In addition, they encountered just the right degree of opposition to the match. His parents wrote from Bialystok that they knew of Avram's family and that they blessed this match with the great-granddaughter of Reb Chaim Klein of blessed memory. But when Rachaeli went to Degania to tell Avram and Rivka, the reaction was different. They looked at each other for a long, consulting moment, then Avram said carefully, "I wonder if it's such a good idea. Not that he isn't a good man, he seems fine and I'm sure he cares for you, but—well, there's background to consider."

"Background?"

"His experience, you know, has been very different. Look, he lived in a city all his life, all he knows is banking. How will he adjust?"

"To what?"

"To this life." He raised a single hand toward the fields in explanation. "You were raised in it, but for someone without the discipline, it's—"

"Why would he have to adjust to this?"

"It's your life."

"It was my life. Avram, we won't be living at Degania."

Rivka shot a glance at Avram: *Let me.* "Well, not at Degania necessarily," she said. "We understand you might want a little independence. Kibbutz Merhavia is growing, or Ben-Shemen. Although here you have—"

"We don't want the kibbutz at all. We're going to live in Tel Aviv."

They went through all the objections and responses of parents and children from the beginning of time: You're young, you don't understand how the differences in background will . . . *But you were the same ages.* But things were different then. It's okay for you, but how about the children? What kind of life is the city for a child? *You think this was the ideal life for a child?* And so on.

It was very satisfying. In one stroke she escaped the kibbutz, defied her parents—all her parents, because eventually Aviva and a number of other members of the older generation of Degania joined in the discussion—and convinced herself that she was doing it for love. Besides, she thought, no child of mine will grow up in a herd. And anyway, she thought, you have each other.

In a society of rebels rebellion is sacrosanct, and so in the end there was nothing they could say. At the end of Shabbat, Avram and Rivka walked her to the road and said goodbye. She watched them walk away, not touching, and between them she conjured the luminous line that bound them. *And anyway, you have each other.* It will be like that for us, she thought.

But it wasn't. They married and found two rooms in Tel Aviv and when Rachaeli looked around those rooms everything she saw was hers. Dov was unquestionably hers. If he didn't fall upon her, burning, he certainly turned to her in their bed at night, and when they slept she was surrounded by him and his warm, dry hand was always cupped over her where her own hand used to be. She was always touching him when they were out, leaning toward him so that he would put a hand on her. *Mine.*

So she didn't understand her own disappointment. She didn't understand, when he reached for her at night, why she was responding so dully. He was still twenty-two, she was still nineteen, and desire charged his healthy body very regularly. But he had chosen her once, and it was done, for him: Chosen. Taken. Good. She waited for him to bury his face in her shoulder again, gasping for love. She waited for the Dov who had once searched hungrily in her face to reappear and to choose her, again and again. She waited for him to shudder, moan in her arms, giving flight to the desire in her. Instead he loved her steadily and kindly and at night he made decent and considerate love to her. She felt nothing.

She dusted the furniture and she cooked meals and hung curtains and she made routine love with him and became his friend. It's like in Degania, she thought. It's like having another brother. We live together, so where's the big excitement?

If his initial flight of passion hadn't deceived them both, if he'd had the same ambition she did for emotional intensity, he might have attempted the lifelong balancing and juggling act that is married love, shifting with her, pulling her in, tossing her just far enough to let her fly, clasping her back, and so on. He might have kept them both burning. But nothing short of that, short of the heat of possession that she had seen charging the air between Avram and Rivka, could have kept her passion alive for him. And he fell far short of that.

Still she was fond of him. She held him in the night when he learned his parents had been deported from the Bialystok ghetto. She sat up and watched him sleep, monitoring him for signs of nightmare and waking him when he thrashed and cried out, shushing him and holding him and tactfully offering her body to soothe him. And when the letter came from his cousins in Warsaw that they'd had word his parents had died in Treblinka, she wept with him and sat *shiva* with him although it was as strange a ritual to her as if it were Hindu.

That was in 1943, in December. He was twenty-four. She was almost twenty-one, and watching him grieve for his mother and father she decided to have a baby.

Nothing had ever been like carrying that child. The simple knowledge that it was inside her, alive and entirely joined to her, brought her constant pleasure. She would feel it move and she would smile, knowing that no one in the world felt it but her. It was the best kind of secret.

The baby was born just before Rosh Hashanah in 1944. Dov's father's name had been Hirsh Leib. Hirsh is Yiddish for "deer." In Hebrew, deer is Zvi, so the baby was named Zvi for Reb Hirsh Leib, his grandfather. "Be gentle, Doobie, with this little deer," she said when she put the baby into his hands for the first time, fifteen minutes after his birth. Flushed with euphoria and the exhaustion of her senses, she was unprepared for what happened. Dov cradled the baby in his arm, instantly expert, and smiled at him, radiant. Lit. Tears ran from his eyes. He blinked them away, still smiling. "Thank you," he whispered.

As if she had made him a gift of the baby.

That was not her intention.

It didn't matter what her intention might have been. Dov appropriated the baby. Here, it turned out, was his talent for passion. He was the lover—absorbed, inventive, versatile. From moment to moment he was what the boy needed him to be—silly, tender, funny, boisterous, all of it. He wooed the boy and the boy did what the beloved does, basked, stretched, and grew in his love.

Plundered, she did her best. She was used to sharing after all, and she knew how to behave with community property. She took the baby to Degania for visits and everyone said what an easygoing, fair-minded mother she was. She was easygoing. She left him with Aviva in the nursery and she went her way like the kibbutz mothers. She visited him at nursing time, nursed him efficiently and changed his diapers, patted his bottom and walked out, just like the others. Better than some of the others.

Where she went then was to the music room. She carried the cello over to a corner of the room and she played for hours, always replacing it in its regular spot and walking away without a glance when it was time for her to go.

She wasn't at Degania when Avram was killed. She was asleep in Tel Aviv, not in Dov's arms but over on her side of the bed. She was pregnant again and she had told Dov she couldn't lie still enough to sleep wrapped up in him. That didn't explain why she turned her back to him to sleep, but he didn't question it.

Avram died just at dawn on a Wednesday morning in April 1947. He was on patrol, the tensions in the country on the eve of partition having caused the kibbutz to triple its night guard. The Syrians came down from the area of Tell al-Kasr, a marauding band. They must have started the fire in the wheat field before Avram spotted them, because his shouts for firefighters were the last words anyone heard from him. When they got there, they found two Syrians shot to death, apparently at his hands. He was lying at the edge of the field, horribly cut, his blood draining uselessly into the steaming soil. The Arabs killed fifteen and burned the field and a barn before they were routed.

A small group of men and women went to tell Rivka and to stay with her. Another group prepared the bodies and dug the graves. In a group, Degania buried its dead and grieved for them. But Rivka moved through the days alone. She tolerated her comrades, she sat with Rachaeli, their hands touching when one of them cried. She even went to the children's house toward the end of the week. She thought, she said, that she might be able to do something for the orphans. But she found them going matter-of-factly about their routines, in Aviva's care by day and with various kibbutz parents at children's visiting hour. "Lucky kids, they have fifty fathers each," she said to Rachaeli. *And I have no one*, she didn't say, but Rachaeli heard it and knew it was true. That was the risk, she thought, of being fired by someone's flame. When he was gone you froze. Rivka was freezing, like one cast into space. Rachaeli held her and she smiled and squeezed back, although both of them knew it was of no interest to Rivka who was with her.

The war began officially in May. The Syrians swarmed toward Degania in waves, tanks and artillery and planes. Dov was sent to Jerusalem and for weeks Rachaeli was cut off in Tel Aviv, uncertain from day to day who was alive. It seemed to her that suddenly she was alone in clamorous exile, with one child who was not hers and another she was holding in her belly in safekeeping for its owner. The baby was born with no one around, neither Rivka nor Dov. She named him Avram, but she couldn't call him by that name and so she called him Avi.

When Dov came home she handed the baby right over to him. Dov was silent and drawn, shaking his head when she asked him about the fighting, but with the children he was his old self. Within two weeks he had established natural ownership. Like a man with two mistresses he juggled both boys, dipping, bending, swerving to catch them where they were and set them flying again. She watched and smiled and kept them fed and clean and gave what she could. Privacy, for example—she taught them to be alone and to cherish their moments of solitude. And things of their own, toys and clothes and books. Dov wanted them to love each other and insisted that they share, but Rachaeli was fierce about this one thing. "That's his! You have no right!" she shouted in a sudden rage one night when Dov picked up one of Zvi's toy trucks to amuse Avi.

"What are you so excited about? Zvi doesn't care, do you, big deer?" The boy watched them both, shifting his eyes from one to the other in silence.

"Don't make him say he doesn't care! He does! He had them all arranged—look—and you just grab one. You don't even ask." There had been five trucks in a row against the wall. Now the other four were scattered.

"I won't make him say anything." He swung the boy off his feet and stood him on the table so they were eye to eye. "Not one word," he commanded as Zvi began to giggle. "Silence from the big deer on the subject of the truck. Right? Silence. Right." With exaggerated care he picked up the little truck, holding it out in two fingers. The boys watched him, giggling, as he meticulously lined the five trucks up, readjusting their positions and checking for minute differences in spacing. "All right, big deer? Good?" He scooped the boy up on his shoulders and bounced him down on the chair where his brother sat. In a moment they were all absorbed in a story.

There was no winning, so she eased gradually out of the game. It was easier for her, after all, that way. The boys played together without too much scrapping and when Dov came home they turned to him and he to them and so she was free. When Zvi was nearly six and Avi three she hired a babysitter and went to work half days for the army's newly official intelligence unit, back in the coding section.

And she bought a cello, secondhand. She allowed herself half of her salary, and she saved it without saying a word until, after many months, she had enough money. She left work early one day and picked it up, walking all the way home with it. She had timed it so that no one would be in the house when she brought it home; Zvi was at school, Avi had gone out with the babysitter to pick him up. She locked the front door and pulled a chair into the bedroom and she sat down, trembling, and began to play. It had been so long, and she was stiff and awkward. The notes yielded grudgingly, giving up only their flattest voices. She had forgotten.

So she went back to the scales. She probed for the notes, rejoicing even at their thin succession. She played a humble and cagey game, expecting nothing and waiting. By the time she heard the children at the door she had found the notes again and was teasing out an old baby sonata.

The knob turned, then turned again, rattled; they assaulted the door with kicks and cries. She laid a lover's hand on the cello—*later*—and went slowly to the door.

"You *locked* it? Why did you lock it? Why are you home? Is Daddy home?"

"I did it without thinking," she lied. "No, Daddy's at work. Come, you'll have a glass of juice, you're red as poppies." When they were occupied with their juice she slipped away unnoticed to close the bedroom door.

But she knew she couldn't keep it closed. She thought of her old cello at Degania and when Dov came home she pulled him in to see her purchase. "This one is not an especially good instrument," she said, "and it's harder to play than I'd remembered. But why don't you learn to play it, too? We can both enjoy it. You'd like it."

"Me? Maybe someday. How about the men, though? What do you say, Zvi, Avi? Want to learn to play this thing?"

For a moment she almost gave herself away, but she pulled a look of calm over her fury just in time and played her old game, the Degania game. "Sure, I wish you would," she told the boys. "It's not such a sissy instrument. It would be good for you to learn to play. Your friends will still be around when you finish practicing in the afternoons. What do you say? I know a nice old lady who can teach you."

That worked, of course. Avi made a face at the cello. "Not me," he declared. "I'm going to play the drums." And he ducked out of the room, beating a quick rhythm on the door with the flats of his hands as he passed through it. Zvi looked apologetically at Rachaeli. "Maybe someday," he said softly. She smiled forgivingly at him. Safe.

It wasn't true, what she had said about the nice old lady. She didn't know a teacher. She went back to the beginning, through all her old exercises, not allowing herself to move on until she had mastered them again. She invoked the voice of Chaim Josef: "Position, Rachaeli, watch the elbow! Long bow, *long* bow on that measure—" and worked herself more sternly than Chaim Josef would ever have done.

It was in fact a lovely instrument, rewarding her as a woman does a man, gradually opening up and granting her its resonances and the several voices of each of its notes. It was to the cello that she came home each day.

She talked Dov into going to a concert one evening that August, a chamber group—members of the Israel Philharmonic playing Mozart and Vivaldi. Dov settled in equably to listen, fixing his attention primarily on the first violin, nodding in satisfaction at the bravura passages. Rachaeli nodded in agreement with him when he poked her, but she had heard the violin only peripherally. She was watching the cellist, a slender man whose black curly hair bounced as he dove into the allegro and who seemed, by the expressions that chased across his face, to be telling himself a story as he played.

She wasn't thinking of him as a man but as a cellist, and so it was easy for her to do what she did after the performance. She waited for the indecisive moment that follows the applause, when the audience is turning to go and the performers haven't moved, and she went forward to the stage apron. "You were marvelous," she said. He didn't look up. She felt Dov frowning at the back of her neck. She raised her voice. "You played beautifully," she said to the cellist.

This time he saw her. He smiled. "What a kindness," he said. "No one ever hears the poor cello, much less talks to him."

"I heard nothing else. You—your fingers fly, and you catch the notes at such dangerous places."

He leaned forward, frowning past the stage lights. "What did you say? Dangerous places? What do you mean?"

"I mean—I always think of the notes as having safe, soft landing places in the middle, bordered by dangerous edges. If you go too far toward the edge, you've crossed over. But the edges are more telling than the centers sometimes." Her face was burning, Dov was changing position uneasily behind her, but she went on. "And you—I mean, you seemed to be using all the edges, in the Mozart."

He let himself down off the stage. "Mozart wrote for the edges. You play." It wasn't a question.

"Badly. Never like you. But—"

"I'm Yossi Levisohn." He held out a hand.

"Rachael Kovner. This is my husband, Dov Kovner." She leaned back placatingly toward Dov. He put an arm around her waist.

"Great performance," he said. *Let's go*, she heard.

"Your wife really hears. That's very rare."

Dov gave in. "She's a cellist, too. She plays constantly." He smiled fondly at her. "We think she's very good."

She felt somehow that she'd been disposed of. She looked soberly at Yossi Levisohn. "I'm no cellist," she said. "Just trying to learn. A student without a teacher."

"Why without a teacher?"

"She doesn't need one. On her own, she—"

"Because I don't know one."

"You would like to have a teacher?"

"Yes."

He took her program and scribbled on it. "My number. Come and let me hear you, we'll find you someone."

She called him the next day and the day after that she brought the cello to the office and walked to his flat with it after work. She located the flat by the sounds of his practicing, and she stood at the door, waiting until he'd finished a passage. Then she knocked.

He was wearing shorts and an army shirt. He smiled, a quick, open smile, and took the cello from her. He lifted it out of its case, looked it over, played two scales on it, and nodded. "Nice," he said. She stood looking at her cello in his hands.

"It's secondhand," she said, "and I wish it weren't. I keep thinking that someone else's playing hangs over it—you know, like cigarette smoke in your bedroom after a party—and I keep trying to exorcise it with mine. In fact, I dread for anyone to touch it." He snatched his hands away from it, raising them in mock apology. She shook her head. "No, but you I don't mind. You can only bring something to it."

"For a non-cellist you're pretty religious about your cello."

"You ought to understand."

"I do."

He did. She told him about the cello in the children's orchestra at Degania and the way she had maneuvered to take it over. She even told him about what she had said to Dov and the children to keep them away from this one. She leaned forward and told him that in complicity, smiling her wry smile. She felt there were no consequences in this room.

He nodded in quick understanding, the joke reflected in his dark eyes. "Give me a woman for strategy every time," he said, admiring, approving. "So how's your technique? Your other technique, I mean. Let's hear."

"I'm slow. I mean, I can play a little, but the fast parts—I'm just not nimble . . ."

"You scheme, deceive, deprive innocent kids to get to play and now you're apologizing? Play."

She played, a little Boccherini minuet. He stopped her once to correct the bowing in a measure. She copied his bowing, looking up at him. He winked: Good.

"You want to be a cellist? Professional?" he asked when she'd finished.

"Of course not; I know my limits. Just to play better than I do."

"Good. I'm relieved. I'd hate to have had to strangle you. You notice we're alone here; I arranged that purposely. God forbid if you turned out to be a Casals in embryo, I'd have had to eliminate you. This is a small country. No room for more than one great cellist. You scared me to death, you know, saying what you did about notes and their dangerous edges. I thought, Who knows what kind of blasted genius is going to walk into my room? Is she too tall to garrote with an A string?"

They laughed. "So, shall I teach you to be mediocre? I warn you, that's as far as I'll go."

"You? But you're not—you said you'd find someone—I never—"

"Me. I myself and not a seraph. An old system for making sure the ranks remember who's on top."

They arranged it: a lesson once a week, there in his flat on Thursday afternoons after work. She went home smiling.

He was by no means an ideal teacher. His only standard was his own playing, and he became impatient when she couldn't catch his technique as soon as he tossed it at her. He would raise his voice in exasperation, then back off, contrite, and tell her a funny story about himself or one of his musician friends by way of apology.

She never asked any questions but she absorbed it all and saved the pieces, fitting them in as she walked home. Born in France, 1916. That made him seven years older than she, thirty-four to her twenty-seven. Emigrated to Palestine with his parents in 1919. Studied at Juilliard in New York from '38 to '43. Parents alive, living in Haifa. No pleasure in his voice when he mentioned them. Lived alone, no woman in his flat, but out there, somewhere in his life, a number of them. One who danced. One with rich parents. One—a newcomer to the music world in Tel Aviv—who'd survived the concentration camps, a clarinetist. He traveled with the Philharmonic: America last year, Europe next spring.

She thought mostly about the women as she walked home in the late summer afternoons with her cello, fitting in the pieces. She thought there was a softening of his voice when he mentioned the clarinetist. She thought he mentioned her rather often. She could have asked about her but he told her all he did, she thought, because she listened with friendly indifference. If she seemed to want anything from him, of him, he might close up. And anyway she didn't have to ask. She was an expert decoder.

It was easy to seem light with him because he was funny. Nothing, not even music, seemed to evoke any reverence in him. "At that first concert your face went through so many changes as you played that I thought you were telling yourself a story," she said to him once.

"Not myself, my fingers. I was promising them wonderful things if they'd only get me through that allegro. Silk gloves, lush women, champagne to dabble in. Then we were negotiating because they tried to hold me up for things I couldn't think of allowing them." He grinned at her blush. "Shame on you! Bartok, I meant. Ives. Decadences like that."

Playing it light, she laid snares for his attention. He was fascinated by the idea of codes and she fed him little anecdotes from her work, making her world seem rich and intricate. She alluded to her childhood on the kibbutz, with seeming reluctance surrendering to him a picture of herself as a special child with mysterious yearnings beyond those of the others. She smiled, indicating that perhaps she was finding fulfillment of those yearnings now. As she laid out the puzzle for him, she wasn't sure how much of the image was accurate, how much she was creating. It didn't matter.

And she didn't think, directly, what she wanted of him, except that sometimes there appeared in her mind a picture of him, not grinning and irreverent but suddenly intense and surprised by his own intensity.

When she dragged Dov to another concert—this time of the full Philharmonic—and spent half the evening searching the faces of the three female clarinetists, weighing one against another, monitoring their stray glances and his for collusion, hating all three of them, she understood for the first time what she wanted. They were playing the Brahms double concerto and to its manipulative sweet tensions she closed her eyes and conjured up her picture of his sudden intensity. Now she knew what she wanted next and she conjured that up, too: saw him open his hands to cup her face, caused him to whisper, "You," and to close over her, gasping for air and for her. She saw herself pull away, search his face, read there what she needed to know and then open to him, playing richly for him, playing him. Wet and educated in the concert hall she opened her eyes and looked again at the three clarinetists, canceling them out and making her plan.

It would have been easy if she only wanted him to make love to her, or if she were willing to make the first move. But what she needed was his total surrender, and that it should appear to him to be his conquest.

It took her six weeks, and then it wasn't on her terms that it began. There was a *hamsim* the day of her lesson and the heat rode her, condensed her, she arrived dazed and enervated at his flat. "Look at you," he said. "Why did you come? Who can play on such a day? The cellos are swollen and cranky. *I* am swollen and cranky."

She pushed both hands into her hair, held it off her neck, stood there all yielding angles. "Take me to the beach," she said, as though spontaneously. "Let's go immerse ourselves, see if it's any cooler that way." This hour of the week is our time, her message ran. If we don't spend it one way we can spend it another.

He got it. They stood waist-high in the water, her skirt ebbing and flowing with the easy waves. She wet her arms and neck, leaving them glistening. "All right, it's been in the air between us for weeks," he said. "Shall we go ahead?"

That wasn't what she'd intended. She didn't want him to yield cheerfully. She wanted him wrenched. She'd pictured him seizing her roughly, overcoming her in desperation, making fierce love to her and never saying I love you until then, until it was torn from him in bed.

She could have waited it out, using silence, hesitation, and vulnerability to force his hand. Instead she took what seemed to her then to be the first adult action of her life. She looked over at him, directly into his eyes, and said, "Yes. Let's go ahead."

So there was no question of a conquest. Still, at the moment he entered her in the unrelenting heat of the afternoon, their wet clothes a tangle on the floor of his room—at that moment a look of intensity, almost of pain, seized his face and he kissed her desperately, moaning in his throat. He didn't say anything at all. It was almost better that way.

So now she had two men, one to hide away and one to break. She did keep Yossi hidden, too. She left him every week without a backward glance, letting on to no one that he was in her life. She saw him only in his flat, or on social occasions when she and Dov went to his parties or he came, occasionally, to theirs. There were no letters, no gifts, not even any more walks on the beach. Those were her terms.

Yossi accepted them easily, so easily that she was glad she had set them first. Her original feeling that there were no consequences in that room turned out, bitterly, to be right. Although he would tear at her skin with his mouth as though starving for the taste of her, although he would gasp at her touch and moan when he slid into her and again when he came, when it was over he surfaced untouched, brisk and funny and impersonal. He let her go with friendly ease. And when she arrived the next time, instead of intensity and longing, he would greet her with a joke and a light kiss.

That was why she didn't break Dov. She could see that she was going to need him.

She wasn't even sure that Yossi didn't have other lovers. He rehearsed or practiced every day, and she saw him in the late afternoons, dropping by unannounced after work a couple of times a week. He was always there, working, and he acted as though she had every right to come to him when she could. But there were the nights, many of them without performances. And worse, what about the nights when there were performances? She imagined him coming out of the hall, a light sweat frosting his curls, the fever of the music still in his body, his fingers and legs alive with buzz and tremolo. She imagined the clarinetist walking beside him, her mouth still tingling Schubert, both of them exuberant, pitched high. She saw them walk into his flat, close the door, saw his legs send the buzz and tremolo through hers, saw his mouth take Schubert, tingling, from the mouth of the clarinetist. She lay on her side of the bed after Dov was asleep and tortured herself, crying soundlessly as she imagined Yossi holding the clarinetist tenderly afterward, running a shaking hand over her hair or tracing with one gentle finger the blue number on her arm, not brisk and distant, but overcome, consumed.

Finally, although her strategy had been to meet his lightness with independence and to ask nothing of him, she was driven to find out. She was brutal with herself, waiting to ask until after they had made love, when he would be least inclined to woo her with lies. He was wiping his damp hands on the sheet, about to reach for a cigarette. "You once told me about someone in the orchestra," she said. "A flutist, I think. A survivor of the camps? How's she doing?"

"Elana? Clarinet, not flute. She's doing fine. About to marry into percussion. A great match, can't you see it?" He caught her eye: *Watch this*. He curled his wrists dramatically outward on the sheet in imitation of a woman's grace, tilting his head back and fluttering his eyelids closed. He writhed slowly in the bed, breathing the nasal song of a clarinet behind his teeth, an exaggerated female sigh of love. Rachaeli giggled. He sat up abruptly, motioning for silence, one finger up: *Wait*. Then he pounced on the bed on his elbows and knees, straddling an imaginary woman. "Ba-bam," he expelled the sound slowly, thrusting in time to it with his pelvis. "Bam—ba ba *bam*, bam—ba ba *bam*." Rachaeli laughed delightedly, watching. He cast her one stern look then flopped back over, fluttering his eyelids, lifting his knees and writhing upward, all the while whining a heated clarinet crescendo. On his knees again, head and shoulders and pelvis thrusting madly—"Bam ba-bam, ba-bam BAM," and again on his back, the spent female, a long descending thin note of exhaustion. Rachaeli echoed the note with a cry of helpless laughter, tears chasing down her face. He opened one eye and looked at her. "They'll undoubtedly give birth to a jazz quintet," he said. "I like to make you laugh."

"And all your other women? Do they laugh, too?" She was giddy with courage.

"Who has time for other women? You think I'm Samson, that I have the strength for anyone besides you and her?" He jerked his head toward his cello in the corner of the room. "It may be lousy for my image to say it, but you two are all I can handle. If I stay away from her for one day she treats me like a stranger, and you—you, my desert flower, it takes all my strength to keep you watered. What do you think, I'm an irrigation canal?"

She turned her head away, smiling. It was true. In bed, at least, she asked for all he had without fear of his refusal. The first two times she had held back as she always did with Dov, wrapping her legs tightly around him when he began to moan and receiving his cresting kiss with an open mouth, but not allowing herself to lose control. The third time they were together, though, she was touching him and she heard him draw in a sharp breath. He swung over her, face drawn as though in pain. "Let me in," he whispered. "Oh my God, let me in to you." When she tentatively let herself feel it, moving with him, he seemed to know it. He groaned with pleasure and she felt him grow harder in her. She let it go then, coming with him, it seemed for hours. Then, terrified, she stole a look at his face. He was smiling at her. "So now you trust me," he said. "Good."

It was true. In bed he was wild for her. She did trust that, and she came to be able to show him her hunger. He was fueled by it, they inflamed each other, and it was for that she came to him. It wasn't all she wanted, he wasn't consumed by her, but it was enough to keep her coming back.

Still she kept her life with Dov on an even keel. Yossi never asked her not to. He seemed content to have her in his flat for a few hours, to give her a lesson, play for her a little, make love to her, send her on her way back to Dov with a joke. She would lie tangled with him after lovemaking, timing her breathing in counterpoint to his breathing so that he would feel her there, waiting for him to say, *Stay with me, Rachaeli. How can you go to him now? How can I let you?* But when she moved her head to see what was in his face, she would find him sleeping or, worse, lying there with his eyes open, thinking. Gone. Then, stirred by her movement, he would unwind himself from her and amble off to the bathroom, returning with a joke or a story. The distance he put between them with his clowning at those moments lay between them, a long stretch of fog. She couldn't see where they had been. She couldn't see where to go.

"For my entertainment today, I'd like to request a chicken story," she said to him once through the fog with a bitterness that took her by surprise. "What's new from the eggs?"

"I don't do chickens," he said. "Cellos, clarinets, the odd conductor, here and there a filthy joke. But no chickens. You must have me mixed up with someone else."

"Silly of me, I do. One of my other jesters."

In fact it was Dov, she thought, it was the fact that she was married and that she left him to go home to this other man, that evened the balance between them. That and the brief moment in those afternoons when passion was laid bare in his face and she opened triumphantly to him thinking, After all he does, he loves me.

Until that one afternoon when he stood dangling the condom, out of

43

her reach, and he said the thing that decided her, sending the cold wind slicing through her when she was least prepared to defend against it. "There's my son," he said, joking even about that, holding his sperm away from her, out of reach, and grinning. He turned away and walked into the bathroom and for a split second she thought of running after him and tearing it from his hand. But she lay still, cold in her own sweat, stunned by the thought that tore through her mind so clearly that she wasn't sure she hadn't said it out loud, or heard it spoken:

Oh no. Not your son. Mine.

She hadn't said it, of course. He didn't hear it, or he would have been more careful in the weeks that followed.

Because all at once it was very clear to her. She would have a child and no one would be its father, and therefore it would be hers alone. She smiled at the thought.

"What's funny?" Yossi asked. "I didn't even tell you my story yet."

"Yes you did," she said, smiling more broadly. She couldn't stop smiling.

"What? What story?"

"Never mind."

"What's gotten into you?"

"Nothing yet." She spilled over into laughter, turning away and rocking with it, laughing at the simple mischief of her idea. When she quieted he was lying on his back, smoking. She didn't care where his thoughts were, and that freed her to be flirtatious. "Come on," she said, snaking a finger through one of his curls. "Tell me some more."

And after all it was as simple as that. When you were the one who laughed, it was the other who waited and agonized, burning toward you through the fog. Only one could be carefree at a time. As simple as that. The mischief ran through her veins, a mineral spring. Time eased, ran at her bidding since there was now no one moment she longed for. She slept easily and deeply, thinking of nothing. She woke up serene. She yearned after nothing, knowing that soon she would be in possession of everything. She grew rosy.

And voluptuous. A continuous, lazy desire warmed her, opened and softened her. It made her smile. She luxuriated in Yossi's touch. Even her skin was open and alive to him. He was maddened by her languid, easy, regal expectation of pleasure. The balance had shifted somehow and he found himself tipping into those slowly closing blue eyes and the smile that quirked her mouth and closed her face to him, even while the scent of her skin and the lavish wetness of her pulled him in.

It was only the slightest shift, but now when she appeared at his door he searched her for clues, interpreting even her fingers' tension as she handed over her cello, even the length of time it took her to cross the sill and close the door. And after they made love, not needing to get up and dispose of a condom now that she was using a diaphragm and anyway not wanting to risk moving from her side, he lay watching her through lidded eyes, hopefully interpreting her lengthening breaths and slightly upraised knees as the carelessness of fulfillment.

In fact she lay on her back with her knees up so as not to lose the sperm.

It was at about this time that Dov had his trouble. If he had seen a change in her over the past few months he had never said so and even now, when after weeks and weeks of passive indifference in bed she began to send unmistakable signals to him of her readiness, he maintained his silence. They had been married for eight years and after the extravagances of the first few weeks, he had entered her body twice weekly during all those years without words, without explosive passion, and without difficulty. But now there was a restlessness, a heat in her body, an expectant catch in her breathing when he approached her, and faced with that he faltered.

They were used to being civil and kindly with each other, and so she said nothing the night he was unable to penetrate her, and when even the caresses that ordinarily brought an instant response failed to arouse him, she did what she would have done if she had been in love with him. She did it out of kindness and out of the knowledge that she would see Yossi the next day. "Let's snuggle," she said. "Hold me, Doobie, the way you used to. Let me sleep in your arms," and she turned over and urged her body back into his embrace, taking his hand and laying it in its old place, pretending sleepiness.

But while his breathing went from shallow and tight to easy and deep, she lay awake thinking. How could she know for sure that Yossi was able to father children? She needed Dov for a backup, and anyway she had come to like the idea that she wouldn't know herself whose child it was. She couldn't have Dov turn impotent now. She went to sleep reminding herself, as she had in the army, to awaken early.

She woke up when it was still dark. Dov slept heavily behind her, one of his legs between hers. It was his sperm she needed, not his passion nor even his consciousness, and because of that she inadvertently provided him with an experience which would torment him later. She eased gently out of his embrace and burrowed under the covers to find him with her mouth, a thing she had never done. He was pungent and she was a little repulsed but she pretended he was Yossi and that helped.

Dov woke up to darkness, wet caressing warmth, and his own electric response. Half conscious, he made a low sound deep in his throat and moved to meet the source of his pleasure, then, as he felt the tightening wet pull, moved more freely and cried out as if in pain. Suddenly she was up alongside him, eyes closed, reaching for him. Desperately he found his place and sank back into warmth, not wary of her demanding heat now but driven by it. She opened her eyes as he came, exploding into her, and saw there what she had sought that first time. He was on fire for her, too late.

She lay back as he babbled his gratitude, raising her knees and husbanding her harvest.

That was in December 1950. By February she knew for certain that she was pregnant. She had carried the other two tight and small and, counting on not showing until much later, she didn't tell Yossi. It didn't concern him, after all.

But as soon as she knew, she told Dov. She had to, to explain her suddenly renewed indifference to him in bed. That night and morning in December had charged Dov like an electric current, altering his ionic structure. It is true that when he and Rachaeli made love for the first time—when she was nineteen and he was twenty-two—he had expected her to be unmoved, and that in the midst of his own climax he was stunned to feel her spasms, to have her lock around him and cry out like that. He was taken aback. And it is also true that when he had sensed that provocative expectancy, that restless heat in her this November and December, he had been put off by it. They had been making very satisfactory love for all these years, he thought. What did she want of him now? But when his body didn't respond at all, when he faltered and terrifyingly failed and then awoke in the darkness to feel her mouth on him and her hair on his legs and himself so powerfully aroused, it was as though he had been to the dead and returned. At the bank that day the sensation of awakening in the dark, being taken, assaulted him again and again. Thirty years old, trembling with his descent to that cold place and with being wrenched back into the warmth of her, he was at last alchemized into the hungering lover he had unwittingly impersonated at twenty-two.

They lay side by side that next night, thinking out their needs. "Look at me," he said finally, pointing to himself, erect and ready. "I've been thinking about you all day."

"Well, let's not waste that," she said smiling.

So for two months her teasing heat drove them both. He thought they had returned from the dead together, and that the new feeling that charged him was answered in her. She thought of nothing but drifted between the two men, rosy and open and smiling.

But in February she was sure she was pregnant, and now she didn't want to be bothered with Dov. So she told him. The other two times she had said, "We're going to have a baby." This time she said, "I'm pregnant." He didn't hear the difference; that may have been because she went on to say that she wasn't feeling very well and that the doctor had suggested she sleep alone for a couple of weeks. "That's pretty drastic, isn't it?" he said. "At least you can sleep next to me, the old way. We don't have to do anything strenuous."

"I'm pretty queasy, I think I'm best off alone." His hand had gone unconsciously to the top of her stomach. She moved it away. "You'll have to put up with me until I feel better."

But with Yossi she came into full flower. In sure and sole possession now of what she wanted, she devoted the afternoons with him to teaching herself what she foresaw she would need in the years to come: the art of finding pleasure with a man—through a man—without yearning after him. It was easy, much easier than needing him and finding him distant had been. She was in control. And she went from moment to moment, enjoying his stories and working at the music and giving herself over completely in bed, so easily and completely that it amounted to taking what she wanted. She threaded her way through his uneven timing, playing off his strengths and coming, not in precarious union with him as in the early days, but in single safety. She closed her eyes, timed it so she came when he did, but she was alone. Then they would lie together in friendly satisfaction and often she would sleep there in his arms till he woke her and told her the time. She could never have slept, in the early days with him, and risked missing a loving touch or word. But the baby was drawing on her strength now and she gave in cheerfully to sleep.

By March she was full of energy once more. She made herself available to Dov again, though not often and not with any trace of passion. She avoided his questioning eyes and the suggestions he whispered in the dark.

On the fourth anniversary of Avram's death, that April, she went to Degania to spend a Shabbat with Rivka. They sat under a tree in the late afternoon, fanning themselves with the cardboard dividers from egg cartons. "How are the chickens?" Rachaeli asked.

"Chickens are boring to the point of being evil," Rivka said. "But lately they're very fertile, so I guess they're not boring to each other."

"Maybe that's the only way they can think of to relieve the boredom. So am I."

"What, boring?"

"Fertile. I'm pregnant."

"Mazal tov! What a good Zionist you are! How are you feeling? What month?"

"Fourth: I'm feeling fine. And it has nothing to do with Zionism—this baby is not for Israel, Rivka. It's for me." She said that strongly, hoping that Rivka would understand and approve. Rivka looked briefly westward, as though she could see Avram's grave from where they sat. "Of course it's for you. But every one of our babies is for Israel."

Not this one, Rachaeli assured her silently. You'll see.

In May Yossi prepared to leave with the Philharmonic for the six-week European tour. She stood in his flat the day before he left, looking around at the heaps of underwear and piles of music. "How will you ever get this packed in time? Come, I'll help."

"Forget it." He came up behind her, kissed her neck until she warmed and let her body ease back against his. "We have better things to do than pack. I have to memorize you."

"You've played me often enough."

"Never the same score twice. You change on me all the time, these days. I never know who's going to walk in here. Let's see." He turned her to face him, undid the buttons of her sundress, letting it slide off her arms. "Today you're a well-fed cat. Just look at her." He finished undressing her, then followed her to the bed, twisting out of his own clothes and leaving them in a knotted trail behind him. He sat on the bed looking at her. "You even look different today. Your breasts are fuller, your skin is gleaming. You look—ripe."

"Take a taste and see."

He found her ripe. Her smell and her taste and the slide of her skin against his overwhelmed him and, frighteningly, he felt a growing urge to press his face against her breast and cry. He looked at her, willing her to see what was in his face. She lay with her eyes closed, a slight sensual smile on her lips and slow spasms of pleasure tightening her eyelids. "Rachaeli," he said. She opened her eyes halfway, including him in her smile. "You feel good," she murmured before she closed them again, shutting him out and urging him farther into her with her hips. She may have seen, briefly, what was in his face, but she really hadn't much interest in that now. They came at the same time but not together—that was how she wanted it—and the next day he left for Amsterdam.

When he came back it was mid-June and she was unmistakably showing. She arrived at his flat the day after his return, as they had arranged. She was wearing a billowy cotton dress so at first he didn't notice.

"Wait till you hear me play!" she said, first thing. "I've done nothing but practice for six weeks—"

"I certainly hope that's—" By this time he had her in an embrace. He backed off, silenced by confusion and shock.

"And that's my other news," she said, following his eyes to the high little mound under her breasts.

"But you didn't have to—I would have—"

"—helped me get rid of it? Why? I want it. It's mine."

"I see." He motioned her formally to sit down. "And his?"

"I don't know. It could just as well be—"

"Mine."

"Yes." She sat on his couch, her forearm resting in an arc on the rounded swelling. He could see it now, and he felt himself stirring. Her wrist rose and fell with her breathing. She looked patiently at him.

"When?" It was all he could think of that was safe to say.

"Early in September."

"Then you can't—"

"Yes I can, for a few weeks. Do you still want me?"

He still wanted her, more if possible. By the end of July, when the doctor advised her to abstain, Yossi had convinced himself that he was the father of the baby, and that she wouldn't look so radiant if she didn't know it and secretly take pleasure in the knowledge. He insisted that they meet right up to the time she gave birth. He pressed food on her and played for her and lay with her on the bed, touching her only to feel the baby move under his hand. Many afternoons she fell asleep that way.

The last week she told him she couldn't come to see him any more. "Imagine if I went into labor here," she said. "It's my third, it could be a matter of minutes."

"But how will I know?"

"I'll get word to you. I know, I'll tell Dov to let you know!" She laughed.

"I'll hold my breath till I hear. Good thing I'm not a trombonist."

She laughed more than the joke warranted. Then she touched his cheek and left, carrying her freighted self out of his reach with no regrets.

BOOK
TWO

A bastard shall not enter into the assembly of the Lord; even to the tenth generation shall none of his enter into the assembly of the Lord.

DEUTERONOMY 23:3

Ramat Gan, September 1951

"Mother?"

"Eva? What is it? You're having the pains?"

"I think so."

"They're regular? How often?"

"Every five or six minutes, I think."

"How long do they last?"

"Not long; it's hard to tell."

"All right, I'm up, I'm getting dressed. I'll be downstairs in five minutes. Eva?"

"Yes."

"Did the water break?"

"No."

"All right. If the water breaks, don't sit on the toilet."

"I won't, you told me. Mother, listen, it's chilly. It's raining. Should
you be coming out?"

"Don't be foolish, Eva."

"Then wear your gloves, all right? And wait in your flat. Shlomo will
ring for you. All right? Mother?"

"All right. Let him ring."

She got back into the bed just before the next one began. Shlomo was
sleeping on his side with one hand over his face. She took the hand and
laid it on her belly without taking her eyes off the clock.

"Unh? Chava? . . . Is that a contraction? You think this is it?"

"The sixth one, every five minutes now. A little less. There, it's over.
Feel it ease?"

"I'm not sure. Should I help you dress?"

"Don't be silly. I'll dress myself, you dress yourself. There's time, they
said—"

"Two minutes. We'll be there in five, ten at the most."

"We have to stop for Mother."

"No. She's not coming. I'll call her later, when there's news. We don't need her now."

"She's waiting for us."

"She's—you called her? You already called her, before—"

She sat up, twisting up her face as though the move caused her pain. When she saw that alarm had diluted his anger she relaxed her face a little and put a hand on his neck. "I didn't want to worry you until I was sure."

She had the best excuse in the world, this time. He let it go. He dressed in silence. She chattered steadily about people to call and casseroles in the refrigerator until it was time for them to leave. At the door she stopped and touched him again. "When I come back through this door . . ." she said, conjuring him with the talisman of the baby.

He relented. "Please God," he said and so they left with everyone happy.

"Name?"

"Eva Konig. No wait, sorry, it's Chava."

"Chava Konig?"

The contraction was hardening, drawing her inward to its center. It wasn't pain exactly but it demanded her total attention. Now it eased and she was able to concentrate on her name.

"Chava Reisner. Mrs. Shlomo Reisner."

In Ujpest—in the apartment with her mother and father and Jacob—she had been Eva. In Auschwitz she was A50062. In Israel now she was Chava. Her mother, Anni Konig, A49488 in the camp and now Anni again, had never called her anything but Eva, and it was only that name she responded to without having to think. Only to the name her mother called her.

But the admitting nurse had barred Shlomo and her mother at the end of the corridor. She was alone in this room in Tel Aviv Hospital, so she concentrated and gave the nurse the information she needed. Chava Reisner, born Eva Konig in Ujpest, Hungary in 1932 to Anni and Sandor Konig. Came to Israel in 1948. Husband, Shlomo (ben Aharon) Reisner, born in Tel Mond, Palestine then, in 1929. Married in 1950, thirteen months ago, in Tel Aviv. His work: diamond wholesaler. Her work: social worker, volunteer. No previous pregnancies.

"Good. Now give me your hand, please, just a pinprick . . . that's all. I'm going to get the doctor now, Chava. He'll examine you."

"Can my mother—can my husband and my mother come in then?"

"No, my dear, you have work to do. Your husband did his share nine months ago, right? You don't need him now. And you don't look like the kind of girl who's going to scream for her mother."

"No, that isn't it—she'll—they'll worry."

"Good. Let him worry a little. You know who's smart? The Persian girls. You'll see, if we have one today. If they know the husband is around, do they scream. They want to make sure he appreciates what they're going through. Clever, eh? What's your husband look like? I'll tell him you're suffering, but nobly."

She mirrored the nurse's quick grin. "Tallish, blond hair, blue *kipah*. Don't say that, my mother will drive him crazy. Tell them—" she put a hand on the nurse's arm, serious now. "Tell them I'm fine, it doesn't even hurt. Tell my mother I know she can't come in and I'm fine."

She was really alone. She looked at the wall and listened hard, but that was silly. Mother was in the waiting room with Shlomo; there was a corridor and two doors between them. She wasn't out there on the other side of the wall.

No one was expecting anything of her right now. She was alone in the examining room, there was not a thing she could do for anyone; even the sheets and the hospital gown she was wearing were no concern of hers. She was perfectly free. A labor pain came, tightened her womb hard and then ebbed. She pushed a strand of hair out of her face, and as she did, the diamond on her hand caught the light. Idly she brought the stone up close to her eye and squinted through it into the light so that she could see a rainbow. She played with the band of brilliant color, absorbed as a child, until the tightening of her womb overtook her again.

"—never get over it." It was a doctor. He had hold of her arm and he was talking. ". . . never get over it," he was saying, fingers on her wrist and counting. She knew better than to interrupt him, so she cocked her head questioningly and waited. The white coats the doctors wore always made her tremble a little so she fixed her eyes on his name tag. Dr. Nahum Arad. Jewish. A Jewish doctor in a Jewish hospital.

He unwrapped the blood-pressure cuff from her arm and fixed a stethoscope on her belly, smiling and nodding to himself when he found the heartbeat. "I've overseen delivery of thousands of babies, I suppose, in the last thirty years, but I never get over it when one comes in like you." He took her left hand and held it, looking at the number. "Where?"

"Auschwitz."

"A triumph. This baby's a triumph, do you know it? The first time a baby was born in this hospital to a woman with"—he gestured toward the number and grimaced—"we all cried. The midwife, the students—the mother. Every doctor in the place who was free found an excuse to come in. We all cried. I don't cry any more. I keep a count. You are number forty-one."

He finished his examination, made some notes on his clipboard, and told the nurse to take her to the contractions room. Before he left he gripped her shoulder with a strong hand. "A triumph. Life over death. Never forget it," he said.

She smiled and ducked her head. But she thought, Not a triumph, just a baby. You don't have to be anything but a baby. And she laid her arm casually in the folds of the hospital gown so the number didn't show.

"No Persians," she said to the nurse when she walked her into the contractions room after her shower.

"What? Oh, right. It's pretty quiet, isn't it?" She helped her into the bed, drew the curtain. "Now just hold still for me, Chava. This is for the pains."

"Wait. What is it?"

"Demerol."

"I don't want it. The pains aren't bad."

"It helps. It won't knock you out, it'll just make—"

"Take it, kid. Believe me, there'll come a moment—" the voice from behind the curtain on her right broke off, and Chava heard a sharply indrawn breath and then a low grunt. "Gottenyu."

The nurse raised her eyebrows expectantly: *See?* But Chava shook her head. "No. Thanks. It really doesn't hurt." It closed in again just then, sharper now and with no advance warning this time. All the moisture left her mouth, her tongue tingled with its withdrawal. Then the pain was gone. The nurse had a practiced hand on her belly. She checked her watch, left for a moment, and returned with another woman.

"This is Mrs. Tamir," she said, "the midwife who will deliver you."

Mrs. Tamir nodded. "Let's just see, dear," she said. She nodded again after she had checked. "Soon now. Half an hour or so and we'll go to delivery. You're doing fine. They'll come closer and closer now. Ready for something for the pain?"

Chava shook her head, smiling. "No, I'm fine." She saw the midwife looking toward her left arm but it was safely buried in the sheet. She looked just like anyone else. No anesthetics, no painkillers, and don't faint, she told herself again. Stay awake for the baby. Stay with the baby. A mother stays with her baby. Nothing else matters. She practiced on the next pain, staying conscious, staying calm. When the tingling in her mouth died down and she could breathe again, she opened her eyes. A breeze picked up the curtain around her bed at that moment and blew it high and she caught a glimpse of the woman walking in. She was tall and slender, except for her belly, and she had masses of black hair. She was walking into the room as though it were her parlor, as though she owned it and she was alone in it. She was smiling. It was an elegant and beautiful smile. The curtain settled down again and she was gone.

When the midwife left for a moment, Chava was luckily between pains. She sat up and knelt cautiously forward on the bed, peeking out from behind her curtain. The woman was sitting on the edge of her bed, slowly braiding her hair. She stopped for a moment and put a hand on her belly, frozen as though listening. Then she smiled again and resumed her slow braiding, closing her eyes and opening them again as though she had been kissed. Chava lay back down again and held the picture of that smile against the next, almost unbearable pain.

———————

Rachaeli finished braiding her hair and lay back. She smiled almost all the way through the next pain. *Soon now.*

———————

By the time they wheeled Chava to delivery at 3:54, the pains were coming almost on each other's tails, leaving her very little time for breathing, but she remembered to stay calm. She knew how to get through it.

———————

Rachaeli wasn't smiling when they wheeled her to delivery at 4:02, but she was concentrating on the succession of pains with a kind of solemn exuberance. *Very soon now.*

———————

Chava did scream when the baby's head crowned but she wasn't aware of it, and anyway it was all right because her mother couldn't hear it. By the time the baby was out and separate she was alert again and with him. He wasn't alone for a moment.

———————

Rachaeli heard the scream and then a baby's cry from somewhere in the room, behind one of the curtains. Then the monumental force gathered in her for one last time and crushed her, split her. She pushed against it to expel the pain, and then it was over and against her own ragged, animal breathing, she heard the thin, indignant cry.

———————

When the baby was clean, they laid it on Chava's breast. "Let your son nurse," they said, smiling. Awkwardly, without having seen more than a dark head, she offered him a nipple, waiting to feel motherhood.

Before the baby was clean Rachaeli reached for him, making them grin uneasily. She held him up for a second, looked him over, then put him to her breast. She smiled as he fastened fiercely onto the nipple. *Mine.* She was never going to stop smiling.

It hurt when the baby pulled at the nipple. Chava was shocked by that; she had expected pain in childbirth, of course, but she hadn't thought that once the baby was born it might hurt her. She was distracted by the sharp little pains and by the problem of the baby's name, so she didn't react right away when the nurse took the baby from her and hastily wrapped him in a blanket.

"Sorry, got to get him to the nursery. They don't really get anything when they nurse for the first couple of times, anyhow. We have a problem here, got to clear the way."

"Problem? Is he—"

"Nothing to do with this young man. We've got three women ready to deliver any minute, one a breech, and they just brought in a busload of injured kids. Not enough people to take care of everyone. Say 'bye to Mommy, big fellow. Say 'See you later.'"

"Wait. When—"

"Come on—uh—Chava. Let her take care of your son. I need that hand for a minute anyway." It was another nurse, holding a blood-pressure cuff. They were both waiting. Chava let go of the baby's blanket and watched the first nurse lay him in a little crib and wheel him briskly out. She closed her eyes while the cuff was inflated.

"When—"

"Shh."

She waited. When the nurse had returned her arm and was checking her pad, she tried again. "When will I have the baby back?"

"Three or four hours. You relax, okay? Warm enough?" A piercing scream blotted her next words. Chava tensed at the sound. "That's mother number one. Listen, it's chaos out there—and in here. We'll get you to your room as soon as we're sure you're stable and someone has a minute, okay?"

"She said a busload of kids . . ."

"An accident. Twenty-two kids, some pretty badly hurt. Why didn't God give nurses four hands and wheels? Anyhow, you just—"

"How old are the kids?"

"Second grade. So they're what—seven?"

Jacob.

"They're alone?"

"*Hey*, don't go getting up yet. Just lie down. Of course they're not alone. That's where all the doctors and nurses went."

"But their mothers? If they're hurt and afraid—"

"Their mothers are being called. They need the doctors more than their mothers right now. And you need to calm down." The patient was showing an extreme reaction, eyes big and dark with fear, obvious signs of panic. Nurse Dagan took her pulse again, considering sedation. Then she noticed the number on her arm. They often had bizarre reactions, the survivors. The midwives were all occupied with births and she herself was needed to assist. She laid a cool hand on the young woman's forehead and spoke softly to her. "Listen, Chava. We'll take care of those kids. They're in good hands, and their mothers will be here in minutes. Meanwhile, your job is to lie here, sleep a little, stabilize so we can get you to your room. Will you do that for me? Chava?" The girl appeared to be engaged in an inward debate. She took a steadying breath and smiled.

"Of course. Don't worry about me. I'll sleep. Really. Oh, wait. Nurse? Does my mother—do my husband and mother know that the baby—that everything is okay?"

"Of course. Now sleep."

"I will."

But she didn't sleep. She watched the nurse hurry to one of the curtained beds to assist at a birth. So the baby was alone; they had taken him away. She closed her eyes and pulled in a long breath, then another and another.

You knew he would be taken away. *I let them* . . . No. Bathed and weighed and measured and examined, the doctor said. And put in the nursery with the other babies. Only bathed, only weighed and measured and examined. *Taken away like Jacob.* No, we went over this, remember? The baby will go with the nurse to be bathed and measured and weighed and examined, and you will lie and look at your flat belly and think about the name. "That's your job," Shlomo said to make me smile, "the name. My job will be to take credit."

And deal with my mother.

He didn't say anything; he held me and he rubbed my back a little so I would know he was awake, so I could go back to sleep.

She put a hand on her middle. Not as flat as she'd imagined it would be. She heard the staccato of the midwife's directions to one of the mothers, other sounds of equipment being moved around and the voice of a doctor talking to someone about anesthesia: "—breech. Best to take it now, before it descends . . . start intravenous . . ."

That's my job. Think about a name for the baby.

But it wasn't a matter of thinking. She knew what the name would be. How to explain to her mother, that would take some thinking. She pulled the blanket around her and, closing out the sounds of pain and urgency in the room, put her mind to the problem.

She could have saved herself the trouble. She never got the chance to explain it to Anni. At the doorway of Chava's room Anni stood aside ostentatiously to let Shlomo go to his wife. Chava saw her through the shifting filter of Shlomo's hair, standing still and watching the two of them impassively. When Shlomo's hug was over she twisted away from him a little and smiled at her mother, inviting her, but she gave Shlomo's hand a little squeeze. "We have a boy," she told them both.

"A genius," Shlomo said. "You can tell by the way he sleeps. Right, Anni?" He was exuberant enough to joke with Anni. Chava gave his hand another squeeze. A reward.

"How would you know which one is ours?" Anni was smiling, too.

"How do I know. The genius is ours. The one who was thinking in his sleep."

"Don't they have names on the cribs?" Chava asked.

"Not yet," Shlomo said. "Some crisis downstairs, so there's only one nurse on the maternity floor. Two boys and a girl in there now. Three more babies coming any minute, the nurse said. You look beautiful. How was it?"

"It's overwhelming at the end"—looking at her mother—"but you always know it will be over." Anni nodded. "Then I held him. He's dark; I expected a blond, but he has—"

"And you did your job? What's our son's name?"

No one looked at anyone. "Aaron." She twisted her hand out of his and laid it on her vacated belly. "For Shlomo's father," she said to her mother.

Anni nodded, mouth tight, face suddenly cold and closed. She kept nodding, a silent, bitter assessment. Chava felt Shlomo trying to catch her eye but she looked down at the blanket. No one spoke. Not a word about why the baby wasn't named for Jacob, neither an accusation nor a defense. It was too late for that.

The rabbi wandered into Rachaeli's room not ten minutes after they brought her there from delivery. He was a tanned, dapper man, about forty-five, with a salt-and-pepper beard. If it hadn't been for the black *kipah* on his head she'd never have taken him for Orthodox.

"That's a da Vinci smile," he said. "Radiant. This is your first? Boy or girl?"

"A boy. My third."

"That's good. That's really good. One for the Jewish people."

"Pardon?"

"One for you." He ticked it off on his fingers, singsonging as in a child's story. "One for your husband. And one for the Jewish people. You never heard that? Well anyway, you obviously have the right instincts."

She kept herself sternly in check until he had left the room but then she whooped with laughter, holding herself because it hurt to laugh. "One for the Jewish people!" she mimicked in the empty room. "He should only know." But when the laughter stopped she was left feeling angry. The Jewish people will have to find themselves another boy, she thought. This one is for no one but me, Rabbi. Finally only for me.

She didn't say anything right away, but that is not because she intended to keep it a secret. What would have been the point of that? Then she would have had to fight Dov for this one as she had for the others. It was a question of picking the time to tell him. She never thought it would be a public affair, certainly. She would tell Dov, they would separate, and she would be another divorced mother. No one would need to know any more.

So when the administrator came in and asked the baby's name, she simply said, "Daniel." Named for no one, this time. Just a name she liked.

When the woman asked, "Father's name?" she said carefully, "My husband's name is Dov Kovner," but when the woman said, writing on her pad, "Father: Dov Kovner," Rachaeli didn't correct her.

And that is probably how it would have remained, a private affair, if it hadn't been for the mixup.

At nine o'clock the nurse brought the baby in. Anni looked at him, then turned away, as though from a flash of light. "Is it the genius?" Chava asked them.

"I think it's the other genius," Shlomo said expansively. "Have a look, Anni."

Anni came over then and stood looking down at them. She said nothing.

Just then the baby began to squirm and cry. The nurse came in and took the baby from Shlomo, saying it was time for his feeding. Shlomo looked at him, then put both his hands in Chava's hair and kissed her, first her eyelids and then her mouth. She kissed him back a little, not enough to prolong the kiss and make her mother feel more left out. Released, she held out her arms to her mother. Anni came and put a cool cheek against hers. Then they were gone.

"Wait," Chava called. "Shlomo?"

He was back, smiling tenderly. "What?"

"Make her protect her fingers. Be sure she puts on her gloves before she goes outside."

He nodded, looking suddenly tired. "Okay." Then he left again.

The nurse was very young and either shy or impatient. "Doing all right with the nursing?" she asked brusquely, handing him over.

"I guess so, but . . . is it supposed to hurt?"

"The nipples are tender? I'll get you an ointment. You apply it after each nursing. Then you wash with sterile water before you feed him." She turned to go.

"Nurse?"

"Yes."

"How are the children? The ones from the bus accident?"

"One is in a coma. Very bad. Two have multiple fractures and another a broken arm. The others have only bruises and scratches."

"So they went home?"

"All but those four."

"And who is with them?"

"What do you mean, who's with them? Look, if you tense up like that the milk won't let down. That's why he's crying. Breathe deep, that's it, relax. I'll be back in a little while with the ointment and I'll show you how to diaper him."

So she was left alone with him. She cradled him gently, surrounding him with her body so he would know she was there, and breathing deeply in and out. She looked uneasily at him and tried out the name. "Aaron," she whispered. He pulled single-mindedly at the breast.

Rachaeli heard the nurse bring the baby to the woman next door, so she knew she hadn't much time. "Would you go now?" she asked Dov. "I'm really tired, and the boys will be lonesome for you."

"Before I see the baby?"

Exactly.

"It'll be a long time before they bring him in—they're short-handed today because of an accident. They really don't want visitors now at all. Please, Doobie. The baby'll be here tomorrow." Finally he left, just in time.

As the corridor door closed behind him the little nurse brought the baby in. Rachaeli had heard him crying all the way down the hall and her breasts were dripping clear fluid by the time she saw him. She held her hands out impatiently for him. The nurse averted her eyes but stood there for a moment.

"You can go," Rachaeli told her. "We know just what we're doing. Only leave me a diaper, eh?"

"What happens if he cries in the night?" Chava asked, handing the sleeping baby back to the nurse.

"I'll bring him to you for his feeding. Don't forget the ointment."

"But what if he cries and it isn't time for a feeding?"

"You need your rest, too. He'll get some water and whatever else he needs."

"He won't be left to cry?"

"No. They'd all wake each other, then. There are six tonight. Four girls, two boys." That was almost a friendly conversation, but she was already on her way out.

"Sorry, my love. I rubbed so hard to get that spot off your bottom and it doesn't come off. A beauty mark, how clever of you. Some girl will love it." Rachaeli snapped the pin shut and lifted the blinking baby for a kiss. "But you'll tell her, 'Sorry, I belong to my Mama.' Right?"

The baby's eyes fluttered closed. He was asleep before she laid him down.

All the babies seemed to come down from delivery at once. Four girls, one a screamer. She woke the others and there was pandemonium, so Nurse Dagan stayed to help Leah Jaffe quiet them and get the new ones charted in. She went over to the blue-ticketed cribs. "What are you complaining about?" she said to the two babies in them. "Two boys with four girls—you have a harem here. Besides, you're older, you ought to be setting an example for—Leah?"

"Yes?"

"Where are the name cards on these two?"

"Never got to it. It's okay, they have their bracelets."

"Who put on the bracelets?"

"I did, just the way Mazal told me. I hope you had time to bracelet these girls in delivery, though. I never want to see another day like—"

"Leah, try to remember. Mazal brought in one baby at a time and gave you the information on each?"

"Yes. Well, that is, she wheeled in both cots at once, but then . . . what is it? What are you looking for?"

"Damn . . . Kovner. *Damn*. Look, Leah, these babies have the wrong bracelets."

"How—"

"I had to help Mazal get this one away from the mother. A survivor, I had plenty of time to look at the baby and to see her name: Reisner. Chava Reisner, a blonde, and it was this baby with all the black hair. But the name on his bracelet says Kovner."

"The other boy baby has black hair."

"It's much finer—doesn't stand up like this one's. This is the Reisner baby. Get the doctor on call, Leah. Do it now."

———

The one thing she hadn't thought of was that Dov would want to hold the baby. She couldn't allow that. She'd managed all right today, but she was going to have to think this through. It would be weeks, wouldn't it, before she was ready to move out with the baby and the boys?

She heard the footsteps in the corridor and sat up expectantly. Yossi—Dov must have made his phone calls by now, and she'd told him to be sure to let Yossi know she would have to miss her lesson. She combed her fingers through her hair and then picked up a book and leaned back against the pillow.

The door flew open, closed halfway, and was banged open again and held by the width of the cot wheeled through it.

"Here's your roommate," the nurse sang out. She was short and round. "You've been all alone in this big room? Here's company now—more coming." The woman on the other cot was about Rachaeli's age, with stylish, short streaked hair. She winked at Rachaeli. Then the nurse drew the curtain between the beds.

Through the open door walked another nurse, holding a little white card. "Came for some blood," she announced, bending the card back to expose the needle and reaching for Rachaeli's hand.

"What for? I've had the baby already."

"Just a followup. . . . *There* you go. Thanks."

The little round nurse pulled open the curtains between the beds with a flourish and bustled out, calling back, "Have fun, girls!" Then the room was quiet.

"Another girl," the woman said. "After all that, another girl. Shit."

The woman had red hair, dark at the roots, and fleshy arms. She lay inert, heavy with drugs. She moaned, even cried, but never opened her eyes. The air in the room was heavy, too, with the smell of the anesthetic she exhaled and with her pain and Chava's fear of her pain. In the ten minutes since she had been wheeled into the room and settled in the bed across from Chava's, Chava had tried twenty times to get up and close the curtain around the front of her bed, but she still sat motionless. When the nurse came in and cheerily demanded her finger and drew the blood, Chava's only reaction was relief to see her. "What's the matter with her?" she whispered.

"Not a thing. Had a caesarean this afternoon. Perfect baby girl."

"She's in pain . . . she moans and cries."

"She doesn't know it; she's out. So if she's not conscious of the pain, don't you worry about her."

Probably the gas didn't hurt. If the women didn't fall on him and crush him before he died. If it was fast and he didn't have so long to be afraid. Probably it was only a minute of choking. And then nothing. Jacob.

She didn't notice the nurse leave. She closed her eyes again, shutting out the woman and her pain that was a separate being in the room, partly hers and partly Chava's. She shut it out and trained her mind on the guest list for the *brit*.

There were three of them in the room now, Rachaeli and Lise—the streaked blonde—and the new one, Tamar. They were eating breakfast and laughing when the doctor came in. He drew the curtain around Rachaeli's bed and stood looking at her a moment, then pulled the wooden chair up to the bed and sat down. DR. SHIMON LEVICH his tag said.

"I feel fine," Rachaeli said.

"Mrs. Kovner, there's been . . . some confusion here."

She waited.

"It seems . . . this morning, just moments before your son was born, another boy was born, to a Mrs.—uh—Reisner. Shortly after that, there was an accident—"

"I know. The kids on the bus."

"Yes, and three births at once and a cardiac—well, at any rate, the staff was under a great deal of pressure and the nursery—this whole floor, in fact, with all the obstetrical patients—was left with only one nurse. She was harried, you see, so that probably . . ."

"Probably what?"

"Possibly. There is a possibility that she misunderstood the delivery room nurse—at any rate, she may have mixed the bracelets. The baby you've been . . . the nurses may have been bringing you the wrong baby. Fortunately, there are only two boys in the nursery, so all we have to do is—"

"You aren't sure which baby is mine?"

"Well, it should be relatively easy to—"

"I've been nursing the wrong baby? Someone else has been—"

"We're going to find out. We've retyped the babies' blood. We've rechecked your blood type and Mrs. Reisner's."

"And?"

"Well, one baby is type A, one is type B. Your blood is type O—"

"And the other one?"

"Unfortunately, the other—Mrs. Reisner's blood is also type O. Thank God the babies are different types, that's the important thing. We will have to bring in the fathers, though, obviously. Will Mr. Kovner be in to visit today?"

"Doctor?"

"Yes?"

"Will you leave me alone for a little while now? I have to think."

"But—"

"Fifteen minutes. Ten. Please leave my curtain closed."

Women. Dr. Levich went next door to Mrs. Reisner. It turned out to be less difficult with her. She was younger, for one thing, and he was able to speak with more authority. She turned out to be tougher than she looked, too. She sat still and composed and listened carefully. "My husband will be here later," she said finally. "Anything that has to be done to be certain, anything. We have got to be certain."

The only little break in her composure came when she asked about her mother. "Do you think—will you have to take her blood, too?"

"No. It won't help, because you're an O. It's irrelevant what type she is."

Her face eased, then tightened again. "She's not to know anything," she said. "About the babies or the blood—nothing. You have to make sure of it."

"Of course. But if it turns out that the babies—"

"Then I'll tell her."

Back to Mrs. Kovner. She was ready for him. "I'll have to have some time to discuss this with my husband," she said. "Alone. Is there a room—?"

"The chapel. I'll arrange it. But your husband's blood test?"

"Doctor, I intend to leave this hospital with my child. Don't worry about the blood tests."

So that settles it, she thought regretfully. It had been sweet, not knowing which one was the father, almost as though there were no father at all. Now she'd have to know, and she would have to tell Dov tonight. No more choices.

The nurses bottle-fed the two babies in the nursery at eleven o'clock; no sense in deepening the mothers' attachments. Rachaeli's breasts filled on schedule, then hardened with the pressure of the milk. When Dov walked into the room, she was cooling the engorged breasts with her hands. They felt as though they would burst. She buttoned her nightgown and pulled on her robe and stood up.

"You can't come in, the girls are nursing their babies. What are you doing here?"

"Came to see you and my boy. Why isn't he in here? Where are you going?"

"Come. We have to talk. I'm taking you to the chapel so we can be alone."

"He's not—is anything wrong with him?"

"He's fine. Did you let everyone know?"

"Yes. Your mother's coming tomorrow."

"How are the boys?"

"Fine. Avi wanted to know when he could take the baby to school. It seems a baby is almost as good as a rifle. But not as good as tickets to the soccer game, he let me know that. Wait, I want to see him."

"He's at the other end. This is the chapel. Come, we'll sit."

The windows were vertical slits in the white walls. They let in slices of light. Rachaeli and Dov sat on the wooden bench turned toward each other, each facing a beam of light but untouched by it.

"There's a problem," Rachaeli said. "They think they might have switched the babies."

"How in hell—"

She told him, drawing it out, telling it meticulously and in order, overriding his questions and exclamations and talking steadily on. "So they checked the babies' blood types," she finished. "One A and one B. Then they retyped my blood and hers."

"What's her name?"

"I don't know. Reisner. Her blood and mine are both type O. So they'll have to type yours and her husband's."

"I know mine. It's—"

"They'll do it themselves. They have to, now. They have to be sure."

"So where are the babies now?"

"The nurses have them. They're being bottle-fed until they know. Listen, Dov. That's not all." She waited, thinking that he would know by her silence. He just sat there looking at her, a crease of bewilderment between his eyes. It irritated her. He should have known. "I didn't mean to tell you this. I was just going to go. But—"

"What do you mean, go? Go where?"

"But now I have to tell you. Maybe it's better, maybe you'll understand better. Dov, the baby may not be yours. I've—there's been someone else. It may come out in the tests, and I thought you ought to know first."

He made an ugly sound, clearing his throat. "How long?"

"What?"

"How long has there been someone?"

"I—why?"

"More than nine months, obviously. Before that, what? How long? Or was it just once?"

"No, not just once. A long time."

"Years, you mean? Months? All that time when—" he swallowed and fought the twisting of his mouth, but he couldn't stop it. He cried, shaking his head impatiently against it and locking the sound behind his lips. The milk throbbed in her breasts and forced its way out, trickling from her nipples. She felt her nightgown getting wet, first on one side and then on the other. She held the robe out so he wouldn't see it.

"I was going to ask you for a divorce anyway," she said.

"To be with him?"

"Yes. Oh—the other man, you mean? No. I don't want to live with him."

"Then who?"

"No one. You wouldn't understand. I don't want to be married, Dov. It isn't good between us."

"You're crazy. What do you want? We don't fight, we have nice kids. And you certainly seemed to want . . . to like . . ."

The milk ran down her ribs in two slow streams. "I can't live with you now. The baby—"

"I don't care whose it is. You can't just—"

The slice of light behind Dov was cut off. She looked up. The rabbi, the one from the other day, was standing with his hand on the open door. The door was intercepting the light. He walked in and let the door swing

73

closed. The light rolled back. "Sorry," the rabbi said. "I just wanted to check something." He pointed to the ark where the Torah scrolls were. "I don't want to intrude, but if there's some need . . . ? I'm Rabbi Becker."

"Rabbi?" Dov stood up, bulky in the narrow pew. He stepped out in the aisle and stood in front of the rabbi. "If there were—in a case of illegitimacy, could a separation be forced?"

She couldn't stop him. He stood in the aisle with the rabbi, the two of them looming over her. She backed up so the light hit her back, warming her. The robe was pulled against her breasts. It was going to get wet. Let it. Let them see it. It was her milk. Let them talk, she had the milk.

"What do you mean, illegitimacy? A child born out of wedlock isn't at all illegitimate, you know, by our law. Only if the child is the product of a union which could never be sanctioned—incest, for example, or an adulterous liaison between a married woman and another man. It isn't easy to be a bastard in Israel." He smiled.

"But in such a case, could a separation be forced?"

The rabbi balanced on his heels, steadied his *kipah* with one palm and looked speculatively at the two of them. He remembered the woman— her third, she had said. The light behind her dazzled him; he couldn't see her face. He sighed. Of all questions, illegitimacy. Don't tell me, he beseeched them silently. I don't want to hear it. "Illegitimacy is no one's favorite subject," he said. "No one wants to think of a child cut off from his people."

"What do you mean, cut off?"

"Let me answer your other question. The consequences of illegitimacy are so grave—so unthinkable—that not only is a separation never forced, it's made nearly impossible. In a kosher marriage, a valid marriage, especially one where there are other children the man has acknowledged as his own, there's a very heavy presumption of legitimacy, and every- thing possible is done to protect the child. It's conceivable, but a man would have to be—wild, obsessed—to cast such a weight on his legal wife and his legal child. And for him to be upheld—well, the woman would almost have to declare her own child a bastard, and no woman would do such a thing."

"What do you mean, cut off?" the man persisted.

The woman's blue robe had slowly spreading wet stains down the front of it. She seemed to be absenting herself from the discussion. What was going on here? Was the husband using him to threaten her? Was this some scenario they played out with every birth? Not with his help. He faced the man squarely and impaled him with a piercing, steady look.

"I mean branding a child a bastard is not a game. It's a life sentence. In fact it's ten life sentences, if not more: 'A bastard shall not enter into the assembly of the Lord, even to the tenth generation shall none of his enter into the assembly of the Lord.'"

"It means he can't go to synagogue?" The man was unmoved by that prospect, but he was searching. He seemed to have something else in mind.

"It means cut off from the people of Israel. It means he can never marry a Jew. It means his children and descendants would be bastards, too, for ten generations."

The woman looked up now, holding her head at an exaggerated angle back. She didn't look cowed; she looked . . . intent. "Who says that?"

In response he waved an arm at the Torah scrolls in the ark. "The Name Himself. Deuteronomy Twenty-three, verse three. No rabbi in Israel may marry such a child."

"And what else? Is he—would such a child be a citizen?"

"Not only a citizen, he could be king if we had one. A bastard who is a scholar takes precedence over a priest who is an ignoramus, the scholars say. He has all rights, even to inheriting equally with his brothers. Only he may never marry, never father legitimate children. That's why no one declares his own legal child a bastard." He looked menacingly at the man. "No one."

It appeared he had made his point. The man's mouth twitched grimly and he held out a hand to the woman. She didn't take the hand, but she stood up and followed him out of the chapel. Madmen. He felt sorry for the child.

———————

"That child was born to you. You're my legal wife. You heard him: the child is legally mine, and you can't just walk off with him. He's mine and I'll love him like the other two, Rachaeli. You'll calm down, it'll be—"

He's mine and I'll love him. Like the other two. It rang in her head, a mockery. How could he have known to choose those words? He must have known all along what he was doing, must have stolen each baby deliberately from her.

Even if it turns out the tests say it's yours, she thought, even then he's mine, not yours. I sucked him out of you. I got him for myself. She turned in the corridor and ran clumsily back into the chapel.

The rabbi was up on the altar, bending over an open scroll. She went

———————

up close and looked up at him. "What if the mother declared the child illegitimate?" she asked. "What about the marriage then?"

Enough. Keeping the Torah between himself and the woman, he looked down at her. "She would have to be a madwoman," he said flatly. "If she were lucky, the husband would keep her and claim the child— give the child sanctuary and get psychiatric help for her."

"He could do that?"

"Unless he were a Kohen, a descendant of the priestly class. A Kohen is forbidden to remain married to an adulteress. He would have to divorce her."

The woman smiled broadly, as at some secret satisfaction. "Thank you," she said and strolled out, still smiling.

Let the crazy marry the crazy and keep each other happy, the rabbi thought, the corners of his mouth pulling downward with distaste. Only why must they have children?

She eradicated the smile before Dov could see it. "I have to change into something dry," she told him when she caught up with him. "And you have to get back to work. Why don't you find a nurse and let her take a blood sample before you go? I'll see you tonight; we'll talk then, eh?"

She looked softer, less bristly. He left her feeling hopeful. Hormonal craziness, he would wait it out. They would deal later with the question of the other man. He swallowed his own sour taste. There was nothing wrong with their marriage. And no woman wants to live alone with three kids, one of them fatherless. No sane woman would choose that.

Rachaeli watched him go toward the nurses' station and then, suddenly tired, headed for her room. She scanned the names posted outside the rooms as she walked. She found it on the room next to hers: ALTEN-BACH/REISNER. She walked by slowly, glancing in as she passed. One woman lay motionless in her bed, hooked up to an IV. In the other bed sat a young woman, blondish and pretty; a man sat next to her, his arm around her, and an older woman stood formally, a little distance from them. The man—the husband probably—was talking and the young woman looked from him to the older woman and back as he held forth. She was the one. A good little girl, Rachaeli thought venomously; she's drinking in the words of her lord and master in his *kipah* and checking to see if Mommy agrees. And after all this, she might have my child?

In her room she peeled off the sodden nightgown and dropped a clean one over her head. "That's some figure you have," Lise said. Closing her eyes to block the picture of the Reisner girl from her mind, Rachaeli eased onto her bed and turned to Lise and Tamar. "Anyone can have a great bustline," she said. "Just skip one nursing." This having roommates was like being back at Degania. It had its uses.

Shlomo and Anni had walked in just as Chava's roommate's baby was being taken back to the nursery. "Where's the baby?" Anni asked. "He ate so fast?"

"He's my son, he's quick," Shlomo said. "Let's go wake him up and check him out."

"Don't bother. The nurses won't let you near him; they're lions," Chava said. "Stay and talk to me." And that would have been all right, Shlomo was already bending over her for a kiss, but the nurse walked in and headed purposefully for him.

"Mr. Reisner?" she said.

"Here am I," he answered, bowing his head.

"Can you lend me your hand for a minute: I just need a little . . . there. Thank you." She was gone. Chava watched her go, silently cursing the doctor.

"What was that for?" Shlomo asked. "They do that to everyone?"

"Just to the good-looking ones. It's their way of getting your attention."

"What's going on here, Eva?" Her mother asked it in Hungarian.

"They need to know his blood type."

"What for?"

"For the records."

"Eva, look at me. I gave birth twice. My sisters and my friends gave birth. They don't take blood from the fathers. Did you nurse the baby just now or not?"

"No."

"He's sick. He needs a transfusion?"

"No. Believe me, Mother, he's fine." She answered in Hebrew but Anni was not to be controlled. She turned and headed for the corridor.

"I'll find out for myself," she tossed back, still in Hungarian.

Shlomo and Chava stopped her in the hall. "Wait, Mother. It isn't that he's sick."

"Speak Hungarian, then. Tell me the truth."

"All right, all right, I will. Only come inside and let me tell you. I'll tell you."

77

She made them sit on the bed with her. She glanced over at the other bed. The woman was asleep again, her head turned sideways on the pillow and her mouth open. "It's just a little confusion," Chava started, and, carefully choosing her words, she explained the situation. She told it without mentioning the injured children.

But it didn't matter. Anni went pale and her two hands tightened on each other. "You're going to have to choose," she said. "You're going to have to choose between the babies."

"No, listen, Anni—"

They didn't move when the doors of the transport car were opened. No one in the car moved, even the kids. The bright daylight assaulted them but those nearest the door just stared out blinking and those facing away, or with their faces buried in their hands or in someone's back, didn't even look up. It was only the shouting that moved them. Then when the first three or four tumbled out, they were all galvanized at once and they pressed out in a body and stood blinking in the light and trying their knees and ankles. Anni flapped her skirt sharply twice and pulled the waistband straight, then combed back Jacob's hair with her fingers, making him wince, and buttoned a cuff on Eva's shirt. They were all filthy. "Fix your braids," Anni said. But they were shouting. "What are they saying?" Anni demanded of Eva.

"'Leave your parcels, get in line. Quick.'"

They made a sort of line. An old man in a uniform quickstepped along it, barking at them to leave their things, move along to the showers. He stopped and looked at Eva struggling with her hair.

"How old are you?" He had a strange look on his face.

"I'm twelve. Sir."

"You're sixteen, you understand? Say you're sixteen. Pull up tall, stick out your chest. LEAVE THOSE THINGS! YOU'LL GET THEM LATER. MOVE ALONG!"

"What did he say to you? Eva?"

"To say I'm sixteen. To stick out my chest."

"Then say it."

"But it's silly, I'm only—"

"Pull off your socks. Hurry up. Now stuff them in the heels of your shoes. Here, put your feet in now, you'll look taller. Squeeze!" Her mother's hands pulled at her shirt, bunched it in front, pulled it out in two points. "You're sixteen. Jacob, come here to me."

The line was splitting. Aunt Lili went to the left with Jeno toddling along, holding onto her hand. Grandfather and old Aunt Marta and the Grunfelds went that way, too. Grandfather gave his arm to Mrs. Grunfeld, who was still weak from childbirth. She carried the baby in her other arm. That looked like the way to go but Mother was looking sharply left and then right as the line divided. "Don't limp in those shoes," she hissed. "Jacob, stay here with me." She pinched their cheeks and her own.

"That way." The man in the white doctor's jacket didn't touch Jacob, only pointed his stick at him and then toward the line of people moving left. "Move." He was speaking pidgen Hungarian.

"Please let him wait for us. He'll get lost, he's only seven."

"You the mother?"

"Yes."

"How old?"

"Thirty-three."

"How old's the girl?"

"Sixteen."

Anni had hastily gathered Eva's hair into a bun and skewered it with two pins from her own hair. It balanced precariously at the nape of her neck. The pins hurt. She held her head stiffly.

"Girl to the right. Boy left. You can go with either one. Same showers. Hurry up!" He poked Anni in the leg with the stick. She didn't say a word, and the man wasn't looking at her any more. Only Eva saw her eyes like that, and then Jacob.

"Go ahead, son. Jacob. Go catch up with Grandpa. I'll find you after the shower. Go on, hurry and catch up. Stay with Grandpa." Then she went with Eva to the right but she stumbled because she was looking back at Jacob.

"Don't cry, Mother. We'll see him soon, after the showers."

But her mother wouldn't answer or look at her and when Eva tried to take her arm to steady her, Anni looked at her as though she hated her and pulled her arm away and walked after the others, saying only, "You stay with me. Keep up."

There was no way to stay with her. She couldn't go the way her mother was now everlastingly going to have to go, but she didn't know it then so she matched her mother's brisk pace even though the shoes hurt with the socks bunched in them like that, and when they were side by side Eva thought that she was keeping up and that they were staying together.

"No. Listen, Anni." Shlomo's voice was flat, his words exaggeratedly slow and distinct. "We aren't going to have to choose. They can tell by matching the blood types. They can tell for certain. It isn't a matter of choosing."

Chava pulled her mother's hands apart, cradling the mutilated fingers and steadily bearing her mother's look. "It isn't a matter of choosing, Mother. This is Israel. No one wants anything but to return the babies to their mothers. There's nothing to choose."

There had been nothing to choose then, either, but Anni didn't say it because she had in fact made the choice. It was her choice, wasn't it, and she had let Jacob die alone. She'd gone to the right and let him go to the left, alone. No choice then either, but she'd chosen.

She got up suddenly and headed for the door again. "Just because they have a little power, they think they can do this to people," she shouted, in Hebrew this time. "Let them see who they're dealing with. They're accountable—" in her rage she swallowed half the word. She was out in the corridor now. "—They're accountable and they'll soon know it. If we have to take both the babies, we will."

"Anni. Chava—"

"Come on, Mother. Let's—"

"We'll take them both. Let them try—there are still places in the world to—"

Rachaeli stood within the doorway and looked out. The older woman must have been a beauty in her time, but her face was lined and haggard now. Some scene she was making. The girl—must be her daughter, she had the same cheekbones, the same almond eyes, only hers were clear and unsunken—looked wretched. The husband looked furious and embarrassed. The girl, catching his look, took the mother by her shoulders and led her back into the room. The husband followed, face grim and flushed.

Rachaeli ducked back into the room. "Would you believe it?" she said to Lise and Tamar. "Everyone in the world wants my baby." She got back into bed and pulled the sheet up vigorously.

Yossi appeared in the doorway. He did look wonderful. He was wearing a white shirt, as though it were a holiday, and carrying a blooming cactus. He kissed her mouth. "Then he must look like both of us," he whispered. His eyes flicked to the other two women and he pulled the chair up close to her bed and sat down, back toward the others. "I brought you a desert flower," he said softly. "To remind you. I don't need reminding."

He didn't. She had a virginal nightgown on and her hair was tangled, but she had shifted her body subtly when she saw him, pulling up a knee under the sheet and clasping it lightly with one hand so that there was a long, sinuous line from her ear to her fingers. She couldn't know, he thought, that her body was sabotaging the closed composure of her face, emanating readiness. He was an expert, by now, at decoding her signals.

Yossi was thirty-five. There were several women in Tel Aviv and one or two in Europe who had devoted their energies to reading him, with varying degrees of accuracy. They interpreted him, trying to play variations of his theme or to bewitch him with easy harmony or with provocative discord. He responded good-naturedly, taking care to find a way to pleasure each of them. Because he was scrupulously honest with them, and because he was considerate of their physical needs and careful never to humiliate or abuse any of them, he thought he was not hurting anyone. But his rages and his fears, his despairing failures and his triumphs he brought only to, and took only from, his cello. And so of course he hurt them all. It had been the same with Rachaeli, except that she was married, so there was a place in her life where he could never go. And except that there was something else unattainable about her—she seemed to affect neither harmony nor discord with him but followed her own undisclosed score. And except that for several months the contrast between her self-containedness and the lush openness of her body had teased him to rage, to fear, to despair and to precarious moments of triumph, all with her.

He was thirty-five and the work of decoding her had begun to seem to be a worthy destiny for him, after music. The pregnancy and now the birth of the baby had only made her more desirable. She seemed to him to be a source, and he wanted to fight his way to it and bathe in it.

He was thirty-five, time to marry. The women were becoming repetitious and wearying. This baby was his; she had protected its life against all logic and had carried it with such obvious delight—even though she rarely mentioned her other children—that it had to be his. Let it be his, then. Let her be his. It was time.

He put the plant down, brushing her breasts as he leaned over her. "So how are you?" he asked lightly, but in their bedroom melody.

"I'm fine. You heard?"

"A boy. I can't wait to see him. I've been thinking—"

"You can't see him. They don't know which one he is." She pressed the buzzer for the nurse. Then, talking quietly, she explained.

"Did that have something to do with the commotion out there?"

"You saw it?"

"The curtain scene."

"That was—I think—the other mother's mother. You should have—"

"Yes?" It was the nurse, the round one.

"Come here. Closer, I don't want to shout. You'll have to type this man's blood."

"Is this Mr. Kovner?"

"No."

The nurse looked at Yossi, then at Rachaeli. Her face reddened. "Fine," she said tightly. "Are there any others?"

Rachaeli suppressed a smile. "Just the two."

The nurse executed a turn and went out, glancing off the door frame in her haste. She returned with the white card and the slide and wordlessly took the blood and left again.

Yossi sucked his finger. "You enjoyed that," he accused. "Wanton. You'll be stoned."

"The nurses' union doesn't handle rocks."

"Listen, I'm going crazy missing you. This is something special, between us. And the baby is mine, you know that. I thought it all out. We'll get a bigger flat . . ."

. . . *Mine, you know that. And the baby is mine, you know that. Mine . . .*

It had been a pure pleasure to see Yossi walk into the room, the kind that doesn't cost anything. She had stopped yearning after him—the cold blast of that moment in his flat last December had taken care of that—but with the end of yearning had come a creamy luxuriance at his hands, and until her body had become solidly engaged with the pregnancy in the last few weeks, she had given over entirely to it. He was unmistakably kindled by her. Even at the end when she lay huge and impenetrable on his bed, he had insisted on undressing her, running his hands over her taut belly and tracing the blue veins in her unresponsive breasts. And now here he was, telegraphing desire. And even bleeding into her sanitary pad, even with the gas pains and with her breasts hardened with milk, his heat breathed over her skin, teased at her, and she felt herself prickle to it. She moved her knee, stretched one hand around it, offering him the curve of her, reminding her body how to curve for him. Let him be her pleasure, then, when she was out of this place.

But then he had to say it, *The baby is mine, you know that.* Was that all any of them knew how to say, *Mine?* She saw it again, him standing naked, dangling the little sac from his hand and grinning, grinning. That was what you chose to do with your son, she told him coldly within the sudden stillness of her body. This one I saved alive, and that makes him mine.

She improvised fast, in that brisk place she'd suddenly come to. It was simple, really, how to sever the baby from him but keep him around for her own needs.

She moved her arm to hold her tangled hair off her neck. "Let's wait until they get the results of the tests," she said, smiling into Yossi's eyes. "Tell me about the concert last week."

The round nurse came in and announced to the window that visiting hours were over. Then, not moving her head, she said, "Dr. Levich wants to talk with you and Mrs. Reisner at one-thirty in his office. We have the results."

"Did you get her home?"

"Yes. I got her home. Raving all the way about her rights. *Her* rights. Listen, Chava—"

"How was she when you left?"

"Seemed all right to me."

"But—how long did you stay?"

"I didn't. Here I am."

"You didn't go in at all?"

"No. I didn't go in. I didn't call up her cronies or make her tea or play audience to her. I took her home and came back to my wife, where I belong."

"How is it they let you in? Aren't visiting—"

"I told them there was a problem with the baby. I told them you needed me. Maybe you'd rather I brought her back and left the two of you alone."

"Don't."

"She'd love that. Anni and Chava and the baby—or both babies, better. A closed circle. Anni and her rights and her eternally grateful daughter and a baby or two to take over and no competition to—"

"How can you? You know how she—"

"I know. How she suffered."

More alien than the pains had been, more terrifying than knowing the baby's head was bursting through the tender bit of skin down there, stretching it, starting the rip that might open unstoppably downward—

83

Shlomo's rage twisted panic in her worse than the hammering of that bursting projectile had done. It had to be stopped, called back before things tore. He had to be made glad, fast. She couldn't breathe this air. Quick, oh fix it quick.

"I don't want anyone here but you. You know that. Please, I can't get up; you come sit here. Shlomo?"

He sat, pulled sulky lids halfway down and grudged her no warmth, but the air was clearing again. One could breathe it without being poisoned. Make sure of it now. Remind him now. She put a hand up to his hair. Tell him another, sweeter thing with your hand while you remind him. Neutralize it.

"She did suffer. She'll always suffer. She wrecked her hands for me."

"To survive. To live. She wrecked her hands to live."

"My father was gone, my brother was murdered, she could never draw properly again with her ruined hands. She only lived for me. To get me through."

"She got you into it—she and your father and the rest of them. You were only twelve and they got you into it with their waiting and their good behavior. She *owed* it to you to get you out alive. And that's a lot of shit, she lived for you. The camp was liberated seven years ago and she's still alive. She makes damn sure she stays alive. Eats for three."

"She starved there. You can't know—"

"You starved, too. You went there with her, remember? You starved, you ate shit."

"She gave me half of what she had. She got me extra food, God knows what she did to get it."

"Did you ever ask her?"

"Of course not. My God, Shlomo. Of course not."

"Maybe she liked it. Whatever it was."

Her hand fell away from him, and down. She didn't move it, leprous, blistered thing. She would have to deal with it later. Now she opened hot stone eyes at him, lidless as a snake, used her silence to shoot venom through him. There was a wild exhilaration in this, feeling this shoot of fury like piss, just like with the guards at the camp, only she could send it through this man and live because he wasn't a god like them with power behind power and no stop to it. He was finished, she could shoot it at him now, pierce him, he wouldn't kill her for her eyeshot. Couldn't. He was out of power; it was all hers now.

But he crumpled then, babbling apologies and pleading with her and making a cloud of wretchedness so that her fury wavered and then dribbled off him and she was left with the same old easy win: Mother protected, Shlomo tender, everybody happy again.

Dr. Levich looked warily at Rachael Kovner as she walked into his office. She walked sedately enough, and she looked tense and subdued. As well she ought to.

"Do you have an answer?" she demanded.

"Yes. If you'll have a seat and wait for Mrs. Reisner to—"

"A definite answer?"

"Certainly. Beyond any question." She sat then, to his surprise, docilely enough.

It was the other one who made the upheaval. She stormed in, clutching a long-sleeved robe around her even in the overheated hospital. She looked grim and disheveled. "You've caused unnecessary pain," she blurted. "Pointless. There was no need, you could simply have taken him aside."

"I'm sorry, I don't—"

"You told me, you promised she wouldn't have to know. All they had to do was ask him to come—I don't know, to fill out some forms or something—and they could have taken the blood where she didn't see. My mother is a survivor of the camps, doctor. She's seen people's blood typed and then watched them taken away to have the blood drained from their bodies for the soldiers of the Reich. She's seen filthy experiments and mutilations—in hospitals, wards like this one with white coats and stethoscopes—that started with blood tests. She's seen babies, children, taken from their mothers and never returned. It doesn't take much to remind her. She didn't have to know, she didn't have to have her face pushed in it, that this baby was taken from her, too. You don't know what you've done."

"Mrs. Reisner, please, I'm sorry. If they typed your husband's blood in her presence it was against my direct orders. But please try to keep some perspective. This baby wasn't taken from her."

She looked pointedly at his bare forearms, unmarred by blue ink. She spoke in the rehearsed cadence of rage. "In a sane world, doctor, you would be perfectly right. In her world—which I begged you not to violate—this baby has been taken from her. Again. She might have been able to see him simply as my baby, her grandson, but you've taken care of that. She walks on a thin veneer. Above it is the new life. Beneath it, everything is filth and terror. This baby's fallen through the veneer for her now."

They had barely been able to make out her last words. She seemed to have run down, though, and she sat suddenly in the leather chair and held her robe around her, silent. The doctor let too many seconds go by.

"Mrs. Reisner, it can't be undone and there's nothing I can say. All I can do is show you our findings and make clear to you how certain we are of which baby belongs to which family. I'll explain it to your mother as many times as I need to, until she understands. May I go on to explain it to you?"

She nodded.

"All right, then." He pushed his chair back and hitched himself up in it. "Ordinarily, in fact, I would bring in the fathers and grandparents for such a discussion, but—"

"Ordinarily?" That was Kovner. Bitch.

"This . . . such a mistake has never happened in this hospital or in my experience before. But when any matter of importance is to be discussed, I like to have all parties present. It prevents misinterpretations due to . . . imperfect reporting. In this case, however, that seems unwise."

Yossi's. It's Yossi's.

". . . glad to speak to—ah—anyone involved, individually. In the meantime, here are our findings. You, Mrs. Reisner, are type O." He got up to write it on a chalkboard behind his desk:

KOVNER   REISNER
♀ O

"Now Mr. Reisner is a type A. That means that you and Mr. Reisner could only have had a type-O or a type-A baby. One of the babies is a type A. Now in the other case, Mrs. Kovner is type O and . . . the father is type B."

It was a game. He thought he was going to force her to ask which one was the father, but he was wrong. She didn't want to know. In fact, she wanted not to know, but she wasn't going to ask that of him either. She sat unblinking and waited.

Reddening, he turned back to the board and emphatically chalked the rest of it in:

86

	KOVNER	REISNER
	♀ O	♀ O
(Mr. Kovner)	♂ O	♂ A
(Mr. Levisohn)	♂ B	
	BABY B	BABY A

The Reisner girl's eyes widened, then she looked at her lap. I'll never see her again anyway, Rachaeli thought.

"So the A-type baby could only be yours, Mrs. Reisner," the doctor went on. "You may be certain beyond any doubt. You and Mr. Reisner could not have had a B-type offspring, and there are only two male babies in the hospital this week, thank God. The B-type baby is yours, Mrs. Kovner, no matter who the father may be."

"Which one did they bring to me before they figured it out?" Rachaeli asked.

"The babies had in fact been mixed. The hospital extends its profound apology to both of you for any pain this may cause you. We have a rule, which was not followed in this case, that the babies must be braceleted at birth."

"There are circumstances in which the rules get pushed to the side," Rachaeli said, standing and looking steadily at him. "It happens." She had one hand on the door when Chava asked, "Can we have the babies now?"

"I believe they've been fed. You don't want to wake them . . ."

"The girl wants to hold her baby," Rachaeli said.

"No, no, I won't wake him. But may we go in and look at them?"

"Of course. And if he's up, by all means . . ."

"Thank you. Come, Mrs. Kovner. Let's go see them."

Rachaeli waited until they were out of the doctor's earshot before saying it. "You don't have to be linked with me. I imagine you're shocked."

"I know that people have reasons, sometimes, for doing what seem like terrible things," Chava said simply. "Will your husband have to know? I mean, I won't say—"

"Thank you. I don't know yet. They got you out of Europe in time?"

"No."

"You were in the camps, too?"

"Yes."

"But—I'm sorry. It's just that when you told it, it sounded as though it happened only to your mother."

The girl just shrugged and smiled apologetically.

They walked on in silence toward the nursery.

Rivka came to visit at five o'clock, just as they brought the babies in. "Let me see!" she exclaimed, holding out her hands.

"Me first, I haven't seen him yet."

"What are you talking about?"

"The last time I saw him he had just been born and he was not at his best." She unwrapped the baby and held him out so they could both see him. He mewed once, then began to squirm and cry. Laughing, Rachaeli offered him a breast. "Ouch. This is more of a relief for me than it is for you, my boy. Sit down, Rivka, I'll explain."

"Can't we get anything right in this country?" Rivka asked when she had heard about the switch. "How's the other mother doing?"

"All right now. She was pretty shaken. Her first baby, and she's a survivor of the camps."

"So she's probably not much of a fighter to begin with." Rivka stood up. "I'm going to say hello. Which room?"

Tight-lipped, Rachaeli nodded in the direction of Chava's room and watched her mother go. The baby was pulling steadily at the breast and swallowing hard—high, hollow little sounds. She brought her knees up and leaned over him so that she was a tent around him. Her hair hung down toward him and his flailing hand grasped a curl and pulled. She smiled.

Rivka strolled back into the room. She went first to Tamar's then to Lise's bed, exclaimed over the babies and made conversation with the women, then ambled back to Rachaeli. "There were a man and a woman with her; it looked like a serious conversation so I didn't go in. The mother has a heavy accent. It's an outrage, you know? When you think of it, if it weren't for that one nurse noticing, we could have had the wrong child."

"I thought kids were pretty much interchangeable to you."

Rivka looked up at the hard tone in Rachaeli's voice. "What do you mean?"

"What I said. Look what just happened here. You came to see me, so you went to visit Reisner and then you had to check in with Tamar and with Lise. It's wonderful, you never play favorites. You'll tell chicken stories to anyone."

Rivka passed a hand over her graying curls. "I used to lie awake at night," she said evenly, "and think about the raids. I counted the paces

88

between our room and the children's house where you were, and then timed myself in the field, running it. I'd lie in bed and run it over and over in my head, fixing every rock and turning in my mind so I could do it in a blackout, in a raid, under fire. There was a plan for evacuating all the children, of course, but then you'd have had to wait your turn. I didn't intend for you to wait your turn. I don't know what the other mothers would have done, but I would have made my run to the children's house, picked you up, and carried you to the shelter. *Then* I would have gone to my station. If they threw me out of the kibbutz for it afterward, so they would have thrown me out. I thought you liked the chicken stories. You always looked a little sad . . . left out . . . to me, and when I came to tell the stories you laughed. I wanted you to laugh.

"Funny," she said, looking at the baby as Rachaeli put him over her shoulder and rubbed his back. "When it did happen it was Avram, not you, and it happened so quietly there was no helping him. I never had a plan to save him anyway. His life didn't seem to have anything to do with violence. I knew he went on patrol, of course, like anyone else, but somehow I always pictured him patrolling the *crops*, you know? Checking the mulch and making note of whatever it was he made note of. Anyway, between the two of us it was always I who was in trouble, not he. I never thought he would need protection."

"It was special, how he loved you. I never saw a man look at a woman the way he looked at you."

Rivka smiled, the kind of brief smile that indicates a subject is closed. "What he was doing was keeping an eye on me so my craziness wouldn't get us both thrown out."

"I wish a man would keep such an eye on me. Once."

"You're not crazy enough to need it."

Then they both turned their attention to the baby, who was still neutral territory.

Dov sat at his desk, feeling the stillness of his body. He matched up his fingertips, laying fingerpad against fingerpad with gentle precision until in those meeting places, at least, sensation was canceled out. He closed his eyes. He could feel the slow generation of the current in his chest, flowing through each arm and meeting in the flat joinings of his fingers, stilled. Her mouth on his cock, her almost despairing cries until he would come in to her. Black hair tangled in her writhings, brown legs pinning him to her.

It could only be a matter of time until she returned to her senses. He shifted in the chair. Soon, he comforted himself. This can't last long.

"He said it was clear beyond any doubt. You can see from the diagram, it couldn't be yours, Dov. And I'm sorry but I don't want you to—I'd rather you didn't have contact with the baby."

"Are you crazy? Where are you going to go with him, then?"

"I'll go to Degania for a little while. Then I'll return to work, get a flat. I'll try to live near you so you can see Zvi and Avi. You're a good father to them."

"This one needs a father, too."

Oh no. No he doesn't. "You can't be his father. It's against the law."

"What are you talking about?"

"You're a Kohen, right? Descendant of the high priest?"

"So?"

"So a Kohen can't be married to an adulteress. You have to divorce me."

"When they rebuild the Temple, maybe. After the Messiah comes."

"Now. It's the law, the rabbi told me. Torah law *is* state law in these matters. You have to divorce me."

"That's insane. You're insane. Wait. Listen, Rachaeli." His voice went soft. "I remember how it was last winter. Do you remember that morning?"

"Yes. I didn't have to do it to you, after all. I'm sorry."

"You can't mean the time I'm thinking of. It was the most—it's been different for me ever since. It had to have been the same for you. You did something *for* me, not to me."

But it was the same time they were thinking of, and she was right. It had turned out to be an unnecessary cruelty.

"Yossi, they have the babies straightened out."

"You don't have to tell me. I knew he was mine when I felt him jumping around in your belly. Swimming—I felt him doing the frog kick. We'll have to take him to the ocean, that's his element. Yours, too. Remember the day you seduced me?"

"It's Dov's baby."

It took him only a moment to recover. The look that crossed his face was still fading when he said, "Never mind, I have rights of collaboration. Anyway, it's the conductor who has the last word and he'll be under my baton. Let's—"

"I'm going to leave Dov—"

"Of course."

"—and go away for a while, to Degania. I don't know what I'll do when I come back, but I don't think I want to be married again."

"You are determined to get yourself stoned. You really want to live in sin?"

"I'm going to live alone, with the boys and my—with my sons."

"You'll change your mind."

She smiled and said nothing.

The daughter had been overreacting. This Konig woman was skeptical but she showed no signs of the devastation the girl had described. He tried again.

"Surely it must be clear to you, Mrs. Konig. The A blood type—"

"I'm an artist, not a scientist, Dr. Levich. And I don't have much faith in experiments."

"It is not an experiment. It's the symmetry of the organism."

"I don't have much faith in symmetry, either."

"Mother, it's time for him to be fed. Doctor, may they stay? They haven't—"

"Of course. Just close your curtain."

They went and got him from the nursery before the nurse could bring him in. The nurse protested, "But he hasn't even been changed."

"Good," Shlomo said. "We'll make the complete survey. Look, I was right. It's the genius. The *first* genius. What did I tell you?"

They laid him on the bed and unwrapped him. Chava picked up his two feet to swab his bottom and cried out, "Look! He has a beauty mark on his bottom just where you do, Shlomo!" Her words rang in the room and everyone laughed. Even, finally, Anni laughed.

"Experiments," she said.

So that when Chava picked the baby up and insinuated her nipple into his mouth and smoothed back his black hair, they were all still smiling, Anni was smiling, and Chava was unprepared to see the smile slip off her mother's face and the face turn gray and inward, the old look. The baby sucked unnoticed now because Chava had to bring her mother back. When she went inward like that, Chava had to bring her back.

"Mother?" Maybe that would be enough. Anni knew what it meant. "Mother?"

"How can it have been so long since I saw a baby nursing? All these years?"

Seven.

"All these years. You think—after seven years you think that everything you saw filthied there . . . you think you've seen it all again somewhere out here since then, washed clean. In seven years you'd think everything would have gone past you once at least, out here, and been cleansed."

"You saw a woman nursing a baby in the camp? I don't remember any babies." She folded herself around the baby. Forty-eight hours old and already the camp. Don't. Don't.

"You didn't see this baby."

Now she tells. Now she dredges it up and tells it. She'll tell me and she'll tell Potasnik and Ari-Bela and Zara and me again and after a while all of us will have the imprint of it. Every time she tells one of us it's a little less blinding in front of her eyes, and after a while she can look through it; she'll see everything through it for weeks like a gauze stage set, but it fades eventually. How long before she can see my baby clearly?

But Anni didn't tell it. How could she? What would it do to Eva's milk? This one she can't. Like some of the others she can never say.

They caught the woman. They brought her into the sorting room, one of them carrying the baby, holding it away from her reach. They didn't have to touch her. She followed, ran, stumbled into the room.

"A baby, Mother? Where was—"

We had to watch. The three of us, caught in the moment, were made to watch. The mother started to talk, her eyes frozen on the face of the one with the baby, but he handed the baby to the other one. The baby was screaming. He handed the baby over so he could undo his pants.

"Your brat is crying. It must be hungry. You should feed it. What kind of mother are you?" *His pants were down now, over his boots. We had to watch. She wasn't sure, so she reached for the baby, watching his face.*

"You'd better take that off, hadn't you, so he can get what he wants?"

"I can just—" *she started to push the shirt to one side.*

"Take it off." *But she knew, she had already understood, and in no time she was naked there in the room. She looked at him.*

"That'll do, right there." *He showed her where to lie, on a heap of men's clothes on the floor. The other one put the screaming baby in her arms. Her breasts, white and flaccid, engorged with milk when the baby found the nipple. The veins stood out blue in them.*

There on the floor he spread her legs and we all watched. He knelt astride her and she tried to move the baby but he said, smiling, "What kind of a mother stops a baby from suckling?" and he caressed the free breast, holding the baby against the other. Then all we could see were his round pink cheeks, sliding slowly forward and back, then faster, he moved like a machine, all the time watching the baby struggling at the breast. Suddenly he leaned back on his haunches, snatched it off her breast and thrust himself, purple and hard, into the tiny open mouth.

She screamed and screamed but he pressed the baby onto himself, his face contorted. When he leaned back, breathing heavily, and threw the baby down, it was dead, choked.

The other one laughed. "At least the little cocksucker died happy," he said.

"Just something I saw," Anni said, looking away from the baby at Chava's breast.

On the eighth day, Chava looked at Shlomo and saw her father.

It was only for a moment and it was because of the way he stood holding the door for them all. She stood behind him, just as she had stood behind her father that day, and Shlomo held the door open for their guests and only for a moment she saw her father, the day he had turned into a woman and held open what could never be closed again. Helpless again, she froze as she had done that time, but then he leaned into the light and grasped someone's arm in welcome and of course it was Shlomo. Not her father.

He was the most congenial of liars, Sandor Konig, and in the suburbs of Budapest in those days, a witty liar who made a living and lied for pleasure rather than for profit was a social asset. Sandor was charming; he was currency everywhere.

Anni, his wife, had no patience for other women or for afternoons of chocolate, evenings of gossip, and the appraising eyes of other people's husbands. And in perfect opposition to Sandor, she applied herself in ridiculous excess to her attempts to see clearly and to draw what she saw accurately. "I think that's true, at least," she'd say with rare satisfaction, pointing to one element in a large drawing. More often she would rip up the sheet, pulling crosswise at the heavy paper, knuckles whitened and face full of contempt. "Maudlin garbage," she'd spit. "Fantasy. What made me think I could draw? I can't even see what's in front of me." Overseeing the household and the children's needs and ripping papers and drawing again took all her time. But Sandor had time for everyone. No taller than Anni but padded with lovingly accrued flesh—not pale and wobbly skin like Aunt Marta's arms but solid and all of a piece, tightened by swims and handball and massage—he was altogether more of a presence than his wife. He was always clean shaven and immaculately groomed, and he always smelled of clean laundry.

He would lie for anyone. "You have a great future; I know music," he would assure the pathetic street violinist as he gave him a coin. Or against anyone. "I happen to know something about friend Imre's so-called prosperity," he would murmur offhand at a gathering, paying out an invented tale of Imre's bad debts and unwise investments and thus ensuring he'd be the first one invited to the next gathering.

It was of some profit to him to lie, of course: he flattered the most decrepit hags into buying useless potions from his pharmacy and he kept Anni constantly off balance regarding his whereabouts so that he could take off an occasional afternoon to beguile one of his women with fervent lies. That was wasted effort, actually. Far from keeping track of him, Anni never paid attention to anything he said.

He was a marvelous father. They could usually find him in the pharmacy, delighted to see them when Anni shut them out. He almost always had a story. "See that gentleman walking out?" he would ask in a tense, secret voice. "He doesn't know it but he has only a week to live. I kept him going for months with a new medicine his doctor didn't even know about, but now even I can't help him. Only a week at most, poor fellow." They would rush to the doorway to look after the man, swearing to each other that they could see the angel of death shimmering around him like a halo. "I shouldn't mention it, perhaps, but that young lady in the Personal aisle with her mother came to me last week with the most pathetic story. It broke my heart. You won't mention to your mother—? She asked me for a formula, a pill to make her hideous to her fiancé. 'I can't bear him,' that's just what she said to me, 'I can't bear him and they're forcing me to marry him. Make me ugly, Mr. Konig, so he despises me or I swear I'll cut up my own face.'" They shuddered at the thought, she and Jacob, and shot eager glances over to her, hoping to see the scars. "Do you know what I told her? I said, 'My dear young lady, your mother may have kept this from you out of modesty, but every girl— without exception, in every culture, every girl is repelled by the man before she marries. You'll see, there's something in marriage that will change your feelings. You don't see all the married women you know looking wretched, do you? Quite the contrary, eh? Patience, patience, you'll soon see.' I believe I saved a match there."

Then later he told them the stories that put the Nazis into perspective for them. "Sure, the Guard came to my shop, what do you think? I put the rose in their cheeks, you may believe me. 'Stand aside for a lady,' I told them. 'You ridiculous cockatoos,' I said, 'take off those caps in my pharmacy. Don't wave your feathers in my face.' Well, they were just boys and they beat it. They know authority when they hear it.

"'You close my shop, you'll be on the Eastern front so fast you'll see your lives pass before your eyes,' I told them. 'You'd better ask your commandant what he'll do to idiot underlings who remove the only professional left in the area who knows how to formulate medicine.'"

"They're letting you stay open because Janoscz is a goy," Anni said. They bristled at the scorn in her voice. "That was in the edict, any pharmacist who owns a pharmacy may stay open so long as the manager is Aryan. For now. You're no special case."

"They never even saw Janoscz," he retorted easily. "And they've closed down many another. Many another." She was always carping at him, lately. They hated her. Her drawings got blacker and blacker every week, and she destroyed every one of them in a rage. They waited for the moment, glad when she tore the paper and replaced it with a clean one.

When the other Jewish fathers were summoned suddenly in March of that year, 1944, to go to the Eastern front with labor battalions for the second army, Poppi remained at home. "Too bad I didn't get to march off with a knapsack like Uncle Imre, eh, Jacobo? But the Jewish community has to have someone here to stand up to the Nazis for them. Mr. Rozensweig himself requested me most urgently to stay. What can I do? A man has his duty." Jacob beamed, tracing the yellow star on his father's coat with a finger as though it were a medal. Eva looked at her mother, daring her to gainsay him, but Anni was looking at Sandor as though she couldn't think who he was, and for once not saying a word.

She, Eva, assured Jacob they would stay in Ujpest until the war blew over, safe because of Poppi's influence, and she told him that he should turn over his bicycle to the collection depot with dignity as she was planning to do because it was Poppi's dignity that was protecting them. Jacob was a model, that day, in the face of his classmates' shameful behavior at the collection depot. But as she told him, he mustn't look down on the other kids either, whose fathers had succumbed and left them with nothing but their mothers and their bicycles. "What if we didn't have Poppi?" she reminded him.

Jacob never saw the thing that happened to their father in the early October morning when the Arrow Cross hammered on the door and he opened to them. He was an awfully slow waker, Jacob, and he drifted out to the foyer after all of them and he stood scowling against the light and surfacing slowly out of sleep and he didn't see it, how their father turned into a woman, standing there holding open his yellow-starred door. How he held it open like any woman for the tall, steely men with the high-heeled boots and the guns on their shoulders. How the tilt of his neck and the placating half smile on his face became a woman's, submitting wordlessly to the soldiers of the Arrow Cross, offering himself, offering all of them.

And how in contempt the Arrow Cross soldiers took account of the womanish, yielding creature and absorbed into themselves the manhood Eva's father had abandoned, adding hardness to their steel and leaving Sandor standing there, holding it open so it could never be closed again.

Jacob saw the showers without water and the naked women towering around him, choking and clawing and falling on him, he saw whatever one sees in the moment before such a death, but he didn't see his father revealed at last as a woman, the woman rejected and despised and still holding it open in frozen petition.

He never saw that and she wasn't sure it wasn't a fair trade.

The Arrow Cross gave them one hour to appear in the square, fully equipped for a three-day march. Fifty kilograms of baggage each. By the end of the first fifteen minutes, Jacob was fully awake and he planted himself in front of their father and demanded, "Why didn't you tell them? We don't have to go. Why didn't you tell them who you are?" Sandor didn't answer and Jacob followed him, screaming his question now. Anni smacked him, hard, and then he screamed some more but he never asked it again.

It was only the metal bedframe behind her and at the door it was Shlomo, opening the door for their guests for the *brit*. Jacob was safe already, where he was. She went and took Shlomo's hand.

Ariela and David, their friends from the camp in Cyprus, were godmother and godfather.

Ariela entered the hospital's small social room carrying the baby, when all of them had gathered. "Welcome," they all called out. She walked in slowly, embarrassed at being the focus of attention but carrying out her function ceremoniously. The mohel was sitting between two empty chairs. She handed the baby to David, who, wincing in humorous sympathy, handed him to Shlomo. Shlomo bent and put his son into the mohel's hands.

The mohel laid the baby on the chair on his right, Elijah's chair. "Elijah, angel of the covenant," he intoned, "see, your own is before you; stand at my right hand and sustain me." Someone made a joke about hoping the mohel was right-handed. There was nervous laughter.

David sat down in the third chair. The mohel arranged the baby in his lap, unwrapping the blue-and-white woven cloth from around the naked infant. "Blessed are You," he said sternly over the voices, "our Lord, Ruler of the universe, Who has commanded us concerning the circumcision." The room quieted.

They all looked away when he cut the foreskin, and Chava tightened her hold on Anni's hand. Shlomo's blessing was drowned out by the baby's cries, but the men responded on cue, "As he has entered the covenant, so may he enter a life of Torah, marriage, and good deeds," and by the time the amens died down the baby was sucking on the wine-soaked gauze, his cries muffled and then quieted. The mohel finished the bandaging and nodded to David to let go of the baby's limbs and hold him up.

"Our God and God of our fathers," he said, now smiling for the first time. "Preserve this child unto his father and his mother and may his name in Israel be called Aharon ben Shlomo, Aaron, son of Shlomo." The congratulations and the jokes swelled to fill the room and only David and Shlomo heard the mohel deliver the final words of the ceremony:

"When I passed by you and saw you in your blood, I said to you: 'In your blood live!' and again I said to you, 'In your blood live!'"

"You are the grandmother?" The mohel had made his way over to Anni. He lifted his glass of scotch. "Mazal tov to you. Tell me, did I hear that you made the baby's circumcision cloth? You don't see that any more."

"Yes. I wove it."

"Magnificent. Tell me, is there a significance to the design? So intricate, I tried to make out—"

"No significance at all, just a design. That's why I'm a weaver. It's pure pattern, representing nothing. No lies, you see, and no truths." She smiled.

"But surely an artist would want to present what he sees."

"It depends on what one sees. Come, have some rugelach, they're homemade by a Hungarian."

"You are the father?" the mohel asked Benjamin, in another small room across the hospital corridor.

He blushed and smiled. "Just the godfather. And this is Miriam Nishri, the godmother."

"They are my oldest friends, from the kibbutz," Rachaeli said. "And this is my mother, Rivka Ben Dor."

"But—is this all? We are so few? And the father?"

"This is all. The father is not here. Shall we get on with it?"

The mohel looked from one face to another. A lot of strain here. Probably a divorce. Or a death, God forbid. He sat down in the middle chair. The mother put the baby right into his hands herself. Allowing himself the mental equivalent of a shrug, the mohel laid the baby on the chair and turned his attention to him. "This is the chair of Elijah," he said in a comforting voice, "who will precede the Messiah, let him come soon, who will turn the hearts of the fathers unto the children and the hearts of the children unto their fathers. Elijah, angel of the covenant," his voice rang in the empty room, "see, your own is before you."

He had to tell them what to do every step of the way. Finally he lifted the drowsing infant in his own hands. "Our God and God of our fathers, preserve this child unto his father and his mother and may his name in Israel be . . . ?" In his confusion, he had forgotten to ask the names.

"Daniel," the mother said.

"Daniel ben . . . ?"

"Just Daniel."

"No, my dear, the child's father's name. Daniel, son of—?"

"There is no father. Call him Daniel ben Rachael."

Gottenyu, a real situation here. He cleared his throat tactfully. "It doesn't matter . . . where the father is at the moment. The child is entitled to his father's name."

"Not this one. My baby is a bastard. His name in Israel will be Daniel ben Rachael. Are we finished?"

He almost dropped the child. No rabbi here, of course, never when you need one. Well, the naming was only a formality, best not to say anything, get it over before this crazy woman caused a scene. "—And may his name in Israel be called Daniel ben Rachael," he said grimly. He relaxed his arms, bringing the baby close to his chest and unconsciously rocking him a little. "When I passed by you and saw you in your blood," he said gently to the baby whose fragile eyelids were trembling closed, "I said to you, 'In your blood live!' and again I said to you, 'In your blood live!'"

When he raised his head, the mother wasn't even looking at the child. She was looking at a blond young woman who had entered the room without his noticing.

"Mazal tov," the young woman said. "I came to invite you all to join our party." She went up to the crazy one. "After all," she said smiling, "they're practically brothers, right?"

He didn't even want to think about how the babies could be practically brothers. He handed the baby to the mother and left the room, trailing a faint "mazal tov" behind him. He quickened his steps, lest the mother catch up and try to press a fee on him. He wasn't about to take money for bringing a bastard into the covenant.

Rabbi Becker looked up when the door to his office opened. He nearly didn't recognize her because she was dressed in street clothes. Then of course he remembered bleakly who she was.

"I know," he said. "The baby is a bastard. You don't have to make another announcement."

"The mohel told you?"

He nodded. "So you accomplished something. The first woman in Israel to declare her own child a bastard. Something else you want?" Then he relented. Surely he ought to offer some guidance, if only for the sake of the child. Nothing legal had happened yet. "Listen," he began.

"I just came to ask you what's the procedure with the divorce."

"Divorce? He's leaving you? Listen, let me—"

"I made a public announcement: I committed adultery, the baby is a bastard. The blood tests prove it. Now you know it and you're a rabbi, right? So he has to divorce me. You have to tell him, right?"

"What are you—"

She put her hands flat on his desk and leaned over into his breathing space. "My husband—Dov Kovner, the hospital has the address and all that—is a Kohen. I'm an adulteress. So now it's up to you."

He really thought he might pass out. The top of his head spun slowly counterclockwise, his ears pulled the rest of him clockwise. "I'll have to get a scribe," he said vaguely, "witnesses."

"Fine. Just let me know when and where. Thank you."

"You're welcome. Wait!"

"Yes?" Remarkable. He said wait and she waited. He sat up straighter. "You know what it will say on your divorce decree?" he asked sternly.

"What?"

"'Forbidden to the husband and forbidden to the lover.' That means forever."

"What do you mean, 'forbidden'?"

"In *marriage*."

"Oh, marriage." She turned to go.

He stood. "And *then*," he shouted, "it will be irrevocable, about the baby's status. A divorce granted on the public evidence of his illegitimacy, you assent to it—the whole country will know. And he will be cut off from his people. Your son will be a bastard, a fatherless one."

"Yes, I know. Don't forget, the name is Dov Kovner."

BOOK
THREE

Even in death, families may be seen standing pressed together, clutching hands.

TESTIMONY, DR. KURT GERSTEIN

Ramat Gan, December 4, 1961

When the bus pulled over to the side of the road and the driver just sat there staring ahead without opening the doors or saying anything, Dani was working with the rope and the handkerchief, trying to get the knots the way his *Magic and Illusions* book said, so at first he didn't notice. Then he noticed because of how quiet it had gotten in the bus. All you could hear was the radio and someone shushing a little kid. Dani listened for a minute, hoping it was real news like an Arab attack. Maybe even their bus would get attacked. He could get behind the Arabs—who'd see a ten-year-old kid in all the confusion?—and disarm one. He started to report the incident in his head, first to Chava and Anni and all of them, then a gorier version to tell Aaron. BOY SAVES BUSLOAD FROM ARAB ATTACK: THREE DEAD.

But it was only the trial again on the radio, more about the trial of the Nazi guy. Eichmann, Eichmann. Every place you went everyone was listening to the radio and shushing people. He sighed and went back to the rope and the handkerchief, so he wasn't looking when the bus driver slammed his hand down on the change machine.

"Bastard!" the driver shouted and Dani looked up sharply, but the driver went on: "Bastards. Those pigs, those filthy bastards," so Dani knew the driver hadn't been shouting at him but talking about the Nazis. It was just a way of cursing. He, Dani, was the real bastard. The Nazi guy was the other kind.

He looked at the diagram of the trick again and waited for his hands to get steady so he could retie the knot. He had something to work out in his mind besides the rope trick, so while he waited he coiled the rope around his left palm and concentrated on the other thing. The bus engine gunned angrily and the bus lurched out onto the road while he was arranging the words in his mind to explain to Aaron what he had found out about how men did it to ladies. Aaron was never going to believe this.

Dani was the only one who got off the bus smiling but it was all right because no one was looking at anyone else anyway. They never did after they listened about the trial.

It wasn't like that when the radios got hold of the story of Rachaeli's adultery and the bastard baby and the rabbinic mandate of divorce; in the comparatively dull autumn of '51, everyone had a field day with it. Everyone had an opinion. The liberal press called it "a disgrace, in these enlightened times, for a baby to be condemned on account of his parents' actions. Should the state legislate," they demanded, "this child's ability to marry and father legal children because the Orthodox claim a stranglehold on marriage and on legitimacy of birth?" The more liberal members of the rabbinate applied themselves to finding an interpretation of the law that was suitable to modern times. The Orthodox said little. The law was on their side, no one was denying that. And the facts in the case couldn't be clearer. There was no hope for this child. No one liked it, but there it was.

"What does the law actually say?" a reporter pressed the chief rabbi's representative. "Is there no way out, in such cases?"

"In earlier times he could have married a bondswoman and set her free, and then their marriage would be legitimate. But there are no bondswomen any more, of course. He has two options: he can marry another bastard—"

"And then would their children be legitimate?"

"No, unfortunately. But the marriage, at least, would be kosher."

"Marvelous. The other option?"

"He could marry a non-Jew. Then, of course, because by law the mother's status determines the Jewishness of the child, the offspring would be non-Jews."

"There is no way for Daniel ben Rachael to father Jewish children legitimately?"

"None. Well, of course he could emigrate. The other branches of the rabbinate might not look into his lineage so closely, and his children might be considered legitimate in such communities. Never in a community that adheres to the law, of course, and so by definition never in the state of Israel."

"So he can be cut off from his people or he can leave his country. That's his choice."

"He can also stay with his people but choose not to marry."

"And who is going to tell Daniel ben Rachael that if he wishes to remain in Israel, he is not permitted to marry or father children?"

"The mother, I presume. This situation is of her making, please remember."

But the mother seemed unperturbed. She never stopped smiling all those first few months, and that drove everyone crazy. She seemed to feel no remorse and no apprehension. It was public knowledge, of course, that she was an adulteress, and worse, an unnatural mother, but it was hard to remember it when one actually saw her that winter and spring, flushed and rounded, moving more slowly than the world around her and languid with triumph. She looked, nursing the baby, like a virgin warming to a secret love. It was hard to remember, then, what she was and the unthinkable thing she had done.

Except at the kibbutz. They were too horrified at Degania to be disarmed by the smile. They felt free, one after another, to make their opinions known to her. She was amused at the uniformity; one after another they said: If you have to have an affair—well, all right, but to insist on divorce? It's wanton destruction. If you had stayed here, their tone said, you wouldn't have had time for such depravity, nor the need for it.

Her old friend Benjamin was now secretary of the kibbutz. "It's a terrible thing for Rivka," he told her severely. "You think it's nice for her, the whole country knowing that you . . . And what about the baby?"

They were standing outside the social hall. Rachaeli held the baby balanced on her hip, bouncing him a little. She lifted him to her, held him up so that her face was partly obscured behind his little head. "You don't know the circumstances," she told Benjamin softly from behind the warm little fortresss. "No one really does, and no one's going to. Don't judge what you don't understand."

"You ought to come back here. Let the baby grow up here, at least, with some . . . with family around."

She thought later what control she'd had. The baby in front of her seemed to muffle her response, distance her from her rage. "Well, we'll see," she said, walking away and thinking, When Hell freezes over.

She went back to Ramat Gan, of course. In fact, she went back sooner than she'd expected to. A man who identified himself as Dov's lawyer called her at Degania to inform her that Dov wanted to meet with her regarding the children. "Let him call me; we'll meet," she said.

"We think the meeting had better take place in my office. Say on Wednesday at eight-thirty?"

Shrugging, she went. Dov was sitting in a leather chair in the lawyer's office. He nodded curtly at her, face stony. "I've decided that Zvi and Avi should be raised at Degania," he said.

"I won't have it," she retorted flatly. "I won't have them raised in that . . . orphanage. Why should they be? They have a mother and a father."

He looked at her. *What kind of a mother?* his look said, but she didn't give him a chance to speak.

"Besides," she went on. "If they live at Degania, you won't see enough of them to suit you. I know you, you'll want them to yourself all week-end. *They* won't permit that; a kid is either living at the kibbutz or he isn't. You'll have to go there and see them during family hours."

He thought it over, then nodded. "I'll take them, then," he said.

"Don't be silly, Dov. What are you going to do with two little boys?"

"Whatever you would do, only in a sane manner. My boys are not going to be raised in that kind of—"

"Mr. Kovner will make arrangements for a qualified housekeeper, of course," the lawyer put in. Rachaeli looked at him. He was bearded and soft-looking, paunchy, and his tone was pleasant enough, but there was something hard in his eyes. He had a stack of books and an open file on his desk. He selected a book and opened it to a marker, but didn't refer to it, just sat with his hand poised on the page. "And as soon as . . . things settle down, you'll be able to arrange visiting times with the boys."

Dov wouldn't look at her.

"That's all you ever wanted," she said. "To come home and have them all to yourself. Open the door and have them come running: 'Daddy's home! Daddy's home! Daddy! Daddy! Daddy!' With no one in the way."

"All I wanted was what I had," Dov said in a monotone. "Now I want what I have left. I want my boys."

"Surely you don't think you're in a position to raise them alone?" the lawyer asked her. "You'll be working?"

"Of course. So will Dov."

"And you have your . . . the baby?"

"I have my baby."

The lawyer looked up at the smile in her voice when she said that. "You'll be better off seeing Zvi and Avi on the weekends. You'll have a little time for them then."

He didn't refer to the book or to the papers in his folder, didn't threaten her at all, but his finger moved gently back and forth on a line of the text. She understood. She would lose them, in a fight. She was notoriously unfit. Dov would get them, or they'd be sent to Degania. She wasn't going to have them raised at Degania; they'd maneuvered her into saying that right off. She was in a box. She sat still, seeing how it was, finally hating Dov.

"I want them weekends and school vacations," she said. "No exceptions."

"No vacations," Dov said. "We'll talk about weekends if . . . when things settle down."

"Weekends—no if and when—and vacations. Or I'll fight you."

"You might want some vacation time to yourself, Rachaeli," the lawyer said, smiling paternally. "Why don't we take them as they come? Certainly if you want Passover, say, or—well, we can work it out. No one wants anything but what's best for the boys. Surely a court fight . . ."

"Every weekend," she said. "And half their vacations."

"That's fair," the lawyer said. He said it in such a leisurely way, and Dov was so still, that she knew she'd given them everything they wanted.

She didn't cry until she got home and began nursing the baby. "The one who has them on weekends and holidays is the one they look forward to seeing," she told herself vengefully, tears running off her face and onto her breast. "I'll spoil them rotten. They'll run to me when I come to get them. 'Mommy! Mommy!' They'll cry when they have to leave me. He'll see what it's like." Then, "He won't be able to handle them. He'll come asking me to take them back. Or he'll die and they'll have to give them to me." Then finally, "They're his anyway. They were his from the beginning." She held the baby up against her, sobbing wildly, until he began crying, too, for more milk. "What are you wailing about?" she cried, roughly giving him the other breast. "You're not losing anything." But then she hugged him to her and rocked him, saying, "Shhh, shhhh," although he was quiet now, sucking steadily. After a while he fell asleep with his mouth cupped loosely around the nipple, but she held him there for a long time as though he were still hungrily feeding.

It wasn't so bad when they were actually gone, living with Dov. He kept the flat and she moved to a smaller one on Herzl Street, a tiny two-bedroom. She called the boys every day after school for a while, then most days, and they came on weekends. The lawyer was right. It was better than coming home after work and having to deal with them when she was tired. She had long, lazy nights alone with the baby, with no distractions. It suited her. If it was wrenching to watch them run to Dov on Saturday nights, forsaking her, it wasn't much worse than waiting braced for that moment every night had been. And she had Dani. She had pulled it off.

On the birth certificate, his name was given as Kovner, and for a couple of weeks she thought about changing it, but she didn't bother. It would have meant changing her name, too, all those forms and papers, and then the boys would have a different name from hers. Why should she let Dov be the only one to share their name? And really, why go to the trouble? The whole country knew who she was and what was hers.

She basked in that. Let them watch her; they would see her smiling. She knew how she looked. She would walk the eight blocks from her flat to Chava's in her loose cotton dress, feeling the power of her body— breasts welling up for the baby, nipples strong and tight, long bare legs flirting the skirt out as she walked, hair shining, skin glowing, smile barely tweaking at her mouth. She knew that men looked at her and she saw herself as a rich, promising package, woman and baby. Not for you, she thought, dismissing them all and sailing the carriage on toward Chava's.

It was odd, but the two women were seeking each other out. It may have been Rachaeli's smile that drew Chava to her, that elegant, free, self-reliant smile that was unlike anything Chava was used to seeing. Or it may really have been what Chava told Shlomo it was, pity for the child. At any rate, she pursued Rachaeli when she returned from her stay at Degania.

Chava and Shlomo lived in Ramat Gan, too, about twelve blocks from Rachaeli in a lovely, roomy flat on Yehalom Street, with a balcony and gardens and a playground. Chava had chosen it even though it was too much room for them then, because something about the arrangement of the kitchen and the shape of the entryway reminded her of Ujpest. Shlomo had money, and he indulged her. He paid for Anni's flat, too, of course. Anni's flat was tiny, spare, and modern, and it reminded her of nowhere she had ever been, which was why she chose it.

Chava didn't dare to visit Rachaeli, but she invited her to come for tea and then for lunch and then for whole afternoons. Rachaeli went. Chava seemed rather a sad sack to her, but her only friends outside of Yossi were at the kibbutz or at work. At the kibbutz they were treating her like one of the criminally insane, and she was on a three-month maternity leave from work, so she took to visiting Chava, formally at first and then unannounced, until at last she simply came and went like a relative. Like a sister. The newspeople got hold of that, too, naturally, and made a great deal of the contrast between the quiet, Orthodox young woman and her notorious friend, even catching the moment when the women took their babies out for their first walk together. There was a photo in the evening paper. It showed the two of them standing on the sidewalk outside Chava's flat, laughing. Chava had one hand on her carriage, the other over her mouth. She was looking at Rachaeli, who had both hands on her carriage and whose dark head was thrown back in laughter. The headline said, SOMETHING TO LAUGH ABOUT?

There was. As they walked, Chava—emboldened perhaps by being out of her apartment and seduced to candor by Rachaeli's ease—had mentioned that she was going to the ritual baths in a few days. "I wish I'd had a girl," she said.

"Why?"

"Well, you know, if it had been a girl I'd have had to wait another seven weeks."

"What?"

"You know. If it's a boy you're unclean for seven weeks. Then you go to the *mikvah* and you can resume—"

"—sex."

"Yes. But if it's a girl, you're unclean for fourteen weeks."

Rachaeli stopped and stared at her. "Unclean. Are you serious?"

"Yes. It's because you add the girl's period of impurity to yours, I think. I wish I'd had girl triplets!"

When they stopped laughing, Chava said, "It's only that I'm so tired. I just don't . . ."

"You don't have to tell me. All I want is to be left alone to sleep. I feel as though I'll never want a man again. But don't worry; it'll pass. Meanwhile," she pushed the carriage so that they would be walking and she and Chava could avoid looking at each other, "you pretend a little and make short work of it so that you can get to sleep. Men are really superfluous at this point, but it's not a good idea to let them know it because you'll want them later."

She smiled as she said it, to belie the hardness of it and to confirm that neither of them believed it, but it was true for both of them. Rachaeli had operated unconsciously on this premise with the first two births. The difference this time, with Yossi, was that it was a conscious design. She had stopped bleeding, she was intact again and weighted with sensuality, but it was centrifugal. Five times a day the baby cried and the milk coursed into her breasts, hardening them and thrusting forward the darkened nipples. Five times a day the demanding mouth fastened on a nipple and drew the milk, workmanlike and steadily. It was perfect. The baby and the breast that nourished him were one complete world, she and her breast and the baby feeding at it were another. No suspense between them, no yearning, no awkwardness at all, just the physical tension of the hardening pressure, the first sweet rush of release and then the slow and steady pumping and the answering tightening of her womb. And the other breast throbbed and trickled in sympathy, waiting for release.

Once a day she slid a soapy hand over the baby in his warm bath. His bottom cupped easily into her palm, the circlet of her fingers slid easily up and down his thigh. The sensation was his and, separately, hers. Perfect. And twice, maybe three times a day she spun into the very center of the centrifuge: first heavy, then weightless, then nothing, perfect sleep. She had barely to reach for it; it all came to her in easy rotation: nursing, bath, sleep, nursing. The last thing she wanted was a man. She said to herself that it was a nuisance to see Yossi, but it was more than a nuisance, it was a wrenching outward from that centrifugal force that held her days.

But she had been back from Degania for a couple of weeks now and she had seen him three times. She had it worked out. He never came to the flat, of course, even if the baby was sleeping. "Let the camel get his nose in the tent," she thought, "and he'll move in, humps and all." He was still saying that he wanted to marry her, and for a while he was ardent about it. That was out of the question of course; Yossi was going to be a complete stranger to Dani, otherwise what was it all for? So she showed him the *get*. "Forbidden to the husband," it said, "and forbidden to the lover."

"So we can't marry," she explained. "No one will marry us."

"That's ridiculous. We'll go to Florence or to New York and we'll come back married. What are they going to do then, whip us with their sidelocks? Sacrifice a goat and denounce us from the steps of the Temple?"

It was part of the agreement with Dov, she told him then, as though reluctantly, her mind switching for the lie to some cool and distant place. "The baby's his," she told Yossi, "and he could probably have gotten custody if he'd forced it. He got Zvi and Avi. I had to promise I wouldn't live with you, to get the baby."

It worked. Yossi was outraged, then sympathetic, then tender and loving. Another easy win. It didn't escape her, how easy it was, and that further increased her distance from him. But she went to his flat, thinking clearly about holding her place with him for the time when she would want him again.

It was a simple matter, really, to keep him bound to her. She had the advantage with him that he'd never dealt with a woman after childbirth, so when she whispered to him that it would still have to be several weeks before they could make love "the regular way," he believed it. She stood with her arms around his neck, raised up a little on her toes so that he could feel her all along his body, and so that her thigh muscles could tighten a little on the bulge in his khakis, reminding him.

He remembered. When she had undressed to a half-slip and lay next to him, trailing her fingers up the inside of his thigh and lightly up to the tip of him where already a drop had formed—when she teased a fingertip over the tip of him, slippery with that droplet, and then sat upright on her haunches over him, moving him with two hands against the slide of her panties—even when he came with that intensity peculiar to passivity, he remembered where he wanted to be. He looked up at her and thought he was marking his place.

And the smile drove him crazier than anyone. She would walk through his door smiling, put the cello down and kiss him, coming out of the kiss with the smile still in her eyes. She would play for him—the technique was still mediocre but there was an authority, anyway, to her readings now, an authority in everything she did—then she would play upon him, play him, smiling that inward smile of hers, so that when he came he was somehow losing to her and he thought more and more of penetrating her, causing her to writhe and gasp, too, and to lose the smile.

For Chava it was more complicated, naturally, because they all pulled outward at her and there was no pleasing all of them. It had been better before the baby was born. She would go to Anni's flat while Shlomo was at work, an hour or two a day, and there would always be something for her to do there. Anni would sit at her loom and Chava would busy herself in the little flat, doing the things Anni had no patience for—cooking, cleaning, organizing paperwork. Anni was at her best working at the loom. The regular rhythm of shuttling, pulling, picking up and laying down seemed to draw off the restlessness and temper her mood. She never minded talking in Hebrew then. They would talk about one or another of Anni's cronies or, these past months, about the progression of the pregnancy and the baby's layette. Walking there in the afternoons Chava always cast about in her mind for something to offer up to Anni in case the conversation flagged—gossip about one of her friends or some event from the news, so long as it wasn't something that would bring up the past. But almost everything in the news brought up the past. Local disputes or governmental excesses were usually safe. Art news was okay. Late in the afternoon one or another of the cronies would drift in and Chava would leave, always reminding her mother what she'd left for dinner, always saying as she left, "I'll see you tomorrow. Okay?" Sometimes Anni would already be involved in conversation with the crony and Chava would have to repeat it. "Mother? I'll see you tomorrow. Okay?"

Anni would release her then: "Sure." Only that, and sometimes even that would be in Hungarian, an offhand shoot from the gabble in the room.

But now there was the baby and so Anni came to Chava's every day. She left the loom behind, of course, so Chava had it all to do, like after the camps and before Anni found the weaving—all the tempering and easing and soothing.

Because after the camps, it was suddenly up to her. She learned that right away, even before they got to Cyprus. She'd been afraid on the ship; she'd had no assigned place to sleep there, and the rolling and pitching and the night sighs of the others, and near their pallet the man and woman silently pistoning under a thin cover and herself anonymous in the disordered darkness had panicked her more than standing numbered and counted for a death call, and she had touched Anni's arm. "Mother? Could you tell me a story?"

"What? Eva?"

"Do you think you could tell me a story?" It was dead dark but she could see Anni's face and she instantly read her mistake. There was a resentful child where her fierce mother had been, and that child's face was blank. No comfort there. She adjusted immediately, pulling her own cover back around her shoulders and pretending to come to consciousness. "What did I say? I'm sorry, I was dreaming. 'Night." She turned over and released her mother and after a while began to tell a story to herself, a story about Anni and her at Auschwitz to pull her through to where sleep was. The fierce mother had existed only after the soldiers came to the door that day, only then, and going to Auschwitz and at Auschwitz.

Eva put one hand on the crack on the ship's deck that told her she was in her certain place and told herself again about the mother she had had at Auschwitz. She searched for a day to remember. Not the first day there, because on that day Anni said nothing at all after the selections, even when they all had to strip and Eva saw her mother naked for the first time and stared at all those round places no one would have dreamed she had. Even when she stared, Anni had no word for her. Even when their heads were shaved and Eva had to say, "Mother?" to be sure which one she was, no word and no sign.

Maybe the next day, when Anni peremptorily pulled together their group of five and left Leonore Zonnenborn out for her sake, Eva's sake. Yes, maybe then, because she remembered Anni quickly picking two strangers—Lila and Ottilie, it turned out to be—and Marika, a friend from Ujpest, but cutting Leonore out even though Leonore almost cried with fear at being left to group up with four strangers for every *Appel* and selection and all the work cadres. "You're too tall," Anni explained brusquely. She directed Leonore's attention to Eva and Lila and Ottilie and Marika, all pretty much of one height and all slender and tightly built. "I can't afford to have Eva looking small by comparison. She has to pass for sixteen." So it was the five of them for roll calls and work detail, and when other women were relieved to have been passed over for the tatooed numbers, Anni kept her mouth shut but saw to it that the five of them were tatooed. "Not one sound," said Eva's fierce mother when it was getting to be their turn for the needle. "If the Germans go to the

117

trouble of numbering us they won't get rid of us so fast. Stand up taller. And not a sound."

A49488, that was Anni's number, and they called Eva A50062. Lila and Ottilie and Marika were A57-something; Eva couldn't remember any more. A family. And Anni found them the quarry detail when others were maneuvering to work in "Canada" sorting clothes, or in the latrines, easy inside work. "You get typhus in the latrine, and after a while in 'Canada' they send you up the chimney so you won't be able to bear witness," she said. So they worked the quarry in the tightening fall days. The men were cracking the earth's crust and the women were hauling pieces of it up to the surface to be crushed into smaller pieces and carted to another place on the surface, so that the face of the earth was littered with its dying inner layer. Their job was to empty earth from its inside outward and they, their cadre of five, were a chain of feet and hands conveying pieces of the center outward. Their fingers and toes swelled and the skin broke and little insignificant bones broke in them and mended whatever way, Anni's hands too, but she wouldn't take the job of pushing the barrow to save her hands. "That's for the child," she said flatly as though Eva were the child of all of them.

"But you're an artist," Marika said. "Your hands, Anni."

"Tell Leonore Zonnenborn about being an artist," Anni said.

Leonore had reported her gift to the authorities. "Artist," she said when they asked what skills. So they sent her to the hospital to work. "It's warmer there," she told them in the barracks that first night, and although she didn't say so they knew there was food there, too. But in the night she vomited and that was because her job in the hospital was to make detailed anatomical drawings of the babies during surgery, and to take photographs afterward. She vomited all the time and at last they sent her up the chimney, but they kept the drawings.

Anni said she could sew when they asked about her skills, and she refused now to take the barrow to protect her artist's hands. "That's for the child," she said.

And Anni made them tell stories, after Eva drifted off in her thoughts one day, dropping a stone from the barrow so that it fell back into the quarry, and was punished by being made to hold up the stones all that long day. Eva knelt on the ground in front of the barracks and held out the rocks in her two hands and the first pains, the ones in the knees and the wrists, were making her bite her tongue along the sides and the guard could see, every time he passed, if she let her arms bend or lower at all and then her mother's voice came at her through the barracks wall: "Eva,

I am going to tell you a story. Listen carefully and don't move, because the story is long and complicated and you might miss something." It made no sense at all, Mother had to be at work in the quarry, she never told them stories, she hated stories, she only liked things to be true, but it was her voice coming through the walls, starting the long story, "Once upon a time, Eva, there were three hunters . . ." and all day long she told it. She must have seen through a crack in the wall because when the guard came over she stopped and when he went away she started again. So she must have heard him laugh in disgust when he saw Eva's puddle of urine and smelled the rest, must have seen him smack her hands with the stick so they almost dropped the rocks, but she only kept on telling it when he went away. "Now listen, Eva, because Petra was in grave danger there in her hollow tree, remember?" All day, the long story full of magic and fantasy from her mother who hated everything but truth, all day long in a storyteller's voice so compelling that it held out her arms, bound her spine erect. It was Mother and not Mother, that voice. Eva never thought, What if they catch her, What if they have a roll call and miss her, she only rode on the voice until at the end the sun went down and they said she could drop the rocks and get up. She couldn't drop them or get up but Marika and Ottilie took them out of her hands and now Mother's voice was angry through the wall: "Get up, Eva, stand up this instant. How long do you think I'm going to lie here and wait for you?" and she was so startled at that—at the picture of her lying in the barracks all day; she'd forgotten that the voice had a body—that she worked herself upright and negotiated the twenty-two steps to the barracks where Mother lay under the lowest bunk, unseeable until Ottilie and Marika pulled her out backward, so flat she couldn't have gotten out alone. How could she have gotten in there, how could she have lain all day so cruelly flat and told that endless tale? And if they had found her there?

"Everyone has to tell a story from her life," Anni told them the next day. "In turn. We have to stay alert. Lili, you first."

"Stories from my life I can't tell with Eva here," Lili grinned. Anni only looked at her until Lili shrugged and led off with a long tale about a man and a bank account. After that they all told their stories in turns and when it was Eva's turn and she would tell about school and friends, they would advise her and discuss her events just as though she were a woman, too, or at least their grown child. The women's breasts were gone—they had wasted to long balloons and then shriveled and disappeared—and they were all bald, so that there was no difference between the four of them and Eva, except that she got some of Anni's food every day and they all knew it was Anni's job to keep Eva alive, get her through this, because they were mother and child.

Then the Germans stopped all work at the quarry—near the end that was, when everyone who could work had to burn corpses and help get rid of the bones—and Anni was sent to "Canada" to sort clothes and destroy evidence, but Eva went with the other three to dig trenches for the bones and they continued with their stories as though Anni were still with them. Then at night Anni would strip Eva and check her for sores and watch her eat the extra piece of bread and pinch her cheeks and they would all stand together for *Appel*.

Anni pulled them all through it, all five of them lived until liberation and even through the weeks after liberation when people were dying extravagantly, yielding to sudden food and release from the routine of terror. She pulled all of them through so that Eva would live, pitching her fierce authority against the sudden dangerous food and freedom.

But it wasn't just that she kept Eva alive, that was the point. In the fearful darkness of the ship Eva called up two of the best times at Auschwitz when Anni was a mother to her. Both were after liberation. One was when the chaplain, the young American rabbi, read from a list of names and told them that Sandor was dead, shot in the forests. Anni blinked once and the young rabbi, having learned that grief looked different on this planet of horror, took her hand and explained gently that because so much time had passed since Sandor's death, they were not required or even permitted to sit in mourning for the customary week. "You can sit for one hour only," he told her, still holding the bent fingers. "Sit right on the ground. Would you like me to stay with you for the hour?"

Anni closed her eyes again, a slow blink, and leveled a look at him and would have spoken only she, Eva, never having heard from Anni the story of how Sandor had gone, said, "No. Poppi," and wailed and burrowed herself into Anni's stiff side. Anni didn't say what she had been about to say but put an arm around Eva—she felt it still, on this hard, pitching deck—and closed her eyes again in resignation and sat down on the ground, pulling Eva down with her. They sat right there while people went by them and around them, and the young rabbi sat with them and listened to Eva's broken descriptions of her father and dealt with her flood of tears that reminded him of grief on his home planet. Anni sat a little apart from them in silence, but at the end of the hour she gave Eva her two hands and helped her up. "Come, Evike," she said, just like a mother. "If you're going to cry for Poppi, now you do it standing up. Come and wash."

The other time was right after liberation, when the women went and found the men and somehow cajoled the life force back into them. Eva was walking past the fence and saw a man on the ground, then saw that it was a man on top of a woman. His bones were stretched out over hers and she was crying out, "Come on, come, put it in me," and trying to get one bony arm down between them. Anni was there, suddenly. She put a hand over Eva's eyes and turned her around, holding her so she couldn't see them. Eva lay rocking with the ship in the random blackness, hearing the pistoning of the people next to her, and called up the giddy moment in Auschwitz when her mother's body blocked the bald, copulating wraiths and her mother's voice countered the woman's cries, "All right, Eva, don't worry, don't worry, all right."

But Anni couldn't do it any more; Eva learned it that moment on the ship and accepted it at once. Anni had traded Jacob's death for Eva's life and then stayed alive to get her through it and she had gotten her through it, but now she couldn't do it any more. It was Eva's turn.

And in the beginning, at the camp on Cyprus where they waited to be allowed into the new country of Israel, it was easy because it was only the two of them, no one else was pulling at Eva's attention. Even after the Israelis came and began to take the teenagers and the older children for training sessions, leaving the adults to sit weaving baskets or draw out their simple routine tasks, Eva would come back at dusk to Anni and tell the story of her day, leaving out nothing so that Anni would have a day, too.

It was no one's fault, really, that the adults were held in storage there on Cyprus. Only a few Israelis could be spared from the struggles in Palestine, and those few had to be used efficiently. That meant working with the children. They'd have had to have different training, anyway, to deal with these adults. These adults were a special case, European Jews who had chosen to remain in Europe and who were bound for Israel now not out of choice but because their Europe had been snatched out from under them. It was still in them, though; they were Europeans by choice and they would never make Israelis, though they had to be cared for. But the children would be Israelis in no time, especially the orphans, and no time was to be lost in mending them and absorbing them.

So they set the adults up with a language class and a few crafts and took the children to the beach to run, pounding barefoot on the sand. They trained them to climb nets and fences and slide under barriers on their stomachs with sticks in their mouths. These young Israelis came from the kibbutzim or from other early settlers; they had always been Israelis and from them the children absorbed a clean, crisp Hebrew and a new set of givens: Jews can win. Must win. Winning does not mean hiding and outwitting, surviving the blows. Winning means holding what is yours and punishing your attacker.

This Eva did not report to Anni as she sat weaving the huge, intricate baskets that she would later abandon. She told her about the other children, about the climbing and jumping and, selectively, about the Israelis.

When she was fifteen, Shlomo came over to Cyprus from Youth Aliyah, and then it began to be complicated because there were more things she couldn't report to Anni, and because now she didn't even always want to report back to Anni.

Shlomo came from religious people, a diamond-trading family that had emigrated from Antwerp to Tel Aviv in 1920. At sixteen he began going out on night raids with a group from the Palmach. He was useful to the group because he was trained in Talmud and among diamond cutters to concentrate and to think through the possibilities before acting. He never mentioned the Palmach group to his family—people in diamonds were trained, too, to hold their tongues—and when Sara Yoffe asked him to go with her to Cyprus to train other youngsters for ground combat, he mentioned Youth Aliyah to his parents and he went.

He was eighteen then, and he had known only pioneer girls, and mostly from a distance. Once he had been with the Palmach group, camped out on the beach, and he had been surprised by one of the girls as he wrapped the leather strap around his arm in preparation for morning prayers. "Good! Shlomo, you're up! Want to swim?" she'd asked. She was wearing shorts and a T-shirt. "Sure," he'd said, "just give me two minutes," and he'd turned east and raced through the prayers, swaying against his own rising heartbeat.

In the water the T-shirt outlined her breasts, the nipples like two new pencil erasers, and she had smiled at him over them as though she were unaware of them. How could she be? He swam hard to exhaust himself, grimly tamed his body so he could walk out of the ocean. She waited for him, pulling the T-shirt away from her skin and flapping it and shaking out her hair. She smiled right at him. "So. That was good."

"Yes. Uh . . . see you tonight? I mean, if—"

"Sure. Why not?"

Why not. That night she gave him access to the nipples and, with cheerful ease, to the rest of her. Later all he remembered of it was his anxiety and ignorance and then relief. He had gotten through it.

It didn't make him much more comfortable around the girls. They seemed invulnerable. They never appeared to feel uncertain or self-conscious. They bantered and teased and offered their bodies or withheld them as it pleased them, all according to an inner scheme he could neither fathom nor influence. Some of the boys had—seemed to have been born with—a kind of calculated nonchalance, an indifferent sexuality. It was clearly the way to be, because the girls gravitated to them, but Shlomo couldn't do it. Something always gave him away: a sudden juiciness in his voice or a surge of heat to his face, or simply his inability to toss easy words with them. No one bantered in his house; words were used to convey information or to weigh options. He had nowhere to practice flippancy, and he wished for someone who would make it unnecessary. When the heat of his body gathered force and geysered him awake in the night he would come to consciousness imprinted with the picture of an anonymous woman's body, but as the throbbing slowed and he rode the flat land before sleep, he would conjure a different girl, whose face was as open to him as the rest of her and who told him in simple whispered words how he was moving her.

His father was beginning to train him to use the loupe and to recognize flaws and cracks in the stones. A diamond was simple; it was perfect, or it wasn't. You could cut it only so many ways, and if you knew how to look, every one of those ways was visible under the loupe. With girls, everything was hidden. You were always guessing. And they were always changing; it was like a game with them. He felt hopelessly stupid playing the game. When two other girls made their bodies available to him, one for a period of two or three months, he didn't understand why, and they never said. They closed their eyes during the act, and when it was over they smoked a cigarette and made cheerful talk. They never said whether he moved them and there seemed no way to ask. He confined himself to commentary on their chatter, learning flippancy.

Eva was fifteen when he first saw her there on Cyprus. She sat with a dozen others and listened to Sara introducing herself and the other leaders and describing conditions in Palestine. Sara made a little joke and the girl responded with a quick smile of understanding. He watched her then. She listened, and her face reflected what she heard with sympathetic frowns and reassuring nods and smiles, as though she owed this in payment to Sara. He had never seen responsiveness like hers before except in much older women, and once or twice in ugly girls. This girl was pretty enough to have closed her face like the others, but her face was open and sympathetic. He stepped back behind the others so that he could watch her unseen.

She was in his morning calisthenics group. She was surprisingly strong; she could hang easily by her hands and jump tirelessly, but she never tried to outdistance the others. She always stopped before the last of them gave out. "You could do more," he said to her one day after their hour.

"Me?"

"You. You could do a lot more. You always stop before you need to. You could be an example for them. They don't push themselves hard enough. You could—"

"They've been pushed plenty. And I'm doing all I can." She got up and walked away from him, but that night she went and found him at evening services with the older people and she waited for him to finish. She put a hand on his arm, thinking that she had to get his attention. Something else new.

"I had no right to talk to you like that," she said. "I'm sorry. You are heroes, you came to help us—"

"Heroes?"

"Of course." She shrugged. "And I yelled at you. I'm—"

"You yelled? I could hardly hear you."

She shrugged again. "Still. You were right, only you don't know what they've—"

"I know."

She shook her head. "I was lucky. We're Hungarian, so we weren't sent to the camps until very late, almost the end. And then I worked in the quarry, so I developed strength in my arms and legs, but some of them . . ."

The crown of her head was about on a level with his nose. She smelled of the talcum the Red Cross had inexplicably sent in quantity. She went on about the effects of forced hiding and inactivity, about starvation and beatings and typhus, and he watched her face. No need for flippancy here.

"I'm sorry," she said abruptly, jolting him alert. "I didn't mean to upset you. You aren't responsible."

He hadn't been paying close attention to her words. "Everyone is responsible," he said, hearing himself with some surprise. "I feel responsible for every one of those kids, for making them ready . . ."

They walked slowly and he went on, inventing it as he talked. The words came from some new feeling of adult maleness that stunned him. He spun them out, enchanted by the feeling. He put both hands behind his back, then, wanting to touch her, stuck them instead into his pockets so that his arm brushed hers as they walked. "I know what fear is," the new man said. "I don't want these kids to ever have to be afraid again."

She had never heard a man say it before. Sandor never said he was afraid. He laughed and said he wasn't, he said he had put the Nazis in their place, but then he opened the door to them, smiling his beseeching smile of fear and holding it open, offering himself. Offering all of them. She stopped walking and touched Shlomo's arm so he would stand still and she looked at his face. "Tell me about when you're afraid," she said.

The new man seemed to know just how to proceed. He heard himself telling her about the raids and the night watches, turning fear into an asset and a proof of worth. It was simple because she listened. She listened with her eyes and body, female to his male. "You're afraid but you do it anyway," she said then, focusing her eyes on nothing as though working out a theorem. "You feel responsible for others, so even though you're sometimes afraid, you do these things."

"I'm afraid all the time I'm doing them."

But he stood there, a man. She suddenly remembered Jacob, the third night at the detention point. Sandor was gone and she and Jacob and Anni were there with the others. Outrage had yielded to immobilizing terror in everyone by now except that Jacob was engaged in some game, marching stiff-legged with a stick upright in one arm. His face was exaggeratedly expressionless. Every few steps he would stop and kick a bundle or point the stick at something and, still pantomiming disinterest, pull the imaginary trigger. She followed him. "What are you doing? Jacob, what are you *doing?*"

"Practicing."

"Practicing what?"

"To be a Nazi."

He was right, she thought. Better to be a Nazi than to be Sandor, whose fear made him into a woman, despised and abused. Best to practice being steel-faced and unafraid, by far better to terrorize than to be paralyzed by fear.

But Shlomo stood there, a man; he said he was afraid but he did the thing anyway, he was still a man. She felt the maleness blow off him like the wind off the sea, more where it came from. His arms were clean, no blue number in the freckled skin. His face was clean—no bravado, no tracks of cajolery and abjection. He could be afraid and still be a man. He could be afraid and still take care of people.

He could take care of her. She had had a father but he had opened to the Arrow Cross, let them in, he had turned in a moment into something else. She had had a fierce mother for a brief time at Auschwitz, whose hands had poked and pinched her into seeming sixteen and fit for work and who had sat on the ground to mourn with her and had shielded her eyes from the skeletons screwing on the dirt; but there was no one now and here stood this man with clean arms and a clean face, and he could take care of her without his face turning to steel.

She nodded slowly, still focusing on nothing, then she looked right at him. It was done, they'd gone across a line. He could have her, he suddenly knew; it required only the working out. Her face was open to him; the rest would follow. All in time.

That was right. They progressed in the old way, from conversation to handholding to tentative kisses to long embraces and so on, with long periods of time between the steps. The slow, friendly progression was new to him and all of it was new to her.

She liked it. Or she liked his passion. Once when he moaned, kissing her, she twisted in his arms so she could see him. "Take me," she hissed. "Shlomo, take me." He pulled her against him and smiled into her hair even though he was rigid and urgent under his khakis. She was just sixteen then. He put a hand into her shorts and touched her with a finger. She was dry. "I love you too much to do that," he said. It was true. Besides, touching her in gentle rhythm with a finger, feeling her warm legs against his knuckles and her crisp bounce of hair under his palm and himself rising fruitlessly against his khakis was more intimate than the complete act had been with the other girls.

"Do you like that?"

She nodded.

"You could touch me, too. Sometime. When you're ready."

She put a hand on him, standing hard against the thick cloth.

"Under my clothes, I mean. Like I am with you."

She was paying close attention.

"All right?"

She nodded again, not moving her hand. He retrieved his hand from inside her shorts and unzipped his khakis. "Sure?"

"I'm sure. Anything."

He took her hand and guided it. She looked up and smiled. "It's warm. And dry. I thought—oh, it's lovely."

"You can touch it harder than that. Don't be afraid."

"I'm not afraid. Show me."

He showed her, and when she was absorbed in her task, moving still too gently up and down, up and down, in too halting a rhythm, he slid his hand back into her shorts and eased a finger into her, advancing by millimeters until he found wetness and then synchronizing with her pumping. He moaned a little and then more wetness came down to bathe his finger.

"I'm sorry." He could barely hear her.

"Why?"

"It's—I'm getting you wet. I don't know why—"

"No. Don't move. That's good. That's wonderful. It means you want me." He was breathing fast and he ground her mouth with his. His free arm encircled her, owning her and making her safe. She thought she did want him. She whispered his name.

"I'm going to come."

"What?"

"Sperm's—going to come out."

"What should I—" It shot up, trickled warm down over her hand. She stopped moving, went slack at the worst moment, but that was only a subtlety.

When after a moment he remembered to say something to her and he began to explain about coming, she said, "I know. That was so beautiful." It was and it wasn't. But she was ready to believe it, and she thought he wanted to hear it.

He did. After a minute he wiped her hand dry and pulled up her underpants, taking care of the girl who found his coming beautiful and told him so. He kept a strong and public arm around her as he walked her to her hut.

And that was so good, to be encircled like that, to be taken care of, she almost let him walk her all the way to the hut. She remembered Anni just in time and quickly turned to face him at the first line of dwellings, so that they were standing separated. He thought it was because she wanted a kiss. She cut the kiss short but smiled wistfully at him, impatient now to get away from him and back to Anni but careful not to let him know it.

"Tomorrow," he said.

"Tomorrow." She turned and ran to Anni.

Too late. Whenever she returned to Anni it was too late, the weight of her hours away hung in the air, counted against her. What had Anni done in the old days, Eva wondered, that she had never seemed to need anything from anyone then? Drawing mostly, and ripping up the sheets of paper. She'd had no friends then, either, but she'd had Jacob and Eva to deal with and the rest of the time she'd been absorbed in her drawing.

"Why don't I try to get you some drawing paper and pencils?" Eva had asked her in the first weeks on Cyprus. Anni had wordlessly laid her two hands on the table, fingers spread wide for Eva to see. The tips were dark with frostbite and two were bent at odd angles. But later, smiling sardonically, she had begun to weave baskets with the others, her fingers arched and supple, working with increasingly slender reeds and making increasingly complicated patterns and shapes. She took to walking on the beach and picking up shells. She would stand and look at one for a long time, turning it in her hands, then lay it on the sand and walk away. The shell shapes—the cockle at first, then others—began to turn up in the baskets, which grew larger and stranger all the time. But she never picked up the work until the others gathered to weave and talk, and when the first of them began to drift off to their huts, she would lay her work down carelessly and leave it without a further thought.

She met Potasnik on the beach. He was carrying a hat filled with shells and he accosted her as she stood handling a broken cowrie. "Hot," he said. He laid down the hat, wiped his face and then his hands with the bottom of his shirt, and then offered his hand. "Potasnik," he said. "Of Budapest, Birkenau, and Cyprus. I got a whole one of those somewhere."

She shook his hand and told him her name. "Also from near Budapest," she said in Hungarian. "Ujpest." He was rummaging in the hat. She laid down the cowrie and turned to go.

"I got it here in inventory somewhere. I was one of the wedding guests, you know. Quite an event."

"Wedding?"

"The Granat Street Cemetery Wedding of the Orphans. June 1944. You missed it? Ceremony at the Granat Street Cemetery, Budapest; reception at Birkenau immediately following. A sellout. Here, I knew I had one." He held out a perfect cowrie to her. "You need it? I'm dealing in shells. This happens to be a rare item, but for a *landsman*, a special price. Give me a glass of tea and it's yours."

"I don't need it, but thank you." She turned again to go.

"I need the tea, I'm parched. I'll walk you. You never heard about the wedding? A major event: a wedding and a trip to the country, all expenses. You know the cemetery?"

She inclined her head.

"There's a group of us in Budapest. We look around. We notice we're starving. We notice we're getting beaten up. We notice we're being thrown out of our apartments and there's talk of deportation. We're not stupid, we figure out that God's attention must have wandered. We were religious in those days, right? So what do you do to get His attention? Andor Rozensweig, should rest in peace, he remembers a *midrash* that says that when orphans get married, God is always in attendance. Perfect. Orphans we've got. We organize the whole thing—a boy orphan, a girl orphan, a wedding canopy on four poles, a minyan—and we march ourselves to the cemetery to marry these two, God should pay attention for a minute to what's doing in Budapest because then He'll save us. Right? Right?"

She raised her eyebrows at him.

"Standing room in a cattle car He saved us. Bing bang, the Gestapo shows up, the whole wedding party is booked for Birkenau—we never knew what hit us. Which one is yours?"

"Excuse me?"

"Which mansion do you reside in?"

So he wound up drinking tea in her hut and when he left he polished the cowrie on his shirt and handed it to her. "Remember us when you need something else. Always glad to show the line. *Au revoir*, my lady. You should be well."

She never even said goodbye, but he returned a few afternoons later and then he made it a habit. She never said much and he wasn't bothered by it. Sometimes he brought others around, another man from Budapest named Bela Munkas, and a woman named Zara. "You're making friends, Mother?" Eva asked her, but she only shrugged. And when Eva came in and found them there sometimes, she would see that they were talking around Anni's silent presence. They filled her hut but not her day. That was Eva's job, to fill her mother's day.

That was all right in the beginning, because there was nothing else pulling at Eva. But now there was Shlomo, and she was pulled two ways. For a long time she didn't even mention him to Anni. She invented meetings and events so that she could be with him in the evenings, but it became harder and harder to tell Anni about her day, leaving Shlomo out.

She decided at last to tell her mother. It was on the night, in fact, when she ran into the hut fresh from his kiss. Too soon to leave him, too late to have kept Anni waiting. She could feel the elastic of her underpants twisted under her shorts; she thought it must show, and to distract Anni she began an animated description of a dispute between two of the youth leaders, but it was too late, Anni had been robbed of her day and as she chattered Eva decided not to deceive her any more. She would share Shlomo with her mother, it would make her happy. Not to tell her everything of course, but to let her know that she had a boyfriend and to explain where she was in the evenings. Anni would be glad for her.

It didn't work out that way. The next afternoon she ran over and found Anni at her basket-weaving. "Mother? Do you have a minute? I'd like you to meet someone, a friend." She took Anni by the hand and hurried her over to where Shlomo stood waiting. They never held hands—Anni didn't particularly like to be touched—but Eva meant to reassure her that she was still her child. Anni's hand hung inert in hers.

"Here he is. Mother, this is Shlomo Reisner, he's one of the leaders. My calisthenics leader . . ."

It went haltingly. Shlomo made conversation, Anni responded politely but without showing any interest, even when he praised her daughter's athletic ability. He tried again. "Chava tells me you make beautiful baskets."

"Who is Chava?"

He gestured, astounded, at the girl.

"Her name is Eva."

"We call her Chava now."

"Why?"

"That will be her name in Eretz Yisroel. Her Hebrew name."

"I don't understand. Forgive me, my Hebrew is very bad. A pleasure to meet you."

That night Eva tried again. "Did you like Shlomo, Mother? Isn't he nice?"

"I couldn't tell. Eat something."

"I am. He liked you very much. He thinks you're beautiful."

Anni's face went hard with scorn. Eva pressed on.

"He's a special friend of mine, Mother. He likes me. I—we've been spending time together."

"When?"

"Sometimes . . . after dinner."

"Alone."

"Yes. Just walks, Mother. But I wanted you to—"

Any number of things could have happened then. Anni could have smiled and said how nice that Eva had a friend, a reminiscent woman's smile of collusion. Or the fierce mother could have reappeared, forbidding the meetings, putting hands on Eva once again as she had in

Auschwitz, to protect her. Then Eva would have had her mother back; or at least she would have had a gesture to rebel against and she could have turned entirely to Shlomo, leaving her fierce mother for her lover.

What happened was nothing. Anni sat exactly as she had been, her face a blank. Silence.

"Mother? You don't mind?"

"Why should I mind?"

No way to answer that one. Why should she mind? Eva was afraid; not embraced and not released, neither forbidden nor encouraged, she would be responsible now for any move she made, and any move at all would be disloyal to someone. She tried once more—if not for permission then to angle out of Anni some concession of a kindred memory. "What did your mother say when you first went out with Poppi?"

"She should have said the prayer for the dead over me. I think she asked who his people were. What does it matter? He lied, I listened, it didn't matter what she said."

"Poppi lied to you?"

Did he lie to her. At one time she would have said that Sandor's whole life was lies and that she despised him for it, but the reality was that she could live with the lies. He lied and she saw things clearly. That was their arrangement.

It started out with her thinking that he would be ballast for her. He was a pharmacist, immaculate and cheerful. Everything he handled was weighed and measured; mixtures were made according to prescribed formulations, and the product was either correct or incorrect, paid in cash or charged on account, taken in hand or sent round by messenger. Anni lived in another realm entirely. She was an art student, a preoccupied and severe beauty, careless of her clothes and her words but inflamed by what she saw and by the process of making others see it. "My *lüftmädchen*," he called her, my cloud-girl, my dream-maiden.

Only she had no dreams, wanted none. She was engaged in a fierce battle with reality—not to avoid it but to pin it down, fix it precisely and unmistakably on paper. She wouldn't even allow herself color until she had the lines right. She never had the lines right, and the struggle took all her energies.

At first they seemed perfect to each other. She saw stability in the precision of his days, and sanity in his easy cheer, a counterbalance for the unpredictability of her work and the despair she seemed always to feel. She thought he would be painstaking and would attend to things. He saw her smudged beauty and thought it indicated a passionate nature. He thought that if she was inflamed by what she saw she would also be inflamed by what she felt. By lovemaking, for example. They married.

It turned out that she was inflamed only by what she saw, and inflamed only with the desire to reproduce it on paper. Certainly the sight of his body was of no interest to her, and—far from being of a passionate nature—she was repelled and humiliated by his clutchings and delvings. She had known, of course, that occasionally he would want to have sex, but she didn't know that it would involve an invasion of all her senses— that he would want to snuffle wetly at her breasts, or be at her mouth all the time, that she would be trapped in his smell and his grunts and whimperings and that even when she closed her eyes her eyeballs would flash his grossly enlarged face. No one had told her, either, that it would take so long to be over each time.

In fact, he was in no way what she expected. He took care of nothing, for example. He must have produced accurate prescriptions—at least no one ever complained—but that was all he did. The accounts, the orders and billing he left to Janoscz and she soon learned that household affairs were her sole responsibility. He was anything but ballast for her. With inane cheerfulness, he would revise reality whenever it suited him—for evasion, for deception, simply for the sake of a good story. Did he lie to her. He lied to her, to everyone, to himself, he lived lying.

So that made it simple for her. He deceived her with a parade of women; she despised him and wrote him off and went more single-mindedly than ever after reality, to wrestle it out of three dimensions into two.

It was even simple with the children. She saw to it that they were nourished and educated, and she made very sure that they were truthful and discerning of truth; when he filled the air with his nonsense she rarely made an issue of it, but they were attuned to her raised eyebrows and pursed lips and to the humorless puffs of disdain she emitted, and she was content that they knew him for a liar.

He told the children his lies all the time, of course, but the one thing he never did was lie about them. He seemed to feel no need to revise them or to enhance them; he repeated their utterances or described their doings without embellishment. They were acceptable to him as they were. It was the one warm spot in their marriage, the justification for enduring his smothering lovemaking and the only respite from her bitter contempt for him and for their life together. He amused the children with his nonsense but they knew it for nonsense, and he was devoted to them.

132

So she let them run to him in the store whenever they wanted; it did them no harm and she worked better, anyway, when they were out of her way.

She could live with the lies, that's what it amounted to. They didn't affect her and they amused the children and he was, after all, a devoted father.

If only he had been capable of one more lie. Or if the Arrow Cross had finished him off when he opened the door to them, before he'd had a chance to push his one truth at her, filthy, repugnant, terrifying thing.

But they didn't. Didn't have to, it was enough just to rap their rifles against the door and bring him running to open it, smiling that inane smile of his. It was enough for them to reduce him to impotence and to stride off, leaving him standing there holding the open door. They didn't have to waste a bullet, he was a dead man.

When the Arrow Cross left she waited for him to put a face on it, to make a story of it for the children so that she could get them through it. This once she welcomed his fantasizing, because something had to be said to Jacob who swayed dazedly in the hallway, squinting at the light, and to Eva who had seen it and heard it and who stared at Sandor now, her face an open wound. Bitterly, Anni took in Eva's look. Was it possible that the child had never seen him for what he was? Was it possible that she had chosen, over her mother's clear signals, to believe his babbling? Then this next lie had better be a good one, because those children were going to leave this apartment and carry their belongings to the square—to who knows what—and it would be endurable only if they could be kept from understanding what was really happening. Anni could get them through it only if they weren't clinging to her in their terror and sucking her dry with refusals and pleas.

He turned around to her. Jacob was beginning to whine and Eva pulled him into their bedroom. "You'd better tell them something," Anni began, but he was talking already.

"We can get away," he was saying.

"How? Don't be—"

"No. We can. They were talking last week, a group going underground. False papers . . . wait it out . . . in the forests . . . you're blond, pretty . . . I could pass . . ." He started to rip the star off his shoulder.

"Running? Hiding? How could the children—?"

He looked away.

"Sandor."

"They'll be all right here. Kids adapt. Anyway, they won't harm children. The Red Cross will see to—"

"You're talking about running and leaving the children? Sandor?"

This once he had no lies for her. He had seen the fire and all his easy lies were exuded in a sweat, his poses melted off, all that was left was a grotesque impotent with a yellow star in its hand. I can't do this alone, she thought over and over, he has to stop it, I can't do this alone.

"*Eva*, Sandor. And *Jacob*. We can't leave them. You wouldn't leave them."

"We'd never make it, dragging them along."

He wasn't even hysterical. He hadn't gone mad, he'd simply been reduced to elemental truth, and the truth was that they were nothing to him. Her children had no father. And he thrust it at her over and over, she had to inhale his terror and to feel his sweat and to listen to his filth, she couldn't stop it. She gagged on it, wanting to heave out his truth, there must be some way to make it not true.

Jacob came running into the hall with a pile of clothing in his arms. He planted himself in front of Sandor. "Why didn't you tell them?" he demanded. "We don't have to go. Why didn't you tell them who you are?"

He, too. He had believed the man's stories, too, had wanted to believe them and not her signals. She was alone with them now; they were going to suck her dry with their terrors and pleadings and refusals and they preferred that lying piece of shit to her.

Sandor turned away and Jacob followed him, screaming his question again: "Why didn't you tell them who you are?" She smacked him in his credulous little face, very hard, and he went on screaming but he didn't ask it again.

Neither of them asked anything. Sandor stayed in the apartment when they left, mumbling something to them about a secret mission. The boy cried and clung to his leg, but the girl looked out of the window as though she hadn't heard him and said nothing. The three of them went to the square, she and Eva carrying their huge sacks, Jacob struggling with a smaller bundle; and then later from the square to the ghetto with about half their belongings and then from the ghetto to the brickyard with a few essentials, and the children never asked where he was or when he would return.

She would have lied to them if they had asked. She did, later, about other things: about the train, for example, and of course to Jacob, promising to see him after he'd gone off to the shower with the old people and the women with infants. She'd made Eva lie about her age, and in the camp there'd been a thousand lies. But it didn't matter any more about the truth. Reality, her beloved wrestling mate in three dimensions, had turned out to have a twist to it, just a little twist that revealed a fourth dimension you could neither believe nor delineate. Two dimensions— paper, canvas—couldn't begin to hold what reality had become. She couldn't remember why she had wanted to try, anyway.

"Mama? Poppi lied to you?"

The child was alive. She had brought her through it alive and intact, and she had no idea what she wanted for her now except that they had to be together.

"Men will say anything when they're after a woman. He was no different."

"Shlomo doesn't. Wouldn't."

"No? So, good. I hope you're right."

She hoped Eva was wrong. She hoped the boy was an impostor and that he would give himself away or leave her, the sooner the better.

Anni's hut was thick with din and chaos the day before they shipped to Palestine, the State of Israel now, but Anni wasn't part of it.

They were packing; they ran in and out of her hut with their ridiculous accumulations, looking for advice and staying to bicker.

"You're crazy!" Potasnik shouted at Bela Munkas for the third time. Eva eased around them, gathering clothes and counting things off under her breath. Anni sat motionless on the bed.

"You're meshugeh, Munkas. You know how many Ben Zions there must be over there? A thousand. So you have to go change your name, you'll be Ben Zion with a thousand others?"

"I'll be Ben Zion one thousand and one, I'll melt right in. You going to be a Hungarian Yid all your life, Potasnik?"

"I'm going to be Potasnik, that you can bet money."

"I'm going to be Ari Ben Zion. New life, new name."

"Wonderful. Right away you'll be a changed man. Blond, a twenty-year-old hero, a straight nose, everything. Anni, what do you think?"

"About what?"

"About Bela's *name.*"

"What difference does it make what he calls himself?"

"Well, I'm going to call you Ari-Bela," Potasnik said. "So in case you decide to change anything else, I'll be ready."

"Anni, you're not packing?" Bela changed the subject, ignoring Potasnik.

"She'll dump everything in one of her giant baskets, she'll be all packed."

"Are they letting you bring the baskets, Annike?"

"What for? I don't want them."

"But—"

"Oh my God. Oh, my God." It was Potasnik, knuckles of one hand against his teeth. He was looking at Zara, who stood dead white at the door, smiling strangely and holding out her left arm. Black stitches criss-crossed her forearm, biting into the flesh. Her dress was soaked through with sweat.

"Darling, what did you do?" Potasnik pleaded.

"Rabinowitz at the surgery did it. I decided last minute, I had to beg him. He was worried about infection on the boat. He's waiting to bandage it, I just came to show you."

"The number," Eva breathed.

"All of a sudden I couldn't get on the boat with the number. I was ashamed."

They looked at their own forearms and avoided each other's eyes. Bela, clucking, pushed Zara out the door and toward the surgery. Potasnik followed them.

Shlomo came in. "I'm going with you! Hello, Mrs. Konig. Chava, I'm going with you to Haifa!"

"Aieee!" She let him swing her around, then remembered Anni and pulled away, but Anni was walking, straight-backed, out of the hut.

She stood on the dirt path and called, "Potasnik! Potasnik!"

Potasnik turned, shocked. Anni had never called to him or to anyone that he could remember. She motioned him to wait and walked resolutely to the piles of her baskets that Eva had collected and left near the hut. She picked up a couple, discarded them, then found the one she wanted. She caught up with Potasnik and handed it to him. It was small, the size of a soup plate, and it had the concentric coils of a nautilus. "For your shells," she said. "You'll need your hat on the boat."

There was only a moment before Anni turned to come back into the hut. Shlomo seized it. "We'll be together on the boat," he said. He crossed his arms around Eva from behind, where she stood looking after Anni. "We'll come into Israel together."

His voice was so loud, Anni must surely have heard him. Eva shrugged angrily out of his arms without turning around. How could he? For a moment she hated him.

"You gave Potasnik a basket, Mother? That's lovely. Come, you never told me what you're wearing on the boat tomorrow."

She hoped he would leave them alone, but he hung around, throwing her questioning looks so that she had both of them to placate at once. They were beginning to pull her thin.

They were married in 1950, in Tel Aviv. She was eighteen, he was almost twenty-two.

She was still a virgin. They had established a ritual and stayed with it: they would kiss, long, drinking kisses, until she would whisper urgently that he should take her, do it, she loved him. He would decline, groaning into her neck or her hair that they couldn't, she knew they couldn't. She knew he would refuse and she loved him for it—he was taking care of her—but she thought she really wanted him. He thought she did, too. He knew it wouldn't be long before they were married, and they would fuse together like two flaming metal wires.

So they were both shocked on their wedding night. She took a long time in the bathroom, trying to shut out thoughts of Anni alone. Deserted. Who was with her? The cronies, Potasnik and Ari-Bela Ben Zion and Zara. But when they left her? When she was alone in the flat?

He knocked lightly on the door, teasing her out before she was really finished with her thoughts, so she lay in his arms still trying to envision Anni comforted.

He was patient. Even with all their caressing, she was innocent of the final act and she must be a little afraid. She seemed tight, a bit abstracted. So he went slowly. He knew she would flame up, would arch her head back and beg him to do it and this time, this time he could.

This time, she knew, he was going to do it. This time she wasn't going to straighten her clothes and go home to Anni. There was a tiny, nibbling feeling of resentment. She squirmed away from it and tried to concentrate on loving him. But it was all different. They were lying down together, not sitting in a dark corner. They were naked, or almost. And there was nothing to stop them. She was numb.

She didn't ask him. That was all right, she was afraid. Her little bit of fear, her virgin vulnerability, only heightened it for him. He had never seen her body all at once. He knelt over her, his two hands traveling down all of her unhindered for the first time. Her stomach muscles tightened under his hands. It was too much. He lowered himself onto her.

She saw: a body. A man, the skeleton of a man, lying face down. No, a man lying on a woman and twitching. Her arm, bony gray arm, snakes between their bodies. He twitches, she claws. They are bald dry bones, humping on the dirt.

He couldn't hold it. She was breathing hard, but not moving and he couldn't tell what she was feeling. But he had to come. Had to.

Her mother's hand covered her eyes, drew her away from the humping bones. "All right, Eva," her mother's voice said. "Don't worry, don't worry. All right."

"Chava!" he cried, coming. "Chava!"

Don't call me that, she thought, feeling his bones dig into her. My name is Eva. Don't call me that name.

The flow of her blood every month was the most wonderful thing. It made everything the way it had been in Cyprus. He had explained the rule to her so delicately the first time. "Not that you're unclean," he said. "Never that. But everything has its time, and this is a time for separation."

So when she felt her period approach, she told him and they separated. That is, they shared the flat, of course, but for the five days of her period and the seven days following, they tried not to let any parts of their bodies touch. She didn't let him see her make his bed or prepare his food; he didn't look at her body. She did serve his dinner and they ate together, but they had a special glass vase they left on the table for the time of her uncleanness—a reminder that although her hands served him, she was out of reach.

All of it was foreign to her—they'd had no religion to speak of, in her home in Ujpest—and he worried that she would be offended. But in fact he hadn't needed to be so delicate about it; for her it was never better than when she was unclean. He would sit at the table, the glass vase between them, and the color would come into his face. "I miss you," he'd say. "I know I can't touch you, but I can't help seeing you and smelling your powder and—I miss you. Hurry up and be finished with it." He would whisper it although they were alone in the flat. She didn't want to hurry up and be finished with it. She was a little shocked that he said those things when she was supposed to be out of reach, but really, it was like being back in Cyprus: the constant yearning, his wanting her but protecting her body, the whispering and waiting. She wanted it to go on forever.

At the end of the seventh day she would go to the *mikvah* for the ritual immersion, and she would return home and take the glass vase off the table and when he came home, his eyes would go first to the table and then to her and he would envelop her. Sixteen days until her next period.

She made a mistake, in those first few weeks. They would lie touching—she liked that, really, on the nights when she wasn't plagued with thoughts of her mother deserted and alone—and at some point he would whisper, "Now?" She would always nod, not sure what he was asking but wanting to please him. After all, his pleasure was the point. Then, when he was little again and slipping out of her, he'd smooth her hair away from her face and ask, "Was it good?" Sure, it was fine, it had all gone the way it was supposed to, so she'd smile and nod and they'd go to sleep. But one night, before they really got started, he raised up on an elbow and asked, "What's it like when you come?"

"When I—me?"

"Yes. What's it feel like?" He circled a nipple with his finger.

"I don't know."

"Come on. I tell you."

"But—I don't—women don't—"

That was her mistake. She should have made something up to tell him, because he looked crushed. He explained to her that she would, should, had to. He worked over her for what seemed like hours, that night, and when she squirmed to relieve the irritation he asked, "Now? Are you ready?" and she hissed, "Yes," in gratitude. Let it be over with. Afterward, he whispered, "Well? Did you?"

She hadn't felt anything different. "I think so."

"What did it feel like?"

"Lovely." She kissed him and curled up for sleep, hoping it wasn't going to be like this every time.

Eventually she learned how to make it go faster and make him feel good about it—she mimicked his gasps and mirrored his movements—but there were times when she'd been so torn during the day between him and Anni that she couldn't—wouldn't—pretend, and they'd separate their damp bodies and go to sleep in silence.

But really, he didn't try very hard with Anni. It was true that she was brusque and unresponsive with Shlomo, but he was the younger one, he was the one who'd had the easy life, he could play up to her a little. Anni did eventually respond when people were attentive to her—look how she was with the cronies now—and she would respond to Shlomo, too, if he'd only be warm with her. But if he came home and found Anni in the flat, he would kiss Chava right in front of Anni and hold her with one arm while he asked about her day, excluding Anni and flaunting their relationship in front of her. "Tell Mother about the man who had the canary stones," she'd urge him. "Mother, tell Shlomo about the loom you're getting." But each of them would direct the talk to her, coldly polite to the other.

It was better when the loom came and then she and Anni spent their time together at Anni's. The cronies would arrive in the late afternoon, and Chava would go home with the picture in her mind of Anni with the four of them—they'd picked up a fifth somewhere, a mournful little man named Grodner who had survived Treblinka and had apparently wandered half starving through the towns between the German and Russian borders of Poland for months before somehow making his way to Israel. In his cups he would recite his Eastern itinerary over and over, a litany of bleakness. But he was another distraction for Anni, and while she dismissed the four of them as "a pack of gossips—nothing to do but carp at each other and eat my food—" she was despondent when they didn't come by, and as time went on, Chava noticed that her mother was drawn into their banter and their wrangling. That made it easier for her to leave Anni in the afternoons. It worked fine, really; she was Anni's daughter in the first part of the day, Shlomo's wife in the evenings.

But then the baby was born and the arrangement collapsed. Everyone—the baby, Anni, Shlomo—was pulling at her at once. It was worst in the first week home from the hospital, because of Shlomo. Anni came over early every day, and that would have been all right except that Shlomo hung around in the mornings and came home early in the afternoons, so that she had to handle both of them at once. She was so tired, and she had to glow all the harder to warm her mother against Shlomo's correctness, had to signal Shlomo to share the baby with Anni, had it all to do for them all. When he finally left for work each day she found herself offering everything up to Anni, all she had held in reserve—the baby, her adulthood, Shlomo, her marriage. It was the baby that worked best; his routine was as compelling and continuous as weaving and the conversation he generated was easy and safe, as long as Chava could keep it focused, keep Jacob out of it. So she deferred to Anni, sharing the baby with her and adroitly shutting Shlomo out of all the little decisions.

After the first week, Shlomo returned without a word to his regular work hours and then for a couple of weeks Anni's cronies came by in shifts and diverted her while Chava pretended to nap, and then there was Rachaeli.

Chava told Shlomo that she pitied the illegitimate baby, and that was why she invited the outrageous woman over so often—because otherwise the child would be a complete outcast. But really, it was the smile that drew her, Rachaeli's inward smile that Chava had seen first in the labor room at Tel Aviv Hospital and that always seemed to hover in her eyes. It was so independent, that smile. It said: I have what I need, I have it all.

That was the point: Rachaeli and her baby seemed to be autonomous. She needed nothing from Chava, nothing at all—not reassurance, not understanding or soothing or praise. Nothing, what a luxury for Chava. And if she had to pay for the luxury—if people were aghast when Rachaeli sailed into the Reisner *brit*, for example, at Chava's urging—it was worth it to be with someone who didn't leech life fluid from her. Rachaeli was the only person in Chava's world who didn't drain her dry.

Peculiarly enough, Anni was drawn to Rachaeli, too. When the story came out about the mother who had declared her own child a bastard and had forced a divorce from the system and the husband, Anni smiled. She was amused.

"Some society you picked to melt into," Potasnik snorted to Ari-Bela Ben Zion. "Not bad enough the woman is trumpenicking around with another man, the whole state helps her make a public case out of it. There aren't enough fatherless kids in the world, she has to go manufacture one?"

"Don't blame the state of Israel for one crazy," Ari-Bela began. Anni interrupted him.

"Crazy like a fox," she said, and although they all pressed her to explain herself she wouldn't say another word. But when Rachaeli began to appear at the flat, Anni treated her with respect, even deference, as though in some way they were peers. It made no sense, but Chava accepted it gratefully. It made everything easier, to have Rachaeli there.

In fact, on the day when Chava went to the ritual bath for the first time after the baby's birth—a Tuesday, it was, in November when the boys were eight weeks old—she left Rachaeli at home with Anni and the two babies, and when she walked back into the flat, the two women were laughing together. Unbelievable. And later in the afternoon, when Chava took the glass vase off the table and put it away in the cabinet, Rachaeli got up and said, "Come on, Anni. Help me get the baby's stuff together, I'll walk you home. Chava doesn't need us here this afternoon." They left, easy together, no backward pull from Anni, and Chava's only feeling was regret that they were leaving her behind.

Shlomo saw right away that the vase was gone, and as soon as supper was finished, he disappeared into the shower. She moved slowly, recalcitrant, taking twice as long as normal to straighten up the kitchen and prolonging the baby's nursing, jiggling him awake when he drowsed off at her breast so that he sucked again absent-mindedly for a moment before sliding back into sleep. Finally, Shlomo took him from her and laid him in his crib and led her to bed.

His head was huge, grotesque, his skin porous and ravaged compared with the baby's. She closed her eyes. He was at her breast. The nipple was hardened and insensitive but she drew back anyway, repulsed, thinking how to sterilize it again for the baby. When he finally entered her, she stiffened, waiting for him to tear open the newly healed skin, waiting for the first stinging and the slow ripping of flesh. Her whole body strained upward against the impending pain. All right, Eva, she told herself. Don't worry, don't worry. All right.

He felt her lift toward him, saw the tension in her face and did everything he knew to hold out, prolong it so that she would come when he did. When it was over, she eased in his arms and her face relaxed and he thought he had done it. He waited for her to open her eyes, let him in. He had waited for a long time to retrieve her from that tightening circle of women and babies.

She opened her eyes but didn't meet his. She smiled briefly, a tight, vague smile, and sat up. He put a hand on her shoulder. "Excuse me," she said. She pulled her robe around her and went into the bathroom. Fighting the heaviness of his body, he followed her.

She was standing at the sink, swabbing her nipples with sterilized water. "I'd have hated to have to do this at four in the morning," she said, smiling softly.

But it was a smile for the baby, not for him.

Rachaeli liked it, spending those afternoons with the two women. They were completely preoccupied with their own baby, for one thing, so that it was safe to bring Dani into their orbit. They didn't want him. And then there was something about the grandmother. She was grim and cynical, but Rachaeli felt a strong pull to her. She sensed that while Chava forgave what she had done—the affair, the bastard child, the divorce—Anni understood, even approved. Anni seemed to see her clearly and to enjoy her. European, nightmare-tainted and troubled though the household was, it was an oddly comfortable fit for Rachaeli. And when Anni's cronies came by in the afternoons, Rachaeli and Chava could leave Anni and the babies and go off on their own for a little while.

The cronies had centered, finally, on Chava's flat. When Anni began going to Chava's every day, they started appearing there in the afternoons—all except Ari-Bela, who had a regular job. He was lucky; he'd been an accountant in Hungary and he had been able to transfer the skill: numbers are numbers. He worked for a plastics manufacturer in Tel Aviv.

The others relied heavily on the reparations the German government paid them. Grodner and Zara worked half time in one of the agencies. Zara's work was to cross-index the names of survivors. Grodner worked in the library, transcribing testimony from the early tape recordings made in the camps just after liberation. They had lunch together every day after work—a yogurt and stewed fruit; Grodner had to be careful what he ate— and then they went to Chava's to see Anni.

They were not lovers. They were together most of the time and they depended on each other, but the light had gone out of Grodner, and Zara wasn't aggressive enough to reach out for him. She wasn't even sure she'd want him; he was morose and silent and passive, except when he was drinking. She did the chattering, usually, for both of them.

When he was drinking, though, Grodner was different. He became flushed and ideas and arguments poured out of him. Then, just when he was becoming a little incoherent, he would look at her and say things that startled her heart and made her feel precarious and daring. "I hold down my feelings for you," he said once, "but if you—"

He never finished saying these things and she never dared respond beyond a look of willingness which he was anyway too drunk to read. But she remembered every one of those sentences, and the afterimage of them kept her female, on edge. She liked it when he was tipsy, except for two things. One: he was inevitably ill and dyspeptic afterward, and for days she was never sure that he wasn't angry at her. And two: the tipsy Grodner inevitably gave way to the drunken Grodner, who lapsed into his bitter travelogue of places where he'd starved, and who turned away from her completely.

It was never out of Zara's mind that the unguarded Grodner felt something for her and she played to it when he was sober and uncommunicative, keeping him informed, watching his diet for him, reminding him that she was there. She couldn't help doing it; some unruly female impulse drove her, even though she didn't want things any different between them. At any rate their real work was to look out for each other, and Chava's flat was a ready screen for it.

Potasnik had a small business. He sold a line of children's novelties to the little variety stores in the neighborhoods around Tel Aviv. He would meander his route in the mornings, picking up a new joke here and there, gathering gossip and opinions like an easygoing bee and leaving boxes of four-color pencils and magic slates and cheap stuffed animals. He usually had something in his pocket for Aaron and Dani, and he always had a story for Anni. Chava suspected that he worked only so that he would have material for his act for Anni.

Everything struck Potasnik funny except Anni. From the first moment on the beach in Cyprus when he saw her turning the shell over and over in her hands, not in madness but with grave professional observance, he had felt a piercing tenderness for Anni. He saw that still face and the intense dignity of her, and he knew at once that she was very strong and unnaturally empty, a vacuum—his vacuum—that she was, simply and finally, his work. He was not in love with her; it was deeper than that, and less mutable.

They all revolved around Anni, in fact—Potasnik and Zara and Grodner and Ari-Bela, too, after work. She was the silence at the center. Or maybe they came to Potasnik for warmth and he obliged them to play to Anni. In any event, they needed to be together. Like alumni of some particularly grueling training academy now closed, or like men who have been in filthy combat together, their frame of reference was fixed in their shared past and they were trapped in it; there was no way to communicate it to anyone who had not lived it. So although they were, all of them, unlikely friends, they had a stake in banding together. They shared the intricate, untranslatable dialect of horror. They owed each other no explanations and they held no pity or reverence for each other.

They had all come out of Europe empty-handed except for Anni. Anni had Eva, Chava, the girl. A child. Chava had the baby, a husband, a flat, meals to get, and it was partly to witness, to rub up against that daily miracle that they came. Simply to be part of a household.

For a little while, Rachaeli provided them with a topic of conversation. This minor upheaval of domestic morality was soothing to discuss, and they were intrigued when Anni stood up for the faithless woman. Inevitably, though, the conversation led them to cases they had heard of in Hungary. It was terrible when one of them named someone from that other life deliberately—already braced, bracing the others with little signals of voice and expression—but it was unbearable when they collided unwarned with some random name. They would search each other's faces, terrified, for the verdict: dead. How dead, where. Seared by the encounter, one of them would go silent and hollow and the others would have to risk everything to bring him back. So finally they abandoned the subject, but anyway by that time Rachaeli was back from Degania and a part of the household and they were getting used to her. She was exotic— Israeli-born, cheerful, healthy, unafraid—and she amused Anni and Chava. They had no quarrel with her.

For her part, Rachaeli hardly noticed the cronies. Communal groups, flocks, were nothing new to her. She was fascinated by the mother and daughter, though. Anni, a tough lady with good bones and a will of steel, had her daughter jumping through hoops. The girl fussed endlessly over her mother and received in return only the most perfunctory attention. The older woman's hands were somehow deformed and she had some kind of back trouble, and the girl was always jumping up to offer, bring, arrange, clear; but more than that, she seemed constantly to be monitoring her mother's moods. It was as though she couldn't be at peace unless there was nothing owing to the mother, and there was always something owing. It was bizarre. Chava and Rachaeli could hardly leave the flat; Chava would keep running back to check on this and that, and then she would be anxious and distracted for half the time they were out.

But there was this: Chava had chosen Rachaeli. Knowing everything, disapproving of her action, still she had sought Rachaeli out. It was she who strung their days together, reminding Rachaeli as she left about their errand for the next day, referring back fondly to last week's joke or even to some event in Rachaeli's past, as though the relationship was building backward and forward at once.

It was only Rachaeli's past they discussed, though. Chava never mentioned her own and Rachaeli was content with that; she didn't want to hear it, really. All that European turmoil ought to be a closed chapter. She liked it, anyway, being known, read, like a novel. She would tell them bits of her kibbutz or army life in the mornings, enjoying their curiosity. She couldn't have known that they were used to neutralizing their pain by listening to stories, that she was momentarily linking the two of them for the first time since the camps with her narratives.

She got started telling them about the cello one morning, and so she told them a little about Yossi.

"You don't have to talk about that," Chava said. "It must be painful."

"Not at all."

"But you must have loved him terribly, to have risked your marriage"—Chava blushed—"and now to be alone with the baby . . ."

"You have it backward. I used him to get out of my marriage—and especially to be alone with the baby."

Chava said nothing, shocked. Anni said, "You planned it."

"Yes."

Anni nodded approvingly and then, still nodding, smiled. Rachaeli smiled back. She was still smiling when she picked the baby up and gave him her breast.

At first Shlomo pitied the bastard child. He agreed with Chava, on the morning of Aaron's *brit*, that the mother and her misbegotten baby should be invited to join their celebration. All he knew then—all Chava had told him—was that the child was probably illegitimate, and he assumed without giving it much thought that the mother was an innocent victim. There were women whose husbands had been presumed lost in the death camps and who had remarried only to find that the husbands they had given up for dead had survived. Those second marriages were not marriages at all, then, but adulteries, and the children were illegitimate. It was a tragedy no one knew how to deal with, and while the children were unquestionably illegitimate by law, neither they nor the mothers could be despised for it. Certainly he was not inclined to condemn them. And then he knew that Chava had held this baby as her own, suckled it and opened her heart to it, and if she wanted to say a last goodbye, he could understand that.

So when Rachaeli came into the *brit* with Chava, trailed by her mother and a few guests, he thought to offer her some comfort, and he was baffled, first by her look and then by her manner.

She was no refugee, he saw that as soon as he caught sight of her. Her bearing, her loose, rich tangle of hair, the offhand way she took account of the party as she stood with Chava, told him that he knew her. She was a pioneer girl. When they were introduced, her accent and the easy humor in her eyes confirmed it. She was no European victimized by the turmoil of the war. Still, she had been caught up somehow in the tangles of family law and the infant she held firmly in one arm was hopelessly outcast. He felt for them. He took her free hand. "You know," he asked gently, "what the rabbis say about illegitimate children?"

Her mock-serious tone should have warned him. "No. What do the rabbis say?"

"That since they are fatherless, God Himself will be their Comforter."

"Your wife is a survivor of the camps?"

He was taken aback. "Yes."

"So you'll understand—forgive me—if I tell you I'm not going to teach him to hold his breath waiting for this comfort."

Later, when he learned what she had done, he was deeply shaken. He might have married such a girl. Flippant in bed and hidden behind a closed face, she could have deceived him and chosen to do a mad, criminal thing, as this one had. Intentionally to condemn an infant to a lifetime of isolation? To toss black solitude over ten generations of children on a whim? It haunted him. He woke one night soon after they brought Aaron home, to find Chava sitting up in bed in the darkness, nursing the baby. She was tousled and smelled of sleep and milk; her head drooped toward the baby's. Shlomo's eyes opened and closed, rocking him between sleep and vigilance. Chava and the baby loomed white in the featureless dark, dense with innocence, inert with trust. Tears cold along his cheeks and the underwater sensation of more gathering to fall tipped him awake. Why was he crying? He cast around in his mind and found the other baby, the lost one. Daniel ben Rachael. He saw himself cradling the fatherless boy in his two arms—that was all, and, comforted, he tipped back the other way, to sleep.

So without thinking consciously about it, he gave tacit approval to the presence of the baby in their home. In his mind he canceled out the mother. When she returned part-time to her work for the government coding office and Chava offered to watch the baby for her on the days when the babysitter didn't show up, Shlomo made no difficulties. It seemed inevitable and right that the child should come under their— his—protection. He came home early, sometimes, on the days when Dani was there, and there were times when Chava and Anni were absorbed with Aaron—he knew better, by now, than to try to break into that ring—and took no notice when he picked up the other child to play with him.

It became accepted in the house: Aaron was under the management of his mother and grandmother, and Shlomo and Dani, free agents, were left to be pals. No one even thought to mention it to Rachaeli.

She was erratic as a mother. Untrained in ownership, she had no talent for the steady, daily mothering that Dov had given Avi and Zvi, but she devoured the boy in short intense bursts of maternity. She would come in from work—especially on days when he was at Chava's—and if he was sleeping she would lift him, inert and solid, and nuzzle him awake with greedy, loving sounds, inhaling the scent of his neck. She was just as likely to give him short shrift, though, especially if they were at home. He was awake and playful in the early evenings and after a few minutes, she found that trying. Usually she would dress him and take him out for a stroll.

Part of the pleasure of ownership, she was discovering, was in having others admire her possession and know that it was hers. It was almost a sexual thing. When they were out—at Chava's, on their evening strolls, in shops—she couldn't help caressing him, murmuring to him, smoothing his hair: *mine, see?* The baby would squirm and buzz his pleasure, baby laugh, and people would watch them. She would lift him out of his carriage, sometimes, for the pleasure of holding him up to her: *mine*. His feet would fidget at her middle, one of his hands would tangle in her hair, she would lay her cheek against his and close her eyes and smile, a dreamy, ripe smile, and she would know how people saw the two of them. She never seemed to look at the people but she saw them watching, and she was stirred by it.

She loved to take him to Degania. On those visits she kept him casually on her lap or she sat on the grass with her long legs crossed and the baby propped inside them, and she compared herself to the mothers she saw there, her classmates, borrowing their babies for an hour or two in the bedraggled late afternoon. When it was time for the babies to go back to the nursery she'd gather Dani up and say, "Time we went home, eh, love?" She would walk one of her friends to the nursery and when that mother left her baby and came out swinging empty arms, Rachaeli would take her leave carrying Dani high on her shoulder, little bobbing flag of victory.

When he was a little older, Dani learned to take advantage of those times. At home she was distant—busy, unsmiling, annoyed—but when other people were around and he did anything at all to get her attention he could bring her close at once. It was a couple of years before he really noticed the other people; they were not the object. Rachaeli was the object, to bring her glow upon him.

His brothers were glamorous but erratic company. They appeared and disappeared. Rachaeli had set up a sleep-sofa and chest of drawers in the living room for Zvi and Avi. She wasn't going to have them invading Dani's room. Dani kept wandering out to where the boys were, though, or dragging them into his room with him. The older boys ignored him, mostly. Callous, loud, exciting, they came in and left the house under their own power and at their own whim. Dani was powerless to follow them. They came on Friday afternoons and were gone by the time he

150

went to bed on Saturday. A man came to get them and took them away with him. He gave them things, called them on the phone. A father.

"Is he also my father?" he asked Rachaeli when he was three or four. "Will I go, too, when I'll be older?"

"No. You won't ever have to go."

"But . . . so then how did they get one? A father?"

"Lots of people have them. You don't need one."

Aaron had one, and Aaron's father lived right in his house with him. Dani mentioned it to Rachaeli, who only shrugged. The next Saturday when Avi and Zvi were getting ready to go, Dani put some things in his satchel that he took back and forth to Chava's. "I'm going, too," he told them. They laughed—only a little, absently, but it enraged him. "I'm going!" he insisted. "I'm calling him and saying to get me, too." He went out to the phone in the hall and dialed some numbers. The phone buzzed in his ear and they laughed some more.

Rachaeli came in. "What are you doing with the phone? Avi, are you teasing him? Why's he crying?"

They told her. "He thinks he's calling Daddy. He thinks he's going with us; he's all packed."

"Come on," Rachaeli said to Dani, replacing the phone and frowning at the boys. "Come on, my boy. You and I will have a party. We'll make—"

"No!"

"Dani—"

He dragged his satchel out to the hallway, screaming, "I'm going! I am!"

"Listen, Dani—calm down, listen, we'll—"

"I don't *want* to. I'm going with them, with him!"

The doorbell rang. The boys ran down the stairs to Dov, and Dani scrambled out after them, sobbing. Rachaeli had to follow, of course, and to pick him up, screaming and struggling. Dov stood on the sidewalk and watched with a penetrating, accusing look, then took each of his boys by a hand and walked away.

She went up the stairs, gripping Dani so hard that her fingers dug into him. When they were inside she kicked the door shut and she hit him. Again. Again, until his rage turned to the simple crying of a punished child, regular, manageable sobs. She wanted to leave him there to cry. He didn't want her, let him be alone. But he was clinging to her, and the crying had taken on the trusting sound of grief, and she closed her arms around him, claiming him again, sealing it between them.

———————

There were things she had to do, now that he was conscious of the people around him. He spent many of his days at Chava's playing with Aaron, and she had to ensure that no one took her place with him. She would walk home with him from Chava's, extracting an account of his day and subtly engineering his loyalty in the process. It wasn't hard, it only required that she shift his opinion of others a little. "Aaron is nice, isn't he?" she'd ask four-year-old Dani.

"He's my best."

"He is. Even if he does always rip up your drawings. You don't mind that, do you?"

"N-no."

It didn't take much. She didn't want him to dislike the others, only to remember their flaws, judge them coolly, and keep in mind who came first. When he was four or five she came in after work and saw him with Anni. He was sitting up close to her on the couch and telling her something. Anni was listening with sober respect, nodding her head quickly in understanding.

"You were telling Anni something important?" Rachaeli asked later, smoothing his hair back off his face.

He puckered his brow. "Oh, yeah. About my dream."

"What was your dream?"

"I forgot. Can we go to the park?"

"Soon. Is it nicer to talk to Anni than to Chava? Like about your dreams?"

"I guess so. When are we—"

"Doesn't Chava like to listen?"

"I dunno. She works a lot."

"But *Anni* likes you."

"Yeah."

"Almost as much as she likes Aaron. That's nice, right?"

"—Right."

"Come on, my own boy. I'll take you to the park."

When the boys were old enough for school, Aaron went into the religious track and Dani into the secular. The boys protested vigorously that Dani should go with Aaron, but Rachaeli was firm about it. "Aaron's family have their ways, we have ours," she said. "Anyway, the time Aaron spends in prayers every day in school you'll be able to spend in clubs. What would you rather?"

Rachaeli took him to school, to register him for kindergarten. School! Like Avi and Zvi! The teacher pinned a flag to his shirt and gave him a glass of juice. Rachaeli sat next to him on a chair that was too small for her. All the mothers sat on too-small chairs. The mothers were the wrong size for the room. It was a place for Dani, not for Rachaeli.

The school lady had a paper she wrote on. "Date of birth?" she asked, when it was Dani's turn. "You tell me, Dani. What's your birthday, do you know? Good. And can you spell your name? K-O-V-N-E-R. Excellent! Very good! Now . . . where do you live? Phone number? Oh, you're wonderful! Do you have brothers and sisters, Dani? What are their names? And what is your mother's name, do you know that? Good. And your father's?"

He didn't have the answer. He looked blankly at the lady, a panicky sense of failure pumping in his chest and throat. He watched her face for a clue.

"No father," Rachaeli said.

"Oh, I'm sorry. Deceased or divorced?"

"Neither. I *am* divorced, you can put that down. His brothers went to this school; you have the information on their father. But this one has no father."

"All right, I understand that, but government records require a name."

"The boy is illegitimate. A mamzer."

The woman reddened; her eyes widened, registering recall. She glanced at Dani. There were people behind them in the line, other kids with their mothers. The room made a little noise. Dani could feel the children looking at him in awe: this boy is already in trouble. His mother said he was something bad. Mamzer. He could feel a distance widening between himself and everyone in the room. Someone tch'd. They weren't going to let him come to school with the others.

"Mamzer palomzer," Dani said, offhand and cheerily, to fool them. "Chalomzer. Dani the mamzer chalomzer."

The children giggled. Rachaeli put a hand on him: *stop it.* But he couldn't stop it. "Dani momzi shlomzi." He looked at the children, grinning. They giggled again. "When am I coming here?" he demanded of the lady.

"Tomorrow morning, eight o'clock."

"And when are *they* coming?"

"Same time."

Aha, he'd tricked them. He was coming to school with regular kids. "Bidibomzer," he said loudly, leaving.

———

"I'm in the Magicians' Club," Dani told Aaron. He was at Aaron's house on Shabbat morning. Aaron was getting ready to go to synagogue with his father. "And I have soccer an hour a day."

"You're learning magic tricks?" It was so easy to make Aaron wish he were him. Dani relented. "I'll teach you how to do some of them. They're easy."

"Come, Dani, you'll pray with us." Shlomo hugged him in with one arm, Aaron with the other. He smelled of soap and clean laundry and something else: grown man.

"We don't have to pray in my school," Dani said. He didn't tell how he always secretly said the blessings Chava had taught him for snacks and juice and after going to the bathroom. He never told his mother about it, either.

"It's all right; you'll make up for it on Shabbat."

He stood with Shlomo and Aaron, stumbling through the prayers, faking the melodies he didn't know. Aaron knew the service cold, but Shlomo smiled at them both. Maybe he didn't notice that Dani didn't know the prayers at all well. Anyway, when it came time for the blessing, Shlomo wrapped the knotted strings of his prayer shawl around the forefingers of each hand and laid a hand on each boy's head. The prayer shawl spread like black-and-white wings around the two boys. The fringes grazed Dani's cheek and Shlomo's good male scent came at him. He inhaled it greedily and leaned in toward Shlomo, looking under his eyelashes at Aaron on Shlomo's other side. Aaron was squirming and fooling around. Good.

". . . lift up His countenance to you and grant you peace."

Shlomo kissed each of them on the head, Dani first. The prayer shawl fell away from around the boys. Dani hugged himself, feeling cold.

There was a time in the mornings when Rachaeli was quiet and easy-going, and Dani had that time to himself. They would sit together peaceably at the kitchen table. Rachaeli would be reading the paper. She would close her eyes, inhale the steam off her coffee. She would light a cigarette and take a drag, let the smoke out slowly and smile at him, acknowledging the little pleasure of the moment, the circle of self-indulgence modestly completed. Then she would finish the coffee, grind out the cigarette, and gather up the dishes. "Come on, old fellow," she'd say. "Time to go."

But then some mornings she went off with her cello, and on those mornings she frowned into the mirror and plucked her eyebrows and had no time for a cigarette. Those afternoons she came home with an air of . . . a scent of . . . an ease of body. He stayed far from her then.

Even on regular days—no-cello days—she was different out on the street, electric, and Dani was uneasy with her. It was like she was a radio sending out a signal, waiting to see who heard it. She had a cool way of not looking at anyone so that you knew she expected people to be looking at her. She would blink once, when someone did look at her; Dani thought it was like a scoreboard adding up goals: *got one.* He didn't like it. He didn't like the feeling that there was something about to happen. When he was little, he would do some kind of act, not to get the people's attention or even hers, but to break the current between her and them: "Want to hear a joke? Want to?" But she'd smile and touch him then, her unreal, too-attentive public smile, and the effect was exactly as though someone had turned a light on her: *Look at this woman.* So then Dani would have to do something to get her angry—act up, get them to look at him instead—anything to turn the smile off. She would glare at him or make an annoyed face, looking like just another mother; they would look away and Dani would be released, triumphant and miserable.

He was older now, ten, and he didn't do that any more. He walked to school with friends, not with his mother. He was always the one the other kids looked at when they talked. He was the center. It was easy with friends, to be the center, and much less complicated than getting

Rachaeli's attention. He would still sit with her in her early-morning quiet time, but then just before she got up, he would dash out to meet his friends, leaving her. Being the one to leave her.

He liked it best when they were at Chava's. Rachaeli was easy and funny there. At home, except for their morning time, she was either busy and short-tempered or she was asking him too many questions, criticizing his friends. But at Chava's she was happy, relaxed. She laughed with Chava and she made Anni laugh. She was the practical one of the three women; she made the decisions and she explained to them about the local news and she told them how to handle things in the city. She'd sit with one elbow on the table, smoking and talking, and if Dani and Aaron came over she would include them, charming them. He was proud of her then.

Rachaeli was a visitor in that house, an event. But Dani was part of the household. It was very different from his own house. Chava was a regular mother, invisible. She put bandages on scrapes and made more lemonade and so on, and she yelled at him and Aaron, but he and Aaron were the interesting things in that house, not Chava.

Dani's house smelled like Rachaeli—her cigarettes, her shampoo, her powder. Chava's house smelled like food.

Sometimes he was a little sick and Rachaeli couldn't take any more days off so she would drop him over at Chava's. They would get there early. Aaron would just be leaving, begging his mother to write him an excuse from morning prayers, and Shlomo would still be home. Dani would sit quietly in the big chair, gloating straight-faced over Aaron's unlucky ordinary good health. Aaron would leave and Chava would begin cleaning up the breakfast things. Shlomo would wander out in his business suit. "What's the matter, Dani? Sick?"

"Guess so."

Shlomo would come over and put his cheek against Dani's forehead, concentrating for two or three seconds. He smelled of shaving cream. "No fever," he'd say, or "a little fever. Your mother called the doctor? What did he say?" When Dani got older, Shlomo would put a hand on his forehead instead. The boy would sit perfectly still, feeling the temperature of his skin meet, ease into, the temperature of Shlomo's steady palm. Then Shlomo would touch his cheek with one knuckle, a kind of salute. "I'll call you later," he'd say, and he would. Dani waited anxiously for those calls, afraid that Shlomo wouldn't call until after Aaron got home. When that happened, he would speak with Dani first, but then Aaron would take the phone, an arrogance of ownership Dani hated him for, and Dani would hear him say, "Hi, Dad. Okay. Good. A ninety-four. He liked my experiment. Yeah, okay, see you later." It was worse than if Shlomo had never called. Dani was the one who had been there all day, though, so he had an advantage over Aaron. He could hold Shlomo on the phone by telling him the news about his household. "Guess what Chava told me today?" he'd say, or he'd report on the cronies' conversation, finding any incident to elaborate for Shlomo. If he tried he could make Shlomo laugh, or better, he could surprise him or impress him. He could make him really listen. Aaron's school news wasn't so great in comparison. Anyway, Aaron didn't even try. He usually wanted to get off the phone and play.

Once when Dani had an earache and Chava had to take Anni to the back doctor, Shlomo took Dani with him to his office. He let him draw on the big white pads, and he showed him how to weigh things on the scales, and even gave him a loupe and some little stones to look at through it. Aaron went to the office with Shlomo sometimes, and he was always talking about the loupe and the scale and the microscope, but Dani wasn't really too interested in any of that. He was watching Shlomo. Shlomo had an outside office and an inside one. The door to the outside one had a special lock and a spy system, and there was a lady sitting at a desk. The inside one was where Shlomo worked. In it there were two safes; Shlomo took tissue packages out of them and unwrapped them and studied the stones. There were two other men who came in and out, bringing messages and asking questions: someone in Belgium had a problem with something, and Shlomo talked to him on the phone; something was happening in South Africa in a month and Shlomo said, "Take it." He talked fast on the phone, decisively, and he joked with the two men, and when the lady buzzed him from the outside office he picked up his phone and said, "Yes, Leah?" He was the boss of all these people, and he owned all the diamonds.

He worked in his shirt sleeves, and when he was on the phone he grabbed a fistful of hair and rubbed it back and forth, so that one side of his hair was all messed up. When he looked in the microscope, he talked to himself. Dani tried to hear what he said, but he couldn't. It sounded like numbers, and while he was looking in the microscope and talking to himself, he drew right on the table with a pencil.

He stayed at the microscope for a long stretch, in the late morning. Then suddenly, without looking up, he called Dani. "Come and look at this. Look what we have here."

Dani ran over. Shlomo stood and hoisted him up onto the stool.

"Close one eye and look into the microscope. Here . . . turn this little knob until everything looks very clear. Got it? Now, what do you see?"

"Lines. Like triangles."

"Good. That's the facets of the stone. What else? Is it all clear? No black spots or white lines?"

". . . I guess."

"Look up to where one o'clock would be on a watch. See the white?"

"No. Yes! I see it!"

"That's a crack in the stone. See how it goes toward the center of the stone? About a third of the way in?"

"Yeah. You got gypped."

"No, I bought a lot of stones. Some will always have flaws or cracks. But how about if we figure out how to cut around the crack? How would you do it? Here, look."

He drew a big shape on the pad of paper, and he drew in the crack. "Show me how we could cut around it."

Dani drew a line perpendicular to the crack, isolating it in one third of the stone.

"Good. That's one way. We could do that and we'd still have four carats or so. But look what's left over. What do we do with the other piece?"

"Give it to somebody poor?"

Shlomo laughed. "If I did that every time, I'd be somebody poor. Look, what if we . . ." He sketched little straight lines on the pad, at angles down toward the bottom of the crack, then more little lines at the other end of the stone. "Now what have we got?"

"A heart!"

"Right! Look how perfectly it works out . . . almost as if it were intended. See, if the planes were different we wouldn't have been able . . ." He went on, sketching and marking the angles. He'd lost Dani, but Dani went on watching and nodding, as though he understood. Finally Shlomo looked up. "A five-and-a-half-carat heart. Pretty, eh?"

"Yeah."

"There's always a way to get around it, Dani. Every time. You just have to think. And sometimes you have to be willing to lose a little, to save the stone. Say, how about lunch? What's good for an earache? Pizza?"

Dani grinned. "And soda."

"Absolutely." He picked up the phone. "Leah, send Yissachar out for some pizza, will you? And two sodas. I don't know, he'll find a place. Clean, tell him."

When the earache got bad in the late afternoon, Dani went to the men's room to take his medicine and the aspirin Rachaeli had given him. He didn't want Shlomo to remember that he was sick and take him home to Chava. This was his whole day, and he wasn't going to give up any of it. He spent the rest of the afternoon drawing diamonds with disastrous cracks, or black spots right in their centers, and making little lines the way Shlomo had, sketching the heroic saving of the stones.

Every year in school he had to explain to the teacher about not having a father's name to put on the yellow and blue cards. He had known for two years now, though, that he had one somewhere. When he was in third grade, a new kid was card monitor. He pointed out to Dani that he'd left the space for "Father" blank. "I don't have a father," Dani said.

"But just his name," the card monitor said.

"No name."

"You have to," the kid argued. The teacher hushed them and collected the cards. The boy pursued the subject at recess. "You have to have a father."

"No I don't. I'm a mamzer; my mother says that means I never had one."

"But you had one once. But he's dead or divorced or something."

"Nope. She says never."

"But when you were born. Somebody put the baby in her belly. My mother says. The man puts it in there."

"My mother put it in herself."

"No she didn't," the kid said with flat authority. "She couldn't."

"She couldn't," Yoram Mizrahi echoed, joining sides with the new kid. In a minute everyone was going to get into it; every kid at recess was going to tell Dani that he didn't know about his own mother. "You don't know everything," he said coldly to the new kid, fighting back the panic. "Come on, Yoram, help me set up my trick. Get me my box. Tell everybody in two minutes I'll do the Magic Broken Rope trick." He turned his back on the new kid and moved to the big rock, center stage. Yoram ran in to get the magic kit, hawking the performance on his way. Dani watched Yoram running back toward him with the box, watched the others drift over and form a ragged semicircle at his feet. The panic ebbed away, leaving him with a kind of angry excitement. He chose helpers from the group, teasing out the selection. They raised their hands

159

to be chosen, just like in school: "Dani," they begged. "Dani!" Chosen, they ran up importantly until he had a cadre of four, and the new kid was frozen out.

All right.

He didn't have to be like the rest of them, with a father's name on the blue and yellow cards. He was the center, and he was going to amaze them all. Trick and amaze them.

He asked Rachaeli about it in the morning. "By the way," he said, "you know what this new kid says?"

"Mm?"

"He says someone has to put the baby in the belly. Like a father."

She pulled the smoke in, *sssss*, between her teeth. It curled out her nose. "So what?"

"Does someone? Have to?"

"Yes, of course. You know about the sheep and the horses at Degania. Every creature has a mother and a father."

"Then who put me in your belly?"

His heart pounded. He was closing in on a father. Rachaeli was looking attentively at him, as though he were telling her something important, but he wasn't telling her anything. He was waiting.

"Someone did," she said finally, "because I wanted you very much. That's all you have to know, and anyway it's late. We have to get going. All right?"

"Sure."

"Dani? When you're older I'll explain it to you. All right?"

"Sure."

Someone did. Someone. One person.

For a while he thought it was Shlomo who put him in Rachaeli's belly. He knew, of course, that he and Aaron had been born together and mixed up in the hospital. They'd heard the story over and over. The women told it sometimes, and laughed. "There you were," Rachaeli said to Anni, "dressed just so, every inch a lady, threatening mayhem and murder. I thought you were going to swallow the poor doctor." Then they all laughed, even Anni.

So maybe Shlomo was his father. But then why didn't he say so? Dani tried being very good when Shlomo was around, and Shlomo liked it but he never said anything about being Dani's father.

He thought of a way to find out. "When did you meet Shlomo?" he asked Rachaeli. She was looking intently into the mirror, pulling the little brush across her eyelashes.

"Shlomo? I don't know, let's see, at your *brit milah?* I guess so."

"At my what?"

"When you were eight days old. There's a ceremony—"

"After I got born?"

"What? Oh, yes. After you were born. Eight days after."

"But maybe by accident you met him before?"

"Maybe I passed him in the street. Why? Hand me a tissue, would you?"

Bereft, he let Shlomo slide away, back to Aaron. It was one of her days to take the cello and when they walked out she put a hand on his shoulder and lifted her chin, smiling over at him. Everyone, look at this woman.

Well, somebody put him in there. She knew and she wasn't telling.

December 4, 1961

Who cared, anyway? He had plenty of things that Aaron didn't have, and he made sure that Aaron remembered it. Aaron got good grades in school, and everyone made a big fuss about it, but that was only when grades came out. Dani had his magic, and you could do a trick any time and everyone liked you for amazing them. They always smiled, even though you'd tricked them. He had the violin, too, his own three-quarter size with blue velvet inside the case and the little amber square of rosin in its own box inside the case.

"We can play duets," Rachaeli had said to him, but he didn't care much about that. He liked to play alone, or to carry the melody in his school orchestra. Everyone heard the violin and looked at the violinist. When he went to Aaron's after school, he usually got there before Aaron and he'd get his practicing in then, with Anni and Chava listening. He liked to play only if someone was listening, and he concentrated on the pieces he did well, ignoring the others. Aaron was learning to play the piano, but the piano was just a piece of furniture. It belonged to the living room, not to Aaron. Dani always persuaded Aaron to put off his practicing until after he went home.

And Dani had big brothers. They were pretty good to have; they sometimes took him places on Saturdays, and they brought him their stuff when they lost interest in it, whole collections of things and sports equipment he was almost ready for. They had no interest in his belongings, being four and seven years older. Aaron had two little brothers—Yakov, two years younger than Aaron and Dani, and Elijah, four years younger—and they were nothing but trouble while Dani's brothers were a source; what he learned from listening in on them made him an authority with Aaron.

Like today. He walked toward Aaron's from the bus stop, still thinking how he would tell him what he'd overheard Zvi and Avi saying last Saturday, and what he'd figured out from it about how men did it to ladies. He passed someone with a portable radio and he heard a woman shrieking at the Nazi guy. Eichmann. He wondered if women screamed when men did it to them. He supposed it must hurt.

———————

The radio was on all the time at Chava's now, all day long, since the beginning of the trial. On the very first day, the cronies had arrived unannounced, in force; they established themselves at the table, turned on Chava's radio, and settled in to listen.

"Judges of Israel," the prosecuting attorney began, ". . . with me, in this place, and at this hour, stand six million accusers."

"Judges of Israel," Ari-Bela whispered.

"Shh."

". . . Their blood cries out but their voices are not heard. Therefore it falls to me to be their spokesman and to unfold in their name the awesome indictment."

Anni nodded, eyes hard. Zara, sitting apart from the others, had her hand in a fist and was biting the knuckle of her thumb.

". . . 'And when I passed by thee and saw thee polluted in thine own blood, I said unto thee, in thy blood live . . . !'"

"What is this," Potasnik demanded, "a bris?"

"Maybe he thinks he'll bring them back to life with this performance," Grodner said.

"Shut up!" Ari-Bela yelled. "Let a man listen!"

They listened. It became a routine: they arrived at Chava's daily and sat through the broadcasts together. When the commentators began to discuss the evidence that was coming out, concluding that resistance had been virtually impossible, the cronies sat in grim amusement.

"Mazal tov," Grodner grunted.

"They're quick, these countrymen of yours," Potasnik said to Ari-Bela Ben Zion. "They catch right on. It's news to them, that it's hard to debate with electric fences and machine guns?"

"It is news to them," Ari-Bela retorted. "It's like we were raped—"

"Raped."

"Will you listen? It's like we were raped, and no one was sure, did we really try to get away? Did we fight back hard enough? Listen, Potasnik, they took us in because we were family, and they didn't ask us any questions."

"Wonderful. They didn't ask any questions, and for thirteen years they've been looking at us funny. Friendless people without papers or guns or where to go—and from here they judge us, that we didn't overthrow the whole SS? You're such an Israeli, Munkas—excuse me, *Ben Zion*—you're such an Israeli, you explain to me what the hell right they have to look at us funny."

"Don't get excited, Potasnik. They didn't know how it was. Did they know? Could they imagine? And we didn't tell them either, did we?"

"We were supposed to publish a statement: Please excuse us, we got murdered?"

"They didn't know," Ari-Bela repeated, "and we didn't tell them. So now they'll know."

"The Israeli speaks."

"So what are you, a Hungarian? You going to go back to Budapest and drink tea with the Arrow Cross? You got a place to go, Potasnik, that's better than here?"

"I'm Potasnik and I don't apologize and I don't explain. Let them read this"—he stuck out his arm and pointed at the number on it—"let them read this and figure out for themselves how it was."

Zara made a little involuntary sound. They all looked at her. She was frowning at the thin welted line on her left forearm. Anni put a hand up to stop her from speaking. "You had every right," she said. "Why should you walk around numbered like an animal? It's no badge of honor."

"You didn't do it. I should have stood up to be counted."

"You stood up enough times to be counted. Let them count someone else for a change." Potasnik closed the subject.

———

Anni, surprisingly enough, made an issue of it in the house. She would latch onto Aaron when he came in from school and lure him to the table with the sweets they were all devouring in large quantities. When he tried to take a pastry and leave, she would push him into a chair between herself and Zara. "Sit," she would say. "Listen. Listen to what this man is telling. Listen and remember." He would fidget and complain, but Dani sat docilely at the table, eating Chava's cookies and fiddling dreamily with his dice or some magic apparatus.

"Look how Dani listens," Anni said in the second week.

"Dani is bored to death. Any child would be," Chava suddenly said. "What do they need to hear this for? Aaron, Dani, get your sweaters. Go outside with your soccer ball." Five faces flashed disbelief, accusing her, but she avoided their eyes and repeated her order. Aaron darted outside, Dani following.

"He doesn't have to hear it," Chava repeated to Anni.

Silence.

"Mother, I'm sorry, but it isn't for children."

"One million children," Zara said, but gently. Anni said nothing and did not look at Chava. After a moment Chava, face burning, walked away, but not far. She hovered in the kitchen for an hour, enraged and afraid, until Ari-Bela came in to say goodbye. "Your mother's upset by all this," he said. He pinched her cheek. She surprised herself by nuzzling into his hand, like a child.

"Why does the boy have to live it, too, Ari-Bela?" she whispered. "Why can't it be finished with?"

"You don't want him to blame you."

"Blame me?"

"Later. You don't want him to say, 'Why didn't you resist? What kind of weaklings were you?' That's what they think now, you know."

"I don't care. When he's older he'll understand."

"This you can't change so fast. He has to grow up understanding. All of them. So in twenty years, God forbid, they shouldn't look at us and say, 'Why didn't you tell us how it happened so we would be warned?'"

Her face twisted into tears, like a child's. "I gave her three children. Isn't that enough to make her forget? What do I have to do?"

"Shh. You're talking foolishness now. Shh."

"When is it enough?"

"Shh, darling. Shhhh now."

It was never enough. It would never be enough to make up for what her mother had traded for her. Her boys would have to hear it all and then they would never be able to look at the world the same again, and still it wouldn't be enough. There was no penance for having survived.

"You're always over there," Rachaeli had said to Dani when the trial was in its third or fourth week. "Doesn't all that Holocaust stuff bother you? Maybe you should stay away for a few weeks until it all dies down. You can come home and let yourself in, you're old enough now. Or come to the office with me. You can play with the decoder."

"No, it's okay. Me and Aaron are building a space station."

Dani had no intention of staying away from Chava's. It was very good there now. Aaron was building the space station alone in his room, even though he was getting into trouble with Anni, who wanted him to sit and listen to the trial.

Aaron hated the cronies. He always had to report to them every day after school; they all had to see his report card and hear his oral reports and so on. Every one of them thought he had the right to yell at Aaron every little time one of his brothers cried that he'd been picked on. They ordered him around—"Get your grandmother a cup of tea. Don't let your mother pick up your mess. Bring me an ashtray, that's a good boy." Except for Potasnik, who usually gave him pretty good stuff, they had no idea what he liked. Zara would go on a baking binge every once in a while and make strange cakes full of chopped-up fruit, which he hated. She always made him a little cake of his own and pushed piece after piece at him every day after school until he finished it. Grodner, whose breath was sour, challenged him to a game of cat's cradle every time he saw him and cackled happily when he got tangled up. And they all spoke immigrant Hebrew, half the words in regular pronunciation, half in an old-time accent. And now, with the trial on the radio all the time, it was worse than ever. They were yelling and shouting, or they were so quiet that you couldn't sit still, and then one of them would cry or moan or mumble something in immigrant talk. It made him squirm inside. He couldn't sit there, even if he got punished for leaving. He slid into his room every day as soon as his mother released him, and he worked on his space station.

Dani didn't mind them. He wasn't bothered by the raised voices or the accents; they weren't his family. He didn't mind listening to the trial, either. Sometimes it was pretty interesting, and in the dull times Potasnik would play cards with him, or Zara would tell his fortune. It was easy; Aaron walked away, so Dani was the good one.

He liked Rachaeli when she was at Chava's these days, too. No one was looking at her at all, and she was sober and quiet and attentive to all of them, a way he'd never seen her. Every once in a while, listening to the testimony, Anni or Chava would give a little cry and press a hand to her mouth, or put her arms around herself and sit motionless, and sometimes Rachaeli would go over to one or the other and touch her. She only tried it once with Anni; Anni started as though she'd been struck and brushed Rachaeli's hand away blindly. But when Rachaeli put a hand on Chava's arm, Chava covered it with her own hand and tilted her head over toward

Rachaeli as though to keep her there. There was no restlessness, no *look-at-me* air about Rachaeli at those times. She would stand behind Chava, arms around her or stroking her hair, and no one was looking at her. She was simply accepted into that silent group of adult witnesses, and Dani was relieved and proud.

It was a strange thing, though. When, as it sometimes happened, Shlomo was home during the broadcasts and tried to take Chava's hand or put an arm around her the way Rachaeli did, Chava shrugged him off, just like Anni.

He took on the job of filling Shlomo in on the trial when he came home. It fell to him; Aaron was in his room, and no one else paid any attention when the front door opened. Dani would meet him in the foyer and bring him up to date.

"What country?" Shlomo asked him one night.

"Warsaw."

"That's not a country, it's a city in Poland."

"Oh. They put them inside a wall. And the kids had to do everything."

"What do you mean?"

"They went through the pipes to get food. And they could get killed for bringing in food, you know?"

"Brave, huh?"

"Yeah! Like soldiers!"

"No, braver than soldiers. And the parents were, too."

"No, they didn't go. The kids went alone. The parents were too big to go through the pipes. Potasnik told me."

Shlomo had gone behind his eyes, the way all the grownups did when they listened to the trial. "No," he said. "But they sent the children. How they found the courage . . ."

He put an unconscious hand on Dani's neck. Dani was thinking that Shlomo didn't get it, really; it was the kids who were the brave ones—but he didn't say it or move. Shlomo moved, though; after a second he mussed Dani's hair. "Oh well," he said.

"Zara cried about the kids getting shot, and Anni yelled at her," Dani reported.

"She did? Loud?"

"No, you know, like Anni yells."

"Mm." Shlomo knew. Anni would have snapped at Zara, withering her without raising her voice. Chava would have tensed right up, quivering like a rabbit, conditioned to her mother's moods, and she would have spent the rest of the afternoon wooing the old lady back to the black

167

silence that passed for equilibrium with Anni. And Chava would be glum and tense herself when they were finally alone. Paying her eternal goddamned debt.

When Shlomo went into the living room, he found that the cronies had gone home and Anni sat alone at her loom. He heard a pounding in the kitchen and smiled sourly, thinking, Chava's taking it out on the meat. He glanced at Anni once more, trying to assess her mood before he went in to greet Chava. Anni looked serene, actually, and in the lamplight you could see that she had been elegant once, a beauty in her life before the camps. How can you know? he suddenly accused himself. Who knows what kind of courage it took, a parent in that place? Could you have gotten a child through it?

I'd have gotten her out, he thought for the thousandth time. Before. How? The new thought shook him. *With what? To where?*

He went over to Anni. "That's nice," he offered, looking at the work on the loom, a fluffy pastel weave with little hairs raised from the wool toward the electricity in Anni's hands. She used quantities of wool. It cost him a fortune, Anni's weaving. "What's it going to be?"

"Another shmatte."

"Where are the boys? Where's Aaron?"

"I don't see Aaron any more. She sends him out. Ask her where they are."

He wandered into the kitchen. Chava was stirring some meat around in a frying pan, staring grimly into the steam. She looked flushed and pretty. He kissed her cheek. She sighed and went on stirring. *Now you,* the sigh said clearly. *What do you want from me?*

Dani got the idea of being a reporter, asking the cronies questions about the death camps and writing down their answers. He got pretty excited about it. He could send it to the newspaper, maybe. Or he could read it on the radio.

He waited until the evening summary was over and the radio was off, after dinner. "I'm writing a report," he told them all. "I have to ask some questions." He had the first question written on his pad.

"Grodner?"

"Hah?"

"Did you work hard there?"

"Like horses. Exactly like horses, only horses they feed. Horses are property, so you take care of them, right? Us they used up till we died."

"You didn't die."

Grodner turned on him. "No one died in my place. Write that. I ate my allotment, no one else's. And I never took a shoe. My feet—you want to see?"

He began to untie a shoelace, shaking. Dani was afraid. Grodner was really angry. Why?

The shoe fell to the floor. Grodner was pulling ferociously at his sock. "My feet froze and turned black—see? See here? Black, like everyone's. You want to know why I didn't die? They didn't get around to me. That's all."

"All right, Grodner," Potasnik soothed him. "Nobody said no. The boy is learning. He's trying to learn something."

"Let him learn that they died for no reason and we lived for no reason. I don't apologize to no one. They didn't get around to killing me. That's it. How about Zara?" he hurled at Dani. "You think she lived because she did something bad? Think she was a whore for the SS?"

"Grodner! The boy never—"

"Every one of the women was a whore or a kapo, eh? Every man killed someone for a shoe or some extra bread. I'll tell you something, sabra boy, if you people never ate shit, if you never stood naked in formation before dawn so some god could decide to let his dog eat your balls or send you to the furnace, if you never made yourself invisible so they wouldn't see you and make an example of you, then don't ask questions and don't judge. You don't know. You people don't know a goddamned thing."

No one spoke for a second. Dani, his face hot, looked steadily down at his notebook and wrote anything, just to show that he was writing. "Dogs ate balls," he wrote. "People ate shit."

"Dani? Come give me a hand with the garbage," Shlomo said. "Hold the door; here, take the papers."

He followed Shlomo outside. Shlomo put the trash in the can and took the newspapers from Dani and put them in, too. Then he lit a cigarette and squinted at Dani over the smoke. "They're angry at us because we weren't there," he said. Dani understood, shocked, that a grownup was telling him the simple truth about other grownups. "They care for us but they can't help being angry, too. You know?"

Dani nodded. "Weren't you in a camp?" he asked, to keep Shlomo out there with him another minute.

"No. I wasn't, your mother wasn't, your grandmother wasn't."

"How come?"

"Because we weren't living where the Nazis were. We were here. We were lucky to be here."

"Yeah," Dani said. "They're mad at us because we were lucky."

He slept over at Chava's that night and by bedtime he wasn't even thinking about the trial or Grodner, but in his dream he was standing naked, tied to some kind of fence, and everyone was standing and looking at him and a big dog came running at him. Everyone was looking and he couldn't move and the dog was charging at him to tear off his balls. Helpless terror. Teeth. A long, desperate scream.

He woke up still tied, but it was Shlomo holding him, and something was strange. Shlomo was in pajamas, so that Dani's face was in the hair on Shlomo's chest.

"Shh," Shlomo whispered, chafing Dani's back with his hand. The hair on his chest was a little soft, a little scratchy. "You'll wake Aaron up. You had a bad dream?"

Dani nodded. His crying had taken on a rhythm that was comforting in itself. He kept it going after the impulse had faded, even when Shlomo's chafing became a little uncomfortable, unwilling to release the furry chest and Shlomo's good smell. Finally, though, he couldn't keep it up any longer and he had to lie back down and close his eyes. He didn't have to worry about keeping Shlomo there, as it turned out, because Shlomo stayed for a long time, even after Dani was asleep.

"Potasnik?"

Potasnik was dissecting a herring, cutting long silver slices and eating them one by one, with bites of a roll. He looked at the boy, tense with energy, wielding his pad and pencil. "It's the reporter. Nu, what?"

"I have a question. What Grodner said—"

"Listen, don't pay him no attention. He gets upset. Go play; it's enough with the paper and the pencil. Where's Aaron?"

Dani persisted. "What did he mean about the shoe? I didn't say he took a shoe."

Potasnik looked around: no one. He sighed. "In the camps you died without good shoes," he said. "Your feet got sores, they swelled up, you couldn't work, and then they killed you."

"So if they wanted you to work why didn't they give you good shoes?"

Potasnik saw the boy, maybe for the first time. Cute, healthy, dimpled, wiry little kid with curly black hair and black eyes, totally innocent of racial inferiority. Never met a goy in his life, probably. Born here, an alien life form. "They didn't want us to work," he said flatly. "They wanted us to crawl and tear each other apart and die, and meanwhile they got some work out of us. We were in fear of them and we were in fear of ourselves and each other. Anyone could steal your shoes. In a second you could steal someone else's, unless you kept forcing yourself not to; in any minute you could be a murderer."

He leaned over and pointed a hand across the table. Big, knuckly hand. Dani tried to picture Potasnik murdering someone. "They had a system," Potasnik said. "In the ghetto they made Jews give them a list of who should die. Which Jews should die, you understand? If the Jews gave the list, *they* were the killers; they picked out who must die. You see? If they didn't, *everyone* died and they were the killers anyway. In the camps, if one person fought back or tried to get away, a hundred died for it. They liked to make one Jew work another until he dropped. They liked to use Jews to beat other Jews. There weren't enough ways they could—"

He looked up. "In only a minute you could steal a shoe, or get noticed and be made to beat up another poor creature. The miracle is that so many of us didn't."

"But Grodner didn't?"

"No, he was lucky. Me too. Lucky Pierre. You writing this down? Going to read it to your class?"

"If it isn't in the newspaper or something. It's pretty important."

"Yeah." Potasnik picked up his knife and fork again and speared a piece of herring. "Tell them I'm alive because those other poor bastards didn't take my shoes, and I'm still Potasnik because I didn't steal some other poor bastard's shoes. Let's see if you can make them understand that."

May 2

It's hot, no breeze to speak of. Dani has been allowed to stay for supper. The grownups are listening to the seven-o'clock summary of the trial. Aaron and Dani sit at the table, too, near the open window, working on their model bombers.

The witness has a funny voice, choppy. "I also met a Jewish boy," he is saying. "About eighteen years old. This SS man wanted to shoot the boy. The boy charged and jumped at the SS man, knifed him, grabbed his revolver, and ran away."

"Yay!" Dani yells, startling Aaron.

"—Fifty Jews were taken as hostages. On the next day the boy was seized. Twenty-five hostages were executed, and this boy."

"What does it mean?" Dani demands of Shlomo.

"What, 'executed'?"

"No— 'hostage.'"

"It means—I capture you. You could resist, maybe; you could even kill me and run away. Right?"

"Sure. You've got to."

"Yes. But what if my people also have your mother and Aaron and Chava? And if you resist or run away, you know I'll kill them, or my men will. Then what?"

"Oh. Like Potasnik said. So is that why they didn't?"

"Yes. One of the reasons."

Still the same week. Still hot. Everyone is in the flat this afternoon— all the cronies, the boys, Rachaeli. They're drinking cold, sweet tea.

"The Germans entered all the courtyards in the ghetto," the witness is saying, "and tore away every child they encountered. They tossed them into trucks, inside which music was playing. Mothers would approach the automobiles and plead with the Germans to give the children back. I saw one mother beseech the guards. 'How many do you have there?' the German asked. 'Three,' said the mother. 'You may have one back,' said the German and climbed into the car with the mother. All three children looked at her and stretched out their little hands. All of them wanted to go with the mother; she did not know which child to select, looked from one to the other, and finally went away alone."

"Murderer," says Anni, looking into the rug with hate in her eyes.

"Yes. Murderers," Rachaeli says.

"Who, Anni?" Dani asks. They look at him, embarrassed and shocked. Can he still be ignorant? But Anni raises her eyes to answer his question.

"The mother," she says, as though it were self-evident.

Everyone makes sounds to cancel out her words but she goes on. "She threw away a life," she spits. "Now there are three on her head instead of the two. Coward. No strength to choose, she gives away a life."

"They made them choose," Rachaeli says. She isn't saying it to anyone; she's trying to decode it.

But Chava answers her. "Yes," she says softly, so only Rachaeli can hear. "Their real crime: they made murderers out of us. Not just the ones who had to choose—everyone. Everyone who lived lived instead of someone else. There's no way to atone. None."

Dani is still looking at Anni, interested in her fury. She must have known that murderer mother, he decides.

May 9

Rachaeli comes for Dani late in the afternoon and Chava interrupts her government gossip to pull her into her bedroom. "Stay with me a while."

"I really can't—" Yossi is expecting her. She'd been hoping to drop Dani at home and steal an hour with him.

"Please." She isn't asking. It's a different voice, set and grim. "The boys are doing a magic show or something for the little ones. I need half an hour. I can't do it alone; I tried."

"What?"

"He said it took half an hour."

"What did?"

"To die. The gas. Twenty-five to thirty-two minutes, one of the witnesses said today. So I have to see how long is half an hour. But I don't want to be alone."

"For your brother?"

"Yes."

"All right. But sit down at least. Don't stand there."

"No. I have to stand." *Even in death, families may be seen standing,* the man said, *pressed together, clutching hands.*

"All right."

"Don't let the boys see. Stay with me."

"Yes, don't worry."

Twenty-five minutes is an endless piece of time. The boys' voices beat against the wall in wavelets, but Chava stands rigid and seems not to hear. Rachaeli stands, too, with her back blocking the door. After the twenty-five minutes have passed, she goes over to Chava, not wanting to break the vigil with words. She touches her arm. There is no response. It isn't over yet. Rachaeli puts her arms around Chava. She is taller than Chava, but thinner, and she wraps her thin arms around her friend's sturdy body. Chava grasps her suddenly and they stand locked. They go to the finish that way, seven more minutes or seven hours, until Chava releases her.

"Now we know," she whispers. Her eyes are wild.

"Yes," Rachaeli says. But she doesn't.

May 16

Rachaeli is outside Yossi's door, listening. The heat has made her irritable and when she hears what he is playing, she bangs angrily on his door. "Do you have to play Wagner?" she demands as soon as he opens it.

His smile holds. "What's wrong? Too hot for Wagner?"

"The Philharmonic doesn't even perform Wagner."

"Oh, you're talking politics. Want to come in?"

She wants to stir it up. Suddenly she doesn't feel like being with him. "Let him die. Let his music die."

"Look, if we only played the music of men we admired—"

"He'd have happily written music to burn you by."

"Aha. The Nazis again. You're all overheated. Shall I give you a shower?"

"'The Nazis again.' Aren't you *listening?*"

"How can I help it? Everywhere I go I'm assaulted—"

"And you can still play his—"

He sighs. He puts the bow down and lays his hands on her shoulders.

"I love you. But nobody tells me what to play. No matter who wrote this glorious stuff, it's inhuman *not* to play it. I shall play it and when the Philharmonic grows up a little, it will play it with me. Meanwhile, we can fight or I can give you a shower." His voice moves down into his throat and he smiles, in control of her. "I can run cool water over you and soap you. You might like it. Soapy breasts and thighs, all of you slippery—"

"You're—"

"Tell me later."

Later, they're lying together. As usual, he's smoking and he has one hand on her. She hasn't moved, she still has one knee up, lazily left as it was. Her head is against his shoulder and her eyes are closed. She isn't touching him. She may be asleep.

"Of course I've been listening," he says. "It could have been them."

"Who?" She can't think what he means. He waves a hand toward the window. What? Oh, children's voices.

"It could have been them in the ovens."

"It could have been us," she says.

"Mm." He nods thoughtfully. He almost believes it.

May 25

Anni and the cronies are all dressed up. Dani has his new white cotton shirt on; he's going with them. It's five in the morning and Rachaeli, sleepy and slow, has just deposited him at Chava's. They have to get an early start, to get the bus to Jerusalem and be in the court when the day's proceedings begin.

Aaron is still asleep; they'll be gone before he wakes up, they'll already be in Jerusalem when he's starting his morning in school. Chava wouldn't let Aaron go with them, even though today is Hungary day in the proceedings. Today they'll begin taking testimony from the Hungarian survivors, and Anni and the cronies are going. Maybe they'll see people they knew in the camps; maybe they'll get to testify, too. Anyway, they'll be there. They have to be there, Grodner says.

Anni is really angry that Aaron isn't going, but Chava absolutely refuses. It's a school day, she says, and that's that. But she's up and dressed now, and she's made all of them a special lunch, and she's pressing smelling salts on Potasnik and reminding Anni to take her painkillers for her back. "I'm sorry, Mother; I can't go," she says.

"You don't have to go," Anni says coldly. "You have your children to take care of." Chava looks slapped.

It's a school day for Dani, too, but Rachaeli thinks it's a good idea for him to go. Anni has promised him it will be the most important day of his life.

As it turns out, it's pretty boring. They aren't in the courtroom where the Nazi is, in his glass cage. They're in a hall near the court, with a screen that shows the trial. The hall is jammed with people and by the middle of the morning, people are crying and yelling things out at the screen and fainting. That part is interesting, but mostly he can't understand their language and Anni and the others are too busy to translate for him.

But on the long bus ride home, he rehearses how he'll tell Aaron about the fainting and the yelling. Aaron will be sorry he missed it.

December 4

Dani stands before the mirror in Chava's room, moving his hand in a slow arc, the hand dreamy, the eyes sharp, fingers around the die in a dancer's delicate arching fan. Up and down, up and down. Aaron's little brother comes over to him. "Look carefully, Yakov," Dani says, frowning. "Tell me what you see."

Yakov looks at the die. "Six."

"Now?" The arc brings his hand down and around to show the other side of the die, held immobile between his two fingers.

"One."

Up again. "Now?"

"Six again."

Down. "And now?"

"One."

"Now watch. This is—" Up.

"Six."

"And?" Down.

"Five! Hey, how did you—do that again."

He does, twice over, and the impossible happens twice again.

He was going to master the trick with the rope and the handkerchief today, but he hasn't; he blames it on the busdriver, pulling off the road and yelling "Bastard!" like that, and shaking Dani up so he couldn't practice the trick—but the dice one always gets people the first time they see it, and anyway he has the other thing to tell Aaron.

"Lock the door," he orders Aaron, pulling him into his room as soon as he comes in from school. But Yakov is outside the door, banging to get in, so the two of them take the soccer ball and run outside, leaving Yakov wailing and Chava dealing with him.

"What's so important? I didn't even get to pee."

"When you hear this . . . but you have to swear. No telling anyone."

"Maybe I don't want to swear. What's the big—"

"It's about doing it."

"Aah. I know that stuff. I knew it millions of years ago."

"So don't swear. And I won't tell you what I heard."

"From where?"

"Avi and Zvi. I heard them talking. You know the trial thing? The booklet?"

There is an interim transcription of the trial proceedings that everyone is buying. Shlomo brought one home last night. There's one in Dani's house, too.

"Yeah."

"My brother was reading about how they raped some women, and I heard them talking. You know what they do?"

"What?"

"Swear."

"All right, baby. I swear."

"It gets big and he pushes it in her."

"I know that. Where?"

"In her wee-wee."

"But what if they pee?"

They are convulsed with laughter, until Aaron has to duck behind some bushes and relieve himself. "But how?" he muses, zipping up. "Does he make her bend over, like dogs?"

"Yes. It must be."

"Woo. Rape." He rolls the thought around, trying not to smile.

"No, not only rape. *That's how they do it.*"

"Everyone?"

"Yup."

"Is not."

"Is too. Zvi said."

"Well, that settles it."

"What."

"My mother never did that. They adopted me."

"Stupid, how could you be adopted? We were born together, re-member?" He speaks with calm reason, enjoying his power.

"There must be another way they do it. My mother would never."

"That's how they do it," Dani pursues, merciless. "His wee-wee in hers. He screws it in. And your mother must have liked it, you know, because she did it two more times. For Yakov and Eli."

A quick, desperate calculation behind blurring eyes. "Oh yeah, well how about yours? She did it three times—and with *two men*. So she must just love it. She probably *asked* them—" Aaron breaks off, eyes wide, waiting to get it. But Dani tilts his head back and seems suddenly taller and dangerously superior.

"That's right," he says thoughtfully. "I think she must've asked my real father. She wanted me to have a special father. Anybody can have kids the regular way. Then they turn out regular, though. Like my brothers and you and"—he waves a hand—"everybody."

Aaron is afraid. He thinks Dani is probably right, and he feels himself becoming irrevocably subordinate to him. "And you're special," he snorts. "I'm sorry to tell you this, but all you are is a—"

"—bastard. *Because*," Dani explains grandly calm, "I was not sup-posed to be just regular. I probably have something big I'll have to do. Very big and very hard. Probably I'll find out in a message what it is."

Aaron strips the leaves from a green shoot. "You're crazy," he says, despairing, knowing that Dani must be right. He hates his mother, who didn't have the courage to let him be a bastard.

Back at Chava's flat that evening, Dani picks up the trial transcript. On the front page it says,

THE ATTORNEY GENERAL
OF THE GOVERNMENT OF ISRAEL
VS
ADOLF, THE SON OF
ADOLF KARL EICHMANN

"Adolf ben Adolf," he giggles. "That's funnier than me. How can he be his own father?"

"Adolf was his father's name, too," Chava explains.

"So I could be Dani ben Dani," he grins, not hearing her.

"Dani, it bothers you?" Shlomo suddenly has a hand on his shoulder.

"No." Dani squirms.

"Because—listen to me—you know you could have another name. You know what you can be?"

"Dani ben Dani." He forces a giggle, prolongs it.

"No. You can call yourself Daniel ben Avraham, because Abraham was the father of all of us, right? And you have a special right to take his name. You really are Daniel ben Avraham, did you know that?"

Dani waits until Shlomo isn't looking, then flashes a look of triumph at Aaron: *What did I tell you?*

Aaron's stomach feels as though he is falling. Queasy with envy, he refuses to look at his father all that evening.

December 14

Shlomo bends over Chava. She is sleeping in the big chair, Eli in her arms. It's late. The tumult caused in the flat by the closing orations of the trial awakened the little one and, powerless to leave her mother's side, she brought him out with her and held him on her lap there in the din and the hysteria. Shlomo, grim, turned out the overhead light and lowered the radio, and eventually the child slept while the grownups sat straining to hear.

Now they have all gone and he has showered and come out to find them asleep together in the big chair. They sleep like two children, wrapped equally and casually in each other. But when he begins to lift the little one out of her lap she startles and holds the child to her with powerful arms. She is wide awake and flushed. She focuses on him. "Oh," she says, relinquishing the child.

She's brushing her teeth when Shlomo has settled Eli in and he comes up behind her and touches her back. "Thank God the verdict is tomorrow," he says. "We'll have the place to ourselves in the evenings again."

She doesn't even get defensive about the way Anni and the cronies have moved in on them, these last months, because she is thinking: *The minute, the very minute the train stops, I grab Jacob and Mother and in the confusion we go under the train on our bellies . . .*

She's finished brushing her teeth and washing her face. Shlomo has his hands on her. She heads obediently for bed.

. . . on our bellies, she sees it, like a film, *between the wheels, and while they're doing the selections we make for the woods. In the woods we find a hole and I see it's a cave.*

Shlomo is kissing her hair, then her shoulder, her breasts. Kiss. Kiss. Kisskiss.

—a cave. Quick, get in, I say
but I'm afraid
Get in!
I wait until they're both in and I pull some earth and moss over the hole and follow them. It's like a room. A little stream runs through it, and at one end we make a fire.
(How?)
Matches. Mother still has her little pack from the train. Matches. What else? We have dried fruit. Bread. A knife. I go up at night and get twigs and some pine branches. Out of the pine we make bowls

She raises automatically to admit him. She clings dreamily to him. Her eyes are closed, but dreamily. He holds back, moving slowly for her.

. . . mushrooms and even quail eggs. I keep them fed and safe and the fire going. We wait it out. I take care of Jacob and Mother and we wait it out

Finally he feels it building up. "Now?"
It's over. Now. We can go up, out
"Now?"
"Yes."

He is panting on her breast. She strokes his head absently. Now Shlomo can sleep.

The Nazis are dead, dying, whipped, jailed, castrated, penned, and it's safe to come out and we're out safe. Jacob is safe, Mother. I saved him for you.

Now Chava can sleep.

May 30, 1962

". . . the town of Dukla. Then Jablunov. Two days in Jablunov. Then—"

"Grodner, shuh, still. Listen—"

"Adolf Eichmann's petition to Israel's president for mercy has been refused. He will be hanged sometime around midnight tonight—about one hour from now—for crimes against the Jewish people, crimes against humanity, and the war crimes of which he has been found guilty."

"—then Zywiec. Bread in Zywiec. Jelesnia, a little bread. Bialskie, the potatoes are frozen. Krasno, frozen. Bystra. Frozen. Limanowa. Frozen—"

"Stop, already, Grodner, with the towns. Is there any more slivovitz or did he drink it all?"

"Look who's talking."

"When should I get drunk, if not on such a night? You heard what the radionik said? We're going to hang the son of a bitch."

Ari-Bela looks up, grinning. "Now all of a sudden it's 'we,' Potasnik? Since when are you an Israeli?"

"Since we're hanging the son of a bitch, ladies excuse me. A toast."

"Another toast? We've gone through two bottles of brandy. Save a little for midnight."

"Zara, you're right. I know, let's have a wedding."

"You're with the wedding again, Potasnik? You want to go find a cemetery this time of night?"

"No, here. Here—Anni, give me your shmatte there. Let me see . . . we have two canes. Give me. You and Grodner will just have to lean a little, Anni, that's all. Now. Two canes . . . how about that? What is it?"

"The boy's magic wand."

"Good. Why not? Now one more. We can't hold up a wedding canopy on three poles. Aw—"

"How about . . . doesn't Shlomo have a rifle?" Zara offers timidly, blushing. They look at Anni. "Would he be angry?"

"From where they are, at the neighbors', he won't see. We'll put it back; he won't know."

"All right. Two canes, one wand, one rifle, one shmatte, makes . . . whoops . . . there, makes a canopy. Grodner, kindly choose a bride."

"You're meshugeh, Potasnik."

"On festival days, the boys choose brides. Don't tell me what's meshugeh. Let's see, four of us to hold the canopy—no, three: Anni, Ari-Bela and me. Ari-Bela, you'll have to hold two poles. And Grodner and who?—Zara? Okay, Grodner?—okay, and Grodner and Zara for bride and groom . . ."

"So who officiates?"

"Potasnik. It's his wedding."

"All right. But after this, Potasnik, no more about the wedding."

"You're absolutely right, Ari-Bela. After this none of us could hold it up anyhow," gesturing at the canopy.

"Grodner can't hold it up now."

Raucous laughter, even a laugh from Anni.

"So after this, let the pishers have the weddings. Fine with me. Let's go."

Anni's shawl, just off the loom, rides high on the four wobbling poles. Zara and Grodner stand simpering under it. Someone finds Dani's magic scarf, the one with all the zodiac signs on it, and covers Zara's head with it. She's unseen now, only a female figure with a bowed head. There is a silence.

"What do I say?" entreats Potasnik.

"Make the seven blessings."

"Of course. Nudnik. What are they, again?"

They laugh, giddy. No one can remember what the seven blessings are.

"Let's each say one," Potasnik decides, waving his pole dangerously. "Ari-Bela, you start."

"Blessed be the bride," Ari-Bela intones, "and may her womb be fruitful."

"Bite your tongue!" Zara screams.

"Forgive me, I got carried away. Blessed be the bride, and leave her womb out of this."

"Amen. I'm officiating here; I'll say one. Blessed be Grodner and may he hold it up a while yet. You next, Anni."

"Almost midnight," Ari-Bela says. They fall quiet.

"Blessed be the hands of the hangman, may he do his work slowly," Anni says.

Grodner, from under the canopy, adds, "Blessed be the fire, let it burn him and his like from bone to ash and ash to powder and let the powder fly into the lungs of their seed and choke them."

"Amen."

"Amen."

Zara speaks, a voice they've never heard comes from behind her veil. "Blessed be my mother and my father, let them look down tonight and call this a blessed day."

In the silence, Ari-Bela speaks. "Blessed be this state, and blessed we who came to rest here."

"Rest is right," Potasnik puts in. "Grodner, save your strength. You've got your work cut out for you tonight. Wait." He pulls on his pole, Dani's wand, and the canopy dips, pulls to one side. Everyone yells. "Take it easy. I'm gonna save Grodner. Here, Grodner. Use this." He holds out the wand to Grodner, leering.

"Potasnik!"

"It's a *wand*," he says, offended. "It's the kid's wand. Magic, right? Here, Grodner, make a miracle. You'll turn the worm into a rod."

He pokes it at Grodner. The shawl sags and sinks over them all, and before anyone moves, Potasnik says, "I got the last blessing. Blessed be the Almighty, Who forgets us daily but remembers us in His will. Amen. Mazal tov."

They pull the shawl off themselves and find Zara and Grodner holding each other. Dani's magic scarf still covers her head and hides her face. Grodner's head is bowed to her shoulder. She seems to be holding him up. They don't move. For a long time, no one moves.

Finally Zara's hand comes up to cradle Grodner's head and she rocks him. They sway raggedly together, like one Jew praying or like someone who is only trying to find his balance.

BOOK
FOUR

Unregenerate arrogance is a strong indication of bastardy.

KALLAH RABATHI

Ramat Gan, March 1963

Rachaeli walked home from work in the late-afternoon sunshine. Strolled. Yossi would be waiting outside her flat; let him wait a little. Still, her body tingled and eased at the thought of him. Forty years old and the most inconsequential things nibbled at her skin, let down her wetness: sunshine, music, the thought of Yossi, spices in the air, swimming. She smiled. I have it all, she thought. She raised her chin and turned her arms outward a little so the air she stirred as she walked would slide over her throat and the underside of her arms, but she didn't hurry. Let him wait a little.

It had turned out to be a very efficient way of holding him, living separately and coming to him in her own time. Better than marriage would have been; he was snared, held taut by not knowing her, not owning her, even after all these years. He had stopped mentioning marriage, and he had no contact with Dani at all. It was only in the last year, in fact, that she had even allowed him to come to the flat when Dani wasn't there. Dani was eleven, and on Friday nights he was out all evening with his scout group, even sleeping over at Aaron's afterward sometimes. Zvi was off in the army and although Avi came over most Saturdays, on Fridays he went out with friends, so she invited Yossi over sometimes on Fridays after work.

He was always prowling the place, looking for clues to her. She was careless; it didn't matter to her what she left around for him to see. Papers from work, notes from friends, underwear, a disorder of clothing and the telling scent of her were everywhere. Only she kept the door to Dani's room closed. About that she was careful.

He had almost forgotten that she had children. The impulse he'd had, wanting to marry her and claim the child, had faded. And he had wandered a few times—flirtations on trips out of the country, brief entanglements over the years. But she seemed always to know, and she pulled him back to her. She never pried or accused, never pleaded. If anything, she seemed to drift away, to relinquish him without regret. But then when he was with her and she kept a distance from him and smiled to keep him out, something about the angle of her body, the composure of her, dared him until he had to try to tease her open. Finally he would begin a little angrily to make love to her—"so she won't suspect," or "because she expects it"—and he would find her . . . succulent, as if with stores of untapped juice. Her lips, her breasts, her eyelids, the hidden channels of her that closed around him, all were swollen with the secrets of her, and his anger would turn to a fury of searching, hurtling against those swelling places. And at those moments she would . . . not lose but fling off the control, the composure, and he would almost have her. He would go a dangerous distance to batter her open, and she would almost meet him there. It would be a floodgate coming, then; two separate triumphs. Later, his triumph would have the aftertaste of despair but she would have him in hand again, brought back to her orbit. She would never say a word about it.

The air she stirred blew hot against her skin. She smiled. *I have it all.*
He wasn't outside the flat. She opened the door and in her living room she saw
—she lurched into free fall, cold—
saw two heads
—she was falling away from them, they weren't moving but she was falling too fast out of control away—
saw two black, curly heads. Heard things: vibrations at a certain frequency, caused by hair against metal. Caused by air against vocal cords. Caused by the intersection of Mozart and two human beings with black, curly hair.
Dani
—she couldn't catch him, she fell—
Dani held his bow suspended before his violin. He looked across the flat music stand, across the horizontal piece of music, at Yossi
his father, who held Rachaeli's bow suspended before her cello and was saying, "Never—"
Never
"—you almost never play legato when you're playing early Mozart, all right? Crisp, always crisp. Bounce right off the string. Okay?"
"Okay." Two black heads bent toward each other across a flat sheet of music. Her son and his father were playing a duet.

She held each breath two extra beats, overfilling her lungs, let it rush out and silently sucked in the next. Her face and her body were otherwise still.

Yossi turned around. "Hi," he grinned. "You're late. Your boy here let me in. We've been having a marvelous time with the—"

Oh, be very careful. *Get him out, get him out, get him out.* No, be careful. She smiled.

"You know the one? The upside-down, right-side-up duet? Mozart was six or seven when he wrote it, I told Dani. One page, see? We lay it flat between us. He reads from the top down, as he sees it. I stand opposite and read from *my* top down. Upside down, the notes make the harmony for what Dani plays."

"He was at a party and he was bored." Dani grinned. The same grin as Yossi's. Had it always been the same or was he catching it all so fast? "So he wrote this. Listen, listen." He gestured imperiously at Yossi with his bow. Yossi nodded once obediently, then a quick glance passed between them, they agreed to begin and nodded together.

"*And*—" Yossi directed. The cello deferred to the violin, muted, holding a steady course for the high, wavering notes to follow. They finished together and looked up at each other, bouncing the same grin between them.

"Bravo," she said. "Dani, you're not at scouts? What happened?"

"I'm going. I just came back to get my manual I forgot."

"They're waiting for you?"

"I guess. I was going to do the Three-Color-Handkerchief trick for Yossi."

"Another time; you've got to get going." *There will never be another time.* "Be careful how you cross the street. You're sleeping at Aaron's?"

"Yes." He took the manual she held out to him, but hovered there, not ready to leave.

"If you're bored at scouts," Yossi said, "write some music."

"No, I'll practice my trick."

"Good. See you next time."

"See you. And next time I'll do the trick for you."

"Great."

"Go on, Dani."

"*Okay.* Well, 'bye."

"'Bye."

The door closed behind Dani. She was quite still now, quite still, and in her mind she dealt out the possibilities, a swift solitaire hand.

She turned a smile on Yossi. "Play for me," she said. "You haven't done that in a long time."

"Now?"

"Mmm. Play some Beethoven. A sonata."

"Which one?"

"The one you played last month. Number three, is it?"

He made a comic face. "You don't ask for much. The whole sonata? Both parts?"

"Just the cello; you can leave out the piano. The opening movement. Please."

She sat on the couch, just out of his line of vision as he played, and she watched him. There was an edge of gray in the black curls, but his arms were brown and tensile and the expressions still chased across his face when he played. She felt her mouth soften and her skin and nipples tingle. He might have been playing all the tender spots of her with the fingers of his left hand—eyelids, shoulder hollows, tips of the nipples, inner thighs—and with his right hand, bowing across the muscles and nerves of her. God, she was going to miss that.

He finished the andante and made a little mocking bow. "You know," she said thoughtfully, "it's true what they say. The music strengthens and deepens as the other powers wane. You're playing wonderfully these days."

He glanced sharply at her. "What other powers wane?"

Right. She'd freed the ace on the first try. She had only to play it out now. "Well," she smiled, "you're—what? Almost fifty?"

"Forty-seven."

A kind shrug. "So you can't expect—"

"I don't please you?"

"Come on, you're fine. Anyway, it doesn't take so much to please me." She got up, stretched, took the bow from his hand, stood over him fingering his curls. "Come and please me," she whispered.

He tried. She lay waiting for him in her bed, and she looked, suddenly, outsized. He sat uncertainly on the edge of the bed. One long, long arm pulled him toward rising breasts, a vast, smiling mouth. He closed his eyes. An indeterminate time held him then, tossed him. He was sucked in, pumped dry, cast up again. He wasn't sure what she felt. He wasn't sure whether he was reaching far enough, there was so much of her. He didn't know what the limits of her were. Anyway he poured into her, a tributary, and slid helplessly out and his member lay puny and flaccid on her thigh.

190

She patted his head. He rolled off her and landed surprisingly nearby, still on the bed. He waited. "You know what?" she mused. His member pleated up, looked for refuge, failed to find it, huddled close to him and waited.

"What?"

"I think it's a myth anyway, about men satisfying women."

"A man can't satisfy a woman?"

She made a little philosophical gesture. "No man has ever brought me over that line," she lied. "I'm not sure it's possible."

He was forty-seven. For twelve years she had moved and moaned in his arms; she'd thrashed and cried out and scratched his back over and over again and all those times she'd been coolly waiting, each time finding him wanting. He'd bucked and gasped and come and come and come and every time he'd lost control in spasms in her arms she'd been watching him and waiting, unmoved.

He rolled out of bed and walked, carefully steady, into the bathroom. He closed the door and washed her off his loins. He managed to clear the mirror twice without seeing himself. He walked back out and pulled on his underpants with his back to her. He reached for his socks.

"What are you doing?"

"Dressing."

"Why?"

"I'm going." He stepped into his khakis. "Someone else will have to disappoint you from now on." He pulled his shirt over his head, tugged it down and walked over to the bed. He looked at her. "But don't think it hasn't been a pleasure."

He kissed her once and he was gone. She lay with a hand on her belly and a picture in her mind of the king played out.

That was that. This was no jealous rage, nothing so hot and tangled as that. It was a cold and final fury. He was out of her life; he would never get near Dani again with his duets and his grin and his mischievous, seductive ways. She'd find other men, perhaps younger, simpler to control, and they'd never come near her flat. The boy was hers and it was going to stay that way.

For months there was no man at all. She thought of it as a brief suspension and she savored it, a new flavor. It tasted of herself, of time slowed down, of uncomplicated choices and no afterthoughts. It tasted like winning; it was sweet. She had left them all behind. She liked it, for now, alone. If her body was restless she would channel its energy somewhere for a while. She began swimming every afternoon after work, longer and longer swims, until she felt her reach lengthening and her legs, precise and powerful, putting easy distance behind her without troubling the surface of the water. She would come home exhilarated and turn her other energies—the impulses of connection, of entanglement—on the boy. He was old enough now to engage in a real conversation and she focused on him, bringing into play all the skills she'd used to pique Yossi's interest. She wouldn't have called it flirting.

It was a strange time for Dani. Things were shifting by themselves into a new light; the old baby ways of acting had become unthinkable and the attentions of women—his teachers, Chava, his mother—suddenly seemed intrusive and embarrassing. He was eleven at the moment when Rachaeli turned her attention upon him; in his whole life women would never be as useless to him as they were then. That was lucky.

Take for example the story about Anni and Chava and Jacob. They were doing family trees in Aaron's class, and Dani looked over Aaron's, neatly lettered in two colors of ink. "There was another Yakov!" Dani said. "Hey, he was only seven when he died."

"The Nazis killed him," Aaron said. "That's why my grandmother is always so mad. She feels bad because she's always thinking maybe she should have gotten killed with him, my father says." He told Dani the story of Anni and the two children as Shlomo had explained it to him.

Dani thought about it, walking home. He liked Anni. Her grouchiness was a relief. She never let him win—she never even greeted him. She didn't put on smiles or talk in a high voice or anything, no fake things. So when he did win or he made her laugh, it was very good. He wondered what the other Yakov was like and whether Anni still missed him. His own mother would have let Zvi and Avi go, he thought. She did let them go. She would have stayed with me. She likes me better. He even pictured it: Avi and Zvi led off, looking back, Rachaeli turning to Dani and walking with him past the Nazis. Unaccountably he felt threatened by the scene. Even in his daydream he felt endangered, being singled out like that. He fixed it up; he ran the picture backward in his mind to the point where Rachaeli decided to stay with him. "No," a decisive, manly Dani said in the new scene. "I'm going with my brothers," and he crossed over to stand with them. The Nazi guards were amazed at his courage, a little Jew of seven, and Rachaeli was left standing all alone. Serves her right, he thought contemptuously, crossing the street to his house. Picking people out like that.

He was always the one singled out. When there was an assembly or a class parents' day or a scouting event, he would move around smiling vaguely, hoping that the strangers there would think that the man nearest him was his father, or at least that his father had left in some orthodox way. Died. At first he'd watched the kids whose fathers had died, planning to mimic their expressions and the way they acted at these events, but they didn't look any different from anyone else. They didn't have to; everyone knew they'd had fathers once. That was all you needed. He didn't even tell his mother about some of these events because when she came, everyone looked at the two of them and he knew it was obvious who they were—the mamzer and his mother, the famous woman who did it. Rachaeli didn't know that, of course. She thought Dani was proud of her, eager to show her off. And lately—it made her smile—he was eager to show off to her, too. That was how she saw it. It was easy to make her see it that way.

It would happen this way: she would zero in on him in the late afternoon when they got home. "How was your day?" she'd ask. "What's new? Come have a cookie with me." Then she'd start in, pointing out little flaws in people he liked, probing for instances of their disappointing him or choosing someone else over him, smiling brilliantly at him, her public smile. It made him uneasy. He'd get restless. She would lift the hair off her neck and he'd see the sweat under her arms, the halting slide of her bracelet. She's always hot, he'd think. She's always spread out. She doesn't sit like Chava; she's never still. Unable to sit across from her he'd jump up. "I've got a new trick," he'd say in a fake-enthusiastic voice. "Want to see it?"

"You cannot trust your eyes; you cannot be sure of what you see," his opening patter went. "Ladies and gentlemen, things are not always what they seem. For example, this block is green . . ."

It was true. She had taught him that people didn't always mean what they said, things were not always what they seemed, and she was right. That was why magic tricks were so good; you could really fool people, and they'd like you for it. Rachaeli liked it, too; she'd sit there beaming when he jumped up to do his new trick for her, not knowing that once he started his spiel he had turned her off. She was the audience, an observant pair of eyes, that's all she was and he couldn't really see her, she couldn't make him restless or catch him in that smile of hers. He would fool her and she would applaud him for it and then he could drift off into his room, away from her. It always worked.

How he wanted her attention, Rachaeli thought. How sweet he was. And, Rivka, this is what a mother is. A mother, a real one, pays close attention to one child at a time. This is what a child needs.

"Hey Dani, did you hear?"

They were at scouts and Yoni, the leader, was late. Asher had started it by telling Yitz something in a low voice and grinning. He put his two fingers together and waved them in an airy sweep under Yitz's nose.

"Get away!"

Asher laughed, flushed.

"Where did you do it?" Shmuli asked. Everyone was edging in toward Asher.

"Do what? What's he talking about?"

"In the woods behind school."

"Who was it?" Shmuli pursued. Asher smiled secretly and raised his eyebrows at Yitz.

"Who was *what*?" Michael pleaded.

"Someone let him do 'fingers,'" Shmuli said. "Come on, Asher, who?"

"Never mind."

"How did you get her to?" Michael was red in the face. They all were.

"*She* asked *me*. She said, 'Want to feel around in there?'"

Five faces looked at Asher, awe-stricken. Then they all grinned and made loud noises of knowing appreciation. "Oo-wah!" Yitz uttered. "She *asked* for it!"

A panicky sweep of certain knowledge overtook Dani. She did it, too; his mother asked for it, and everyone in the whole country knew it. He wanted to kill Asher, cancel out everyone in the room, and he was afraid that he was going to throw up. I don't care, he thought, not crying, swallowing hot sourness. *Who cares, who cares?*

He asked once when he was going to see Yossi again. A bewildered look crossed her face. "I don't know," she said. "He hasn't called me since he met you that time. Well, maybe soon."

But Yossi never called. "Never mind," Rachaeli told Dani. "He's probably busy with his music." Dani knew the real reason. The man hadn't liked him, although he pretended to. He shrugged. Rachaeli hugged him. "If people don't like us, who needs them. Right?"

"Right." He squirmed cautiously. She didn't let go. Suddenly he had to get away, it was urgent. Smiling blandly he ducked out of her arms.

"How about showing me your new trick? It's with colored scarfs?"

"Not now." Her hand still lay on his neck. He wriggled away. "I have to go to the bathroom," he lied. "Anyway, I forgot that trick."

He never forgot a trick. He learned them from books mostly, and practiced them alone in his room, standing in front of the mirror and keeping a sharp eye on his hands. He had a whole repertoire now, and a carton full of equipment. A lot of it he had made himself, some he had ordered from catalogues.

He had spent all his Chanukah money for the Buatier Pull and four silk handkerchiefs, and when it arrived, Avi made fun of him for wasting his money. "Two agorot worth of plastic and string," he scoffed. But it was a wonderful thing. It was a flesh-colored, pear-shaped container, with the narrow end attached to a black silk cord. At the other end of the cord was a tiny clip. You threaded the cord through your sleeves and clipped the end of it to the right shirt sleeve. You had to get the length of the cord just right, so that when your arms were relaxed the container dangled into your left palm, and when you pulled your right arm just a little the container retracted into your left sleeve. You could let the container down into your palm, push any small object into the wide end and vanish it. It worked smoothly because the container was slick plastic, properly shaped and weighted, unlike the cardboard facsimiles he'd made.

He usually tried the tricks out on Chava and Anni. Anni was the perfect audience, because she hated to be fooled. Rachaeli and Chava would applaud indiscriminately, whether the trick came off well or not, but Anni would watch intently and pounce in triumph on the slightest slip. "It's in your sleeve!" she'd exult, and Yakov or Eli would run up to him and look up his sleeve to find it.

He sat them down in a row the day after he got the pull: Anni, Chava, Eli, and Yakov. Aaron wasn't home yet. While they were settling in and the boys were jostling for position, Dani shrugged his shoulders in the jacket a couple of times to feel the pull drop and retract. He moved gently, so as not to dislodge the knotted string of handkerchiefs—blue, then green, then yellow—that he'd pushed into the container.

He launched into his spiel, showing them that his hands were empty, calling Eli up to check between his fingers. Mostly this trick depended on misdirection, so he did a lot of patter and finger-counting as he offered to produce a green scarf. He made a fist of his left hand and pulled and the blue end came up. He looked embarrassed and shoved it quickly into his fist, shrugged the pull up and showed two empty hands. Again he promised green. He let down the pull and this time produced the yellow end, again shoving it shame-facedly back before it was fully out. Finally he said, "Well, we've had blue and we've had yellow, so together they should make—green!" and he plucked the string of scarfs out of the air, green knotted between yellow and blue.

It had worked perfectly. The boys' eyes were wide. Chava clapped, delighted to have been taken in, and Anni frowned. "You're a charlatan," she said at last.

He bowed deeply, flushing. "Thank you," he said, accepting the tribute.

When he straightened up, Aaron was standing in the doorway, impassively taking in the scene. "Did you see Dani doing his magic trick?" Eli asked. "Aaron, did you?"

"What? No. I just got here."

He had seen it. His mother was making one of her big fusses over Dani. Be nice to him, be nice to him, that's all he ever heard. Things are very hard for Dani, Dani has no father, don't be like that, Aaron, you have everything, Dani has nothing.

For their information, Dani had everything. The big star, the magician, the one with the funny cracks and the quick answers. And he never had to do anything. If he, Aaron, didn't bring home a perfect report card, if he wanted to sleep late on Shabbat, if he talked back to his parents or—worse—his grandmother or her thousand stupid cronies, he was a criminal. But nobody cared how Dani did in school; he didn't even have to study Torah, and if he showed an interest when Shlomo talked Talmud he was some kind of angel. If he even showed up for services on Shabbat, Aaron's father treated him like the Messiah.

For example. Father sits Aaron down after supper to test him on the week's Torah portion. Aaron is reciting the part about God sending Moses to Pharaoh. Moses says, "What if they do not believe me?" and God tells him to throw down his rod and the rod turns into a snake, and then God says, pick it up by the tail, and it becomes a rod again. Aaron recites the verses perfectly. Dani is sitting at the table, fussing with a loop of string. "I know that trick," he says suddenly. "I know how they did it."

Shlomo smiles. He treats Dani like a grownup. Polite. "How did they do it?" he asks.

"It's not a rod at all. I read about it, it's an old Egyptian trick. It's a snake all the time, some kind of cobra. A *Naje* something. If you put pressure just below its head, it gets paralyzed, so it seems like a stick. You know—"

"Rigid?"

"Yeah. Then when you throw it on the ground it gets unparalyzed and it moves. That's all."

Aaron's father tips back his chair and holds his chin in three fingers. "You grab it below the head?"

"Yeah."

"But here it says, 'grasp it by the tail.'"

Dani shrugs. "The guy didn't know the trick."

Shlomo only smiles. "Maybe He did. Maybe everybody did, all the magicians in Pharaoh's court."

"Right, so—"

"So maybe if Moses grabbed it by the *tail* and it turned into a rod, Pharaoh's magicians would know—"

"—that Moses had a better trick!"

"That God's magic—"

"—was better than Pharaoh's! I bet *that* got them."

So Aaron's father and Dani grin at each other and Dani is a star. Without ever reciting a word.

Or, for example, the business with Yakov and the closet. It was really Dani's idea. Yakov was being a pest and wanting to be everywhere they were, so they said he couldn't be with them because he was a crybaby and he said he was not and they said he'd have to have an initiation to prove it. They did a lot of stuff to him and he didn't cry, so finally—it was Dani's idea—they blindfolded him and tied a scarf around his mouth and tied his hands down to his sides and turned him around to mix him up and led him out of the flat and back again, and into Mother's closet. They told him it was a deserted place where no one but the crazy janitor ever came and then they locked him in and left him. They left him there for half an hour; then they tiptoed back in and Dani stamped around the room, limping like the janitor and jangling his magic-set keys and saying, "Someone's going to get it," low and in a funny accent like the janitor.

Yakov must have started screaming long before Dani got to the door, although you couldn't hear it because of the scarf around his mouth, because by the time they opened the door he was all red in the face and he'd wet his pants. They took the scarf off his mouth and he started to scream like crazy and cry and try to get away and that's why Aaron sang the song, to let him know it was them, to shut him up.

It was the one they always sang to him when he was being a crybaby, the Sabbath song. "God said to Jacob, Don't be afraid, my servant Jacob"—that's as far as he got and then Yakov tried to get them and fell down and he was screaming, "You lousy bastards, you bastards," and Aaron was singing, "Don't be afraid, my servant Jacob," and that's when his mother and grandmother came into the room.

Dani was just staring at Yakov, looking scared, and Yakov was on his knees, blindfolded and tied up and screaming, and Grandma went crazy. She stood there yelling Yakov's name and then she started shrieking at Aaron, "Enemy of the Jews! Murderer! Enemy of the Jews!"

His mother went out of her mind. She was holding Yakov and trying to untie him and screaming at Aaron, and Dani was comforting Anni, shushing her and saying, "He's okay. See, Anni? Yakov's fine, he's okay.

Shh, Anni," and he was crying, too. The faker.

So Aaron got hit when his father came home, and that was almost a relief after the way his mother and grandmother were all afternoon, and nothing happened to Dani. He made a big fuss over Yakov, going to sit by him when Mother put him to bed and refusing even to come out for supper, and of course Aaron's father went in there and stayed for years until he came out with his arm around Dani and Dani was crying. Faker. That's all he was, a big, stupid faker.

He was going to ignore Dani and his stupid magic trick. He followed his mother into the kitchen. "I got ninety-eight on my math test."

"That's wonderful," she said absently. "Go see what Grandma wants."

He knew what Grandma wanted. She had dropped her spindle again and she was waiting for someone to pick it up. He'd heard her "tch" and he was ignoring that, too. She was always dropping her spindles; ever since they moved her loom here he was always having to run and pick them up for her. She sat in that chair of hers covered in threads and weaving away and then she'd drop a spindle and go "tch" and make that little annoyed moan and wait for someone to pick it up. He hated that. He always waited until she asked him to do it.

He stamped back into the living room. "What do you—"

Never mind. Dani had it already. He was holding it behind his back and pulling a coin out of the air with his other hand. He bent and offered the coin. "You dropped something, madame?"

Grandma would get him now. She hated to be teased.

"Come on, Houdini," she said. "My spindle."

"Oh, a thousand pardons, I thought that *was*—oops—" From behind a fan of fingers he produced the spindle. "Is *this* yours?"

She took it, shaking her head fondly.

"Next time four drachmas, lady. Me and my camel got to live, too."

"Get out of here," she said, smiling like a fool.

"You want to play?" he asked Dani. He hated himself for asking.

"Sure."

"Let's trade cars." Dani was a lousy trader. He'd give away anything except his magic stuff. Rachaeli was always yelling at him for it, but Dani didn't care. Even if he didn't care, though, it was like winning to outtrade him. Almost like winning.

A vagrant piece of the earth's blazing core, tumbling downstream in the Vaal river, was snared abruptly in a bit of wire mesh. It rolled there, carried by its long motion: leaf to earth, earth heated and digested to mulch, mulch sorted out patiently to carbon, carbon pressed and heated in the centrifuge to crystal, crystal pried loose by slow geologic shifting and shuffled, swept, tumbled toward the moving body of water and into a diamond-seining sieve.

The earth had closed around the little gap left by the stone: sifted in, settled, tamped, and for miles around it, particles were moving and shifting in consequence. The river bank was deceptively still. The diamond lay obedient and inevitable in the sieve. Roughly eleven carats, blue-white under its dull film.

Tel Aviv, September 1964

Eleven carats is nothing as rocks go. Measured that way, the rocks the women carried up the hill from the quarry at Auschwitz were thousands of carats apiece. But those quarry rocks swallowed light and kept it, unlike diamonds which, faster than the eye can see, catch white light, bend it, shoot it back splayed into reds and blues and so on. Those other, thriftier rocks at Auschwitz were not coveted and therefore were neither measured nor weighed.

But eleven carats is a respectable weight for a raw diamond of good color, and therefore Shlomo studied it himself before it went to the cutter. Little windows had been polished in it and he held it under the light and, magnifying loupe in his eye, looked for flaws.

When you look into a diamond you see intersections of planes of light. Convergence is what the fire and brilliance amount to—new light striking old convergences. What you want in a diamond is unstinting refraction. There are sometimes cracks in diamonds, white, dull interruptions of the light, and sometimes there are specks of untransformed carbon—

tiny, cocky holdouts—and you try to eliminate those in the cutting, because they give back less light than they take in.

Then too, the same heat and pressure that cause carbon compounds to harden and crystallize into structures which admit light and refract it will sometimes leave stresses in a stone. A polarizing microscope will show these stresses as blue and pink bruises. A cutter has to know about the stresses in a stone because sawing or cleaving creates heat, and that last, seemingly incidental, bit of heat striking the stress will cause the stone to shatter.

Shlomo turned the stone and looked in through another of the windows polished on its surface. So far it looked to be flawless. But something about the stone made him uneasy. He took it over to the polarizing microscope and looked in and caught his breath at the pity of it. Off center toward nine o'clock was the faintest smear of mauve and blue. Still holding it under the microscope, he pulled over a pad of paper and began to sketch the salvaging of the stone.

But as he sketched, random thoughts traveled across his mind: snatches of the Torah portion Aaron would chant at his bar mitzvah next week; a glimmer of Chava turning away from him to sleep; a reminder to test Dani on the Haftarah chant he was teaching the boy in secret—their surprise—and behind it all, the feeling of pity. He took the stone out from under the microscope and looked at it whole. Eleven carats, nearly perfect in color, and invisible at the center a lick of blue and mauve that made it vulnerable.

He wasn't thinking directly of the boy who was not his son as he crumpled the cutting sketch, carried the stone back to his desk, released it into its tissue folder, crossed it off the cutter's list and, cradling it in his palm, walked to the smaller office safe and locked it away untouched.

But he thought of the stone and Dani together on the day of Aaron's bar mitzvah. Aaron chanted the Torah reading perfectly, of course, a long and tricky one, and then came Shlomo and Dani's surprise for all of them. The gabai called the bar mitzvah boy up to read the Haftarah, but it was Dani who stepped forward to chant what Shlomo had taught him.

Shlomo watched Aaron step back to yield his place and Dani come forward to read, and the pathos of the boy's solitude up there—no father, no uncles or grandfather to stand with him before the congregation—caught at his throat, but he was prepared for that. He'd been thinking about it for days. He wasn't prepared for what happened next, though. "Calling . . . the bar mitzvah boy, to read the Haftarah," the gabai sang out, and now when Dani stepped forward, the gabai inclined his head to

Dani, waiting, then repeated to the congregation the name that the boy had given him: "Daniel ben Avraham," the gabai proclaimed, and Shlomo was undone.

The boy had claimed the name Shlomo had told him was rightfully his all those years ago: Daniel, son of Abraham our father. Tall and skinny in his new prayer shawl, Dani heard his new name called out for the first time with composure, and immediately he began the blessings. Named, once and for all.

He chanted the Haftarah perfectly and then joined Aaron in saying all the blessings following the reading, and at the last word he looked up to grin triumphantly at Shlomo. Pity and admiration surged in Shlomo for the boy who had named himself, and the flawed stone came suddenly to his mind. They belong together, he thought, and in an instant he ceded the stone over to the boy: let it be an inheritance for him.

It was all flooding his thoughts, and so he forgot himself and said the thing he shouldn't have. After the service had concluded and he had kissed his son and received an awkward hug back, he turned to Dani and took the boy's face in his two hands and said, "'Whosoever teaches the child Torah is deemed to be his father.'" He didn't smile when he said it, and neither did Dani.

Rachaeli looked up sharply when she heard it, but by then Shlomo had dropped his hands and she made a joke of it. "Careful, Shlomo," she said. "What will Chava think we've been up to?" Chava smiled, because it was unthinkable that Shlomo would deceive her and because she thought Shlomo was just being kind. "Shlomo feels sorry for the boy," she was always saying. "He tries to make up to him for being . . . fatherless." She went over and took Shlomo's arm and gave it a little hug, to thank him for the sweet gesture he'd made to her friend's child.

Rachaeli waited until they got home, and then she brought it up lightly, carefully. "I never expected that," she said. "A religious bar mitzvah!"

Dani shrugged. "Shlomo asked me if I wanted to learn it. You know, to surprise everybody."

"You certainly surprised me."

She was more than surprised; she felt betrayed and threatened. She had gone to the synagogue with Dani—to Aaron's bar mitzvah, she thought—and while she sat watching the comings and goings and enjoying the painless nostalgia of seeing Aaron come of age, her own child had appeared in a prayer shawl and begun to chant blessings and verses, acolyte in an alien ritual. Without so much as a word to her.

What had she thought it would mean, owning the child? She was determined—she had gone to extraordinary lengths to see to it—that his allegiance should be only to her. Certainly he was purely her child, unlike her other two sons. She saw habits, mannerisms, attitudes in the older two that they'd picked up from Dov. Every time she got them for the weekend she scented him on them, heard his stodginess and prim caution in them like an accent acquired during a visit to a foreign country. Dani looked like Yossi, of course, with the curly black hair and the quirky grin, but he was entirely hers. As his body lengthened out and lost the baby fat, she saw her own leggy body in his. He was androgynous still, softness in his face and her own pitch in his voice, and she could almost believe that there had been no other agency in his birth. They were a sight together. They walked in the street and people looked at them, her in her ripeness, him a young shoot bending off her, and she believed that they saw some invisible extra charge of life in the two of them, and for that brief moment it was everything she'd thought it would be. *Mine*, she thought, smiling her radiant public smile at the boy. Sometimes someone would stop and watch them go by and Dani would blush. He knows it, too, she'd think then; we're something special.

So there were two shocks when she saw him called to the Torah. First of all he looked . . . separate, suddenly. Too tall for a child, towering over Aaron, and his face startlingly male. His voice, when he chanted the prayers, was deeper than she expected. She would have to hand him over to the army, she thought, shocked. Even this one. It seemed terrifyingly imminent, so that she wanted to snatch him down off the *bima*, down to size.

And then there was this choice he'd made on the sly. When had he learned all this mumbo jumbo? And why? He would have his real bar mitzvah at Masada next week, with his classmates, as Zvi and Avi had done. Why wasn't that enough for him?

The cronies had rustled and buzzed behind her in the press of people leaving the sanctuary. They hadn't noticed her. "Since when is the boy religious?" Ari-Bela asked. She didn't turn around. "I don't know," Potasnik answered, "but listen, it could be a good thing. Their holiness and her chutzpah—the boy could turn out to be just the thing, a messiah with balls." They had snorted and giggled and shushed each other, and Rachaeli had moved stonily into the crowd. She would deal with this.

203

"You certainly surprised me." She was smiling. "I didn't know you were so holy. Or was it just because Aaron was doing it?"

He shrugged.

"When did you learn all that stuff?"

"At Aaron's. It was boring, just listening to him practicing all the time."

"So Shlomo taught you, too?"

"Yeah. Well, I learned at the same time." It wasn't true. Aaron had learned the Torah chanting at school. Shlomo taught Dani alone, while Aaron practiced. They would sit like conspirators in the bedroom, and every time Dani read the melody for a complicated phrase from the little dots and lines under the words, Shlomo would nod his head and smile excitedly, urging him on. They kept their voices low, and the first time Dani chanted the whole Haftarah through correctly, Shlomo grabbed his shoulders and nodded vigorously, beaming.

"Are you going to grow your hair and wear fringes and pray three times a day?"

"No."

"You want to be put into the religious school track?" It was a threat. She was still smiling.

"No." He smiled, too, camouflage under enemy fire.

"Well, I don't know. You even picked up a new name. Or was the little man hard of hearing?"

"The gabai? When I was called to the Torah?"

"I suppose. What did he call you?"

"Daniel ben Avraham."

"For my father?"

"No, you know, for Abraham our father." He saw immediately from her face that he should have lied. He didn't care. Let her hear it. "Shlomo said it's a name anyone can use who doesn't have one."

"You have one. Your name is Daniel ben Rachael. Listen, Dani—"

"Anyone who doesn't have a *father*, I mean. Anyone who doesn't have a Jewish father—like a convert, say—can be ben Avraham. You need a name to give—your father's name—when you're called to the Torah."

"Listen to me." She took him by the shoulders. He set his teeth and focused on two gray hairs that chased through one of her black ringlets. "You don't need a father or a father's name. You're not missing anything so wonderful, believe me. You know how many kids call a man Daddy who had absolutely nothing to do with siring them? Or how many kids look at their fathers and dread growing up to be like them? Not for you, my boy. You have a clean slate. You're my kid; that's all you have to know." She had said all this to herself often lately, a speech. She liked the way it sounded, rolling out.

"That's not all I have to know."

"What?"

His throat was closing up. If he said a word now he was going to cry. He shook his head, eyes down.

"What did you say?"

"That's not all I have to know," he said loudly. He twisted out of her hands and ran for a tissue. "A person has to know his own name," he shouted. A door slammed.

She followed him, yanked open the door to his room and stood incredulously watching him blow his nose. "What *is* all this? Because you needed a father's name for some antiquated ritual?"

"Because I always need it. Because I'm the only one who doesn't. Because you had to have some affair." He was shouting.

She was afraid for a minute. His anger was almost like a man's. She had known, of course, that this would come up some time; he was bound to be curious. That was why she'd worked up the speech. But she'd expected that she would explain it softly, with womanly heroism and that he would understand, approve. She wasn't like all the other mothers. He didn't want her to be, she'd been sure of it. So when he hurled it at her like that, a furious accusation, she panicked for a moment. It was too late, suddenly; he was a strange, angry, masculine figure, condemning her. But then she caught the little uncertainty in his eyes. She went over and laid a gentle hand on his neck. She hadn't had a chance to say the beginning of her speech. It fit in now. "I didn't have you because I had some affair. I had the affair to have you."

A long moment passed.

"So . . . *purposely* to have me like this?"

"I wanted a child—"

"You had *two*."

"—of my own." He was staring at her. "Anyway, what difference does it make? Half the kids in the country don't have fathers."

"They aren't bastards."

"Oh, for heaven's sake, who cares about that?"

"Everybody. Everybody knows and everybody cares. I never met any-body in my whole life who didn't know."

It was true, then. He said it to her and she didn't deny it. His last hope had been that she was an innocent victim, she had been falsely accused or at least forced. But there she stood, conceding equably that she had had an affair, on purpose. She had a hand on his neck, just like some girl in a movie. He shook her off, one quick twist of rejection. "Everybody I ever met knows that I don't even have a father's name. 'That's Dani, he's the mamzer.'"

"Do you want to know his name?" She loomed over him in her green silk dress, breasts at his eye level if he looked up and he had to look up, because if he didn't she was going to say a name and then he would always know who it was, every minute of his life he would know the man's name who didn't claim him.

"No," he said quickly, looking right up at her through her breasts. "I'm not interested." His heart thudded but he stared her down.

"Fine. Then don't let me hear that ben Avraham stuff again."

"You won't."

She didn't hear it from him again. She never heard the name at all until nine years later when they came to tell her, using that name, what had happened to him in Golan.

At Auschwitz the earth's crust is twenty-five miles thick, a veneer. Below the earth's crust, in the heat and turmoil, the business of exchanging energy goes on unilluminated and that is where the diamonds are made.

On the earth's surface at Auschwitz no diamonds were made, but an unusual number of them changed owners. In little rooms, pellets of Zyklon B were dropped through special openings. Upon exposure to air, the pellets changed from the solid state to a gas, hydrogen cyanide. There were humans locked in the little rooms and when the gas was released, the humans asphyxiated. Then as their bodies lay about on the surface of the earth, diamond rings were pried from what had been their fingers and anal and vaginal cavities and cleaned.

The diamonds were added to the rest of the loot traveling west in the returning emptied freight cars, and deposited for the time being in a cave not unlike the one in the Golan where Dani would later face the Syrian.

It was dark in the cave where the diamonds rested, a chamber cut from the earth in earlier days when the diamonds were still unformed. There was no light there for the diamonds to catch. They rested, cooled, sloughed off leftover vagrant cells from their previous, temporary carriers. They themselves were finished with molecular change, barring great heat.

The looting was one of the industries at Auschwitz. Another was the work of turning the earth inside out, quarry work. Chava thinks of that now as she moves piles of Anni's belongings from cartons to shelves and drawers. They are moving Anni in to Chava and Shlomo's flat, finally. Rachaeli is helping empty the cartons. They pass things from hand to hand.

Chava is wearing a diamond on her right hand, but she never looks at it any more and she is unaware of it now as she smooths her mother's nightgowns into a drawer and tries to think of a way to answer Rachaeli's questions.

That is why quarry work came to mind, because Rachaeli asked her about letting go. "Won't you and Shlomo miss the privacy? She'll be right on top of you."

Chava frowned no. "There's plenty of room."

"But . . ." Rachaeli gestured at the partition wall between the rooms, Anni's bed on one side, Chava and Shlomo's on the other. Since Rachaeli moved out of Dov's place, she has never made love with anyone else present in her flat, and even with Dov it was just the children, babies then. She can't imagine making love with her mother listening. "What will you do about making love?"

Chava rearranges the nightgowns in the drawer. "What do you mean?" Rachaeli can't see her face.

"Well—I mean, will you be able to be . . . can you enjoy it?"

"As much as I ever did."

Rachaeli is sitting on the floor, her long legs bent on either side of the carton, her hair pinned up in two crossed hairpins. Still, she looks elegant. Chava is always a little awed by that elegance. It makes her feel childlike and devoted and she always answers Rachaeli's questions, however importunate. Rachaeli studies her.

"You never let go?"

This one Chava can't answer, because she knows that Rachaeli believes that people live on solid ground, or she couldn't ask such a question. She doesn't understand about the veneer the way Chava does. Chava knows that everything is a veneer at best—humanity, law, money, love, decency—so you have to be very careful how you walk about on it because there's nothing underneath. You can't just let go. Rachaeli can, only because she's never fallen through. Chava knows that you must put all your efforts into maintaining the veneer because that's all there is, but she doesn't tell this to her friend, any more than she would to her children.

So the quarry comes to mind. At Auschwitz their job was to turn the world inside out, hollow it and toss pieces of the core onto the surface. It leaves a shell. You would have to be very careful how you walked on such a planet, knowing you had had a part in the hollowing. She is.

"She doesn't interfere," she says finally, sidestepping lightly. "And I can never do enough for her. I owe her everything and I haven't . . . so many things I should have done I've held back on."

"What things? What else could you do?"

"I didn't name my first child for my brother Jacob, for example, although I should have."

"Should have?"

"Well, you know. He died and I lived. I owed her that, at least, to name my—"

"You owed her? Because he died you owed her?"

Chava feels the anger you feel when you start out to explain something to someone, knowing he wishes to misunderstand. "She could only go with one of us. She went with me, so I lived."

"She thought you had a chance. She knew he didn't."

The chill in Chava's voice is as much anger as she can show. "This is the same discussion I have with Shlomo every time. He doesn't understand and you don't, so if you don't mind—"

"I'm trying to understand. So why didn't you name Aaron after your brother?"

"Because he—my brother—was a victim. I couldn't. I was afraid—"

"—the name would be bad luck?"

She likes Rachaeli. They are very close in some ways, and she doesn't want to insult her. Besides, Rachaeli couldn't know how stupid that was, how beside the point. Bad luck. And Chava can't tell her; no one who'd been in the camps would talk about the taint of that death. She'd been afraid of passing on the taint, but there is no way to say it to this innocent. This virgin.

"Yes. I was afraid it would be bad luck."

"But then you . . ."

"Then why did I name the second one Jacob? Because after you have one child you understand that he grows up in his own way, he becomes a separate person and the superstition about the name is silly." That is true. Jacob's taint doesn't reach her Yakov. The camps don't touch her children at all, she sees to it. Even against her mother she sees to that.

"So you got to pay your debt to your mother."

"Yes. That bit of it."

"You're a good daughter."

She is not a good daughter, Chava knows. But she acts like one. She can't stand the feeling when she doesn't act like a good daughter. She smiles a little, accepting the compliment.

"Doesn't Shlomo mind, though—having her here all the time?"

"Shlomo minds. He tells me all the time how he minds."

"So—"

"So he minds."

She says it easily but it is not so easy. She has to be attentive to her mother, has to brush Shlomo aside so her mother knows she comes first, and every time she feels his anger. It twists the panic around her lungs, makes the air feel too thin, poisoned. Like being locked in and gassed. She can't say anything to appease him or Anni would hear it, so she keeps quiet. But she has discovered something: eventually her silence turns into power. He comes to understand that he's wounded her, and he needs to be forgiven. Then it is a matter of letting him come back to her, and for a time everything is pleasant.

Rachaeli persists. "But you must mind, too. I mean—if you're never alone, when do you talk out your decisions?"

"What decisions?"

"Well, like about the children . . ."

"Where they go to school, the religious training and all that—that's all settled. The rest there's no need to discuss. I handle it as it comes up. I don't bother him with it."

Rachaeli freezes with one hand in the carton. "Wait a minute, wait a minute," she says. "All of a sudden I understand. You have it just the way you want it, don't you? Like me. Only," she nods slowly, admiringly, "you didn't have to make such a noise to get it that way."

"What way?"

"The boys are all yours. You've maneuvered them away from Shlomo without a word."

Chava speaks warily. "He has his influence."

"Yes, I suppose. The religious thing—he made a Jew of you, eh?"

"Hitler made a Jew of me." Cold and final. The bitterness might be for Hitler or for Shlomo or for Rachaeli. Then she relents. "The children are both his and mine," she lies to her friend. "His as much as mine."

In fact, Shlomo has nothing to do with the children. They are her offering to Anni, a rope ladder for the two of them across the thin veneer. Having them at all was an act of profound cynicism. But out of kindness, and because she cannot translate the thought into Rachaeli's language, she does not say so to her elegant, innocent friend.

She holds out her hand for another pile of clothes. The diamond does its work: catching the light from the window, it bends it and shoots it out again, refracted. If it could reverse the effect, taking distorted rays and sorting them out, giving off straight light, things might be different in the room. As it is, everything the diamond catches is bent, and that seems normal, beneath interest, to the women.

Ramat Gan, April 1967

Because she had borne her boys with such deep cynicism, Chava was afraid to be separated from them. She could never be sure what might happen to them; anything might, and she knew whose job it was to fight the odds, keep them safe. She did it by being home all the time, whenever they might need her. When they came home from school she was always there. Aaron was fifteen now, and Yakov thirteen, and even Eli at eleven was pretty independent, but she insisted on knowing where they were at all times. Still she almost got home too late, that Thursday in late April '67.

It wasn't her fault. The older boys were dismissed from school early to dig trenches, and she was at the supermarket when they got home. She didn't expect them home for two hours yet.

It was her third market that day, actually. The civil-defense people had published an instruction booklet about stocking the shelters and she had organized the one in their building, collecting the money and buying the provisions and seeing to the sandbags and all that. That was a couple of weeks ago, but now she was laying in supplies for her family, preparing to dig in or to escape. She went out every day while the boys were in school, and she scoured the city for canned and dried and packaged foods. She lay awake at night, thinking it out. Dried fruits and nuts and meats were best, obviously, and then rice and flour, but those had disappeared from the shelves at once. Next best were small cans of fish and tubes of nut butter. The water was a worry; it was so heavy and the plastic jugs were so bulky. In two places in the flat—in the hall closet, sewn into a raincoat and four bedrolls, and under the bed in boxes—were the basics: cans of fish and vegetables, packages of dried and dehydrated meats and grains, packets of biscuits, chocolate and halvah, cans of juice, matches, can openers, small knives, Sterno, antiseptics, burn ointment, penicillin tablets, soap, cigarettes, batteries, radio, ammunition. The jugs of water were lined up in both places, ready to be hand carried. The diamonds were in an old hat of Shlomo's in the hall closet.

It had taken her a long time to get the diamonds from Shlomo. He had joked about it, made fun of her, until the night she cried. He paid attention then, finally, when she dug her fingers into his arm and—not crying simply, but gasping, steaming with rage—spat it at him, that when Tel Aviv fell and the Arabs came and no one stopped them, when the world looked on and let it happen again and they were raped and slaughtered and had nowhere to go again, and the diamonds were all that stood up, again, to get them out, buy them out, then wouldn't he be glad to have them safe in his vaults where he couldn't get to them, wouldn't he laugh then, to watch his sons split and burnt, raped, forced, butchered, for want of his diamonds?

He brought her two dozen of them and she stayed up all that night sewing ribbon pouches for them that they would tie on under their clothes. She hid the ribbon pouches in the old hat in the closet. Then she went back to thinking it out, about the provisions.

She had been prowling the stores that day, looking for things she might have overlooked, and when she got home she was weak from the heat and her head ached. She heard the radio, of course, as she came through the door. Shlomo left it on day and night, listening for news and for his reserve group's call-up code. It was like the loudspeaker in the camps—you had to listen to whatever the radio chose to blare at you, every single minute. When there was nothing else, they thrust music at you, battering your nerves like in the camps. Over the noise now she heard Anni calling Aaron, determination in her voice.

"What's he done, Mother?" She set down her package, smiled automatically at the cronies, and took off her shoes.

"Nothing. I have something to give him. You too. Here." She held it out. It was a little capsule.

"What's this? I have penicillin."

"It's not penicillin. It's to put away, to keep on your body."

"Anni, for God's sake. What are you, Eva Braun? Throw it away." Ari-Bela wasn't smiling. He went to take it from Anni, who snatched it back.

"Idiot. You think these grow in the streets? You'll come to me when you'll need it. And don't tell me again this is Israel."

"This is Israel. You don't need to go passing around the cyanide. You're safe here." He spoke gently to her.

"Safe," Grodner grunted. "Putz, you never learn. In this world nothing is safe. Who's going to save us? The U.N.? England, maybe. Or France, like before, eh? They're going to watch us burn again, Ben Zion, and write our eulogy by the firelight. At least this time we can choose our death."

"Mother? It's cyanide? You were calling Aaron to give him—?"

"You too, Shlomo, all of us."

In another minute she would have been too late, Anni would have gotten to him. You never knew where the danger was going to come from. Chava took the pill from Anni's hand and gentled her voice, like Ari-Bela's. "Mother, Aaron believes that he's safe. Invulnerable. Israeli. You protected me, right? And I have to protect him. That illusion is his protection, because take it away, let him see how close it is, and he'll—"

"What? You think this ignorance, this protection of yours, will stop them killing him? When they come for him he'll be invisible because you lied to him that he's safe?"

"No. I think that when—if—they come for him, he'll fight like someone who expects to win. What will he draw on if we infect him with our fears?"

"What. You called me?" Aaron was dressed in his khakis, a counterfeit uniform he'd rigged up, impatient to go out. "I have to be at the meeting place in five minutes."

"What for?" Chava asked him.

"To dig trenches. Everyone is. And when the war starts, my assignment is to deliver mail in this district. I'll be home every day at noon."

"Go dig. Grandmother just wanted to know where you were. Aaron— if there's any trouble, you come right home as soon as it's safe. We'll need you here."

"I know." The door slammed behind him.

It was Dani who settled the thing with Anni. He came in half an hour later. Ari-Bela and Grodner were arguing loudly over their taxes. "—if you were a man you'd send yours in early, too," Ari-Bela was saying, "when your country needs it."

"Take your finger out of my face. What kind of moron pays his taxes early? My ulcer I'll send them."

Anni was at her loom, silent. "What's up, Anni?" Dani asked. She shrugged. "What's good in the kitchen?"

"Go see."

"Come and show me. How's your back today? Want a hand?" They made their way into the kitchen, his hand under her arm. He was taller than she was now. The men were shouting at each other in the other room. She dipped a cabbage roll out of the pot and ladled it onto a plate for him.

"Where's Aaron?"

"Digging ditches. Trenches." She snorted, disdainful.

"Me too, I gotta go soon. Where's Chava?"

Anni only shrugged: Who knows? Who cares?

"Hey, what's wrong? You mad at her?"

She didn't mean to tell him, but over the radio and the shouting of the men she couldn't hear herself begin and it was hardly like telling. Anyway, it was just Dani, not family.

He got up and came and stood over her and put an arm awkwardly around her shoulders. He invented a thing to say to her. "Hey, never mind, it's okay. Don't you know the army has those capsules? They give them out if they think—well, you know, that people will need them. They have one for every person. Didn't you know? It's regular emergency procedure."

She studied him. It must be true, he looked so certain and matter-of-fact. "It's all right that I told you, then? I didn't spoil it, that you thought you were safe?"

"It's all right, Anni, you know you can tell me anything." The authority had passed into his hands like magic. "Anyway, I never thought I was safe."

He said it for the effect, but of course it was true.

Shlomo went. Dov and his boys, Zvi and Avi, went. The men all went and the women and children and old men were left. For two weeks in all Israel no one's father was around.

Some of the men were going to die. Dov might die, Dani thought, and then Zvi and Avi would be fatherless; they would finally have that in common with him.

The rabbis consecrated the park as an emergency cemetery. People covered their windows and painted their light bulbs and car lights blue and then before they knew it—a war in six days—the fathers were back. It was over. The radios were still on for several days—speeches, reports, evaluations—and then they turned them off. They began to hear about the deaths. A few of Dani's classmates had lost their fathers. Dani was writing for the high-school newspaper, and he took the job of putting together the memorial column listing the students' fathers and older brothers who had fallen, their army service and divisions, the dates and locations of their deaths. It ran on the front page, bordered in black.

Dani watched the mourners when they came back to school; they were dignified and solemn, but he saw them smiling and joking, too. Everyone was courting them. It didn't seem so bad to lose a father that way. He wished he were one of them; he envied them their grief and the stature it gave them. It turned out that he did benefit from the war in a way, though: there were a lot of fatherless kids around now, and some whose fathers were alive but not all right, so for a while the teachers were very careful not to put too much emphasis on fathers.

He thought about his own father. It was possible, wasn't it, that he had fallen in the war, too? He probed himself for a reaction: *The man who gave me life is dead*, he intoned to himself and he pictured a powerful man lying broken in the hills of Jerusalem, but he couldn't feel anything. It wouldn't be of any use anyway, even if he had certified information that his father had been killed in the war, even if he could grieve publicly like the others. No one would feel sorry for him because it wouldn't be like losing a real father; he'd just be a famous bastard all over again, in case there were two or three people left in Israel who didn't know about it. But he liked the mournful mood he'd set, so he tried imagining Rachaeli dead. Say she'd been hit by a stray shot. He could picture that all right; the picture swam up, immediate and realistic. He probed for grief again, found panic and relief twinned but no sadness until he pictured himself breaking the news to people, and then a poignant self-pity pricked his eyes until they stung: alone.

Anyway, Dov came home, and Zvi and Avi and Shlomo. Zvi had taken some shrapnel in his leg, and it was pretty badly torn up, but they were all alive. No mention at all was made of Dani's father.

One of the things the radio told them that week was about the Syrians and what they had done with some of their prisoners, the pilots. Stripped them, smeared them with honey, tied them up, left them alive in the desert for the flies.

"That a human being could do such a thing," Shlomo said. "It's unbelievable."

The cronies looked at him. Shlomo was a good man, but an Israeli. They said nothing.

Gradually Chava began to put the emergency food away in the kitchen, but she kept the diamonds hidden in their ribbon pouches in Shlomo's hat. Anni kept the little capsules she had stashed in an old medicine vial.

When he returned home, Shlomo talked incessantly about the weapons. It had come to him in the desert, in the night, that if they lost they would all be trapped and dealt with, another Holocaust. It could be him, this time, and Chava and his boys and Dani. Easily, in a few days, if the war went badly. The thought had come to Dov, too, and to Yossi, fifty-one and fighting his third war, afraid again for his hands, too old for all of this. The voices of the European Jews on the radio in the days of the Eichmann trial had seemed to belong to another kind of people, victims. But in the night and in the heat and turmoil of the days Shlomo and Dov and Yossi thought about losing. They thought, for the first time, how little it would take to change their voices to those radio voices.

Shlomo didn't tell Chava about those thoughts he'd had. She was so tight with anxiety, more fears would only drive her further into her silence. And for other reasons he didn't tell her about his senseless tears in the desert at Nahel.

They were mopping up in Nahel; the last of the Egyptians seemed to have fled and scouts were checking the area. Shlomo, filthy, sand in his eyes and nose and teeth, asked the unit's doctor whether the well water was safe for drinking. The doctor grimaced. "Safe but hardly better than thirst," he said.

The doctor was right. The water was cloying and greasy-tasting. Shlomo spat it out but dipped out more to wash his face and hands. This bleak spot was the wilderness of Paran where Hagar and Ishmael, banished by Abraham at Sarah's insistence, waited to die. "Is this filthy stuff the best the Almighty could do for them?" Shlomo said to the doctor.

"Who?"

"Hagar and Ishmael."

"You're thinking about our brothers?" The doctor waved a hand toward the makeshift enclosure and the Egyptian prisoners in it. "Ishmael our brother?"

"Not really. Our brothers are trying to wipe us out. I'm only thinking about the woman and the child in exile. Not Sarah's finest moment."

"No. Funny, she was so giving, too. Endured everything for Abraham except the one thing: couldn't abide the presence of his child, another woman's child. Willing to send them out to die—it was murder, really—just so she didn't have to countenance the child. It wasn't sexual jealousy, you know, it wasn't Hagar she minded. It was the child."

"I know." He saw Hagar lay the boy down on the hot sand and turn away from him: let me not see the death of the child, she said. Shlomo was exhausted and nerve-worn. He'd had six hours' sleep in three days. He saw the child, parched and feverish, black curls trickling sand as he tossed, fatherless now, no one to protect him. Tears made hot tracks through the stubble of his beard and he had to turn away so the doctor wouldn't see it.

"No jealousy stronger than a woman's on behalf of her child," the doctor was saying, but Shlomo didn't hear him. He was splashing the stinking water of the wilderness of Paran on his face and trying to control his weeping, thinking senselessly, *Let me not see the death of the child.*

The cronies listened to Shlomo telling about the new Centurion tanks. Potasnik said, "If we'd had these weapons, Grodner, we'd have been heroes."

"It's true," Shlomo said. "And if we *didn't* have them there would have been another Holocaust. Can you swim, Potasnik?"

Grodner shook his head. "Such a simple thing, eh? Such a small difference. Tch." He looked Shlomo directly in the eye for the first time in all these years. No one but Grodner knew it was the first time, not even Shlomo. It wasn't the kind of thing he'd notice. But it seemed to him that Grodner's voice had deepened. Strange in an old man.

The year that Dani was seventeen, Rachaeli began to see that the task of pruning his allegiances was getting out of hand. It had to do with girls, of course.

At first she watched him preening before mirrors and making phone calls in an exaggeratedly casual baritone voice and she smiled nostalgically as though it were another harmless stage of development, like learning to walk. She had been nineteen when she leapt into the passionate trade with Dov—her secret heat for possession of him—and left behind for all time her parents' circle, but she didn't make the connection between herself at nineteen and this red-faced child of hers talking with a girl on the phone.

Then he went to a social at Aaron's school and he met the girl. Shira Something. Skinny little thing, quiet, not especially pretty, but there must have been some appeal. He began calling her at night, lying on the hall rug with his feet up on the chair and the phone held close to his mouth, talking in teasing, confidential tones. It was a whole new voice, irritating, and Rachaeli couldn't keep herself from mocking him about it.

Rachaeli wasn't at home on a Friday afternoon when he left to go over to Shira's. Shira's parents were, though, and the mother, Mrs. Ofek, got hold of Dani at the door. She explained it kindly. "You're a nice boy, Dani. We all like you. But I'm afraid you'll have to . . . Shira's not allowed to date." Her face was red but she looked right at him.

"She went out with Natan," Dani pointed out.

Now Mrs. Ofek looked away. "Look," she said. "We . . . Dani, parents have to worry for their children. It's certainly not any fault of yours, but you . . . I can't let her date you."

The father appeared behind her. "You know what the law is, son? Did anyone ever explain it to you?"

"The law?" He was beginning to panic. What law? Had he broken some law?

"Look, it isn't for me to . . . I'm not the one who ought to . . . ." Mr. Ofek shifted his skullcap with the flat of his hand. "Look, you want me to explain it?"

"Sure."

"You're illegitimate. A great kid, healthy, nice—it has nothing to do with anything except the way you were born. But the law says you can't marry. In this country you are unmarriageable."

"We weren't planning to get married!"

"But things get serious sometimes; they get out of hand. What parent wouldn't want to spare his daughter from starting something she can never finish?"

Never finish. He went home and found Avi in the living room with his girlfriend. They were there for Friday-night dinner. She was sitting between his legs on the rug, doing her college homework. Rachaeli came in just behind Dani, carrying groceries.

"You're back," she said. "You didn't say where you were going. I got you a shirt for the socials. You went out last time wearing—"

"Take it back."

"What?"

"Take the shirt back. I don't need it. I can't go to any socials. It would have been nice for you to tell me."

"What are you talking about?"

"It would have been nice for you to explain it. But it's okay. Mr. Ofek explained it all. I get it now." He turned to go.

She grabbed him by the arm. "Explained *what?*"

"How since you had a lover I can never get married. You know I never met this man before last week? But he knew all about how I'm a mamzer. Everyone in this country knows, you know that? And I'll never get near a girl, so take the shirt back. Or give it to some normal kid."

Thinking about it later, it was not his complaints about his bastardy that stood out in her mind. Adolescents exaggerate everything. What came clear to her, suddenly, was that there would be girls. Women. Sooner or later, one woman. It was inevitable. And if she wasn't careful, he could latch on to some father-figure, too, in school or in the army. Kids did that when they rebelled against their parents. All right; since she couldn't keep him tied to her, she narrowed her objectives. Let him prefer her. Let him not cleave to someone else in rejection of her. Let him see them all as pale substitutes.

She could only buttress him in advance. She began to remind him, whenever the opportunity came up, that he couldn't rely on the strength of any other adult's commitment to him. "No one is for you the way I am for you," she said over and over. "Why should they be? No one will fight for you the way I do—don't expect it."

He disapproved of her now, she saw that. Adolescents disapprove of everything. But if he was going to feel that way, let him at least see her as an unusual woman, not bound like everyone else—bold, female, with emotions too powerful for the normal bounds. Let him at least have to overcome that, finding a woman. Let him try to find a woman to equal her. She went to work on that, playing to him with the kind of energy one expends on a potentially straying lover. "I don't understand how Chava fills her days," she often commented to him. "No work, no real hobbies—nothing but cooking and cleaning. It wouldn't be enough for me." He was impassive, or he agreed absently, but she believed that he was taking it in. She talked to him about her work, exaggerating the importance of it, playing up the excitement. She let him find her playing the cello, too, and she inveigled him into playing with her, letting her cue off him in the difficult quartets. She felt herself to be rich, vital, burring with female pulsations, and if Dani felt that too, well—let him try to find that in a woman.

It was about this time that Alon came along. Rachaeli had had a series of brief affairs, mostly disappointing, and then she'd met him in the newly formed neighborhood string quartet. She went after him directly, not at all the same tentative girl she'd been with Yossi. She was used to playing openly to Dani and she played openly to Alon without any interior debate. He fell easily into her hands, perhaps too easily. He was younger and he was married; that was fine with her. She could only shine brighter compared with some young, dull thing. And she didn't really want more of him than she had. She was forty-six, she was surging with energy, she was the eternal female. She had Alon for sexual excitement, Chava for friendship, and Dani for keeps.

More and more she had Chava for friendship. Chava didn't require the effort that Dani did, or that men did. She didn't care how Rachaeli looked. She didn't flirt or betray her or threaten to withdraw. Rachaeli was Chava's lifeline outside of the European tangle. And the part of Chava that was Rachaeli's was solidly Rachaeli's. She was her unconditional friend. Rachaeli was keeping that unconditional friendship for her old age. Some much later time.

Dani never asked a girl out again after the scene at the Ofeks'. He asked

Shlomo and Shlomo confirmed it; he could never marry. According to the Law, no rabbi—and therefore no one in the state of Israel—could marry him, except to another bastard or a convert. In any case, he must never father a child, because the taint carried for ten generations. Shlomo looked wretched, telling him this, as though it were a death sentence. "You can adopt children, though. You can marry a convert and adopt children. I've thought it through; there are Scandinavian girls coming to some of the kibbutzim. After the army you can join one of these kibbutzim and meet one, marry, adopt children. You'll love them just the same, Dani, you'll see . . ."

Shlomo went on about adopted children, as though that had anything to do with it. How was he supposed to care about having kids when he couldn't even get a date? Nobody was going to be allowed to go out with him. Every time he asked, some father was going to have a chance to call him a bastard. Forget it.

He found ways to exist in the social atmosphere of the high school without liability. The newspaper was very good for that purpose; as a reporter, you could be a celebrity by aiming the questions at someone else. People liked answering questions about themselves, and simply by using their statements you assumed their power and increased your own.

The other, even more effective ploy was a simple one, available to no one but him. It came to him just after the confrontation with Shira's parents. He began to play up his situation, especially with the girls. He made a joke of his bastardy. "It's just me, darling," he'd say, "the eternal bachelor." It was tragic, really, like a fatal illness, and he was brave and charming about it, but his eyes were always a little sad. Haunted, the girls said, hating his mother for what she'd done to him. He was a romantic, unreachable figure. It worked excellently.

The real fun was with new people. It was always on his mind when he met someone: does he know who I am? He looked for the flicker in people's eyes when he gave his name; it was always there. Then he would say it outright, *mamzer*, tossing it at them so they got tangled in it, caught off guard, and the advantage was his. The most sophisticated would engage him in long discussions of the backward legal system, making him a political hero. The others would flounder, embarrassed and apologetic, and leave feeling they owed him something. They were right, he thought; they did.

Finally there was always the magic. People were always wanting him to show them a trick. He knew now what he hadn't understood as a child: quick hands were only a small part of it. The real thing that made magic tricks work was that people were blinded by their own expectations. They knew so well what they expected to see that they could hardly see anything different. So you played to their expectations and they did three quarters of the work, deceiving themselves. If they expected 1-2-3, for example, and you did only 1-2, they imagined 3 and it took them a second to realize that 3 was missing; by then you'd done the trick and the dazzle of it made them forget everything else. Adults were the easiest to fool because their expectations were really hardened and their reflexes were slow, besides.

He did magic shows for children occasionally and for school events, where he used the teachers for stage dupes. They'd try to look blasé or knowing, but they'd be flummoxed into reaching for the wrong hand or picking up the wrong hat. The audience loved that, and the teachers would have to smile and say "great trick," as though they enjoyed it.

He didn't really want the adults to smile and applaud. He wanted to trick them so they would be angered, shocked, frightened. He wanted them to doubt everything they saw, after his act. He dreamed of a great, monstrous trick, so undeniable and so inexplicable that people who saw it would be enraged and made permanently unsure. Certain people he would never do it to. Shlomo because Shlomo liked him, and because he knew for certain that Shlomo couldn't be his father, would never have let him be a bastard. And Anni and Chava and the cronies because they'd already had the worst trick done to them. He liked them, besides. He did all his regular tricks for them to amuse them, to make them forget. He actually liked it when they smiled.

But except for those seven, the monstrous trick would be for everyone. They would see him manipulate reality, dance it around their heads, wrench things away from any possible expectation, and they would see, too late, what they had let him do. The women would despair. The men would turn icy cold. You little bastard, they would say.

B'vakasha, he would answer with a flourish, smiling from behind the illusion. By your leave.

Tel Aviv, July 1969

Grodner wasn't an old man when he died, Rachaeli thought. They drifted across her mind, appearing and reappearing like the spots you see from the heat—Grodner, Anni, Rivka, Avi, Dani. Things were fraying like one of Anni's crazy, unfinished weavings cut off the loom too soon, and after the six-day war was when it began. With Grodner.

He was only sixty or so then, not old, but he was in decay. If you are a year away from your death, you're old no matter what age you are, Rachaeli thought. If you're sick you're old. She tuned to Alon's A, catching the look he sent; it rested blatantly on the bow she was drawing between her legs on the A, then fixed on her eyes: *Later. Yes,* she smiled back, but she sighed to herself. He wasn't subtle. Everyone in the group knew. She didn't really care so much; she insisted on the secrecy only because it gave it an edge. Anyway, you can't have everything; young men aren't subtle. But they aren't old, either.

Grodner was in decay after the six-day war, and he died the following year. Ulcers, colitis—starvation and dysentery, terror and rage and their acids—had devoured him, burned him from the center out. It frightened Anni and the cronies out of their wits, and Anni had never quite recovered hers. That one of them should die *now?* Anyway? That there was another death for them after the one they had cheated? They were stunned. Rachaeli remembered them sitting in Grodner's room the day he went to the hospital. Grodner lay on the couch, dressed and ready. His shirt was one button off, done up crookedly, but no one wanted to move him to fix it. There was stubble in patches on his face. Anni sat straight up in her chair, hands folded, like a visitor. Ari-Bela fussed with the blinds and the curtains, to block the sunlight that lay across Grodner's face. Zara held one of Grodner's hands. The hand was bony and still and rested impersonally in hers. Potasnik pleaded with Grodner to take a little applesauce, open his mouth, try it, Grodner, it wasn't as good as slivovitz but it was a start. Shlomo walked in then—he'd come to drive Grodner to the hospital—and perhaps that triggered Grodner. Anyway, he suddenly spoke up. "You're not to say Kaddish for me. Understand?" They each pulled in a breath but he cut them off. "Do you? I said it already for myself when I died the other time, in the camp. He only gets one death from me. He only gets one Kaddish."

"Personally I'm not ready to say Kaddish for you," Potasnik said. "You don't want to die now, Grodner, it's the rainy season. It would rain on you for weeks, you'd sink to the center of the earth. We'd all get soaked at the funeral. Have pity, Grodner, hang on."

He had no humor left; he was in that last selfish spiral of illness. "No Kaddish. I forbid it."

Shlomo said Kaddish for him for the eleven months and a day. Chava told her about it. Stupidly, it comforted Rachaeli.

Why did she keep thinking of Alon as a boy? He was hardly a boy: thirty-five, ten years younger than she was. Well, eleven. He was no Yossi, certainly. The sophistication, the edge of authority were definitely lacking. On the other hand, he was so easily influenced and controlled. It was good with a younger man; he was passionate and demanding, jealous. She smiled. And he wasn't so young that he couldn't please her, move her. He'd outgrown the inadequacies of very young men—

Like Dani. Nearly eighteen now, just beginning with sex, probably. Soon anyway, in the army.

She wasn't going to think about that.

—and he was accomplished in lovemaking. He could bring her there, stay with her—

He tapped on his stand. They looked up, nodded. They were doing one of Beethoven's string quartets and they were bad. Amateurs, of course, but Alon and Shoshana, the dark little Moroccan violinist, were pretty good. Rachaeli and the second violin were the weak ones. This time she was going to hold her own.

Rachaeli was forty-six. There were lines slanting downward from the flare of her nose to the corners of her mouth. The skin on the backs of her hands was minutely webbed, crosshatched. She made a fist every time she looked at them, to pull the skin taut. She had to think about eating certain foods, lately, and she found herself wooing sleep as once she had wooed Yossi, opening herself to it and willing away her anxiety lest the anxiety chase it away, succumbing gratefully and then waking too early, betrayed.

Alon was young. That was the bite to it. He was hers, wild, possessive, but he would leave. Eventually her little wrinkly places, the flaccid swing of flesh, something would repel him. He would go. It equaled the pull between them, made it sweet to her. She enthralled him but she didn't, couldn't own him.

Anni knew about Alon. Or most of the time she knew. It tickled her to hear the stories Rachaeli told about the men. It was incongruous—Anni was austere, really, and of course lately she was often despondent—but she had always relished Rachaeli's outrageous behavior. She listened with vindictive, bitter humor. Lately Rachaeli tailored the stories to evoke that response. It was better than the apathy Anni had fallen into.

Anni never went out now. Grodner's death had left her ill; he did indeed die in the rainy season, and they had to walk though mud and stand in rain at the funeral, and Anni caught a cold. It went to bronchitis and in the brisk routine of medication, thermometers, cough syrups, rubs, sponge baths, no one noticed her sliding into the strange mood. Finally the fever broke and the X rays were clear and the weather lifted so that they could get out. Rachaeli and Chava walked with Anni between them. They got as far as the Ramah movie house and Anni stopped short. She looked queasy. Her eyes were fixed on the queue in front of the movie house. People were standing packed together, a long line. "I want to go home," she said. They almost had to carry her. Now she resisted going out at all. At first crowds, the jostling and the press of bodies, disgusted her, then to be thrown together with even a small group of strangers—in a bus or *sheroot* or in a shop—agitated her. There were times now when she forgot where she was. There were moments when she turned on her own work in a frenzy and slashed it off the loom. There were days when only Rachaeli could talk to her. Or Dani, when he was there.

He'd be gone soon. In two weeks he and Aaron went to the army. Rachaeli wasn't going to think about that now. Watch the crescendo here, she told herself; watch the break.

It was all fraying. Avi was gone three months now—a *yored*, one who had made the descent from Israel, gone to live in the United States. Driving a cab. Rachaeli hadn't been seeing much of Zvi or Avi since their high-school days; they'd been spending weekends and vacations with their friends, or traveling. But Avi was really out of reach now. They were both, although still in touch, out of her reach. Dov was silent and embittered about his son's defection. Zvi was scornful. Rivka was hysterical. She couldn't face her friends; she was humiliated, bewildered. "Avram's namesake has left this country to drive a cab in America," she said to Rachaeli over and over. "For what? For an easy life? That's what he wants? You should never have left the kibbutz, never."

225

She said it every time Rachaeli went to Degania to see her, every Shabbat now. She was sixty-eight. She had high blood pressure and circulation problems and she'd had to slow down. She worked only a couple of hours a day, easy work—"The beginning of the end," she cracked—and she didn't know what to do with herself.

Of everything, Rachaeli thought, that was the worst. Rivka was always on her mind, demanding, needing. Come to see her. Bring her dinner, she doesn't feel like eating in the dining hall. Take her clothes to the laundry, she can't burden her friends. What was she reading, bring her a book. *When are you coming again, it's good to see you.* She was like a child. She had no right, no right, she was supposed to be the mother. It was all right for Rivka, Rachaeli thought; she left *her* family in Plotsk. She never had aging parents; they were a generation without elders, children together in the promised land—lovely until they got old and didn't know how to behave. *What do you think about the leg, Rachaeli? Does it look swollen?* Rivka, how do I know? I'm not a doctor. Ask the nurse. *I can't keep asking the nurse, she has others to look after. Why did Avi leave, Rachaeli? To drive a* cab? *It's so important to him to have a stereo?*

And still, with it all, any person who walked into the room got Rivka's best; Rachaeli was forgotten. An old kibbutz buddy? Give him juice, give him the cake Rachaeli brought, get involved talking kibbutz politics, let Rachaeli sit there and wait it out, enduring the waste of her day off. And any child, any child could wander in during family hours and get a story, more than a story—get Rivka as she could be, bright and funny and strong. Any child but Rachaeli. Still.

"—watch the *triplet*, Rachaeli. Back to B, please. And—"

Any child but Rachaeli. For Rachaeli she had only demands and criticism: Avi was a tragedy. Zvi, who was doing so well in the bank, was a waste. "We need another banker? Let him do something for his country. That's all they know— 'me and mine.'" Only Dani had Rivka's approval. "Look how excited he is to be going to the army. He'll wind up in the paratroopers, you'll see."

Not this one, Rivka. This one is mine. Two weeks now before he left. Rachaeli was wooing him, waging crafty war against his army excitement—fixing him tidbits, ironing his clothes, teasing him out on evening forays for ice cream or to Jaffa for the clubs. He'll remember this, she kept promising herself, when he's eating rations and lying on rocks.

They would clip his black curls. He was beautiful, her boy. And so young.

Alon was young, that was the thing. She glanced at him. He was sitting on the edge of the wooden chair, legs apart and eyes closed. He was wearing a T-shirt and she could see the muscles shift and tighten as his left hand moved on the neck of the violin. Young. Taut, smooth, agile. Easy.

She pleased herself, with him. She did whatever occurred to her, whatever she wanted at the moment, and he was content to let her lead. More than content; it was the hot core of his dependence on her. It wasn't that she angled down on him at this moment, or raised her legs and encircled him with her feet at that, or that once she waited until he was standing at the side of the bed and suddenly sat up to face him and took him in her mouth as he stood before her, holding him there with light fingers and a lazy tongue. It was that she wanted these things and took them. In this one place he didn't have to be the aggressor. She decided everything, even when it was time for him to come. She closed on him then and pulsed it out of him, like a flood. He rode her like a current, any way she went.

He saw the little lines etched into her belly, the wrinkling of the skin around her navel. He saw the gray hairs isolated in the black thatch between her thighs. He saw the blue veins in the fold under her bottom. They were erotic to him, tokens of her luxuriant authority over him. She made no effort to cover them or to distract him from noticing them; she knew. She was riverbed and river to his tumbling stone and she polished him to her vagaries. He was so young, there was plenty of time to shape him.

And when she finished with him each time and he fell into that quick, light, trusting sleep in her arms, she had a moment to think before he woke up and the dominance shifted. In that moment, cradling his curly head, she usually thought, Let him remember *that* when he looks at a young woman. Let him try to find that with some girl. She never slept. She needed that minute to say it to herself, having lost more to him each time than he knew. Sometimes she had to think it several times over.

Tel Aviv, August 1969

Shlomo is locking up on Friday afternoon, getting ready to go home. When he finishes with the regular vault he opens the little vault to add a pink to his collection of colored stones. The blemished one is still there. Five years now since he laid it in the vault, eleven carats of good color with the hint of stress at its core. He comes upon it now and then, of course, and he doesn't always focus on it, but he can recall without difficulty his cutting plan for it, his strategy for skirting the stress and salvaging the stone. It would make sense to cut it and sell it, especially since Chava has insisted on keeping her hoard of stones all these years, thousands of lirot worth, but he leaves it untouched. He picks it up now and unfolds the tissue from around it, imagining that he can see the bruise in it, that the mauve and blue lick is visible to his naked eye like the faint streaks in the sky before sunrise. He imagines polishing the stone himself, faceting it around the bruise, flaunting it, so that the colors of it would be mirrored hundreds of times, triangles and parallelograms flashing blue and mauve, a stone that would break your heart.

He folds the tissue deftly around the stone again and lays it in the vault and sets the lock and closes up the office and heads for home.

The boys are leaving in a few days to go to the army. It will be good for Aaron to get away from the women. The three years in the army will break their stranglehold, move him once and for all to manhood and a world of men. He thinks, impassively, that his son has a lot to learn from the men. But Dani, he thinks, they'll love Dani. He's just their meat: brazen, cocky, tough. Some training officer will get hold of him and spark him, inspire him—help him to hit his stride, there'll be no stopping him then.

He can see the officer—tall, easy, commanding, clever. A fitting father for the boy. Sinking in jealousy and loss he turns the corner onto his block. There is a little crowd of people; he thinks it's a ball game until he sees that they're standing pretty still. Then he gets close enough to hear the voices and see the black hats of the Hasidim, a father and a son it looks like, walking home from the ritual bath in white shirts and clean pants, with their plastic bags in their hands.

"—hurt you to cover your head like your friend," the man is saying, kindly enough, to Dani. "You're a Jew, aren't you?"

Dani and Aaron, Shlomo sees now, are with three of their friends. They've been hanging around together for days, finished with school and all charged up about going to the army.

"God thinks it's important for me to cover my head?" Dani asks sweetly.

"Of course. You're a Jew, you know to cover your head."

"But He doesn't care if you sit back and let me go to the army to cover your ass while your son stays home. And," he takes a step back, widening the circle, "he doesn't give you enough sense to cover your pecker."

The man's fly is open. Evidently he left the *mikvah* in a hurry and forgot, and through the gap of his undershorts a bit of flesh is showing. It is broad daylight on the busiest afternoon of the week. Shlomo stands back and watches the man adjust his clothes and stride away with his son, the boys snickering and jostling each other. He feels as though his own face has been struck.

Dani and Aaron, weak from laughter, clump their way up the stairs with their arms around each other. Aaron's *kipah* slides off his head and Dani replaces it for him. "Cover your ass, man, don't you know you're a Jew?" he says, and they start to laugh all over again.

They get to the landing and open the door and see Shlomo coming up behind them. He looks grim. Poor Shlomo, he never has any fun. Dani feels sorry for him, trudging off to work every day. He feels sorry for anyone who isn't eighteen and going to the army. "Smile, Shlomo, it's Shabbat; you've got tomorrow off," he calls.

"Dani. Come with me, please."

"Sure, in a minute."

"Daniel." His voice is angry, formal. He marches to his bedroom and holds the door open for Dani. Dani shrugs, goes and stands before Shlomo. What the hell? Shlomo gestures him in and closes the door.

"What you said to that man."

"The Hasid? What about it?"

"You humiliated him. It was easy, eh? You put him in his place."

Dani shrugs, fights a grin, ducks his head.

"What did Rabbi Elazar of Modin say about that? We studied the Ethics of the Fathers, you and I. What does he say?"

Resentful now and uneasy, Dani frowns, indicating that he doesn't know what Shlomo is talking about.

"'He who puts his fellow man to shame,'" Shlomo prompts.

Okay, I'll humor you, the boy's demeanor says. He singsongs: "'He who puts his fellow man to shame in public, even though he has knowledge of Torah and good deeds to his credit, he has no share in the world-to-come.'"

"Why?"

"Why what?"

"Why would such an action forfeit one's share in the world-to-come?"

"You tell me."

"Because—look at me—because you destroy a man in his own eyes and in the eyes of the world, and in him you destroy a reflection of God. And because it can't be undone, never."

He goes on and on. Lessons. Torah. Bullshit.

Who does he think he is?

The boy plays his cocky role, but he's taking it in. He still needs to be guided, Shlomo thinks, relieved and tender, and he maintains his sternness long enough to pound the lesson home. Then he gives Dani a hug, cupping his head briefly in benediction. "All right, son," he says, feeling the little trembling in the boy. "That's enough now."

Aaron, pretending to be busy with some papers, watches them come out of the bedroom. He knows his father so well he even knows what lecture Dani must have gotten. Rabbi Elazar of Modin, he bets, Perek number three, Mishnah fifteen, it starts on the third column of the page. Lucky thing it happened the way it did, he congratulates himself, I was just about to open my mouth to the guy. Then it would have been me in there with my father, and Dani would be out here. If I'd opened my mouth faster, he thinks, turning his head from the two of them, I'd have been in there. And he would be out here.

Rivka was right, Dani had planned all along to go to the paratroopers; he was going right into the parachute training camp at Tel Nof.

Rachaeli was furious. She had raged, threatened, bribed, reasoned; nothing would move him. "Let them find someone else to be a hero for Israel," she fumed now to Anni and Chava, pacing the flat. "Let some other kid throw himself into the worst spots. *Not this one.*" She couldn't understand it; she had used every argument on him, he had only kidded and cajoled her, bouncing her words off playfully like beach balls. He was already registered.

"Don't worry," Chava said. "He'll be all right." Someone had to say something. Anni was deep in a brooding silence, no telling what she was thinking or what she might say. "Dani can take care of himself," Chava told Rachaeli, but in her mind was only relief that Aaron had chosen the armored corps, the tanks. She saw Dani hurtling out of a plane, tumbling through enemy air, parachute opening, airborne prey for bullets, nowhere to hide. Aaron would be in a tank, enclosed, armored, hatch closed, safe, safe. Like being safe in your own secret cave only better, because of the huge guns. Aaron would be the aggressor, Dani the soft, dangling prey. She went to hold Rachaeli, whose breathing was turning into gasps.

"Name."

"Daniel Kovner."

"Address."

"Thirty-nine Herzl Street, Ramat Gan."

"Next of kin."

"My mother, Rachael Kovner."

His heart pounded but he answered quietly. The guy was cool, though; he showed no response to the name.

"Hold your hand out for the nurse, please."

"Fingerprint?"

"Blood type." She jabbed him, a perfect red pearl of blood balanced on his fingertip until she smeared it onto the glass.

"I thought everyone in Israel knew my blood type." Get it over with, let them say it.

They smiled vaguely. "You been typed so often? Not sick are you?" The sergeant opened his folder.

"No. I'm the one."

"What one?"

"Daniel ben Rachael. My mother's Rachael Kovner."

"So?"

It burst inward in his chest, points of shock, it tingled on his tongue. He looked at the two of them, the impatient bearded sergeant and the army nurse and he memorized their faces, the first two people in a new world. Step off now, into the chasm; test them.

"I'm the bastard."

Puzzlement, a quick trade of questioning glances. They didn't. They really didn't know. He changed all the combinations in that moment. No one had to know. If he didn't tell them, they wouldn't know. He was just another soldier. He had only a second now before they framed the question. Distraction and misdirection, change their focus and pull off the trick. "Just a joke. Do we really get sworn in at the Wall?"

"Of course." The sergeant lifted his chin. The girl smiled. They'd switched from curiosity to pride. Easy marks.

"By Danny Matt himself?"

"All of him. You'll get your tags later in the day. Uniforms to your right."

Play it quiet and he could be like anyone.

Colonel Danny Matt towered over the rabbi; as they passed each other, changing places, the red beret sailed high over the black *kipah*. Dani stood among the others, another uniformed eighteen-year-old. They'd each been handed a rifle and a Bible when they took their oaths and he hefted their weights in his two hands, by force of habit finding their balancing points.

Colonel Matt made sense, too. The rabbi had droned on and on—no one listened to him—but the colonel spoke right to them. "You're a unit now," he said, "and you'll be together for at least a year and a half, most of you for much longer. Your leaders will come from among yourselves and you will depend on each other for life and safety. You stand before the Western Wall. Paratroopers took it, paratroopers will safeguard it. You walked twenty-five miles to get to the wall. You'll walk, run, and crawl a lot of miles together, until every inch of this country is as familiar to you as your homes."

No homes any more. Mothers and fathers, that was finished now. Dani smiled.

The colonel was wishing them a hard and painful training, sweat, thirst, and exhaustion. Dani fixed his eyes on the towering thin man in the red beret, accepting his benediction.

He was constantly probing, testing his anonymity. It seemed to be holding. He had a name, of course, like anyone else, but the name didn't mean anything special to any of them and they assumed he was from an ordinary family.

Not to offer information meant that you were in control. He'd always known that; he'd certainly used it to keep his mother and Chava off his back, and it was the basis, besides, of magic and illusion, but this was trickier than either the magic or evading his mother. Here he was the illusion.

Mostly he listened. It seemed there were a lot of families that weren't ordinary. They were all telling stories about their families in those early days of basic; it was the first time most of them had been far enough from home to have occasion to describe their parents, so there was an orgy of talk. Dani listened, he drew them out and he never offered any stories in trade, and no one noticed.

Listening, he began to think that Rachaeli was right: a lot of fathers were no bargain. Shemtov Merhavi, the Yemenite, for example, talked about his father as though he were his grandfather. His parents spoke Arabic, Shemmy spoke Hebrew. They lived near Petach Tikvah, and as far as Dani could tell, the old man spent his days squatting with a water pipe, waiting for the End of Days. He'd taught his children to beg, and that seemed to be the sum of his involvement with them. The mother taught them amulets, incantations, all the tricks they needed to armor their souls against the evil eye and the curses that threatened them from every side. Shemmy was a misfit; he didn't beg, he willfully went to school and even through the vocational high school. His uncles took him sternly to task for failing to bring money home, wasting time in—they spat—the schools of atheists and libertines. He seemed to be related to a whole tribe of people, answerable to all of the men and somehow responsible for all the girls.

Nissim ben Haroush had come to the army to escape his father and because he wanted to drive a car. He'd arrived at the induction center in tight pants, a tight flowered shirt, and pointy shoes. He had his hair slicked back in a complicated sweep—even after his army haircut he kept trying to smooth it back—and he spoke with a heavy French accent. He was Moroccan. His father worked in the bromide plant at Sdom. He cursed the yellow stuff and its stench, cursed the country he'd come to where he worked like an animal in the airless heat of the Dead Sea, cursed his children, seven mouths to feed. Three times a day he put on a prayer shawl and phylacteries and prayed in a shrill voice—it was the only Hebrew he knew—and as often as not turned around to beat one of his worthless sons. They enraged him; everything enraged him. Nissim's mother, a soft, gentle woman, lived in terror of her husband and of the careless assaults of fate. She had no one but her children in this devilish place he'd brought her to. When it was time for Nissim to register for the army she became hysterical, clutching at him and imploring him to stay home. A neighbor's son had claimed mental illness and had been exempted from the army; Nissim's mother followed her son for days, keening and tearing her bodice, begging him to do the same thing and save himself from the army.

Nissim had no intention of missing out on the army. To begin with, if you claimed mental illness they labeled you a psychotic and it went on your papers and you could never get a driver's license. Beyond that, he had been waiting for years to get out of his father's house. Three years in the army; he'd return a man. His father would never dare lay a hand on him again.

Lev came from Kibbutz Ginegar. Dani thought he knew about kibbutz families, but Lev didn't talk about his parents the way Rachaeli did about hers. They seemed like good friends; in fact, it took a while for Dani to catch on that Ehu and Onat were Lev's father and mother and not just some of his friends. Lev talked incessantly about his friends from Ginegar without any explanation, seemingly unaware that no one in the barracks knew them. "Well, you know Shimon, he's always doing that," he'd say, expecting that they did. He talked about stars and planets, too, with the same myopic familiarity. He was mad for astronomy. The sergeant said he would be useful on night marches.

Atsmon didn't say much about his home, but they all knew who he was. The first night in the barracks someone poked Dani and pointed at the pale redhead who was quietly and methodically lining up his kit. "His father is Motti Atsmon," the kid said.

"The general?"

"That's the one. Air force. The 'sixty-seven—"

"I know."

Everyone knew Motti. He'd run the series of low-flying raids that ducked the scanners and took out the Syrian air force in '67. He flew the missions himself. He was photographed after the war with his hand gripping the shoulder of his fifteen-year-old son. He'd just come home, still bearded and haggard, his uniform rumpled. "We had no choice," Motti Atsmon said to the reporters that time. "It had to be done, and that was the only way to do it. So now my boy and his mother can sleep at night."

The picture had gone around the world. Dani might not have noticed it—he was fifteen then, too, bored with the news—but he'd happened to be in Chava's kitchen when the evening paper came. Aaron was having his piano lesson and Dani had followed Chava into the kitchen to get a snack. He was rooting around in the refrigerator when she picked up the paper and turned a page, and he heard her grunt as though she'd had a sharp, surprising little pain. He went over to her. "You okay?" She was staring at a picture; she looked as though she might cry. There were a lot of pictures of dead heroes in the papers these days. He glanced at the picture. "Someone you know?"

She put the paper down and wiped a fingerprint off the refrigerator door, shaking her head.

"So why do you look like that?"

"Nothing, Dani. I was thinking about my father."

"He looked like that guy?"

"Hardly." She huffed an angry little laugh. He'd never seen her like this, it made him uneasy. He was glad when she went to answer Anni's call. He picked up the paper and studied the picture. Another father returning home to his kid. So what. Israel was full of zillions of fathers going home to their kids.

He looked at Judah Atsmon now, the kid from the picture grown up, minding his own business, quietly arranging his things. So what, Dani hurled at Atsmon in his mind, not knowing what he meant.

He studied Atsmon after that, spied him out, pitted himself silently and grimly against him. In fact it was probably because of Atsmon, because of him and his father, that Dani became an officer and led his boys into the cave in Golan. And it was because Dani listened and drew them out in those first weeks that Shemtov Merhavi and Nissim ben Haroush and Lev the astronomer followed him later where he led them. Because he paid attention to them and because of the way he was in the darkness.

Almost half their early training was in the dark—night marches, interrupted sleep, pathfinding, survival, blindfold weaponry. The Arabs feared darkness, hated to move around in it, almost never fought at night if they could help it, so the IDF trained their boys to use the night—move in darkness with daylight agility, fight in it, handle weapons without looking at them.

It turned out that Dani had a genius for darkness. He liked it, liked blackening his face and merging with shadows, understood at once about using the dark, finding the patches of blackest night and moving noiselessly in them. And he was unusually dextrous. He actually did better with the rifle—stripping it down, cleaning it, reassembling it—in darkness than some of the others did in full light. He just shrugged it off. "I fool around with magic," he said. "I'm used to doing things without looking at my hands."

Lev had an easy time with the pathfinding on clear nights—he read the stars like street signs, as the sergeant had predicted—but he was easily tripped up by the terrain, seemed never to anticipate its clutter, the rocks and holes and tripwires. Atsmon was brave and observant and dogged, but he fought the darkness. Dani swam in it, easy waters, known haven.

Shemtov, though, was terrified of the dark. When they got to parachute school he turned out to be an excellent jumper—fearless, dead accurate, agile, everything. But he'd never have gotten that far without Dani.

He froze up on the first night march when they split up for pathfinding. Dani was first to find his way to the objective, after an hour of threading lightly through darkness, feeling himself invisible and potent. No one knew who he was; no one knew where he was. Cagey, untricked, he matched himself against the night's subterfuges and it was powerless to defraud him. When he checked in with the sergeant he was still charged; it was hard for him to sit still and wait for the others to straggle in. Forty minutes later everyone was in except for Shemtov, and finally the sergeant sent Dani out to find him. "Find a way to bring him in if he's hurt himself," the sergeant said. "If you can't manage it, make sure he's armed and secure and come back for help."

"Why don't I just bring someone along?"

"We can't spare anyone. Eight of us fell in an ambush. You'll have to try to handle it alone."

"Right." It was a game. Himself against the night, the enemy, and the dead weight of Shemtov Merhavi. Watch this, Atsmon.

As he made his way back along the wadi, he rehearsed the fireman carry. He hoped Merhavi was unconscious; if he was in pain—a broken leg, say—he'd be that much harder to handle.

The darkness parts, sudden glimmering of light off the eyes and palms of Daniel Kovner, an otherwise unheralded appearance to the hushed crowd. How did he come upon them without a sound like that? A matter of balance, a shifting of weight, mesdames and messieurs. No expression crosses his face as in one silent, smooth, powerful motion he presents— hey, presto!—the motionless body of the Yemenite, a shadow in the blackness on his outstretched arms. He lays the body, dusky and featureless, at the feet of those assembled and straightens, stands still for a moment, nods once, modestly: Thank you.

The Yemenite was way off the path when he came upon him, blundering noisily in the wrong direction and making some kind of noise. A sort of high-pitched whining song. He had his arms wrapped tightly around himself and he didn't seem even to be looking where he was going. He wasn't hurt at all.

"Merhavi," Dani hissed. The Yemenite kept going. "*Merhavi*. Over here." No answer, he just kept stumbling along. Dani ran right up close. "Hey, Shemmy." Now he could make out the sound. It was Arabic, something rhythmic. The kid was saying something over and over in high-pitched Arabic. Dani put a hand on his shoulder.

Shemmy gasped, then fell slowly away from Dani's hand and lay motionless on the sand. Dani knelt down. The kid's chest was rising and falling, so he was breathing. He shook him, shook him again, harder.

"You sick, Shemtov?"

Shemtov opened his eyes, darted a look around, focused on Dani, slid his eyes away. Sat up, swallowed. "It's just you. Dani?"

"Yes?"

"I can't do this."

"You sick?"

"I can't find my way in the fucking dark. I'll go into regular army, I'll transfer over."

"You'll learn."

He shook his head.

"Why not? It's only the first night."

"It doesn't get you?"

"What?"

"The . . . it's so dark. Noises, things come at you . . ."

Dani didn't really understand Shemtov's terror or feel any special compassion for him, but he had a showman's compulsion to release the boy
from the spell, bring him up blinking and smiling. All the way back to the
objective he talked to Shemtov about how everyone had fears, how
Shemmy would get over it and be a great paratrooper. He made jokes and
kept touching Shemtov, little guiding prods and pats. At one point the
boy stopped. "You won't tell them?" he asked.

"Why should I tell them? You going to stay?"

"I'll try it."

"Good man."

That was the only time Shemtov spoke the whole way back. When
they got to the objective the others in the unit were sitting on the ground
in a group around the sergeant, Gershon, who was talking about edible
roots and berries. They all looked up. "He was looking for the lost tribes,"
Dani said.

"How do you think they got lost in the first place?" a kid named Bloch
cracked. "Some sadist sent them out in the pitch black with gunpowder
on their faces and mud packed on their shoes and told them to find Point
A, two miles to the left of the Little Dipper. They're out there yet,
wandering around looking for their sergeant."

That was all, but Gershon looked keenly at Shemtov and nodded a
"well done" at Dani. Dani bowed his head once modestly. *Thank you,
my friends.*

What you have, Shemmy knew, is family. He knew it as an Arab would know it; they had both learned it in the same terrain: I and my brother against my cousin; I and my cousin against the stranger. He lived within a *hamoula*, a network of men who were bound in clanship for protection and for family honor. Your father and uncles went before you in the world; they and your brothers and cousins stood behind you, as well. It was all that you had to cover your nakedness in a treacherous world.

He was Yemenite and Nissim was Moroccan, and they knew something that the others—the white Anglo-Saxon Jews—didn't know. They knew the Arab when he stood in a position of power over them. Shemmy had been born in Israel, so he didn't know it from his own experience, but more frighteningly through outbursts, whispers, silences he had listened to all his life. He hated Arabs and he feared intensely the darkness that hid them and all the other menacing figures his mother had peopled his imagination with. Daylight could be relied upon, and your *hamoula*, and the men you bound to yourself as brothers. That was all.

Nissim had come to Israel as a boy. He remembered it all: the unprovoked attacks, the fear, the humiliations. He remembered stepping aside to let an Arab pass, remembered his father, who was a tyrant at home and who terrorized Nissim and his brothers, toadying to the Arabs, bargaining for less and less and finally abandoning the business and leaving with nothing, degraded and defeated. He remembered hearing the talk of vandalism, burning, brutal killing—random, unannounced, virulent.

He remembered hearing about two teenage boys, neighbors. They were jumped on their way home from services, beaten, kept in an alley and released hours later, when their mothers were nearly berserk. Nissim's father and the other men talked in hushed tones about what had been done to the two boys. Nissim wasn't allowed to hear it, and that was worse because he imagined horrors that aroused and terrified him. No one was ever punished, of course; it was out of the question even to report it. A lot of discussion followed. Someone in the next town had been robbed and beaten and left for dead. Someone else had had his shop burned down. Was it the beginning of a new pogrom? The adults were afraid. His own father was afraid. Everyone Nissim knew was afraid. That was just before they left.

It was funny. Tourists in Israel didn't know the difference between him and an Arab. He would see them pass him, tense with mistrust, then turn in relief to an Anglo and ask directions. He hated the tourists for it. He was no Arab; Arabs were animals. They'd cheat you every time. They'd wipe you out in a minute. His balls pulled up every time he passed more than one Arab man on a quiet street. When he was a boy, he had wanted to run. Now he wanted to kill.

There were Jews in this country who didn't even look like Jews. Blond, towering, the women milky white. He wanted to make them see him and he thought that would happen now, because together they had a task: to keep the Arabs out. He was going to be valuable to them. They were going to forget that he was black. Shemtov Merhavi kept trying to buddy up with him, but he couldn't stand Merhavi. Superstitious, fearful, ignorant, he was the worst kind of black. Nissim wasn't going to be lumped in with him, the two Sephardim. He snubbed Merhavi and studied the Anglos. No one was going to mistake him for an Arab when he got finished in the army. He was going to be respected.

He and Shemtov had one thing in common, though. They knew Arabs. The Anglos were like children; they didn't understand their enemy at all. They thought it was some kind of game. Gershon talked about the Egyptians stepping up raids on the border, and he and the other Anglos saw a military maneuver. Shemmy and Nissim saw the black edge of nightmare. The Anglos bantered cheerfully—"Slap 'em down," they said; but Nissim saw his own face under the Arab's foot, a knife at his crotch. It was him or them. That was what the laughing Anglos didn't understand. They would learn.

Gershon drilled them in techniques for disarming an opponent in hand-to-hand combat, and Nissim ran the exercise with ferocious intensity. He sweated and his heart knocked hard against his breastbone. Parachutes and night hikes were fine, but this was what it was about: killing. He was better at hand-to-hand than anyone, and every time he disarmed a partner and stayed his arm in a ready position, he saw himself finishing it. He saw the Arab's face smashed under his rifle butt: one less.

At the end of the six weeks' basic they were all edgy—apprehensive about the jumping course and unsettled from the lack of sleep. Gershon, for the final week of basic, had let them sleep only five hours a day, in irregular patterns, and he drove them harder than ever. It was dawn when the fight broke out between Shemmy and the Moroccan, but they'd been up for hours. Gershon was in his tent, on the phone. They were scattered, eating an unidentified meal, perhaps lunch, and no one heard the argument begin. They turned around when they heard the voices sharpening and then suddenly Nissim was shouting, "Your words in your mother's teeth," and Shemmy was going for him. Dani and Atsmon started over to them to break it up. They lost sight of them over the rocks but in the early morning haze their voices were amplified.

"*Bondouk.*"

"What'd he call him?"

"Bastard."

"You *bondouk*. Of your mother and the men your father pimped for her. Spawn of a whore."

The words came at Dani, rebounded off rocks, confusing him. He stood still in the noise, heart pounding, but Atsmon kept going and pulled them apart. Atsmon shouted, Atsmon talked, chastised, settled them down while the sun dazzled Dani and the noise locked him to his foothold. By the time he reached them Nissim was smoothing his hair back with aloof, arched fingers and Shemmy was huddled with Lev and Bloch. Gershon never knew about the fight. One for Atsmon.

It was ten hours later—two meals after the fight—that Gershon noticed. "Shemtov, you're not eating?"

Shemmy shook his head grimly.

"You're not well?"

"I'm fine. I'm not hungry."

One of the kids told Dani later in the day. "Shemmy's fasting."

"What for?"

"He thinks Nissim cursed his food."

Dani snorted a laugh.

"Don't laugh. They're saying he could starve. It sometimes happens."

Dani went to find Nissim. It was getting dark. Nissim was in the latrine, peeing.

"Shemmy thinks you cursed his food."

The stream halted, started again. "Pfff. Let him think it."

"Did you?"

Nissim turned around, zipping up. "Women do that, cursing people. I don't do it. If I want to get him I'll do it face to face. You think I can't?"

"Why are you fighting?"

"I despise him. He's disgusting. Afraid of the dark, a child. A girl. He makes us look bad."

"Us?"

"Not you Anglos. *Us.* Blacks."

"You think people judge you by him?"

"Of course. Don't you?"

"Never once thought of it." In the darkening room Nissim's face gave him the lie. "Anyway, aren't you afraid of anything?"

"You think I am?"

"I know *I* am. To begin with I'm not too happy about jumping out of that Super Hornet next week. Are you?"

Nissim shrugged.

"Anyhow, Shemtov's not running away. He does the night marches, even if it's hard for him. You have to give him credit for that."

"Credit. You hold his hand—no offense, Dani, I mean it with respect—you baby him through the night marches."

"Last night he did one completely alone, and he wasn't the last one in."

"Probably ran all the way— 'Mommy, there's a demon after me!'"

"He did it. I hope I do as well jumping out of that damn helicopter. Listen, Nissim, I can tell him you didn't curse his food, or you can. You might need him someday."

"Hah."

"The longer he fasts the more people will notice, and that won't be good for you. They'll figure he's just another superstitious Oriental Jew. You can help him get their respect or you can confirm their prejudices. I don't care which you do." He walked out of the latrine.

At ten o'clock, before they went to sleep, they had another meal. Nissim looked up from his bowl. "Merhavi. I hear you did well in last night's march. I had a little trouble with the Uzi he gave me. It jammed. What'd you have?"

A pause. "A Kalachnikov."

"Any trouble?"

"No. No trouble."

"Hope I get a Kalachnikov next time. The Uzi is a bitch. Eat well, Merhavi. Good appetite."

Shemmy nodded, looked around defiantly, and bent his head to his bowl. He ate. *One for me, Atsmon.*

They didn't start out jumping from the Super Hornets. First they went off the wheel, then the tower, then the stationary airplane fuselage up on the blocks. Shemmy was a star. He seemed to control his falls—to float, choose his moment and his target, kiss down on it, tumble tight and easy, only for the sake of the choreography. Every time he finished a jump he looked up, ready for another.

Dani could do the jumps but he was unnerved by them. Jumping involved too many variables he couldn't control. From above, objects could be illusory in too many ways and there was never time to sort them out. He could manage his fear, the shock and lurch of freefall, the panicky timing of the pull. He could even, after the first few times, will himself to enjoy the moment of suspension after the chute opened— *ladies and gentlemen, the amazing floating human*—but it was only a moment and then there was the approaching earth, flying up to flatten or impale him—tree tops, rocks, veils of sand over treacherous abysses. Each time he jumped there was an instant when he felt himself in the clear, saw solid terrain below and waited, flinching into his bowels, for the ground to open, for the vicious, wheeling waters or the hidden blades of rock. Every time he came out of a tumble on innocent ground he knew he had accidentally hit right, one more lucky time too many. He counted. Six more jumps to qualify for the red beret.

The night jumps were the worst, an exercise in pure fatalism. This was not the darkness that hid him on the ground, yielded itself open to his easy delvings. This was black deceit, unseeable malevolence. Standing in the racket of the Super Hornet, the unrelenting noise magnified by the blackness took even the illusion of decision from him. *All right*, he said each time to the night, *take me then*, and let himself go, so far past fear that his bowels didn't churn or his mouth go dry and he almost forgot that he must do things to pretend to control his fall. Some separate part of his mind counted . . . four, five . . . and moved his hand to pull the cord. He was thinking, nonsensically—This must be what it feels like to be a girl—when that separate function jolted into action, focused downward, found shapes, pulled tendons in, tumbled him over, meeting earth. He learned nothing from his safe landings; the three night jumps were all the same—the passive hurtling into certain death, the curious passionless resignation and the inexplicable feeling that this was how it was to be a girl, and the sudden unwilled rush of energy that landed him. If there were fifty night jumps they would all have been the same.

Some layer of self was peeled away in this falling, and that may have been why he got drawn into the talk in the late night and found himself inventing a father.

"My old man would think the End of Days was here," Shemmy chortled, "if he had to do the jumps. Those old people, when they airlifted them from home—from Yemen—they had to pry their fingers from the plane."

"Mine is a paratrooper," Bloch said. "He was with Danny Matt in Jerusalem. He says they never really jump in combat any more."

"If my mother knew I was jumping out of planes—" Nissim started.

"Mine, too," Dani put in. "She had a fit about my signing up for paratroopers."

"Ehu's air force, you know," Lev said. "He was stand-by for Motti Atsmon's raid, in fact. So this is no big thing to him or Onat. Same for you, Judah?"

Atsmon nodded.

"When my mother started making a fuss," Dani heard himself saying, "my father soon took care of it. Women."

"Yeah."

He saw him, a tall and solid man, taking Rachaeli in hand and calming her. Winking at him: I'll take care of this, son.

"—do? Dani?"

"What?"

"What's he do?"

"Who?"

"Your *father*."

He cast around. What does a father do? "Diamonds."

Whistles. "So you're loaded."

"No. Well, let's just say he's in diamonds. I'm not supposed to talk about him. Okay?"

Respectful nods. They understood. He almost had him for a moment, the big, solid man who didn't discuss his work, who easily controlled Rachaeli, and whose hand gripped Dani's shoulder. Then he lost him again. They were kidding Lev and he laughed with them, too loud.

They are in the Galilee, camped out by the Jordan, an afternoon in the first six months of infantry warfare training. By now they are trained to sleep four hours a night, any time and anywhere, to put consciousness down easily and pick it up instantly. They are learning to be sudden and deadly, hand killers. Grappling, throwing, judo, silent throttling. They can shoot at a distance, too, or handle demolition and they can assault in cadre, but sudden hand-to-hand attack is primary. "The Arab is afraid of night; we fight him at night," they are told. "He is mortally afraid of hand-to-hand combat; we engage him hand-to-hand. He who frightens the other by playing on his weaknesses has won. Surprise. Darkness. Hand-to-hand. Whenever and wherever possible."

In comparison the guns are pleasant, a puzzle, really. They make Dani long for his Buatier Pull and the scarfs and hollow balls, and that is how he comes to try the Jumping Stone trick on the others. They've spent hours today on weapon drill. Blindfolded, they're handed a weapon and they have to figure out instantly how to work it. Exhausted and thirsty, they're yelled at, pummeled, startled by loud reports, and someone shoves a firearm—Russian, British, American, Swedish—rifle, sub-machine, pistol, assault gun, anything—into their hands. They have to disassemble, reassemble, load, stand to fire. The blindfold is calming to Dani—he concentrates better with it on—and the gadgetry intrigues him. Like magic tricks it's all balance, fit, settle and click, shift and reshift, and—hey, presto!—fire away.

So he's high and excited there in the Galilee in the late afternoon after weapon drill. Hands still buzzing, he fiddles with his flashlight. Unscrew it, drop out the batteries, then the spring. Now back: spring, positive end, negative end, insert top, screw and again unscrew. He thinks of the Jumping Stone and he smiles, pockets the spring, ambles off to gather things up.

"Where you going? It's almost time to catch a snake for dinner."

"Latrine. Back right away. I don't think I want any snake tonight. I may have a root or a berry. Don't sit on my supper while I'm gone."

He gets his bowl, snatches up a few sugar lumps from supply and hunts around for a little stone, hefts a couple in his hand, finds the right one. Now what? Lev's harmonica. He paws through Lev's gear—a tangle, as always—and comes up with the harmonica. Good. Shoving everything into his pocket he fills the bowl three-quarters full with silty water from the river, then sets the flashlight spring into the water, standing it upright like a little cylinder. He peers in. Not perfect but good enough; it's obscured. He tries one sugar cube. Not heavy enough to weight the spring. He adds another. Two does it. Ready. He tosses out the wet sugar cubes.

He goes back toward the group, carrying the bowl carefully before him. "The Galilee lives," he intones. They look up. "Even the stones of the Galilee live."

He sits cross-legged on the ground facing them, palming two sugar lumps onto the spring under the guise of settling the waters and quickly drawing their eyes to the stone in his left hand. He holds the stone up, turns it in his fingers, sets it deliberately in the bowl of water, balancing it on the sugar cubes. "Watch." He begins to play tunelessly on Lev's harmonica, keeping his eyes on the bowl of water. He is the only one who sees the little stir in the water as the sugar cubes melt away. He reaches out his hand just as the stone springs from the water. It seems to leap obediently into his palm. He passes the stone to Nissim, meanwhile pouring out the water and palming the spring. He passes the bowl around. "Even the stones of the Galilee live," he flourishes.

"Terrific."

"How did you—"

"Do it again." Nissim, grinning a challenge.

He ignores it, turns away from Nissim.

"Do it again."

"Without putting your hand in your pocket first. I'll fill the bowl for you." Shemmy, laughing with Nissim.

Dani shakes his head in solemn refusal. "The Galilee moves at its own will. It cannot be forced." They hoot and laugh some more. Atsmon smiles over his cigarette. Dani hides his anger and joins the clowning. Later Gershon takes him aside.

"Don't feel bad," he says. "These Oriental kids aren't easy to fool. They're refugees, you know, from another world. They see things more clearly than the rest of us, because everything's new to them here, and they can only afford to believe what they see. No illusions, you know what I mean?"

Like Anni. "Yeah."

"So they're tough to fool with magic tricks. It makes them great soldiers in this kind of unit, though, because they're used to looking around fast, getting a fix on a place, picking up whatever's useful—adapting to where they are and what they have. And just try to take something away from them . . ."

"Yeah—"

"See, so they're great material. You don't fight it, you use it."

"Right."

Gershon was talking to him as though he were an officer, as though it were assumed between them. And in fact everyone assumed it. When Gershon gave them the questionnaire after basic that asked them to write down the names of those among their group they'd like to have as officers, everyone wrote down Atsmon's name and many wrote down Dani's.

He wrote down his own name. You didn't have to have Motti Atsmon for a father, to be an officer. He'd be a better officer than Atsmon because he'd had to be his own father, so he knew how. Baby Atsmon was going to follow his daddy. He, Dani, would be father to his men. They would follow him into the jaws of hell when Atsmon was sucking his thumb in the desert. Chew on it, Atsmon.

He began on Shemmy one night after supper. He got him alone.

"Shemmy."

"What?"

"Tell me about the night. You know, darkness, how you feel."

Shemmy looked at him, betrayal black in his eyes, but Dani wasn't deterred.

"Because . . . was everyone in your family like that? In Yemen?"

"What are you talking about?"

"Is it just you—like some people are afraid of heights—or, you know, is it a cultural thing? Because if it is, we can really use it."

"Go shit in your yogurt."

"Shemmy, this is important. You can tell us what goes on in their heads, out there in the night. What they fear, how it makes them react." He sounded convincing to himself. He liked the sound of it; it had a rhythm and a power.

"You said you wouldn't tell them."

"I won't tell them. But *you* could tell *us*. Think for a minute, will you? You're in the desert. It's pitch dark. Out there somewhere is a Syrian unit. You're going to kill them or they're going to kill you. You've got to use everything you have, right? Right?"

"So?"

"So one of the things you have is, you know what's going on in their heads. Everything they've been taught to fear. You can play on it, use it, turn it against them. Shemmy, you're a *resource*."

Shemtov looked at him, uncertain now. Wary, wavering. Like just before a trick breaks and the audience is ready to yield to wonder.

"And if you talk about it maybe you won't feel it as much. Anyway, we're a unit, right? Shouldn't we help you with it and shouldn't you be a resource for us?"

"They won't want to hear it."

Ah, he's over. "Sure they will. Shemmy, you're going to save a life. Somewhere, some time, one of us is going to live because of you."

So now Shemtov Merhavi sat on the ground and told all of them about being afraid. They were nineteen years old and they listened without looking at each other. Shemmy talked and talked, now that he had begun, looking fixedly at an invisible screen and reporting what he saw on it. Dani kept quiet but sat at a little distance from them and nearer to Shemmy, and he caught their eyes from time to time so they'd remember who was running this.

"You hear things. Something . . . seems to be behind you, waiting. You feel it there; it sees you, you don't see it. It gets hard to breathe and you want to run"—Shemmy looked swiftly around but no one was making fun of him—"but no place seems safe to run to, it's all dark. They have a saying, 'The night holds a thousand enemies.' So you stand still. You *feel* it, like it's sending waves, your throat closes and you think you might do something stupid—"

"And if someone jumped you?" It was Atsmon, frowning in thought.

Shemmy's arms pulled in close to his ribs. He shook his head.

"Would it be worse if you heard him coming?"

"No." That was Nissim. "Because if you heard the footsteps you'd at least know where it was, and that it was human . . ."

Shemmy nodded, eyes on Nissim in grateful surprise.

"So if someone came up silently on you—" Dani jumped in, nailing down the point before Atsmon could open his mouth again.

"You'd plotz," Bloch said, breaking the intensity. They laughed.

"I don't know that word, *plotz*, but it sounds right." Shemmy was okay now. "Dani came up on me that night when I was lost pathfinding and I—I fainted."

"My God."

"You got it. That's plotzing."

"I'll take an unconscious enemy every time," Dani summed up triumphantly.

"So we should practice sneaking up," Atsmon put in. "Except not on Shemmy."

"No, I think I'd be better now. And"—Shemmy was in command now—"grab for the throat. That's where all the panic is, in the back of the neck and the throat."

They started to fool around then, grabbing at each other, and Dani organized them into pairs. Gershon watched and saw it happen again, a bunch of kids turning themselves into a unit.

They were learning to be sudden and deadly and to kill close to, with intimacy, and when they had leave they looked urgently for girls. Nearly all of them needed to get rid of their innocence—it took longer to lose than simple virginity—but as far as he could tell, only Dani had a policy about it. He had to be careful.

He'd never heard the barracks word for penis before—*zayin*, weapon—but he recognized its truth the first time he heard it and he made a joke about it. He told it only to himself, of course. Right, but mine's loaded, he thought. One shot and I make a bastard. I should carry a sign: "Beware, loaded *zayin*. Deadly bastard-bullets, cripple for ten generations."

He was nineteen, almost twenty. No one in his unit knew the truth about him, and none of the girls he met were old enough to have heard the story or to connect it with his name, but still he wasn't free. He was what he was, a weapon of destruction.

He was nervously waiting his turn with a whore for the first time when it struck him: Shlomo was right. He was tainted. His kids would be bastards, too, even if he did nothing wrong. And *their* kids, and so on. He had no particular feeling for children, so he made the decision simply and painlessly, savoring the nobility of it there in the hallway of the whore's flat: he must never father a child. He fingered the condom in its foil wrapping in his pocket—army issue—and he decided to use it. That was going to be his policy. He felt older at once, and in command.

"You don't need to use that, honey; I'm clean," the whore said.

"Don't be offended. It has nothing to do with clean. I'm protecting my kids."

"*You* have kids?"

"No."

"I don't get it."

She didn't have to get it. He was in control here. No kids; he was going to see to it.

Whores were boring, though, and demeaning. It was all an act with them, and he was the dupe in it. He looked for girls to date; there were no fathers to answer to in the army, and there were plenty of girls who weren't asking any questions. He avoided the flashy ones, although they looked at him. They ran their fingers through their hair and smiled teasingly, and they made him uneasy. They seemed dangerous to him, untrustworthy. The safer, quieter girls presented another problem—he couldn't relax with them. They wanted to know him but he couldn't allow that, because any little detail might give him away and then they'd reject him. It got so that he was angry at that kind of girl on the first date. The soft looks, the probing questions, and the opening confidences would irritate him until he'd play with the idea of telling the girl, shocking her. He never did, of course, because then everyone would know, so instead he would treat the girl to an evening of offhand rudeness and rough combat talk until she'd get the point and begin to edge away.

He tended, after a while, to the breezy ones who got by without too many words and who didn't mind being interchangeable. Most of them were on the Pill, but they didn't care if he used the condom, and if one ever asked about it he mentioned that he was a carrier of a rare genetic disorder. They didn't dwell on it much; settling down was far from their thoughts. Anyway, he became very good at taking their minds off it. He got to be good with women.

It was Dina who had taught him. She was the only one he'd explained it to, and that was because she was the first. He'd never been to bed with a woman who wasn't a whore. It was, in fact, his first date since Shira Ofek. Dina was older, twenty-six, a divorcée. She was a ballistics instructor, and right away their first time out, he told her his joke about being a loaded *zayin*. He told himself that he needed to find out what a woman would say, but it was really panic. He couldn't think of another thing to talk about.

She was shocked. "Ten generations of *what*?"

"Bastards. That's how it works."

"Oh my God, what garbage. Why? Just because your mother wasn't married?"

"No, because she was." He explained the law.

"Well, that's crazy. Listen, I'm not planning to have children, but I'll tell you what I'd do if I were and if I got pregnant by a—by someone like you. I'd *have* the kid and never say a word. I'd bring it up like anyone else."

"That would be wrong. That's why I'm always going to take care of things—contraception—myself." He liked this conversation. Her face was flushed and she was heated. She leaned forward to make her point, her breasts grazing her arms. They were going to do it that very night, he could tell; they were already talking about contraception. It gave him an edge, having this policy. It made him the controlling one. "Because you have to keep things straight. Bloodlines. I have no idea who or what my father was and therefore I'm never going to father children."

"You're—what, twenty? You'll change your mind." She smiled at him but he didn't like the smile. It put her at a distance, feeling older and smiling at him.

"Not about this. Anyway, I think a man ought to protect a girl. She shouldn't have to think about anything but . . . her feelings." He looked directly into her eyes until she flushed again and looked down. Ah, better. He had her.

But later, in her bed in the dark, it went very fast and at the end it was like the night jumps. It wasn't like what he knew, his own hand, and there was so much at once—the scent of her, the shock of her nipples touching against his skin, the little murmurings, her electric touch, that by the time he entered her he could only think, *All right, then, take me,* and jump out untethered into black freefall, abandoning himself to whatever might be reaching for him to swallow him alive. Afterward, when he collapsed panting on suddenly still terrain, she ran comforting fingers through his hair, over and over, as though he were a child sobbing himself to sleep there on her breast.

Worse, later they talked about it. "I have to please women," he said, asking her. "I can never be a father or husband, so I have to give them something. Pleasure."

She took a long time to answer. "You'll learn," she told him finally. "Pleasure isn't what you think; pleasure is what happens along the way."

"You didn't—"

"It's okay. Next time we'll go a longer way around." She was assuming that they would meet again; cold with humiliation, he resolved never to see her again, and he wouldn't have, but he was still in her flat an hour later, they were sitting on the couch smoking and trading army stories, and she started him up again. He was wearing an old robe of hers and she opened it and touched him lightly. He jumped at her touch. "You're beautiful," she said, and something had changed in her face and the rhythm of her breathing. He felt himself stir. "I bet you'll hold on longer this time," she whispered.

He followed her wretchedly into the bedroom, cock straight out under her ridiculous robe. She held out a hand and smiled indulgently. "Come on." There was no way out. Smiling women. Laughing women. They thought you were a child to be controlled. He wriggled out of the robe and dropped it, following her into bed. Longer, hold out longer this time. Count to fifty, pull the cord. He went to enter her. "Not yet. Touch me. Should I show you?"

She showed him. He was quick; he caught on and he had good hands and suddenly she was moving her hips in a slow, demanding way, reaching for him. He tried to hold on to his resentment but he was kissing her and mixed up with her, breathing with breathing, sounds with sounds. She set the pace; he abandoned himself to those relentless hips, warm whirlpool. *All right, then, take—*

"Take me," she hissed suddenly into his ear. So instead of falling he jumped open-eyed, jolted to it, a longer, slower plunge.

"Told you," she breathed.

Shut up, shut up, I'm in my own good place. He put a controlling hand on her, to quiet her down.

So he kept coming back to her until her reserve duty was over, learning the click and shift of it, getting the balance, improving the act.

Aaron is with a whore. He's letting her undress him and he isn't saying a word. This is his sixteenth woman, thirteenth whore. He likes to go with regular girls but he likes the whores best because of two things: keeping quiet and being blown. With regular girls you can score—it isn't really scoring with whores because they have to; you pay them—but it's like being home all over again. You have to say what they want to hear, you have to be a certain type they want you to be, you have to figure out how they're feeling and what they're thinking. And then once you start with them, they surround you. He's had enough of that.

It popped into his mind about the day he left for basic. His mother insisted on coming to see him off and he was sure she'd do something humiliating, so he was furious before they even started out. Normal mothers didn't behave the way she and Anni did—hovering, studying you, inspecting you, conferring over everything you said and didn't say, panicking all the time. Crying. He hated them for not controlling themselves. Anyway, there she was at the bus and he was waiting for it to happen and then she was . . . blank. No emotion at all, like she didn't care. Just waved him off. Then what the hell did she come for?

The whore has him naked now, and she leads him over to the sink. "You don't say much," she offers.

"I'm enjoying just being quiet."

"That's good. Some guys talk you deaf."

She soaps his balls and cock and he closes his eyes. He doesn't even want to see her in the mirror.

He loves the army. It's a relief, not having to worry about everyone's feelings all the time. And he loves the tank corps. He's met guys from other services who said they wouldn't be able to take it in the armored, having to follow orders without even discussing them—it's the only service in IDF that operates that way—but he likes it. First of all, it makes sense. You couldn't operate blind in a tank without someone directing you. Secondly, this way you aren't responsible for things. The captain says load, you load. He says turn, fire; you turn, you fire. You can't be wrong. You can't disappoint anyone. All his life he's had to be a mind reader. *Grandma wanted you to go with her.* She didn't say it. *She shouldn't have to say it; you should know.* Read Mother's moods, don't leave her alone when she's blue, don't send her into a panic by being late. Don't ever be late. Figure out what you can and can't mention to the cronies. Figure out what answer the teacher wants to hear. Figure out what Father expects you to say about the page of Talmud. All of them waiting with their mouths shut for you to be wrong. He doesn't need three years of that in the army.

"Lie down, honey. What do you want?"

"Would you mind blowing me."

"Fine with me, honey. Want to go around the world? It's twenty-five lirot more, but I'm good."

"Okay."

He closes his eyes so she has no face. This is what he loves. No emotional scenes, no talking at all. She prods him to turn over and he feels it warm and wet on his asshole. She could be a slave; she has to do this. Ministering to him. All he has to do is lie there. It's up to her.

He wants more but she rolls him over and goes to work on his cock, and he lets her. He's not moving or saying a word. It's all up to her. He covers his face with the bend of his arm, in case anything is showing. Slave girl, he could do anything to her but he's good, he lies helpless as a baby and lets her do him. His legs are splayed out and he's heavy, immobile, speechless, faceless, she's doing it without a word doing it without a word doing it without—

During the next year and a half some of them used what Shemmy had taught them about darkness and fear. They were fighting in a sporadic, undeclared war. Incidents occurred on the border like dusty dreams: they were engulfed in them abruptly, the incidents seemed to have no definition or expectable duration; then they burst and dust drifted away and someone was dead.

They were nineteen and twenty, twenty-one. They had memorized Israel by foot, sand dunes and gullies from the borders of Lebanon to the borders of Egypt, but now they were pinned to the banks of the Jordan and the land wouldn't stay still to be learned. The sands shifted so that Tuesday's landscape was like Monday's and not like it. You couldn't count on getting a fix on anything.

Every other night, in shifts, they lay in the dessicated riverbed from 8:00 till 5:00 A.M. and waited for terrorists to try to infiltrate. You could tell where things were moving by the clouds of dust they raised in the moonlight. But if you moved they would see you as well by your cloud of dust. You could point a projector at the enemy and illuminate your target, but if you did that, you pinpointed your own position. So you lay still and concentrated on piercing the dark by ear and waited; you had one chance to spring. Or you used the dark and the night wind and crept up on them, drawing on Shemmy's lesson and—sudden, deadly, knife to throat—you killed.

These weren't regular Arabs, though; they were Al Fatah—tough, motivated commandos. And they were picking the moments to infiltrate. They had the advantage; they knew *when*.

Before he made his first kill, Dani had nightmares. He dreamed of shrinking, suddenly, in the face of an oncoming man, so that distances were immeasurably lengthened and his strength was desperately inadequate. The dreams were protracted, unresolved, draining. But they weren't as bad as the other dream, where he killed. He had that one just before he actually made the first kill. In it, the scene was from regular life, some benign everyday place. A man approached and Dani knew (dream-knowing, instant and certain) that it was his father and that he had all the time in the world (dream time) to decide how to speak to him. Bankrolls of time uncurled at one end—time to plumb the man, assimilate him, use, choose, have. Then as he framed the first question the man glimmered into something else, a threat. Infiltrator. A parched riverbed was all there was between them, he was coming fast and Dani was unprepared. Desperate, he raised a knife and the man glimmered back into father. He shifted like the demonic sand, father/terrorist/father, until finally Dani, wailing fear and outrage, had to plunge the knife into the body, whoever it was. Then he woke up, carrying dream-certainty with him, unshakable in daylight: the man had been his father.

Because of the dream he hesitated for a second before striking the commando who came upon him the next night. The darkness turned in an instant into a moving form and Dani moved automatically, pulsed by adrenaline, to kill, but the dream befuddled him for a moment so he held his arm a second and then had time only to thrust the knife heavily through oncoming weight. Accidentally it hit right and the man died, not swiftly and silently but in a hot rush of sticky, animal-smelling blood, and with loud, unnerving groans. Then there was dead weight, thud and recoil, silence.

Oh, it was simple, death. An unrepeatable, perfect trick: now here, now simply gone. Dani vomited in quick response and was left with the sour taste and the sourer thought that came next: so was birth. His own birth was a simple thing, too: the piercing of the wall of one thing by another in an instant, and he was made. Randomly connected up. That was a terrible thought.

There was a lot of talking when they weren't on border patrol or in ambush. On camp patrol they talked on the phone to each other, incessant small talk. They talked face to face and with walkie-talkies, and when they had to keep quiet they framed stories for later. The killings they told over and over but Dani wasn't ready to tell his when he got back to camp, because it felt heavy and shameful, like a failure, and because he had to sort it out from the crazy dream he'd had. Everything was shifting; nothing held still to be what it was. Nothing was simply one thing. Sand blew at you; you couldn't trust what you saw; you couldn't trust anything.

Avoiding sleep, he sat patrol with Shemmy at camp that night and listened to one of the Yemenite's convoluted stories of family vengeance in the old country.

"They went in strength, you know? Fifteen, twenty of them, maybe more. The thing had to be done. Even the boys went, two or three of them under twelve . . . their father, after all. You, Dani, you'd do it for yours."

"Hmmm?"

"I say, you'd avenge your father's name. Even—"

"No."

"What?"

"No, I wouldn't. I haven't got a father, Shemmy."

It had to be said. He was so tired. He was tired of keeping up the pretense. He was exhausted by the effort of blocking out of his mind the heavy fall of the body onto his knife, the sound and smell of the blood bubbling out, and the flickering knowledge that the dead weight was his father. He couldn't begin to rest until he told someone about the killing, and he couldn't begin to do that until he explained about his father and the dream. He was desperate for things to hold still. He needed someone here to know him, to help him hold them still. For the first time, he longed for Aaron, his old easy mirror. It would be a simple thing to tell Aaron the dream and the killing. But there was no one here except Shemmy. He had no choice but to tell Shemmy.

"He died, Dani? My God, I'm sorry. When?"

"He didn't die, or anyway I don't know. I never had a father. I'm a bastard."

"But the . . . you said diamonds—"

"A lie. My mother was married, she had . . . some other man. It was a whole big case in the papers. I'm a famous bastard, in fact."

"Oh my God." Shemmy said it wide-eyed, behind a spread hand, like a girl. "You have no one?" He was horrified.

"Sure. My mother, two older half-brothers, friends."

"But . . . your own people? Who stands up for you? Who do you go to?"

Dani wanted to smile, thinking of Shemmy's tribe of toothless old reprobates puffing away on their water pipes and awaiting the Messiah. But the boy was sincere; he looked as though he might cry for Dani. It was good he had told; he felt in control again. He gave Shemmy a little arm punch. "Wouldn't you stand up for me?"

"My word on it." The kid was deadly solemn.

He killed more Al Fatah before he went to officers' training, and he learned that it was always somewhat accidental, or seemed so. It always came at you too fast. You always moved a little too slowly. That was all right, once he got the feel of it. If that was all there was to it, he could be an officer.

To command means to betake oneself to the point of greatest danger.

There are no excuses for staying behind. When no order has been received, imagine what the order would be.

In case of doubt, strike. The shortcut to security is the road to the enemy's hill.

Do not attack head-on; there is usually a better approach.

If you must attack head-on, arrange things so that you don't present a broad target.

When the troops are really exhausted, stop and let them rest.

Do not put off combat for want of provisions; provisions are probably on the way to you.

When you are caught in enemy fire it is better to move than to dig in.

Always try for surprise in one form or another.

When you attack, dare, dare, dare.

—GENERAL S.L.A. MARSHALL

Audacity and ingenuity. Those were the prime qualities they looked for in officers, especially for the paratroopers. Atsmon went to officers' training, another guy from the unit went, and Dani went. Atsmon had natural command and courage, so he could manufacture a kind of dignified facsimile of audacity, but Dani was the real thing. He knew he was.

To command means to betake oneself to the point of greatest danger.

Damn right. In the months of officers' training he learned command techniques, supplies, communications, offensive and defensive tactics, and the rhythms of assault. Staging. It was a game, a puzzle; you could practice it and master it so that the dazzle, the startle were in your hands and so that the enemy, dazed, off balance, took the extra moment to respond. Timing and dazzle, that was mostly it. He dreamed the staging of an assault; he rehearsed it in two scenes.

Scene: He waits. It is the real war, future time, and they've been sent in behind enemy lines to take out the antitank missiles. Their tank corps is stymied, paralyzed by constant electronic ambushes. He's been dropped with his small, hand-picked unit to free them up. There is no moon. A little wind. In the darkness he puts a hand on Shemmy's shoulder. Shemtov gives him thumbs up: he's fine. They know what to do. Bayonet in hand, Dani goes forward himself to see if the area is mined. He picks his way deftly over the control wires littering the ground from the spent missiles. His men can't see him in the dense black night, and they don't stir. He will assay the night for his men and they will advance in his path, in safety. They know that. They wait.

He comes back. To the west it's mined. To the east, it's safe. There are three missile sites: here, here, and here, heavily manned. Silently he deploys them, his boys, but he is the first. Follow me. It's synchronized, a spare choreography of dispatch. Three teams cut through the night and hold their positions: Ready. Ready. Ready.

He is the diversion. He sets off his flares by remote, draws their notice. Messieurs, your attention please. Dazzle and startle, three Arab missile teams shift their eyes. Dani's boys, three perfectly trained ambush units, drop, seize, throttle, knife, destroy. Without missing a beat, he spots the officers, two of them and their lieutenants. He shouts to them in Arabic— "This way!"—and, thrown off, they stop, turn. He shoots while they waver, picks them off crisp and fast, disappears them into pockets of night. Top that, Atsmon.

> Scene: Chava's flat.
> Cast: Chava and Anni, weeping in gratitude, background. Aaron, stage left, in civvies, passive. Center stage, Dani, on crutches, in uniform, fatigues and older. Upstage of Dani, Shlomo, hands in pockets, a little shaken.

Shlomo speaks: "Did you know it, when you took out the antitank missiles, that they were preparing to fire on your bro—on Aaron's unit?"
Dani: "No. We just knew there were tanks stuck out there."
Shlomo: "Five more minutes, ten, they'd have fired on them. Aaron would have been killed."
He lays a hand on Dani's shoulder. A benediction passes from man to man. No one can ever give Shlomo what Dani has given him. Certainly not Aaron.
Pause.
Hush.
House lights.

Later, in the fall of that year, 1972, he told Ronit that fantasy of his. He was telling her everything. She didn't smile when he told it to her; she put one palm against his face and kissed him. She meant to kiss it away, replace it with herself, but instead she sealed it. She couldn't have known that.

He was out of active service and in the reserves then. He had Shemmy in his unit, and Nissim and Lev and Bloch, as well as a bunch of younger kids. He kept up with them, Shemmy especially, right after they went off active service. Shemmy had a job as a typesetter. Nissim's hair was growing in; he was working in a garage, saving up for a car. Lev and Bloch were at university. After a while they had to manufacture occasions to see one another and their contact tapered off.

Dani missed them. It was jarring, stepping back into the world he'd left. It was like emerging from the stage lights; you went backstage and everyone knew it was just you; they could see all your props. The civilian world was old, full of people older than him. Funny, the army had seemed to be the zenith of maturity when they were in high school, but now the generations had fallen into place all around him and he was just a kid again, surrounded once more by people any one of whom might know his story, people who could pinpoint the salacious details if they wanted to jog their memories. He had no chance for anonymity in this world. Well, let it go. It was just a kid thing, really, keeping the big secret.

But he missed the freedom of first names and he missed the pulse and tension of defense and he missed the nighttime maneuvers, the easy darkness. There was no one in this pallid, workaday world he wanted to seek out.

Aaron was at Bar Ilan, studying criminology. He liked it, studying what made people do criminal things, how to balance out evil with justice. Dani saw Aaron now and then, when they met at Chava and

Shlomo's. They had very little in common. Dani wasn't in school, for one thing, and Aaron seemed childish to him with his studies and his university circle of friends and his solemn commitment to an ordered world.

Dani knew there was no order in the world. He'd learned it from Anni and Chava; they'd never seemed to notice that he was around when they talked over his head, and certainly no one had ever tried to protect him from the talk. And now his work taught him daily that chaos was the natural order of things and that the hardest task in the world was establishing a single fact. Not truth, just a fact. Facts hid, people hid them, time blurred them—even fractions of a minute did—they flickered out and re-emerged as other, slightly different facts.

He was a newsman. It turned out to be his ticket back to the nighttime world. Out of active service he'd gone to work for *Maariv* as a part-time stringer. Before long—they were short-handed and he was nervy and persistent—he got them to take him on staff. He worked graveyard, putting the paper to bed at nine in the morning. It suited him perfectly. For just a few minutes, early in the morning they had in type an accounting of the previous day's events, fixed insofar as their information went. Sometimes you actually pinned something down. Sometimes two facts or two events crossed and made a truth. At any rate, no one in Israel was less deceived than he was, he and his co-workers in the early hours of every morning.

Then too, he was just getting going when everyone else was tired, so he was always catching his subjects off balance. He'd get up, shower, have a coffee and a roll, and head off to check things out. It would be the very end of everyone's working day and they'd be tired, off their guard, one foot at home already. "So what's today's version of the truth, General?" he'd ask, and follow it with a series of good-humored, tricky questions. Half the time they'd say more than they meant to. Half the time was enough.

Best of all, he was on a different schedule from everyone he'd ever known, especially Rachaeli. There was no question of his being able to afford his own flat, so he was living at home, but it worked out fine once he was on the graveyard shift. She was gone when he came home to sleep and he was just getting ready to go to work when she came home. He didn't even think of it as living with his mother. He was twenty-one. Home was a place to sleep and change clothes.

She had him home. She'd unpacked his stuff every time he'd come home on leave, searching for clues, and each time she'd repacked clean clothes and reminders of home. Gifts. The clues were in what was missing: she couldn't teach him not to give his things away. He didn't seem to care what belonged to him and it infuriated her.

"You left your shirt behind?"

"What shirt?"

"The new one you took with you last time. Plaid, from America. No-iron."

"Plaid . . . oh, I think I lent it to Nissim."

"Wasn't he the one who took your pocket knife and never gave it back?"

"He lost it, I told you a thousand times."

"Therefore you lent him the shirt."

"He was going out."

Some kid with greasy hair and body odor was wearing the shirt she gave Dani, the one that opened just so at the neck, and he'd never see it again. Or he would but it would be everyone's going-out shirt, common property. She was fighting tears suddenly, so enraged she was afraid to speak. She wanted to hurt him, dig her ten fingers into his arms and leave ten marks. "Stop it, you have to stop it!" she wanted to scream at him. "You have to stop giving everything away!" But screaming was like begging, and she was damned if she'd beg. Anyway, she could handle him. She smiled pityingly and rubbed her hand over his curls. "My Dani," she said. "He'll be your friend as long as you keep giving him things?"

He looked annoyed. "What are you talking about? He's just a guy who needed to borrow a shirt. It's just a shirt."

She was clever and she said nothing, but she thought she'd planted a seed. And she decided that when she gave him things, she would have them monogrammed.

But she had him home now and she was keeping track of everything. She checked his comings and goings, she listened for recurring names, she teased confidences from him. He'd gotten through the army unscathed: no intense friendships, no idols, no older man whose protégé he'd been. So far there was nothing to fear.

He had the late court beat. He was looking for an angle, and the editor suggested that he investigate the night kids—young delinquents who hung around on the streets at night, in gangs. He'd never come into contact with them before. Day people didn't, unless they had their pocketbooks snatched or made use of the street girls.

The girls were young teenagers; they did a big business in Arabs. Dani wrote an article about them for *Maariv*. ARABS ARE FUCKING US, his headline said. The article went on to say that one of the secondary effects of the '67 war was that Arabs could now get on a bus to Tel Aviv and screw Israeli girls rather than buggering each other, previously the only outlet for boys who had no access to girls of their own culture. The night editor killed the story but he let Dani do a series on the kids.

They were fourteen, fifteen, sixteen. They'd dropped out of school. They came from the areas south of Tel Aviv—Or Yehuda, Hatikvah—and from development towns like Kiryat Shmona and Bat Yam. They came from broken homes, or their parents were helpless to control them, or their fathers brutalized them, or there were just too many kids in the family. The older kids who might have controlled them were in the army. The ones who were left were army rejects—illiterates, degenerates, kids with prison records, the unbalanced ones—and they taught the young ones every kind of hustle. No one had to teach them vandalism; that they invented on their own.

There was a gang that hung around the alleys of Jaffa. Dani moved in on them. He wandered around the nighttime streets in black jeans and an open shirt, keeping quiet. They couldn't make out who he was. He wasn't exactly a grownup. He didn't seem to want anything from them. He didn't carry a notebook, never wrote anything down, never asked a name. They tried picking his pocket; he was too fast for them, but he reacted with good humor: "Slow hands," he said. "You've got to make it fly to you, right out of the pocket—whoops—like that." He materialized a coin, seemingly out of the kid's pocket. "Then you've got to stash it before anyone notices." He disappeared the coin. "Like that, right?" Then he pulled a coin from behind the kid's ear. "This belong to you?" He was weird, they decided, but not weak and not dangerous either.

The girls offered their various specialties, figuring him for a shy customer. He gave them cigarettes, kidded them, but never went to bed with any of them. They chatted away in the slow times, told him about their customers. After a while he told them about his editor, trading stories, gaining their confidence.

He wasn't hiding who he was, it was just that they had no conversational skills so they had to keep bumping him, like dolphins, to find out what he was and what he wanted.

He wanted their stories. They gave them up, fact by fact, with little shrugs and frowns as though he should have known all this.

Shalom Khaduri was fourteen. He had nine younger brothers and sisters. His father was crippled: he earned a living by having kids. More kids, more welfare. "He drinks and waits for the welfare check," Shalom said.

"I have a friend whose father smokes and waits for the Messiah."

"The what?"

Dani explained. The kid shrugged. "The welfare comes sooner."

Shalom's hustle was purse snatching. He was good. He'd never been caught.

Zadok Raz was on parole already, for vandalism and theft. They'd caught him stripping a car. He liked it better in jail than at home. At home his father chained them to the bed to discipline them. Half the time he went out and forgot them. Or worse, someone would come in and find them there, chained up like a dog. "Don't write that," Zadok blurted. "You write that, I'll get you."

"I won't," Dani assured him, and he didn't, although it was questionable whether Zadok would ever have known; half these kids were illiterate.

Avigdor Gabai had no father. He lived surrounded by women at home—mother, grandmother, sisters. Even the social worker was a woman. There was one uncle living with them, his mother's brother, but he was a drug addict so you could hardly call him a man, Avigdor said.

"Why not?" Dani asked.

Avigdor looked at him. "Addicts can't get it up. They can't do nothing. They don't even *want* to. Didn't you know that?"

"No."

"You don't know much."

"I know about not having a father. I don't have one either."

266

"Yeah?"

"I never had one. I'm a bastard."

It was the first time he'd said it to anyone since the night he told Shemmy. He said it deliberately, magnanimously, thinking that he'd finally found a use for his illegitimacy. It was a connection; they were both outsiders, it would open things up between them. But Avigdor's face closed over, the careful distance of superiority. He dragged on his cigarette. "Mine died," he said. "And my mother, she doesn't go with men. My sisters either; I see to it."

His mother doesn't go with men. A toothless, raggy, dim-witted woman with tits down to her knees, Dani told himself in a startling rush of fury. Her brother's on drugs and her son knocks down old ladies for their handbags and breaks telephone boxes for the coins and he's trying to tell me they're better than my mother and me? He conjured up Rachaeli, tall and pretty, smiling, flushed, her hair curling carelessly around her face. Perfume. Wit. Codes. Music. Style. "My mother's dead," he said coldly to Avigdor. "She died when I was born. She was just a girl." He strode away from Avigdor thinking, Stupid bastard, I wish you died. You stupid bastard, I wish you died. I wish you died—a spray of rage that spattered Avigdor Gabai, Avigdor's virtuous slattern mother, Rachaeli, Dani's nameless, faceless father, and himself.

Still, he thought of it as a connection. Even after the series of stories had run—his first byline—he thought of himself as the champion of these kids. He began to speak of himself as a bastard, an outsider having a special rapport with other outsiders. He believed it was true.

On Friday mornings he got paid, and he usually cashed his check at the bank before he went home to sleep. He was walking to the bus stop one Friday morning in the early fall, fingering the bank envelope in his jacket pocket, when he saw the kid. He was a young one, maybe thirteen, still had that half-girlish look about his face. He was working the corner opposite the bus stop, begging. Actually he was offering bundles of weeds, thrusting them in front of people and asking for money for them. People were swatting him away like a fly. Dani walked across the street. The kid was pushing his flowers at a couple now. The man was in jeans and an expensive shirt. He had a Nikon around his neck. The woman was in a shirt and jeans, too, new ones, very tight around her rear, with a sweater tied around her shoulders. Americans.

"Should I give him a quarter?" the man was saying.

"I don't know. I think he's an Arab."

"Well, obviously he's an Arab, begging in the streets. But still—"

Dani stepped between the kid and the Americans. He steered the kid away, propelled him across the street.

"Hey, let go of me! I had a sale, you—"

Dani kept the kid moving. They went halfway down the side street. Dani backed him into a doorway. The kid was scared now, looking around for an out. He'd dropped the weeds. "You a cop?" he asked defiantly. "I wasn't—"

"Take it easy; I'm not a cop. I'm not going—hey, hold still a minute. I'm not going to hurt you. Who sent you out to beg?"

The kid shrugged.

"How old are you?"

"Thirteen."

"Dropped out of school?"

"Listen." There was no one on the side street with them. The kid's eyes stopped darting around and he looked directly at Dani, smiling now. "What do you want from me? That your corner or something?" His voice hadn't changed yet.

"No it isn't my corner. I just want to give you something."

The kid tensed. Dani saw it and understood, but he knew what he was doing. The boy didn't have to stand on a corner and let people stare at him and talk about him. He didn't have to be singled out like that, for any stupid tourist to discuss. Dani could do without his paycheck, and for the boy it would be a miraculous infusion of dignity. Power. In a minute now the boy was going to hold out a tentative hand, unbelieving, and take power and dignity from Dani's hand. And turn his back on them all. Let them find someone else to gape at.

"No strings," Dani told him. "Just a trade. I give you this"—he held out the envelope—"and you cut out the begging. It's a thousand lirot."

"A thousand lirot! Mister, I can't take this. Money like this, someone'll come looking for it. You keep it, okay? Or give it to someone else. I won't work this spot any more, I swear."

"No one will come looking for it; it's mine."

This was taking too long. He'd intended to give the kid the money, stave off his gratitude, and leave. He was getting annoyed. "Just take it, okay?" He pushed it toward the kid, arm's length. The kid took it, wavered. "I've got a bus to catch. Don't thank me." He left the kid standing there and ran for his bus.

But on the bus he pictured the kid counting the money, suddenly rich, like magic. Let them pick their own weeds, kid. He smiled.

Aaron was aghast.

"You gave away your paycheck?"

"No, I gave away cash. What would a street kid do with a check?"

"You gave a week's pay to some kid on a street corner."

"A month's. A thousand lirot. Enough for a new start."

Everything looked different when you'd been away. Aaron had always thought of Dani as the older one, the one in charge. Dani had always dreamed up the plans, and in the end they'd always done what he wanted to do. There had been a glamour about him and when Aaron had tried to imitate his careless manner, he'd either looked like a fool or gotten into trouble. He saw now that Dani was all flash, a poseur. He had no idea of responsibility. He wasn't even building a career. There was nothing to him.

They heard Shlomo's key in the door, then Shlomo eased in carrying a huge board.

"What's that?"

"Shh. Where's your grandmother?"

"Out with Mother somewhere."

"Good. Help me with this. How long till they get back?"

"Five; she left a note. Where's it go?"

"It's for Anni's bed, under the mattress. Give me a hand, we'll set it up before she gets back. Hello, Dani, you here for dinner? We don't see enough of you. Shabbat shalom."

"Shabbat shalom. Yes, I'm here for dinner. I'm not around when normal people are awake, usually. Anni's back still troubles her?"

"Who knows what troubles her. Yes, her back is a problem; she has pain. That, at least, we know." He looked at Aaron, who closed his eyes and nodded slowly, an acknowledgment that they shared an understanding. Man to man. That was different, too, since he was home from the army. He and his father on one side, the women on the other. He was emboldened to show Dani up, just this once.

"Dani's been playing Rothschild."

"Watch the door, ease to your left. Playing Rothschild?"

Aaron told his father about Dani giving a month's pay away. "I was just about to tell him what we're studying now—that you don't simply throw money at the antisocial element. They need to be helped to internalize our standards."

The boy was so smug. When had he acquired this pompous manner, this fat, papal voice? Shlomo felt antipathy turn in him for his son, smirking with self-congratulation across Anni's precisely made bed, so certain he was right. Aaron was going to do what was prudent and considered, no more.

Like his mother. Every five days except when she had her period, Chava put in the diaphragm and scrubbed her face and brushed her teeth and put on her nightgown and checked on her everlasting mother and closed the door noiselessly and turned out the light and came to bed and lifted her nightgown over her head and laid it aside and lay down and opened her knees and admitted him. Nothing much happened to her when they made love; he knew that now. She closed her eyes and opened her legs and put her hands on his back and when she felt him coming, she kissed him. Sometimes she clung to him and raised herself to him— it had to do with the time of the month, he supposed, or with some private grief or fear—and he would feel himself surge; he would help her arch to him, he would hold back and try to move some passion in her, and then when he came and kissed her, her mouth would be softer, her breathing less even. But no matter how it was, in a moment she would raise up on an elbow and listen, returning to her mother's service even before she closed her knees. She would roll right out of bed then and open the door noiselessly and go into the bathroom and clean herself behind the closed door and tiptoe back to bed and arrange herself for sleep, not touching him. Finished for five days. Still, the curve of her back as she slept, the vulnerability of the hand curling over her face as a shield moved something in him, an ache of tenderness, and he accepted that in place of passion. But Aaron didn't have his mother's sweet vulnerability.

Shlomo turned his head to look at Dani, lounging against the dresser. He couldn't help returning the boy's grin. "Sometimes you just feel for someone, eh, Dani? And you act on impulse, just to be doing something to help. Even if it's a bit silly."

The boy smiled at him. He needed a haircut and he wasn't getting enough sleep so there were dark rings under his eyes. "I probably ruined the kid and now I'm broke, but it felt great. Incidentally, I scared him half to death. I think he thought I was going to knife him or land him in jail."

"Lift the mattress; slide the board all the way under—all the way. If she sees it sticking out, who knows how she'll react. She's capable of imagining herself back in the barracks, poor woman. Where are you off to, Aaron?"

"I have work to do before Shabbat. Excuse me." Let his father and Dani make the bed for Anni. They didn't need him.

Dani had in fact landed the kid in jail. He hadn't even gotten to the corner when a policeman saw him stuffing the bank envelope into his pocket and brought him in for questioning. They couldn't contact his mother and father, so they kept him overnight. It was just luck that Dani was following a court stenographer and spotted the boy being escorted into juvenile court, late on Sunday.

The damn kid didn't have a chance with the judge. Who would believe his story, a dirty thirteen-year-old with ill-fitting clothes and a thousand lirot in large bills? Dani let the stenographer get away and followed the kid into the courtroom, thinking it should be easy enough to explain and get him off.

The judge, a dumpy-looking woman, listened to the officer's statement, then turned to the boy. "Haim Monsour, is that your name?"

"That's right."

"What is your family situation, Haim? You live with your mother and father?"

"My father."

"Good. And your mother is . . . ?"

"She's dead." The boy hung his head. Dani looked around to catch people's expressions and missed the boy's quick sidelong assessment of the judge's reaction. The judge's face was unchanged.

"I see. How long ago did she die?"

"Uh, two years ago."

"And you're . . . thirteen?"

"Yes."

"You're in school?"

"Sure." He avowed it with innocent astonishment.

"What school, what grade? We'll check on it, Haim."

"Well, I don't always go. My father needs me, and—"

"You dropped out. How many grades did you finish?"

"No—I—"

"How many?"

"Seven. But I—"

"So where does a thirteen-year-old get a thousand lirot? Do you go to work?"

The kid's face was red now and his voice was very tight. He stood before the judge's bench in his too-short pants and cheap shirt, looking about ten or eleven. It was time to save him. Dani took a step forward.

"Your Honor, I gave the boy the thousand lirot on Friday afternoon at four o'clock. He didn't steal it or anything; in fact he was reluctant to take it."

"Why?"

"Well, I guess he—"

"No. Why did you give him this money? Do you know him? Identify yourself, please, and your relationship to the boy."

"My name is Daniel Kovner. I don't know the boy at all—"

"Address?"

"Mine? Thirty-nine Herzl Street, Ramat Gan."

"Place of business?"

"I'm a reporter for *Maariv*. That's how—"

"And you didn't know Haim Monsour before you gave him the money? Was he a source for your reporting?"

"No. Look, can I just tell you?"

"Please."

"*Maariv* recently ran a series of my articles on the street kids. You know, pickpockets—"

"I know."

"So I'd just been paid and I saw the boy hawking flowers—"

"Begging."

"Yes. Look, he's thirteen. He was begging on a corner, not too well fed looking, ragged—some Americans took him for an Arab—"

"So you gave him, what? Your paycheck?"

"I know what it is to be on the outside, Your Honor. I am a bastard in a country where that means I'll never be permitted to have a wife and children . . ." He paused long enough to let that register. Let them hear. Rub their noses in it. But the judge was expressionless. "And something about this little kid touched me. Someone has to care for these kids."

"So you gave him a thousand lirot and you figured you'd helped him out. Haim? Did this man give you the money?"

"He's the one. I *told* them." The boy nodded violently at the judge, pointing accusingly in Dani's direction.

"Did he want anything from you? Did he ask you to go anywhere with him, for example?"

"No, nothing. He gave me the envelope—the money—and he ran away."

"And what were you going to do with the money?"

"I don't know. Buy a TV, maybe."

"Would you give the money to your father?" She was looking at Dani. "So you could eat better and go back to school and have clothes that fit?"

The boy said nothing, but Dani saw the trapped, hostile look on his face. His own face burned. Enough. "All right," he said to the judge. "You can let him go. He hasn't done anything wrong."

The judge turned to the court officer. "See that someone checks the home situation," she said. "I want this kid back in school. Check with welfare—"

"They won't take us," the boy blurted.

"What do you mean?"

"My father, he wants the welfare to take us, but—"

"Take . . . ?"

"Me and my sisters. He says it's too much for him, but the government won't take us."

"You were going to change his life with your thousand lirot, Mr. Kovner."

"Someone has to be for these kids."

"I agree. So I sentence you—"

"*Me?* What for?"

"—I sentence you to six months' social service with this boy. No, eight months, until the end of the school year. I make you responsible to this court for seeing that Haim gets to school and does his work, and I will check it with the school authorities. Leave your address and phone with the clerk. He'll give you back your money. You may give it to Haim as an allowance, if you wish. I'll see you back here in June with Mr. Kovner, Haim. You're lucky; he wants to help you." She slapped the folder shut and looked past them, ready for another case.

Dani and the boy glanced at each other, mirrored looks of entrapment and disbelief. The boy's eyes dipped, returned in solemn innocence to Dani's face.

"Don't worry about it, mister," he said. "I'll go to school. On my mother's soul, you don't have to worry. I was going to go anyhow. My father wants me to."

"It's really better for you, you know."

"Yeah, I know. Well, thanks. See you."

"Wait. Haim?"

The boy turned around.

"You promise you'll go? Shake on it?"

"Sure." He stuck out a grubby hand, smiling, pumped Dani's hand once, and ran out of the courthouse.

That was the end of it; they had a deal. Dani didn't follow the boy to school, of course; he figured he'd check with the teacher in a few weeks and make sure the kid was doing all right. He meant to buy him some clothes and take them to his house, but he never got to it.

When the call came—it woke him up at midday a few weeks later—he couldn't even remember who Haim Monsour was. "Picked up for shoplifting," the voice said. *Who?* "And truancy, of course. Judge Doron expects you in court at two-thirty this afternoon."

He remembered: the little bastard, he'd broken the deal. He set the alarm for one-thirty and went back to sleep. At two-thirty, groggy and aggrieved, he arrived in court. The kid wasn't in the room, but there was the same dumpy judge.

"You're in very serious trouble, Mr. Kovner," she said.

"*Me?* Listen, this has gone—"

"You were under orders of this court to oversee Haim Monsour's return to school. He hasn't been in school a day since he was last in this court. He was caught shoplifting this morning. You are responsible."

"I'm *not* responsible. I don't even *know* this kid. He gave me his word—"

"You are certainly responsible. You are under court orders that make you responsible. Now, do you want this court to act against you, or do you want to see that Haim Monsour gets to school every day from now on?"

"I can't. Look, I work nights. I'm a reporter, I work the night beat. I cover this court, as a matter of fact. I got up especially to come here today, but—"

"You'll have to change shifts."

"*What?* You can't—"

"Watch me." She picked up a form and a pen.

She was a lunatic. He took a breath. He spoke in a reasonable, warm voice. "Judge Doron, you've made your point. I made a stupid mistake in giving him the money." He smiled boyishly at her. "My mother used to yell at me all the time for giving my things away. But it isn't a crime. Now—"

"Soliciting a minor is a crime."

"Soliciting . . . I did nothing of the sort and you know it!"

"You don't want it on your record, though, do you? Accused of soliciting a minor?"

"What is this, a vendetta? Why me?"

"Because you are handy, Mr. Kovner. You're a godsend. The boy needs observation; you're young and energetic, righteously indignant. I read your articles. Very moving. Victims of society caught between cultures, smudged angels of the night."

"Smudged angels. I never—"

"No, you have your own style. Much more cynical. That's fine. The less you expect with these cases, the better." She put down the form. "You don't have to raise him, you know, just keep him straight until June. All you have to do is get him to school; they'll make sure that he stays, once he's there. As for changing to the day shift," she looked him over, "it wouldn't hurt you. You look terrible." She turned to the court clerk, dismissing Dani.

"You're crazy," he said. "I'll fight it."

She lifted up her glasses and looked steadily at him. "That will look fine in the papers," she warned. "NIGHT KIDS' REPORTER REFUSES COURT ORDER TO ASSIST STREET URCHIN." She replaced her glasses on her nose. Light flashed off them. He blinked. Everything was glaring bright in this nightmare daylight.

"Don't get yourself so excited, Mr. Kovner," Judge Doron concluded. "He's just a little boy. He won't eat you up."

"This boy is a liar and a cheat," the principal said flatly. "He skips school, he never does the work, and then when he drops in to class— usually when it's raining or cold—he disrupts the whole flow of things. He has excuses and stories for every day of the year. What am I supposed to do with him?"

"Educate him. His father can't do it, his mother is dead—"

"He told you that? He said his mother was dead?"

"He said it to the judge."

"His mother is in Tel Hashomer, the mental ward. And if you ask me, the boy will be either in jail or in Tel Hashomer, too, in ten years. He isn't going to go to school, and if he does, he isn't going to learn. You'd have to educate him with a stick. He has no idea of the difference between lies and truth."

"Neither has anyone else. Neither have I."

"I beg your pardon?"

"He is going to go to school. I'm going to bring him every morning, and you'd damn well better keep him here and teach him whatever you teach everyone else."

He walked back out into the corridor and braced his arms on either side of the boy against the slickly painted cement wall. "No one knows more about lies than me," he told the boy pleasantly. "I am the king of illusions, and my business is to flash one story or another at the public, day after day. So I don't give a shit whether you say one thing or another to me, because I don't believe anything. Get it? All I care about is that you get your body into this school and into your classroom every day, all day, and that you show me your homework every morning. I'm not interested in explanations—I get lied to by experts all day long—so there'll be no explanations and no excuses. You do as I say and we'll be fine; maybe I'll even teach you a few magic tricks so you can fool people and get applauded for it. We'll see. But if you mess up, I tell you now—believe it, Haim; this is as true as it gets—that I will drag you back to that court and tell that bitch of a judge that you're a hopeless truant. No one is ever going to make you this offer again: after this it's jail or Tel Hashomer." He turned to leave.

"Every morning?"

"What?"

"You said I had to show you my homework every morning."

"Right."

"But . . . you're not going to come every morning."

"I am going to come every morning and you had better be there. If you're not . . . I know all kinds of people in your neighborhood. *All* kinds."

"What are you butting in for? I got a father."

"Yeah? Well, he doesn't do much for you that I can see."

The boy's eyes blazed. "I wasn't in any trouble until you came handing out your money. What is it, you like boys?"

"Seven-forty-five, on your front steps," Dani said, murder in his voice. "With the homework."

———

He changed shifts. He had loved that nighttime world, the after-hours, loosely linked universe. Even the courts, in that quadrant of time, were offbeat and imperfectly balanced. The expectations were different at night, also the requirements. At night you didn't have to have a regulation social life, for example; you had friends at work, and women of an undemanding type. There were no couples at three and four in the morning. Now he'd shifted to the standard cycle and he was out of step. He'd have to deal with a wide-awake, balanced world at work and with pairs of people, families, in the evenings. It unsettled him in a way that real ambushes, real enemy attacks never had.

Haim was there every morning at seven-forty-five, on his front steps. He looked surprised to see Dani every morning but he had nothing to say. Dani would glance cursorily at the homework—messy, scratched out, the answers given in short sentences or cryptic phrases. Then they would walk to the school in silence, each humiliated by the encumbrance of the other, each comforted in a strange, unacknowledged way by the routine hostility of the other. When they parted the day lay before each of them, laced with snares. This at least was known and balanced.

Inevitably there was a day, two or three weeks into the new arrangement, when Haim had no homework to show him in the morning. He tried to tell Dani there'd been no assignments. "I check all facts," Dani told him. "You'd be surprised how often they turn out to be . . . uh . . . incomplete. Which way is your classroom?"

"You coming in?"

"Did you doubt it?"

And when Haim stood trapped between his teacher and his keeper, the assignments clear on the blackboard in front of him, there was a little smile on the boy's face, almost a look of satisfaction, and for the first time in this daytime world Dani felt at ease. "You do that work at lunchtime," he said. "I'll be here at three o'clock. Mrs. Haravi had better be able to tell me then that you're caught up."

He was there at three o'clock. Haim thrust the completed work into his hand, miming sullenness, but the little edge of satisfaction showed. "It's done," he said. "Are you happy now?"

"I'm neutralized. Just. Where does he sit during tests?" he demanded of the teacher.

"His desk is there." She pointed.

"Can you move it? I want him in the front, where he won't be tempted to look over any shoulders."

"Oh, that's not necessary. Haim is doing fine."

"It's necessary. In the front row on one end or the other. It'll make it easier for him. Right, Haim?"

The boy glowered at him, but as they left the building together and walked down the street he bumped Dani's arm with his, a tentative kind of hug. Dani slowed his pace and decreased the distance between them by inches, an acceptance.

Actually, the work wasn't bad in the daytime. The people weren't so much different from the night staff, and he got to do more hard news. Then he really had a break; they assigned him to cover the Langer bastardy case. His editor knew that Dani was a bastard, of course— everyone knew it by then; he traded on it—and he asked whether covering the issue would be a problem for Dani. "Are you kidding?" Dani grinned. "I was born to report this case."

It was an upheaval, the Langer question, because in a country of unending debates, it demanded a decision. A brother and sister, Miriam and Hanoch Langer, had chosen mates and applied for marriage licenses. They were informed that they were bastards, and therefore not permitted to marry.

They were WASPs, white Ashkenazic Jews with Protectsia—connections in the society—both born in Israel; both had served in the defense force. It was news to them that they were bastards, since their mother had been married to their father. It was news to most of the nation that they were actually being forbidden to marry. It was big news. It was a picnic to cover the story.

"You know the background?" the editor asked. "Their mother, Eve, married in Poland before the war. The man was a Christian but he converted to Judaism after the marriage. They moved to Palestine and the marriage broke up in 1942. Some rabbi told Eve that the man's conversion hadn't fulfilled all the requirements of religious law, and that therefore she had never been married and didn't need a divorce. She remarried in 1944, a man named Langer, and they had these two children. Langer died in 1952. When Eve planned to marry a third time, the Rabbinical Court looked into her first marriage and ruled that her first husband's conversion had been valid after all, and therefore that her first marriage—a kosher marriage—was still in effect, never having been legally dissolved.

"But that rabbi told her—"

"His mistake, her problem. They forbade her to marry; they declared the marriage to Langer an adulterous liaison and that made the two

Langer children, Miriam and Hanoch, illegitimate. But they never informed her or the children that they'd been labeled bastards. Miriam and Hanoch found out, when they applied for the marriage licenses, that there's an undisclosed list of mamzerim, and their names were on it."

"A blacklist." He wasn't surprised.

"Damn right. However, this is 1972. The boy is in active service, a parachutist, and he went straight to Moshe Dayan. You can imagine Dayan: 'What do you mean, one of my boys—born here, one of us, a parachutist—isn't permitted to marry? Are you *insane?*' He's ready to unseat Golda's government; Hausner and his liberals have a bill in the works now to take the marriage monopoly from the rabbis."

"Allow civil marriage."

"Right. The Orthodox are spitting fire. They say there will be no Jews left in Israel; it won't be a Jewish state. They're talking excommunication. Meanwhile it gives the liberals, the secularists, and the feminists a chance to holler about barbaric family laws and a final break between church and state. You may see Golda's coalition fall apart. You may see the whole definition of this country change."

"We'll see a lot of commotion and no change."

"You're wrong. Get on the story, you'll see. People are outraged. You know who's involved? For example, a woman born in Russia or the U.S., wherever. She had a civil divorce—the guy wouldn't give her a religious divorce or she just didn't bother with one—and then she moved here, married, had kids. *All those kids are bastards.* Big change is coming, Dani. People are hysterical, you'll see. All those mothers are hysterical."

Rachaeli was amused. "The whole issue is ridiculous. Women don't make bastards; it's the rabbis who are making those children bastards, with their dusty laws no one gives a damn about."

"You're wrong," Dani said. His voice was cold. "The laws are necessary. The system makes sense."

Chava laughed, uncomfortable with the discussion. Rachaeli and Shlomo looked sharply at Dani.

"It makes perfect sense," he repeated. "It's a matter of bloodlines, keeping them clear."

"There's nothing wrong with your bloodlines," Rachaeli snapped.

"Think of it." He spoke to Chava and Shlomo, smiling blandly and ignoring his mother. "Thirty thousand people in captivity, in exile in

Babylonia. They're living among people whose norm is idolatry, child sacrifice, incest, bestiality, who knows what. Two generations of carelessness and this little group would be a genetic cesspool. So they make laws. One: Don't marry one of Them. Two: No incest. Three: The woman bears children by one man only, so the community knows where the children are coming from. It's brilliant; it works."

"Good. That was thousands of years ago, in Babylonia," Rachaeli retorted.

"It applies."

"You feel tainted?" She asked it mockingly. The color was high on her face.

"Of course I do. I am. Tainted and deflected, bounced off sideways from the people. Unclaimed, unidentified, and therefore potentially dangerous to the genetic pool."

There's nothing wrong with your bloodlines. You want to know who he was?"

"You know I don't. I could go back and read the newspapers."

"His name wasn't in the papers."

"I don't care who it was, Mother. It doesn't matter; it only matters that I don't father any children. I'm a dead end. I want it that way."

"Dani." Shlomo had to say it twice before he got Dani's attention. "There are two opinions, even in the Torah. The Law also says that the children are not to be punished for the sins of the parents."

"Tell that to the parents," Dani said. "Let them commit crimes that don't leave children as living evidence." The words filled the room, pushed against the walls. Chava looked up quickly, stiffening as though she was the one who had been attacked. Rachaeli reached for her hand, quieting her, and pointed a finger at Dani, about to answer him.

"Dani? Are you in trouble?" Anni spoke up, suddenly cogent. Everyone smiled brightly at her, as though she were a precocious child.

"No, Anni," Dani answered, kneeling down to pick up the pad of paper and charcoal pencil she'd dropped. "No more than usual. Are you?"

"No more than usual," she snapped back. The two of them laughed.

There were hundreds of them, all varieties of bastards, and he interviewed a lot of them. "One Mamzer to Another," he called the file. Usually he provoked good quotes from the other bastards by stating his point of view about bloodlines, but when he was among regular people he would inveigh against the law and the rabbinic stranglehold on marriage and divorce. It made people uneasy to have him bring it up. There was a power in that.

Just after Golda appointed Shlomo Goren chief rabbi—obviously a move to change the rabbinic ruling on the Langers and slide away from national confrontation, *Maariv* was saying—Dani was at a party. He'd begun by discussing Goren's appointment with one couple, but a small crowd gathered and he found himself addressing a group. He turned up his wattage. "After the Holocaust, what difference does it make who's legitimate?" he demanded. He picked out a girl way over to his right. She had a lot of auburn hair pulled back off her face. Pretty, a bit angular. Serious-looking. "When you think of it," he said directly to her, "our Father denied us all, in Auschwitz and Dachau, so how are you different from me?"

She colored, but she smiled. "I'm not."

"There, see?"

"I'm a bastard, too."

"Oh? Actual or symbolic?"

"Actual, according to this idiotic law."

Resentment washed over him. Suddenly the world was full of bastards. "What's your story?" he asked bluntly, thinking. She wants to take center stage, let's turn the lights on her and see how she likes it.

"My mother was married in Austria, before the war. She and her husband were sent to the camps and they told her, after the war, that he had died in Bergen-Belsen. She came here and after a year or two she remarried and had me. Five years ago someone she knew from Vienna said he'd seen her first husband in Haifa. He'd survived the camps—the records were wrong—but he'd never found her. He thought she was dead. He was here as a tourist."

"So you're one of those hide-and-seek bastards?"

"Hide-and-seek?"

"God's little game. Now she's a widow—hey presto, now she's an adulteress and you're illegitimate. I've talked to a dozen like you."

"Have you?"

"At least a dozen."

"And what kind of bastard are you?"

Someone snickered.

"The purest kind. Child of simple, straightforward adultery. Available for parties and small gatherings." He made a flourish and smiled crisply, dismissing her. People looked around for someone to talk to; pairs formed and turned away from Dani. He shrugged and went to get a drink. She was in a corner, talking to an older man. Her face was lit; she was nodding, sketching something in the air with a finger. Dani ambled over.

"—bowel resection," the man was saying.

"Simple enough. Two or three points in the procedure—"

"Yes, but it's a new technique. You'll want to show the details."

"Fine. Just make sure I have adequate lighting this time, and that the surgeon understands I'm there to sketch and lets me near the table."

"Don't worry. Your experience with Rafi was unusual."

"Unusual's hardly the word." She smiled briefly. The smile changed the angles in her face to light-catching curves.

"You mean I'm not the only strange man to give you a hard time?" Dani asked.

The man frowned at him, but she said evenly, "By no means. But usually they use scalpels for cutting."

"I'm sorry. It's my job to be . . . aggressive with my questions, but I shouldn't have—"

"It's all right." Her face showed no expression, but she was blushing again. She turned back to the other man. "Operating Room C? Six-thirty?"

They made arrangements, something about the lighting in the operating room; Dani, excluded, held his ground in stubborn silence. The women in the nighttime world were easy. Dina had been easy. They didn't make things complicated with blushes and rejections; they played the game with shortened rules. There must be women in this daylight world who would do the same. If he were smart he'd go and find one. But he stood there waiting for this unsmiling daytime girl to give up and turn back to him.

Finally the conversation floundered between her and the man. Dani claimed her. "Are you a photographer?" he asked. "My name is Dani Kovner. I'm a reporter for *Maariv*."

"Ronit Gordon. I'm a medical artist. I do the anatomical drawings that go into textbooks and encyclopedias and so on."

"How did you get into that?" Chitchat. The long rules of the game. But he was going to get her to smile for him, apricot skin curving, cat's eyes softening for him.

It took a long time to get that smile. She smiled—civilly, coolly, in amusement, wryly. He amused her and she grinned. He took her to movies and she laughed. He told her funny stories about the people he'd interviewed. She smiled and smiled. But those smiles held him off, closed something in her face to him. It wasn't until he broke a date with her and she saw him with Haim that she smiled for him, let him in. He understood her terms then.

They had a date for Wednesday at three o'clock. She was going to meet him at the Press Center and show him the new exhibit at the museum. At one o'clock, Haim's teacher phoned and asked if Dani would come to school at three. He called Ronit. "I have to be somewhere at three, but I should be done by four. Can you make it then?"

"Trouble?"

"No, I—this kid I'm involved with seems to be in some trouble at school, and I have to talk to the teacher."

"Nice of you to care."

"No, actually it was a court order. I'll explain at four, if you want."

"I do."

Mrs. Haravi was smiling. "We have something to show you," she said. Haim was standing by her desk, unsuccessfully trying to scowl.

"Show him, Haim."

The boy held out an envelope. It was a report card. Math, C. Hebrew Spelling and Grammar, C+. Composition, A−. History, B−. English, B−. Science, C+. Deportment, Improving.

"What do you think?" she demanded, beaming.

"I think he'd better show me a little work in math and science and language. The rest is okay." He turned to the boy. "Come on, I promised you something if you did all right. Thanks, Mrs. Haravi. You must be a genius."

"He's a little mischievous, but he's trying hard."

"Thank Mrs. Haravi, Haim."

"Thanks. Where are we going?"

"Downtown. Come."

They stopped at the hobby shop and Dani bought a length of rope and a Buatier Pull. Then they went over to the Press Center. Ronit was waiting outside. They went in and found a table. Dani sent Haim to the cafeteria counter for some doughnuts. "We won't make it to the museum," he told Ronit. "I owe the kid. You mind?"

"No, of course not. But tell me—"

He told her briefly, while Haim waited for the doughnuts. "Pretty stupid, eh? To think I'd fix everything with a thousand lirot? I'm paying now."

The boy came back. He handed Dani the change. Dani said, "What about the rest?"

"What rest?"

"This?" He made a coin appear from behind Haim's ear. "And this?"—from midair. "Can't you keep track of a little change?"

"Hey! How'd you—"

Dani pulled the rope from his pocket. He tied it loosely around a Coke bottle. "Be careful, I have powers." He tightened the knot, pulled tighter and tighter until the rope seemed to cut through the bottle. He snapped the knot out between his two hands. "Want to do that?"

"*Yeah*. Lemme—"

"Sit down. Lower your voice. Watch me. *Watch* me, Haim."

It took an hour and a half to teach the boy two simple tricks. He was putting his own jacket on Haim to show him how the Buatier Pull worked, fussing over threading the cord through the sleeve, when he glanced at Ronit. She was smiling; something in her eyes had opened to let him see in. It was a woman's smile, collusive, offering him room and time to come in. Just like that.

"You like kids," he said later, walking her to her flat.

"So do you. I'd never have guessed. You should have seen yourself with Haim."

He shrugged, denying it, but liking hearing her tell him about himself.

"Sorry." She smiled. "You gave yourself away."

Those were her terms. She wanted to know him. She would open herself to him if he would open to her, a simple bargain. He had no intention of meeting her terms, but he could easily create the illusion. It would be worth the effort; she was so reserved, so serious—unlike Rachaeli, for example, who smiled all the time and seemed always to have the flush of easy generosity about her—that when the smile touched her face, she was transformed. What was behind the reserve would open, too; she would be wanton, delicious. He would show her how. He would give her whatever illusion of knowing him she wanted in exchange.

She was confusing to make love to. He went slowly, he used what Dina had taught him, and Ronit's nipples hardened and she got very wet—she said she was ready—but she turned her head away, barely moved, made no sound at all. He couldn't tell what she felt. She smiled, later, and told him it had been good. He didn't know what that meant to her.

She hated the condom. She whispered that she wanted to feel him in her, not a lifeless rubber skin. She used a diaphragm, after the first time, and after a little while he relaxed and accepted it. The sensations without the rubber shield were unexpectedly intense; he could feel himself bathed in her wetness, and he had to struggle for control. There was a moment, each time, when he had to abstract himself from the lovemaking to maintain control at all, and still she hid her face in his arm and lay silent and yielding.

But one Friday, he'd been at Chava's with his mother for dinner. Anni was sending bulletins from her own crazy time warp and Chava was pretending that nothing was wrong, and Rachaeli was smiling, smiling—and later he came to Ronit without preliminaries, just seized her, hurting her arms. "You're the only thing that's real," he whispered, and that was true.

His breathing sounded like crying to her. She couldn't be sure. She felt herself heat and soften and she cupped him, guided him into her. He drew his breath in a gasp, and moved recklessly in her, unevenly, a rhythm of need.

Something happened—a little cry from her, a change in her breathing. He looked at her. Her eyes flew open, a look almost of terror, of staring into the abyss, and he suddenly remembered freefall. He remembered feeling himself plunge into the night, out of control, and thinking, This is what it feels like to be a girl. "Go ahead," he whispered. "Go ahead. I've got you."

"Hold me."

"I've got you. Go."

She tightened everything on him—arms, fingers, legs. She sucked his tongue into her mouth, closed wet and hard on his cock, made no sound at all, held, held, then everything went soft and she breathed out, a slow, pulsing release and he came into her downward-opening, slowing gyro, so she felt it, hot stream, felt herself close in reflex spasms on him, and was waiting for him when he emerged.

It took her some time to understand that he was asleep.

When he woke up after his brief sleep, he felt great. She was awake, sitting curled up in the big chair with a book. She had a robe on. "What are you doing way over there? Come back," he smiled. He remembered then that it had been different. "You came, didn't you?"

"Mmm."

It had something to do with the kid. She liked his being with the kid. "Come on." He held the sheet up demandingly, waited until she closed the book and got back into bed. He lay back with his arms behind his head. "You know what I think?"

"What?"

"I think about all those kids, the bastards. The little ones, nine, ten, twelve." It was coming to him as he spoke. "Alone, you know? Like I was. Well, everyone knows me by now. Dani Kovner, the third most famous mamzer in Israel. And the Langers will get out on a technicality, Goren will make sure of it, but there's no technicality for me, right? I'm always going to be a mamzer when all the others have found an out." He raised up on an elbow, really seeing it now.

"So I'll never have kids, right? Everyone in Israel knows it. It leaves me free, don't you see?"

"Free."

"To be there for all those kids." He stopped a moment, but not for an answer. He narrowed his eyes and nodded, holding the floor. "Maybe that's what I was born for: let every one of those kids think of me as his father. I'll do it. I'll claim any kid who wants to be the bastard's bastard."

"Claim them? Then what?"

"Well, then they can come to me."

"And you'll teach them a trick."

"You mad at me? Ronit?" She was crying. What the hell? "I thought—"

"Never mind. Silly of me. My problem."

"What problem?"

"Nothing. It was special for me. I've never—you were so—I've never seen you like that. And then when I was . . . you *knew*, you said . . ."

She swallowed. "I've never been so trusting. But it's ridiculous for me to expect—never mind. Go on. They'll come to you."

He had to think for a minute, then he caught on. "You think it wasn't special for me?" Her eyes were swollen and her nose was red. She turned away for a tissue. "You think I didn't know you were trusting me? I fell asleep for a second, I couldn't help that, but now I'm—look, I'm trusting you with my idea."

His idea. He was onstage again, all charged, using her for an audience. That's what he thought trusting was. He'd forgotten already about shaking in her arms, needing her. Well, God help the kid who believed this man's rhetoric. She'd never fall for it again.

She fell for it over and over, because it wasn't really rhetoric. There were times when he did need her, and that flayed off her defenses every time. He began to let her know him, then he insisted that she know him. He told her his history urgently and after a while she learned that the price of his openness, his vulnerability before lovemaking was his abstraction afterward. But it was a cycle; he came around again. She had only to wait.

Meanwhile, she used the time after lovemaking to learn him. He would plunge directly into sleep in her arms, sometimes while she was still trying to get her breath back, and then, suddenly awake again, he'd roll over and reappear, brisk and collected. He wanted to talk about everything, then: Goren's handling of the case, politics, his editor, his family, the other family—Shlomo and Aaron and those poor women— and she was clever. She forbade herself to let him see that she was bereft while he chattered on. She smiled and teased him and looked, she thought, like a strong and independent woman. She learned to smoke.

That lasted a month or so. They'd been to a *brit milah*, the circumcision of the first son of one of his army friends, a boy named Shemtov, a small wiry fellow with a beautiful wife. A girl, maybe eighteen. Ronit was going everywhere with Dani now, and Shemtov, beaming with importance in his tiny home, teased them about getting married. They smiled and changed the subject.

That may have been why she risked making the demand, because of the talk of marriage or because of the beautiful, slender girl balancing her baby in one easy arm. Or it may have simply been that damned sweet talk of Dani's. They went back to her flat and undressed slowly, playfully, full of wine from the *brit milah*. She pulled off her panties and saw the fresh red stain, and she quickly pulled them back on again. "Sorry," she said briskly. "I wasn't expecting it till—"

"Why are you getting dressed?"

"Well, I—"

"You religious?"

"No, of course not. It's just your sensibilities, I—"

He walked into the bathroom, came out with a towel and a wet washcloth. "Don't tell me about my sensibilities." He pulled her panties down again. They got stuck on a foot and the red stain flashed in the tangle. He freed the panties, tossed them into the bathroom, where they lay on the floor.

"Lie down."

"No, listen, you don't have to—"

The washcloth was warm. He'd even thought to make the water warm. His voice was tender. "Did you listen today? Twice the rabbi said, 'In your blood live.' I love you, I want to make love: I don't care if you run rivers of blood." She read his face. He really didn't care.

It was like a first time. She kept scanning his face, unsure, and he kept smiling, kissing her. He took her like a bride, gently. She let her fingers wander lightly over his arms and back. *I'm not holding you to this*, her fingers said; *you can stop any time*, until she caught fire, reckless with trust, and began to move on him.

"Say it!" he gasped.

"Say . . . ?"

"Tell me you love me. Please love me, damn it."

So that she laid claim to him at last with her fingernails and teeth and she closed around him, saying it three times as they came, the casting of a spell. Then before he could drift, she broke her rules. "Don't you dare leave me," she said, not hiding her tears. "I don't care, I don't care; you can't drift away now. Don't you leave me out here alone."

He was sinking; it yanked him awake. "I love you," he offered placatingly, not knowing what she wanted. He rolled off her and put an arm around her. She nestled in and threaded her fingers through his hair, surrounding him. She didn't seem to want to talk.

He held her until the blood dried on them both and his arm went dead under her. When he tried to move, he found that she had fallen asleep, fingers still caught in his hair.

Rachaeli is playing the cello, a fugue. She is alone. She plays slowly and deliberately with no intonation, just getting the notes right.

Alon drifts into her thoughts and she pushes him away. Never mind; she always knew he'd find someone younger. Let him go. She rehearses his faults again, an incantation of ridicule. I am still appealing to men, she tells herself again. All I have to do is look around a little. I have more freedom than ever, too. It's not as though I have to worry about Dani any more.

Because Dani is out of her hands. She tightens on the neck of the cello, fingers of flexible steel urging the vibrato out of the A string. She smiles grimly at the pain of it. Finally, after all her years of fruitlessly trying to train him to ownership, there is something her son is keeping for himself. Someone. The girl, Ronit. And why is he so possessive of the girl? Because she demands it, clever bitch. She requires him to own her, not to share her. She gives herself pitilessly and he is totally enmeshed.

She ought to have known that a mother could not possess a child. Not this one, at any rate. To begin with, he carries Yossi in him—not just the cockiness, the black curls, and mischievous grin, but the elusiveness. No one will ever really own him, not securely. There will always be someone after him and he can be kept in hand only in ways not available to a mother.

She had thought that because he'd never marry, never be distracted by children, he would be hers forever. She understands now, a bitter understanding, that she has only ensured he will be less hers, not more. He is free and talented in love—one has only to see him with the girl to know what he's capable of—and he will burn for one woman after another. And the amiable boredom of marriage will not bring him back to her.

Dani is what she wanted him to be for herself: hungry, thirsty for connection—an easy forgiver, no judge—charged with news, avaricious for more. Eternally available, he is going to deceive her again and again, a lifetime of choosing others.

No point in trying to bring him back by discrediting the girl, either.

She's tried that and failed. He turned cold, an unendurable state, and she had to demean herself, cajole him out of it.

There is one possibility, the one thing she's never considered. She might have to give it a try.

She stops playing, momentarily lost. There are too many voices in the fugue now for her to continue to play without paying close attention. She's been making a lot of mistakes.

––––––––

Chava is packing for Aaron. He's leaving to study in the United States, only for a year, he says. She has to keep the younger ones from mentioning it near Anni because there's no knowing how she might react.

Anni has deserted her. Sometimes a child and sometimes an aged invalid, she is never a mother. Chava, who spends her hours tending to Anni's brittle limbs and endless, querulous demands, has been orphaned. The cronies come by every day and they infuriate Chava. They observe her treatment of Anni in tactful silence and with reassuring platitudes, but Chava believes that they divine her impatience with Anni, and that they are judging her.

When they are alone in the flat, Chava and Anni, Anni hides in the recesses of time and from her hiding place badgers Chava with demands and complaints, switching hiding places in an instant so that when Chava tries to answer her, she finds herself abandoned again. Or Anni sketches in grim silence, page after page of drawings of foreign streets and gardens, detailed views of rooms. Bicycles. Dresses. Counters in some kind of store. No people. She'll tear out a sheet, hold it up, mutter something in Hungarian, then the sheet will slip out of her fingers unnoticed and she'll be engrossed in another sketch. Something about the way she holds her body when she sketches, something in her voice and the concentration in her face call up the old Anni, Mother before the camps, except that she won't acknowledge Chava's presence then at all. Chava hates her when she is drawing.

She has resorted to the most despicable tactics to conjure her mother back to her. She has even, when they were alone in the flat, made her own voice like a child's and called to Anni, such unforgivable things as, "Mama, they want us for roll call. I'm afraid, Mama, do you hear me? Come and stand with Marika and Ottilie and Lila and me." Or, "The stones are so heavy, Mama. My fingers—tell me a story now so I don't drop one." Then she's appalled at herself and she brushes out Anni's hair with the soft hairbrush or rubs her hands with lotion in penance, but none of it matters. Anni never responds.

The worst of it is that Chava thinks about the camp all the time now. It's as though Anni, whose job it was all these years to stand between Chava and the camp, has sidestepped and now, suddenly, there's only Chava and Auschwitz. Chava sees the dangers and the threats to Jews everywhere now, and she talks about it incessantly.

Several times Anni has flickered back on like a faulty radio. It's impossible to tell what the cause is, but it seems that the cronies are always there when it happens. There are things Chava needs to know from Anni, she has things to tell her, but they have no privacy. With no warning Anni will suddenly begin talking reasonably to Potasnik—"Oh, you're here; I've been sleeping. Potasnik, why do you look so old today? You're not well?"—and Potasnik will take her bony hand in his two red ones and chat with her, easily, and the truth is that Chava half believes that if she speaks the spell will shatter and Anni will flicker back out again. So silently, with a fraudulent smile on her face, she watches Potasnik steal Anni's few cogent moments, one by one.

Her back is aching from bending over Aaron's trunk. She straightens up and looks around his room, barricaded with cartons and littered with hangers. Without particular purpose she goes into the kitchen and picks up the phone. Whom should she call? Rachaeli, between men for the moment, is moody lately. Chava doesn't want to hear about Rachaeli's problems. She dials Shlomo's office, just to see how he is.

———

Purim: Shlomo is tipsy. They've been reading the scroll of Esther all morning, stamping their feet to drown out Haman's name each time it is mentioned, and passing around dwindling bottles of whiskey. The goal is to blot out the killer's name, as he intended to obliterate the Jews of Persia. It's hot. Shlomo flaps his prayer shawl to get some air. He steals a glance at Dani, who stands on his right. Eli and Yakov are wandering around somewhere, probably catching the candy the girls are throwing from the balcony. Aaron is in the States and Dani, who hasn't been to services with Shlomo since the army, appeared unexpectedly this morning with his girl. Shlomo suspects the boy thought he would be lonely without Aaron and came to keep him company. He doesn't really miss Aaron, but it's good to have Dani with him, after all these years. Dani's girl is upstairs with Chava, Shlomo imagines.

———

She's a serious little thing, all bones and hair, but pretty in a way. Beautiful eyes, cat's eyes. She's mad for Dani, obviously. He remembers when he would lay his hand on Dani's head to bless him after services, and how the boy would turn his cheek toward Shlomo's chest and insinuate himself by degrees under his prayer shawl. He used to pity him. Does he pity him now?

The bottle comes his way again. He takes a mighty swig, passes it to Dani, who grins and follows suit. Dani's face is flushed, he's swaying and stamping like a Hasid. He loves life, this one.

Does Shlomo pity him now? He supposes so. They'll never be able to marry—or, since the girl is a bastard too, technically speaking they could marry, but they could never have children. But in a way . . . look, they're in love. Nothing dilutes it—kids, routine, nothing. If they stay together, it's because they're crazy about each other despite everything. Just because she wants him. It can't be marriage and children she's after; she just wants Dani. How she looks at him with those eyes.

Hot, it's hot. He loves this boy. He does, and that's the truth. Freely, without having to. All his life this boy is going to be loved freely; no one will ever have to.

"Does she keep her eyes open?" he asks Dani suddenly.

"What?"

"Your girl. When you make love. Does she open her eyes?"

Dani looks stunned, then he laughs. "Sometimes."

No. I never asked that. Shlomo turns a little away from Dani and begins, desperately, to drum his feet with the others.

She does open her eyes, because he asks her to, even though it is so dangerous. Her face had always twisted shut when she came and he felt lost, cut off. So he whispered it to her, once, "Open your eyes, this time. Will you? Let me in."

He thought she wasn't going to, because as she came close she twisted her head away, grazing his arm with her teeth and crying in her throat. But suddenly she was back, hands gripping his hair and eyes burning. He saw through her to the centrifuge of her coming, spinning open. Her eyelids closed momentarily as if against pain or brightness, opened again to him. He spun in, pouring helplessly into the twisting and tightening vortex. There would be nothing left of him this time.

She shuddered in his arms, quieting slowly. "I'm so naked to you," she whispered. "Even my skin is off."

There was a little core of him left and with it he pulled mightily inward, wrenching himself back from her. Raggedly reabsorbed, whole again, he pretended to sleep. Never again, he thought. It's too much.

But now she opens her eyes sometimes and every time she does he rushes in, he is sucked in and left an exploded husk. He loves it, hates and fears it, and helplessly loves it again.

Haim has chosen the seat over the rear wheels of the bus. Dani and Ronit and Avigdor Gabai are sitting three rows ahead of him. Avigdor is sixteen, he doesn't want anything to do with Haim. Haim doesn't care.

They're going to the Nahal instruction center so Avigdor can see it. Nahal is paratroopers. Haim is hoping to see somebody jump out of a plane.

Dani is trying to get Avigdor and Zadok Raz to join Nahal when they're eighteen. Raz wouldn't even come today. Raz is stupid, he can't even read and he's older than Avigdor. He's mean, too. Dani got Raz and Avigdor to join Working Youth; they're in Gadna premilitary training together, but Haim knows that Raz will never make a paratrooper, even if Dani is able to teach him to read. Raz has been in jail once. You get disqualified for being in jail. Anyone but Dani could see that Raz was a loser. Avigdor too, the fag. Lucky thing Dani doesn't try to teach those two magic. They'd never be able to pull it off.

Haim only pretended to put the money Dani gave him in the bus's coin box. He went in with a crowd, dropped two agorot to make it sound like his fare all went in, and palmed the rest. He did the same thing when they went to Jerusalem last November to cover the riots. He's getting a lot of money from these trips.

It was good, in Jerusalem. There must have been a million people there. "You want to see a demonstration?" Dani had said.

"What's a demonstration?"

"A lot of people protesting against something."

"What something?"

"Eight rabbis said that two couples could get married. They got married."

"I don't get it." But he went. He'd never been to Jerusalem. It was okay, only it was full of people screaming and tearing their clothes.

"How come?"

"They say they're in mourning. They say the Torah has been burnt."

"Was it?"

"Not actually. I'll explain later. Go with Ronit, now."

He explained on the way home. It was boring but Haim had to listen. Dani said he had to understand the news. He took him places and made him write a report every time. Haim got to use Dani's typewriter at *Maariv* to do the reports though, so it was half good and half bad.

Dani said Goren's rabbis had a secret meeting and decided the Langers were never bastards, so they could marry after all. Dani said it was a neat trick how they avoided having to make a hard decision. Moshe Dayan went to the weddings. Orthodox people tore their clothes and screamed. It was pretty good.

Dani is a bastard, too. It means his mother was fooling around with some other guy. Haim has met Dani's mother and he can't imagine it; she's pretty old. He's met Rivka too, the grandmother. They've gone to Degania twice. He likes Rivka a lot. She's funny. Once when Ronit started crying and Dani sent Haim to Rivka's room, she told him a long story about chickens and roosters, with chicken and rooster imitations. It was a kid's story, but it was better than standing there watching Dani and Ronit making out.

He thought it was stupid, what made Ronit cry. Some little kids walked by with their teacher and one said, "Hello Dani, father-of-no-one! Hello girl, mother-of-no-one!" and then of course they all had to say it, Hello girl, mother-of-no-one! and she started bawling.

Ronit is in bad moods a lot lately. Haim presses the ball of his foot into the floor and bounces his foot a couple of times until his leg jiggles up and down independently, like a motor. He cracks eight knuckles. He looks to see whether Dani and Ronit and Avigdor are talking. He looks away. What does he care.

"Tell me about having babies."

Ronit smiled girlishly when she said it, but Rachaeli knew enough about the girl to discount the smile. She was a strong-minded little thing. Rachaeli had made it her business to get to know her. They got on very well, a bonus. She couldn't manipulate Ronit much—the girl was too straightforward—but that was turning out to be unnecessary. Ronit wanted what Rachaeli wanted.

"Are you pregnant?"

"Of course not."

"So what do you want to know about having babies?"

"Is it awful?"

"Yes. And lovely. They lie on your belly . . . it's still high and swollen, you know? And they go right for the breast—Dani pulled at it so fiercely that they all laughed." She smiled and frowned, remembering. "And when he did, I felt my womb close and draw, close and draw. Pain and pleasure and . . . I don't know, pity. Poor baby, you think. Poor black wet battered head." She smiled, a woman's dreamy half smile that pitilessly included the girl. "But a tyrant at the breast, and you . . . submit."

"Like making love."

"No. Better."

It was going to work. She was much cagier than Ronit, and besides, it was only natural. Every woman wants a baby.

Ronit wasn't thinking about it at first. Loving him, she didn't recognize the childlust when it began to work on her. It was not that it was in her mind to deceive him; the impulse was somewhere in her seedbed. It was her time.

Even when the little thought surprised her, weeks before the fight, she didn't focus on it. It was just a vagrant little picture then, on a chilly late afternoon in the midst of an especially sweet tangling. They had the blanket around their feet and he was over her, the dying daylight veiling one side of his face and playing over his hair. He held her eyes with his, moving so slowly in her that the light never left his face and she felt him running in her veins like sweet warm light, swelling her. He hardened and held still in her, that little breathless halt on the precipice, and she saw it then, had a momentary picture of him pouring into her, filling her. "I want it," she keened to herself in the stillness, not understanding what she wanted.

After that she said it to herself often, fiercely now, picturing the rush of it into her and feeling inexplicably let down when she lay in his arms and felt it trickle out of her, wasted. She began to hate the diaphragm.

But it was beyond discussion. They couldn't marry. That is, they could but he wouldn't think of it. There were ways. They could leave, for example. They could get married in France or the United States, plenty of places. No one would ask questions. Their children would be legitimate in any of those places. She'd do it in a minute—she'd rather be a mother than an Israeli—but Dani refused. His job, his paratroopers, his delinquent boys . . . all too important to give up.

So they could do what other people did: marry and adopt kids. Or even have them; that was Rachaeli's suggestion and it made sense to Ronit. Have them and figure the law would change. But he wouldn't hear of that, either. "We can be lovers, but we can't marry and we can't have kids. We can't, that's all. Anyway, what do we need it for?" She'd thought about it. She could have her tubes tied. There would be nothing to come between them then. But she couldn't even keep the thought in her mind. Sterile.

"That bastard," she blurted once when he made her laugh and she hugged his arm and felt how she was locked in to him. "That bastard. He made me for you, didn't He?"

"Who?"

"God."

"God? He's no bastard. If He were, He'd have a little compassion. That's His whole problem; He's not human. He's created a people who are morally superior to Him."

"You believe in God?"

"Of course not." He smiled. "Yes, you witch. He made you for me."

So why did he insist on living by that evil law? Another of his poses, maybe. Rachaeli thought so. She said Dani wouldn't feel that way if Ronit were actually pregnant, if he could put a hand on her and feel his baby moving in her. Rachaeli mentioned that it had really gotten to her husband, Dov, feeling his babies kicking in her.

Still, she never intended to deceive him. He should have believed that. If he'd thought about it he would have remembered how it swept over them both that night. He was just home from his six weeks in the reserves, still in his uniform, and they'd planned to go to the wedding, Nissim's wedding, and leave early. She was all dressed, as a matter of fact, and they'd have gone straight out except that he wanted to shave. He stood at the sink, bare to the waist, drawing the razor through the lather on his face and telling her about Nissim's plans in misshapen words through half a stretched mouth. She went up behind him and put her arms around him. "Missed you," she whispered. He stood still. "How do you expect me to shave?" he moaned. He could have given her a kiss and saved the rest for later, but suddenly he was wiping the shaving cream roughly off his face with a towel and turning to her, groping for the zipper of her dress, and then she didn't have time to think about anything at all, so that when he asked it she couldn't think what he meant. She wasn't even sure what he'd said.

"Is it in?"

Oh. The diaphragm. She held still under him. His face was wild, twisted. "No—I forgot—"

He was out of her then, rasping "Touch me." She groped for him, desperate to guide him back. "No. Just hold it. Take me quick, *quick*, I'm coming." Then it was warm on her hands and cooling on her belly, wasted, and he was gasping on her breast like a runner. She was left. He raised up abruptly over her and fixed a stern, inquiring look at her.

"Don't ever do that again," he said finally.

"*Me*? Do what?"

"What if I hadn't asked?"

"If you hadn't asked, it wouldn't have been spoiled."

"Spoiled? You'd have been pregnant, little one, and then you'd have had all kinds of trouble." He disentangled himself from her, but didn't release her from his look.

She pulled the sheet up around herself. "Trouble."

"You don't think having an abortion is trouble? Well, I do, and someone has to think—"

"But I wouldn't have had an abortion."

"What are you saying?"

"I've seen them done. You think I'd destroy your baby? My baby?"

"Your baby and mine would be a *bastard*. You wouldn't do that." He was searching her face now, from a distance. He was going far away.

"It would be a baby, Dani; we could go somewhere where it wasn't a bastard."

"There's nowhere for us to go. And anyway, any child of mine would be a bastard, anywhere in the world, and to the tenth generation. I'm not fathering any babies, Ronit. I told you that. I thought it was understood."

"It was decreed, not understood. You never asked me."

"You want a baby?"

He looked assaulted. His voice was controlled, tight. It was ice against her ten thousand open pores. Pull him back now. Warm him. "I want your baby." Yes. That was true. She recognized it, now it was said. "I think about nursing your baby, Dani. I think about a little black-haired, curly-headed boy of yours. I think of putting him in your arms, giving him to you."

He closed his eyes and pulled a hand down over his face, stopped with his palm barricading his mouth, his fingers gripping his chin. His eyes opened over the barricade. Pain in his eyes.

"Dani."

"You would have done that? Gotten yourself pregnant?"

"*I wasn't getting myself pregnant*. I never had a chance. We just—"

"You want it so badly? Ronit?"

"It's part of wanting you. I . . . my body wants it, the way it wants you."

She couldn't hold his eyes. "I love you," he said from far away. "Too much, maybe. You're enough for me."

"So are—"

"But there'll be no more bastards in this line. I can't. Even for you."

"It's a thing you say. You haven't even thought about it. It's one of your pronouncements."

"I've thought about it for twenty-one years, day and night."

"*You* don't mind being a bastard. You glory in it."

There was a silence.

"Come on," he said finally. "Time we got up. We'll be late." He got out of bed. "One thing, though. I won't hold you. If it's something you need so badly, I'll let you go. You deserve to have what you want. You'll have to decide."

Dani was furious with her, Rachaeli read that plainly enough. He blamed her for his problems with the girl. The rabbis really meant it, really made an issue of it; who was to have known that? And he, for some reason she couldn't fathom, was using it to hold the girl off.

"Why don't you marry her?" she burst out once, exasperated. "You *can* marry her; she's illegitimate, too."

He looked coldly at her. "You've been researching it with the rabbis? How I can get married?"

"I asked someone a question. If I don't do it—"

"Did you also hire a band and pick out the ring?"

"Did I—oh stop it, Dani. Don't be a child. You should be glad to know—"

"She wants children," he said, deadly quiet. Suddenly he seemed to loom there, a man. Frightening. "She's a normal, sane woman and she wants to marry someone and have his children."

"Good, so—"

"So I'm sterile."

"What are you talking about?"

"Legally sterile: I can't have kids. *They* can't have kids. Their kids can't—"

"Oh, that's nonsense. You can—"

"What? Move to New York, like Avi? Hope that the children don't ever figure out what they are, and that they never want to come back here to live? It's a great set of options, Mother. Stay here where my life is and live like a man, doing my work, but live without woman or child—or go somewhere with her and have kids under a pretense and drive a cab like Avi and hope that the Klan doesn't get organized in time to kill us."

"Klan! Dani, you're—"

"I'm a bastard, Mother. You wanted a bastard, you got one."

Ronit would have let it go, or she would have waited for him to come around, but it was on his mind all the time after that. He asked her every time, even the sweet times, even the times they were wild to get to each other: "Is it in?" And every time he asked, she felt accused, punished, and something in her slid closed.

"*Yes*, it's in," she said once. "I *always* put it in." But still he asked every time.

"Why don't you get married, at least?" Rachaeli said to her. "The damned law permits that. Get married and the rest will follow."

"I would, but he won't do it. I'd even—I think I'd even be sterilized for him."

Chava, who had been chopping fish, looked up sharply. The cleaver hovered an inch over the chopping board. "You can't do that," she said. "Jews don't get sterilized. After Hitler?"

"We're not Jews, exactly," Ronit said bitterly. "We're bastards."

Rachaeli put her two hands on either side of the girl's face, fingers in the thick auburn hair. Chava saw, fleetingly, the young Rachaeli in the labor room, elegant and self-contained, smiling from that deep-centered female equilibrium of hers. "Don't even think of it," Rachaeli said tenderly, a voice Chava hadn't heard in years. "A woman deserves to be loved, and to have babies to love. Both."

"He wants me sterile."

"He doesn't know what he wants. He'll come around. Don't get sterilized; don't even discuss it. Just make sure he can't live without you. He'll marry you." It was Dani, her voice said, who was the alien in this. She and Ronit were of one core.

But Ronit couldn't think of him that way. He could be pierced, laid open to her. All the bravado, all the poses and flash fell away from him when they were together, and he was not alien, he was . . . they were connected. One current ran through them both. She needed that; she seemed to need it to live. She couldn't tolerate a barrier, of either his mistrust or her deceit. She had to be open to him.

So when, very soon after the conversation with Rachaeli, she was with him and he asked again, was it in, she cried, "Should I get sterilized? Then would you relax?"

"No. You can't do that for me. That's not what I want, to maim you, deprive you."

"I don't understand you. What's the difference? You want me sterile but not sterilized. What do you want of me?" She couldn't stop. She had to batter him open. "You have some grand picture in your mind. Page one, with a headline: DANIEL KOVNER, GENETIC HERO. RENOUNCES IT ALL TO SAVE THE JEWISH PEOPLE FROM CONTAMINATION."

"Not the Jewish people. My children."

He said it so quietly she was afraid. She lay back down next to him. "Hold me, Dani."

He held her. They were two separate people in the bed. She could feel his separate heartbeat. The fear swelled in her throat, feeding on silence, until she had to risk it. Jolt him back to her. "I've been offered a job."

"A regular job? I thought you liked free lance."

"I can't support myself forever on free lance. It's for a medical series. In New York."

It was a long time before he spoke. "Are you going to take it?"

"I don't know."

"Maybe you should."

"I don't want to leave you. It's a long time, maybe a year."

"I can't give you what you want."

"I want you."

"And children."

"No, not if—"

"Yes you do. You'll want it more and more. Maybe you'll find someone in America. You could have American babies." He was crying, the muscles in his face tugging uncontrollably. He felt her trying to look up at him but he held her immobile, saying nothing to betray his aberration. Tears slid into her hair, but she never felt them. She started talking, but he was thinking that he couldn't keep holding her; he fought for control and amassed it, hearing her sounds but unable to connect, stunning himself into control so that he could let go of her.

To her it sounded like silence. It sounded like dismissal. If she had known he was crying, she would never have left.

The girl is sitting as though composed, but one of her fingers rubs her thumb hard, back and forth, back and forth, and its knuckle is white. "I'm never going through it again," she says. "Never. Love. It's viral, vicious. It's an abnormal invasion of healthy tissue. I won't have it or feel it ever again."

Rachaeli had wanted Dani to marry this girl, settle down, burn out, relax into tepid marriage. She had planned it, moved for it, seeing it as the way to reclaim him. She doesn't remember that now. Pity turns in her, opening a dangerous chasm. She walks over and takes the girl's hand, prying open the fingers. "You will, you'll see."

A silence.

"You sold your flat?"

"Yes."

"You'll meet American men."

The girl shrugs. Rachaeli strokes her hair. Damn Dani. God damn them all, the oblivious bastards.

Ronit sits fully dressed in the plane's bathroom, shut off, suspended over the ocean. She is crying, rocking back and forth, the tears running hot, turning cold on her cheeks, running hot again. But she won't comfort herself, won't put hands on herself in pity: not to hold her face, not to cover her mouth, not to hug her arms and contain the rocking. If you're going to cry for him, she tells her twisting mouth and her throat in fury, you'll get no help from me. No pity here.

Finally she tears a tissue out of the wall holder and blows her nose, but that's as far as it goes. The tears run hot and turn cold and the body rocks unballasted. *Fool. Cry, then.*

Dani waves off the cabdrivers outside the airport. He's been standing there like a fool, watching her plane. It's up now; released, he can't think where to go. It's terribly hot, too heavy to move very fast. He can feel the blood crystallizing in him. He will turn to stone.

He takes the bus to Petach Tikvah. He finds Haim on the front stoop of his building. Haim is in clean shorts and a white shirt. "Hey!" he cries, grinning widely. "What are you doing here?"

"Thought I'd take you to the hobby shop. You're about ready for the hollow balls."

"I can't."

"Can't?"

"I have to go somewhere with my father."

Dani stares at him. The father? Now?

"We have to go see my mother. It's her visiting day."

There are two Danis: one standing there stupidly staring at the boy and thinking, Now? The father? What right?, and one organizing the retreat, shooting adrenaline to the limbs and making light sounds of *see you, another time*, and even, masterfully, accomplishing a wink.

Ridiculously, he strides four blocks before turning his head, making dead certain he will not have to see Haim's father. Father. What right?

He is turning to stone. Someone, someone. He sees a sign for a telephone and goes into the shop to call Shemtov. The phone rings twelve times. No one there.

Somewhere, then. Just somewhere. Her flat is gone, he'll fall right through space. Chava's? No, Shlomo will be getting home and he'll put his solid hand on Dani and Dani will shatter, splinters of stone and a terrible noise of breaking.

He heads for the bus. His place, his mother's place. Three blocks now. One after the corner. Here, now.

Rachaeli is sitting on the couch. She gets up when he opens the door, and she walks toward him. She is almost upon him when he turns smartly and attains his room. He locks the door and sinks carefully onto the bed, arranging himself in a semicircle around the molten stone, waiting for the rest of him to crystallize and become inert.

BOOK
FIVE

And when I passed by thee and saw thee polluted in thine own blood, I said unto thee: In thy blood live; yea, I said unto thee: In thy blood live.   EZEKIEL 16:6

Diamonds are elementally pure: unadulterated carbon. Dani's hands are blackened with newsprint. An impure form of the element, graphite is chemically identical with diamonds; the difference is the intense heat and massive pressure that force the carbon to crystallize. Dani washes his hands now in the men's room at work and the carbon sluices down the drain with water and soap. You can make soap of lye and any fat. Animal fat, for example, or more specifically human fat. It's been done. This is a less exotic soap, though, and the water is just water. Dani is washing up to go to Chava's for the holiday. It is October 1973, the eve of Rosh Hashanah.

Anni is in a car. She sits quite erect in her dress and gloves, her arms pressed to her sides, and she shies away from contact with her grandson Eli on the one side and Chava on the other. The heat is intense, even with the windows open.

Eli is in uniform; he's on holiday leave from active service. Anni is silent and rigid. Only her eyes move. Perhaps she feels too sick to talk. They are bringing her home from the hospital, although she is very ill. Her heart is starving her body. She is very ill but not critical and so they've sent her home; they're making room in the hospitals because of Syrian troop movements on the border.

The car stops for a traffic light. Anni turns eyes burning with hate on Eli. "Water," she demands, no trace of abjection in her voice. "If you are a man, a little water for the boy." Eli, of course, has no water to give her.

Aaron's plane taxis in at Lod. For the twentieth time he fingers the parcel in his pocket. It's a new suit, very elegant. He bought it through a contact in New York. He looks like an American in it. He worries that the parcel will pull the jacket out of shape, but he's had it in his pocket the whole trip. Only a yokel would carry diamonds in a briefcase or a box; Shlomo always transports them in a pocket. When the Hasid gave them to Aaron to take to his father, he watched to see where Aaron would put them. The man was getting ready to laugh at him, Aaron knew, and he took pleasure in dropping the stones casually into his pocket like a dealer: Fuck you, Zimmerman, you can fucking laugh at someone else. Although he had to restrain himself from fingering the pocket as he walked away and the anxiety made him queasy, he wasn't going to give the bastard the satisfaction. A city, a world full of thugs and these arrogant, showoff bastards carried fortunes in their pockets. Asking for it.

Aaron takes his raincoat from the overhead compartment and folds it over his arm. He'll take a cab to Shlomo's office and he'll walk in and greet his father and then, with a gesture of ease, he'll take the parcel from the pocket of his elegant suit and drop it on Shlomo's desk. "From Zimmerman," he'll say, passing another test.

They've settled Anni in the living room. She seizes a phone bill and a pencil from the end table and writes laboriously across the face of the bill. She holds it out to Eli, who takes it. Smiling ingratiatingly, she reaches out to him. He bends over her. She touches the epaulet on his shoulder. "Is that right, sir?" He looks over the shaky writing. It is dated July 17, 1944, and it says, "I am all right. I am at Waldsee. I am working." Eli looks helplessly at Chava. Anni has spoken and written in Hungarian; he doesn't understand.

"We were all made to write those when we got to the camp; they sent them to the people at home," Chava says. "Tell her it's all right, Eli. I can't stand it," she tells Rachaeli. "Every time he passes her, she touches the epaulets and talks to him in that groveling way. I can't take it."

Rachaeli smiles and passes a hand over Anni's thinning hair. She sits down next to Anni and takes her hand, absently stroking it. "A friend of my mother's told me a story once about a woman he remembered from Poland," she says to Chava and Eli. "Meshugenah Malkah, they called her. All year long she was perfectly ordinary, a drudge of some kind, but every spring she went crazy. She'd appear in the streets all dressed up like a coquette and when she saw a soldier—you know, a cossack—she'd rush up to him and kiss his hand, flaunt her poor old raggy body at him. They'd hear her out the window of the schoolroom, saying outrageous things, making obscene offers to the soldiers." She laughs, patting Anni's

---

bony hand and chafing the bluish fingers to warm them. "She went crazy by the season—when she thawed out, I guess—and Anni is a little crazy in her old age. Maybe it's not even craziness, you know? Maybe it's just giving in to what was always there. Power, strength," she muses. "You want to touch it; you want to *be* it. Maybe you don't have to be crazy, only realistic."

"Maybe." Chava takes the bill from Eli. "Go ahead, honey, call your friends. You don't have to spend your leave time dealing with Grandma. Only be ready for dinner early, all right? It's the holiday."

Potasnik is old. There are pouches under his eyes that look as though they hold reserves of tears. His hands seem bigger and they tremble. He is grimmer; they all are, Potasnik, Ari-Bela, Zara; the humor seems to have been leached out of them. *Be funny, Potasnik,* Rachaeli begs him silently, but he shifts irritably in his chair and grimaces. "I suppose Grodner would say we should make the first strike," he says. "Kill the sons of bitches before they move in on us." He often says Grodner's lines for him, these days.

"Don't worry, we'll be ready for them. Let them try to cross the Bar Lev line," Ari-Bela says. "What are you worried, Potasnik? It might take us seven days instead of six this time?"

"Golda won't make the first move," Dani says. He's sitting between Rachaeli and Anni. Everyone is there at the table: Shlomo, Chava, Aaron, Yakov, Eli, Anni, Dani, Rachaeli, Potasnik, Ari-Bela, Zara. The men are in white shirts, the women in light dresses. It was brutally hot during the day; the fan hums and squeaks in the background. "Israel can't attack; we can't afford to be the aggressor," Dani goes on. "Golda has no choice but to wait it out. There's enormous pressure on her to make the first move, but she can't do it."

"Who says we got to be better than everyone all the time?" Potasnik objects.

"Let's get started, Shlomo," Chava says. "The meat will be overdone."

Shlomo stands to make the blessing. Chava brings him the pitcher and bowl and towel. He pours water over one hand, then the other; the water catches the light from the candles. Shlomo, hands dripping, gets on with the blessings. "Blessed art Thou," they all finish, "O Lord our God, King of the universe, Who has kept us in life and has preserved us, and enabled us to reach this season." Zara sighs, thinking of Grodner. Potasnik pats

---

her arm, frowning. Rachaeli watches Dani. She can't tell whether he's thinking of the girl. Chava, scanning Anni, finds her unperturbed and goes to deal with the roast.

"She's asked me twenty-five times where is my bicycle," Aaron growls. He and Dani are taking the garbage down to the cans. Aaron holds the bag at arm's length. He can just see his new suit stained with gravy. "Then she talks to me in Hungarian. Then all of a sudden she says, 'Aaron? You've been away so long. How is it you went away? You're in school?' So sometimes she's okay, then—ah, I don't see how they stand it. She's a drain on everyone's time, energy, money. They ought to—"
"What?"
"'What?' You sound like God the Judge. You know *what*, put her in a home. It's not like she was ever so wonderful. I sometimes think the only reason she saved my mother was to ensure that she'd always have a handmaiden. She always ruled this place, you know."
"She could have gone to the left."
"What?"
"With her little boy. She could have gone to the left with him and she'd have died a saint. Without having to choose. Without starving or breaking her hands on stones, without enduring terror and humiliation, day after day. She did the other thing, though—went to the right with the kid who had a chance of making it and toughed it out with her."
"Sure. But that—"
"She's a crazy, abusive old lady who did God knows what to outlive those sons of bitches and keep one kid alive. I hope she blesses me before she dies."
Aaron raises the lid of the garbage pail. The garbage has been cooking in the heat; the stench rises and overwhelms him. He closes his throat and holds his breath, pushes the garbage bags into the pail, and jams the lid back on. Disgusting. Why doesn't this country have incinerators?

"Dani, what's your unit's code name?" Shlomo asked it casually one evening between Rosh Hashanah and Yom Kippur.

"'One Stick.' Why?"

"No reason. Just curious."

It had been a long, raucous session, choosing the code name. Bloch suggested Onan, "because when we come, we'll scatter on the ground." Lev argued for Ursa Major. "Circumpolar, you know," he said. "It never sets." He was ignored. Oded Peretz, one of the younger members, suggested Shadrach.

"You crazy?" Shemmy asked. "You want to bring fire on yourself?"

"In my life," Nissim uttered. "He thinks the code name's an amulet. How about Safe and Sound, you like that, Shemmy?"

"How about One Stick?" Dani suggested.

"I don't get it."

"Ezekiel: 'I will take the stick of Joseph and put it together with the stick of Judah and make them one stick in My hand.' Something like that."

"'I will gather them on every side and bring them into their own land,'" Shemmy continued it. "'And I will make them one nation in the land, upon the mountains of Israel.'"

"What did you do, Shemmy, memorize the Torah?"

"He's got extra time, nights. When you're married it only takes ten minutes."

"Are you kidding? Shemmy's record is twenty seconds."

"Well? How about One Stick?"

"Why not? Easy enough to remember." Bloch put a hand on his fly, grinning lewdly.

"He said One Stick, not one toothpick."

"All right, all right. One Stick, done?"

"Done."

Shlomo asked about the name because if things were going to heat up he wanted to know which codes to listen for on the radio. As it turned out, of course, no one was listening to the radio when they were called up.

———————

There are no radio broadcasts in Israel on Yom Kippur. Rachaeli was at Chava's for the day, as it happened, and the radio was on, emitting static sounds from time to time. Shlomo had forgotten to turn it off before sundown, and then it was the holiday, so he couldn't. It wasn't bothering Rachaeli. She'd brought her cello to amuse Anni, and she was playing some Scarlatti. She was babysitting Anni, who had made a scene when she saw Shlomo and the boys ready for services, dressed in their white robes, faces unshaven. "You're in shrouds?" she'd shrieked. "Why are you in shrouds? Why are you in shrouds?"

Chava had to give her one of her pills, and they decided they couldn't take her to services even for a little while. They had no choice but to ask Rachaeli to come over. Anni was quiet now. She sat wrapped in one of her shawls, eyes hooded.

"How are all your men?" she suddenly asked. Rachaeli stopped playing. "What happened to the violinist?"

Rachaeli lowered her eyelids and made a face of broad, comic resignation. "Gone," she said. "Found himself a young girl. I hope she's exhausting him. It wouldn't take much. Aren't you hot in that shawl?"

Anni looked down at herself, a brief survey. She shook her head. "What do you want with them?" she asked curiously. "Men?" For a moment Rachaeli saw her as she must have been at twenty.

"I'm not sure," she began, and then the siren cut through the flat, right through the room and between the women, isolating them on either side of the divide. It stopped abruptly and there was a moment of static and then the voice erupted out of the radio at them. "At ten minutes before two," it said, "the armies of Syria and Egypt launched an attack on our forces at the borders." Silence, more static, a disconnected bit of music. Prokofiev, Rachaeli thought. No, maybe not. Get Anni to the shelter. Where's Dani? Zvi? At the front? No, it's okay, they're home. All right, then, nothing to worry. They're not in it.

———————

Shlomo was at the synagogue. It was two in the afternoon, Yom Kippur. He had reached the point in his fast where he had gone beyond awareness of hunger and thirst. His body was lightening, a thin shell now for his wandering thoughts. Dani was not with him today; he'd smilingly declined to come to services, saying he wanted to spend some time with his boys. His boys. Three delinquents who would break his heart. They took everything Dani gave them and repaid him with more demands, lies, disappointments. He claimed that it was a triumph that the young one was in school, the older ones in training for Nahal, but Shlomo knew that Dani spent half his life checking up on them, intervening for them, bribing them and berating them. His boys. They made fun of him, called him Uncle, mocked his standards. Everything he gave them they twisted. Shlomo closed his eyes. He felt Dani a small glowing thing in the center of his breast. He imagined curving all of himself around the glowing thing, so that his pulse and his breath and the energy of his life fed into it. Let it be a year of good for him, he prayed. Let him be inscribed for strength.

Aaron pushed Shlomo's elbow upward, jolting him. Time to stand up. Shlomo stood and took the edge of his prayer shawl in his right fist and, along with all the other men around him, began the ritual confession of wrongs. He thumped his chest over his heart with each recital, battering at the shell with a tight fistful of prayer shawl. "And for the sin of hardening our hearts," he repeated. Yes, that one, he accused himself. Hardening my heart against Anni, not her fault, not her fault, unhappy tortured soul. Try, he urged himself. She hasn't so long to live; try to be kind.

Aaron read through the list in an even voice. "For all these," he chanted now, "forgive us, pardon us, grant us atonement."

The boy, too, Shlomo pierced himself. Hardening my heart against my son, too. A man, now, a good man. What kind of way for a father to be? Try. And her? He ran unfiled film behind closed eyes: himself sharp with Chava; himself pretending not to hear Anni so that Chava always had to be the one to answer her. Himself punishing Chava with indifference and silence. She doesn't have enough pain? He conjured her image, sleeping balled up against her terrors. He saw himself curl around her, absorbing it all from her into his bigger, calmer body and leaving her soft and easy. Oh, try. How could you forget?

They sat. The cantor began a long passage. Released, Shlomo bent his head and reran all the scenes, one after another, pitilessly—all the times he'd knowingly turned away, hardened his heart. He saw what he might have said and done, so simply. One after another he recalled the cruelties no one else had seen, added up the account against himself. Anni.

Aaron. Chava. It took a long time. When he focused on the service again, they were reading that strange little prayer for the people of Sharon who had lived in uncertain balance on the unstable earth.

"And for the inhabitants of Sharon who live in peril of sudden earthquake," the prayer went, "may it be Thy will, O Lord our God and God of our fathers, that their houses may not become their graves."

(It happens. On August 24 of 79 A.D., for example, the day of the first recorded eruption of Vesuvius, the earth, with no warning anyone knew how to recognize, tossed a piece of itself inside out, releasing heat that melted rock and smothered living things in their homes, among them Pliny the naturalist.

Volcanoes are pipelines to the unfathomable center of the earth, vents for the hot molten core too far away to keep in mind. The blue soil in South Africa interleaved with diamonds is volcanic in origin, stilled now and cool. So the igneous rock that melted and crushed the life from Pliny the naturalist was the stuff diamonds are transported in: hot, fast upward chutes bearing crystals and death.

Pliny made a mistake, incidentally, speaking of diamonds. Hammer may be broken and anvil may be shattered, he said, but not the diamond which lies between them. He was confusing hardness with infrangibility. It is possible for matter to be very hard but anyway to shatter if cleaved along a tenuous line. Diamonds, for example, are extremely frangible, having perfect cleavage. In each crystal there is one plane in which the molecules cling together less intensely than in any other direction in the atomic lattice. Strike that plane and the crystal cleaves open simply and cleanly. That is how the diamonds looted from humans at Auschwitz and the diamonds in Chava's stash and the diamond, the uncut flawed one in Shlomo's small safe, came to offer up such flat surfaces into which one might look and imagine the cold, silent fire of galaxies.)

May their houses not become their graves. Shlomo turned it over in his mind, playing with it, and so he saw the soldier make his way up the side aisle of the synagogue several seconds before it registered on him. The soldier clapped a *kipah* on his head with one hand. A white paper fluttered in his other hand. He approached the rabbi, bent over to tell him something. The rabbi got up, took the paper, put a hand on the cantor's shoulder to silence him, and went to stand behind his lectern. "At ten minutes before two," the rabbi said, "the armies of Syria and Egypt launched an attack on the borders of Israel. The following are called to service." He read a list of names and men began to exit at a run, some still wearing their prayer shawls. Both Yakov and Aaron were called, but not

Shlomo. Shlomo stood hurriedly to touch them before they left, letting the prayer book fall from his lap. He put a hand on the side of each boy's face. "Eat something," he said after a moment. "You can't go fasting. And find your mother. Don't go without seeing her."

He caught the soldier on his way down the aisle. "How about 'One Stick'?" he asked. "Are they called up?"

"I don't have units, just individuals," the soldier said. "What's the name?"

"Never mind. He doesn't belong here; you wouldn't have the name. Is it only infantry and tankists?"

"It's everything."

We should have been warned. They should have blown the shofar, Shlomo thought with helpless rage. What's it for, if not that? What the hell is it for?

———

Like all the men in the little synagogue, Nissim's father was rocking fervidly in his Oriental robe, shrilling prayers alternately with Berber incantations against the evil eye. The din was unnerving. Nissim closed his eyes and rocked a couple of times to relieve the pressure on his toes. He smoothed a hand over his new suit. Beautiful, he was elegantly turned out. Tall and tight beside his grubby little father, who was wailing for pity like an Arab.

When Nissim was little he would wait on Yom Kippur for God to call his father to account. God would find him out and punish him, strike him before everyone and he'd be finished, he'd never touch Nissim again. His father's prayers had seemed powerful then, loud enough to confuse God. Nissim thought that when he was grown, his voice would be more powerful and he would cancel out his father's noise and God would suddenly pay attention and deliver His wrath. He didn't even bother to raise his voice now, though; his father simply disgusted him. Amulet-clutching little tyrant in his filthy silk robe, groveling to God.

If you felt elegant and thought elegant, people would treat you elegant. He, Nissim, went to work looking good and he treated the whites like they were no better than he was. He'd purged his language and his gestures until he was just like anyone else, and he was going to be accepted that way. If they didn't return his invitations that was only because he couldn't teach his stubborn wife to cook like the whites and to speak up like a white woman. The other women were like birds, strong and bright and full of song, and all his Bracha did was giggle behind her hand. Nissim sighed. It was easy in the army—there was no one attached to you, dragging you down. You were a man with men.

His father was off again, outwailing the others. One Arab had wailed like that when Nissim held the rifle on him at the Canal. He felt his cock stir, remembering how he had pulled the trigger and cut off the wailing just like that. Just like that, Nissim thought dreamily, the caterwauling stopped and the Arab was canceled. You stood, a man with men, and you cut down the vicious dogs and, if you were lucky they wailed like that when you raised your gun and you had the pleasure of silencing them for once and all.

He hadn't seen the soldier go up to the sexton with the list. He was looking, in fact, into the shine of his shoes, so when the fellow tapped him on the shoulder he started.

"Nissim ben Haroush?"

"What?"

"That you? Nissim ben Haroush?"

"Yes, why?"

"You're called up. Meet your unit at the rendezvous. Full pack. Got it?"

"Sure. Thanks."

He whipped off his prayer shawl and folded it. "I'll say goodbye," he told his father, who showed no signs of hearing. The old man didn't blink until Nissim was halfway down the aisle. "Where are you going?" he shouted then, as though to a child.

Nissim turned. "There's war," he said above the heads and the babble. "You dassn't, today! It's Yom Kippur."

Nissim smiled at his father across the fence of rocking bodies. He read the din accurately; they were all listening, carrying on their prayers automatically but tuned to his reply. "When there is war, *abba*," he said clearly, "the men must go. May you be inscribed for a good year." He was still smiling when he thumbed a ride to the center. It had to be war. This had to be it.

Dani was at the beach with his boys. The sun was brutal and he was beginning to worry about Haim. Although he'd slathered the boy's skin with sun cream, he thought he could see the pink tingeing his shoulder blades and the backs of his knees. Maybe the fast was too much for the boy. He was dizzy himself, a little. But if he let Haim drink something, the older ones would start in on the kid again. Just now they were all batting a soccer ball around, not bothering each other or anyone else for a change. Let them be for a few minutes.

He'd been scooping up handfuls of sand and sifting it down over his legs and feet, so that they were almost covered. The muffling of sensation in his feet and the steady scoop and trickle through his fingers were narcotic. It was peculiarly quiet on the beach: no radios, no vendors, no sounds of traffic or work. Only the surf and wavelets of voices. There was a scuffle for the ball. Haim's voice pierced the heat. "You fouled! You fouled!"

"It was good!"

"Liar!"

"Your mother."

Everything twitched in Dani. Sand fell away from his shin bones in two clean lines, but before he was up, Avigdor was holding up both hands. "Sorry. Sorry kid, just an expression. Okay?" Avigdor shot a look at Dani, who kept his face blank. The kids went back to their scrimmage.

Dani closed his eyes. A second's decency from the little animal. Finally. He felt the blood slow in his veins again. Have to let them play a little longer now; can't break it up after that. The ball made a steady, solid sound, bouncing from shoulder to toe to elbow, Zadok, Avigdor, Haim. He got up and ambled toward the water, stood ankle-deep in the surf to get used to the cold. Something glinted at him from the sea bottom and he tried to locate it between waves. Gold? A coin? He thought he saw it carried out a little way with the undertow and he dived in for it, the cold shocking the breath out of him. Gasping, he brought it up. A bottle cap. Ladies and gentlemen, things are not always what they seem.

You ought to have learned that from her, once and for all. Ronit. Rachaeli was right about that, at least.

Stop. Never mind.

"Avigdor? Zadok, Haim? Want to swim before we head home?"

"Wait."

"Yeah."

"No."

"Yeah."

"Okay."

The big ones plunged in, horizontal, their backs like the backs of porpoises. He waded out to meet the kid, who wouldn't admit he couldn't swim. He picked him up under the arms and plowed through the water with him, feeling ribs, excitement, tension. "Want to jump them?"

"Sure."

"Wait for me to tell you."

"I know when. Let go."

"I'm not holding you. *Jump.*"

He held him and the buoyancy and tumult of the water let them both deny it.

The cold pierced them, held them until they got almost to Dani's, where the hallway was dense with heat, ovenlike. There was a red envelope under the door. A call-up. He tried the radio and found the bulletin: War, finally. "Avigdor, get out the Uzi. Move! Check it, see that it's clean and reassemble it. Haim, get my stuff. Don't forget the sleeping bag and the windjacket. Find what the hell you did with my compass, too. Let's go. Zadok, go home. Fast, thumb a ride—"

"Who do you—"

"Tell your mother you've been called up. Get your boots and a couple pair of socks and put on some clothes that fit, and get back here. I'll wait twenty minutes, then I'm going."

Zadok left, whooping; the door slammed behind him.

"He's not army!"

"He's going with me. By the time they figure it out he'll be behind lines somewhere."

"Then I'm going, too."

"No."

"Fuck that! I'm—"

"No. Listen, Avigdor. You'll be army next year. You'll have a chance to make officer. Screw it up now and they'll never take you. Zadok is older; he'll pass for long enough to get into action, and there's no other way he'll ever make it. You know that. He's illiterate, got a record. This is his only chance. Besides, I need you to take Haim home."

"What. I don't need—"

"Shut up, Haim. I need you to get him home, Avigdor. The city is going to be crazy today. And you look after him while I'm away. I don't want to hear any shit about truancy or any other wiseguy stuff, when I get back."

"Who do you think you are? You're not my fucking father." Avigdor was near tears. Dani turned away, dialed a number, said, "Naftali, that you? Tell the old man I'm called. My files are on the desk, tell him. See you. Yeah, thanks." He looked at Avigdor. "I'm not your father and I care about you anyhow. I don't have to and I do; remember that. You stay straight and keep him straight or I'll come back and break your fucking neck. Is that Uzi ready? Let's go. Haim, get my black case."

"The magic stuff? You taking *that*?"

"No, stupid; you are. See if you can figure out some tricks instead of getting yourself into trouble while I'm gone. Move."

He was right; the boy had had too much sun. In the filtered light of the stairwell you could see the pink along the skinny shoulder blades and down the backs of his arms. He'd be hurting tonight.

When Vesuvius erupted in 79 A.D., the explosion sent a column of ash and pumice twelve miles into the sky. It must have looked like a monstrous smokestack, like the ones at Auschwitz and Matthausen, only more surprising. The next day, the burning column collapsed and covered Herculaneum with ash, hot gases, and molten pumice. It is estimated now that it probably took less than five minutes for the inhabitants of Herculaneum to asphyxiate or burn or be crushed to death by geologic debris.

It took slightly more time than that to asphyxiate a roomful of people using Zyklon B gas, and then there were still the bodies to deal with. A man may be asphyxiated by breathing air containing about .12 milligrams of hydrogen cyanide—Zyklon B—per liter of air. Zyklon B destroys the capacity of the red corpuscles to transmit oxygen to the tissues, so death is accomplished by means of internal suffocation. The bodies, of course, had to be burned elsewhere, in order to preserve the little rooms with the gasproof doors for further use. It takes a fire of eighteen hundred degrees about two hours to reduce flesh and bone to ash. There was always a column of smoke issuing from the chimneys at Auschwitz, but it was only smoke and it drifted harmlessly into the air.

Men in tank crews are issued protective fire-vests and gloves and head covers. But it gets cruelly hot inside a tank, airless, and the fine sand sifts in and under everything, and the squeak and rumble are unrelenting and inside a tank you cannot see, and men tear off their head covers and gloves and vests in desperation. It happens all the time.

It was like that in the sand dunes on the Egyptian front on the third day of the Yom Kippur war. The heat was intense; there was no visibility at all in the dust and the black smoke of the artillery and the Katyushas. Aaron was gunner. He was following directions. The voice came over the intercom: "Gunner. Shot. Eight hundred. Tank. On!"

"On!" Aaron barked.

"Fire!"

"Firing!"

It made a rhythm; your voice and right hand were working parts of it, and the rhythm made you safe. Enclosed in plate steel, unseeable, engaged in rhythmic response to orders heard in darkness, Aaron felt safe. He'd taken his head cover and gloves and vest off, like the others, and sweat ran into his eyes, sand was in his teeth and nose, the desert wind was up and the grinding tank noise and the crack and thunder of shooting and the wind were concentric pounding circles, but the voice was human and steady against the din.

"Fire!"

He fired and his thunderous shot covered the noise of the shell that found his tank, so that in all the cacophony his own death was the sound he didn't hear. It was an armor-piercing shell and it went through their tank at two o'clock on Monday, October 8, at Hizayon, eight hundred yards from the canal, and it made, instantly, a furnace of the tank, roasting the driver, the loader, and Aaron, the gunner. In such a case it probably wouldn't have helped if they'd been wearing their protective gear, because their protection was their doom, their house their grave, like the houses of Sharon and Vesuvius and the little rooms in Auschwitz. He was twenty-two years and one month old. His incinerated body, reduced to ash and bone fragment, was returned to his mother and father.

Potasnik opened the door to them. They rang the bell on Wednesday the tenth. Potasnik opened, and at first they couldn't make out who it was. There were two or three of their neighbors, one a woman, and their family doctor, and a stranger.

"Mr. Reisner?"

"No, he's out."

"Can you reach him?"

"Well, he's at work. I don't—"

"Is Mrs. Reisner—"

"Chava dear, we've come—"

"No."

"Sit. Come, we'll sit—"

"No."

It was almost like chirping, the noise in her ears that jammed the radio and the murmurings and the rising arc of questions and the staccato of the phone call, only it was too fast a rhythm for chirping—blood singing in her ears, that was it, because it was pounding all through her, rocking her so she almost couldn't—

"All right, darling. Shh, all right, Shlomo is coming."

"Who?"

"Shlomo."

"*Who*, which boy, which of my—"

"Aaron is fallen, Mrs. Reisner."

Potasnik still had his hand on the doorknob. Tidy old man in shirt sleeves, his trembling spread hand covered the knob forgotten.

"You opened it," Chava shrieked suddenly at him. "Why? How could you? Woman, *woman*, you opened it and you let them in." Her voice filled the building now, big and inexorable, deep from her chest "I hate you. How could you oh my God how could you let them in?" Hungarian from old pipes, the visitors couldn't understand it. The doctor dropped the container of pills back into his pocket and unsheathed a hypodermic.

"Eva, stop it."

"Woman-n-n-n! Useless—"

"*Eva!*"

"What, Mother? We're even now, I'm even with you now, son for son, right? I don't owe you now. Son for son. And anyway"—turning to face her now—"you let him open it. You let it happen."

"Chavele—"

"Potasnik, she didn't mean it, she's out of her—"

"Shlomo's coming—"

Shlomo was coming, running through the streets.

Let me not see the death of the child.

He thought it would be his call-up; he'd been expecting it every moment and he was ready to go. He was going over invoices with the girl when the call came, Ari-Bela sounding grim.

"Shlomo? It's Ari. Listen, I—"

"I'm called up? Read me the notice."

"No, I—you'd better come home, Shlomo. There's been . . . the notification committee came, a colonel Magen—"

He hung up and ran. For every two steps a breath scraped in, hold it two, push it out. They came at him one after the other, four boys torn from his veins, Aaron, Dani, Yakov, Eli; one after another he bounced them back, kept them, by agonized effort, in suspension. *If I see one clearly he will be the one, let me not see, let me not—*

She was awake, sitting upright in her bed, drowning in air. Shlomo had run into the house; Rachaeli had come; the neighbor woman had followed Chava everywhere, ludicrously guarding her from self-harm until Rachaeli sent her away; Potasnik had held Anni in his awkward old-man arms until she stopped shaking and then murmured to her endlessly in a corner; Shlomo had cried and then slept and all of it was at a remove from Chava. Aaron was dead, burned, and that was at a remove, and Chava slept. But now she was awake, the drug dissipated, it was black night and silent, Shlomo slept, Aaron was burned. She saw him flaming, no, my God, flaming in agony and terror, my God, no, think of the cool earth, so she conjured herself bedding his scorched fragments in cool earth, saw herself hollowing the earth again with nails and claws, turning the world inside out again for Aaron in flames, trapped, flaming, screaming—

"What? Chava? Oh. Ohhhhh."

He went to hold her, she waved him away, away, but he grappled her in anyway and held her motionless. She said something.

"What?"

"Tell me a story," she heard herself senselessly say.

She would think, later, that it was because he didn't falter, didn't hush her, didn't ask do you really want a story, what kind of story—that it happened because Shlomo, who had really no stories in him, began immediately to tell it. He kept her locked against him, muffling everything, and threaded his voice through the black minutes for her to hold to.

"Imagine a place deep within the earth, quiet, quiet, beneath the noise, below rivers and roads, below agriculture and digs and below roots and soil."

"Cool."

"Yes. Cool and dark, and quiet. Now imagine a bit of carbon, maybe as big as a man's fist, and it finds its way to this deep and dark and quiet place. It's only a bit of carbon, a few stray elements in it, shapeless. Now give it time, a lot of time, and it sloughs off the stray elements so it's only carbon. Pure carbon, all right?"

"Yes."

"All right, now move the earth's plates around it a little, so that there's a pressure on it, massive, steady pressure, and heat—no, shhh, earth-core heat, geologic heat—and give it time, a lot more time and do you know then what the bit of carbon is?"

"Crushed. Smashed."

"No, it does a miraculous thing, I'm going to tell you. From somewhere in its own workings it shifts its molecular structure; slowly, in the heat and the great pressure its molecules shift so they are four-legged lattices, stable, unbreakable. It's a crystal now, still carbon, but crystallized so that now it's perfectly clear and very hard and very, very precious. A diamond, Chavele. So precious." He was crying.

He means me, she thought. Me and Mama, all of us from the camps, but especially me.

That wasn't really his meaning at all; the pain and the nighttime disorientation had fused a synapse in his mind and if he had gone on talking he might well have come to the flawed stone, to Dani, and then things would have been irrevocably closed between Chava and him, but she was pulling away from him, her nightgown was over her head, she was naked, she was pulling at his pajamas. The scent of her came at him, unscrubbed and immediate, and his skin pricked up.

"You want me to take them off?"

She nodded. She was half up on her knees, her hair wild and her eyes fixed on his face. He got the pajamas off and put his hands on her shoulders, uncertain. She pulled him to her, pulled him over her, reached for him.

He was still crying; he could hear himself now, but her palm and her fingertips made him hard and then she guided him in to her and wound her arms and legs around him and found his mouth with hers, so now he was crying muffled sounds into her mouth, and she began to echo, match his cries with indrawn breaths as though drinking them.

She saw the two skeletons humping on dust, luminous bones screwing death, and she embraced them too, with him, cushioned them all in her thighs and breasts, *all right, all right*, and went heedlessly through the veneer, closing in spasms on the hardness of it, so it all poured into her. *All right. Shh, all right.*

"Lieutenant Daniel Kovner?"

"Right."

"Got your unit together?"

"All but two. Ben Meir's abroad and I couldn't reach Gabai."

"They'll have to catch up. Your men equipped?"

"I need a helmet and boots for this one—"

"Name?"

"Raz. Zadok Raz. He's hooking up from another unit. And an Uzi for him."

"No Uzis. Got to give him a Galil."

"Right."

"Okay, let's have your cards. Here's your prisoner's cards: Kovner, Am-Shalom, ben Haroush, Bloch, Lev, Merhavi, Peretz. If you're captured, you can give name, number, blood type, vaccinations, that's all. Don't give rank if you can help it. Got your identity disks?"

"I want to change mine."

"Change what?"

"The name. It's spelled wrong."

"Now? Do it later, man. Let's see—you're going to the Golan. Report to Elisha, the thirty-first."

"Elisha, thirty-first. Right. Change it now, will you?"

"Do it when you get back."

"I might not get back."

"All right, but you'll have to type the new one yourself. I have no one at the machine. And let's go, make it fast, eh? This is some time to change your tags."

The machine was off in a corner. He made the one for Zadok and then for good measure he made a new tag for himself: Daniel ben Avraham, 2141053, Blood type B, crisp engraving in new steel.

"What should I do with the old one?" he called to the deployment officer.

"What old one? Oh—I don't know, throw it out. Ready?"

"Ready." He tossed the old tag into a wastebasket where it hit the side, ricocheted, spun, rocked, settled. Before it settled, he was gone.

They hitched to the front in a *sheroot*, dodging other loaded vehicles and passing hundreds of other reservists thumbing rides to the Golan, standing in little groups on the road, helmeted and booted and in every variety of dress. "Half the goddamn country is hitchhiking to the Heights," Am-Shalom said. "We'll tip over into Syria, it'll be all over."

"No, the other half is hitchhiking to the Canal," Bloch cracked. "Blessed be God, Who surrounds us with enemies so we shouldn't lose our balance."

"Who's the kid, Uncle?"

"Zadok Raz. Say hello, Zadok. He's infantry, but he's hooking up with us."

"Smart kid. You can get killed in infantry, you know. They shoot right directly at you, in the infantry. With us, they got to find us before they shoot at us. We do night work; we leave the dangerous stuff to the other schmucks. Right, Shemmy?"

"Sure. And me, I don't show up at night at all."

"Yeah, well the whites of your eyes would show, except that you shut them tight whenever it gets scary."

"Your sister."

"Your mother. Got a smoke, Uncle?"

"Here. What's that, Oded?"

"My chemistry book. I have an exam on Thursday."

"Shit, this thing had better last past Thursday. I've got this girl in my hair. By the weekend, she'll be back in Copenhagen and I'll be free and clear."

"She wants your virginity?"

"Yeah, twice a day. Shit, this war's a *relief*."

Zadok caught Dani's eye and winked, beaming. A man among men. Even when they got close enough to hear the racket of the fighting and the others fell silent, Zadok was strung tight with excitement. He knew it would be like this.

They had no idea it would be like this. It was all turned around. The Syrians were everywhere, pouring down into the Golan, tanks, artillery, rockets, missiles, endless rolling tanks. Wave after wave of them rolled right over day into night, crushing, breaking, spitting death, there was no rest. You couldn't see them, sometimes, until they were upon you, or you were upon them, because the Golan hid them—the rocks and the tels and the brush and the hills masked them. You couldn't see to brace yourself; you couldn't see anyway because of the smoke and dust and the fire flashes. And you couldn't hear. Ammo and vehicles were exploding from every direction, the noise ricocheted off the rocks and came at you twice, three times, amplified, untraceable. And you couldn't move; there were burnt-out tanks and half-tracks everywhere you turned and everywhere you were was the center. There were no lines.

Night should have come, you expected it, and it got very dark before the moon showed out, but in the darkness they kept coming, thousands of tiny infrared eyes, rolling through everything. The darkness was supposed to stop them, but they kept coming. The night wouldn't cover you either, no black place was really safe because their commandos had night-vision telescopic lenses. You couldn't see the man next to you, but some invisible Syrian saw him plainly, picked him off beside you; you couldn't see your own hands but the Syrian could triangulate your death, neat and precise. Then the moon showed out, light and very bright, and you were picked out in high relief and your target was behind you, coming fast.

It took the kid until dawn to get afraid. He'd seen the movies; this was wide-screen war, just as expected. He bounced along in the truck, fingering the AK 47 Dani had found for him—he couldn't handle the Galil—and complaining about "leaving the battle." He still thought there was a battle you could leave. They were going behind Syrian lines on the Bnot-Jakov/Kuneitra road to take out a roadblock. He thought there was a line. He didn't understand yet that it was all turned around. The rest of them had their eyes fixed on Dani's scrawled drawing of the roadblock, and there was no talk. Zadok thought that was normal. He had no way of recognizing how skewed it all was.

That was why he didn't panic until dawn, probably. They'd been put down in the wrong spot. Disoriented, they'd climbed up an escarpment, right into a gun site. They'd stood in the bright moonlight, they and the Syrians, frozen, until it all erupted. Zadok was slammed into rock; there was the thin pop of the Uzis and the hiss and crack of grenades, then sobbing, or breathing that sounded like sobbing. Am-Shalom was dead, sprawled out, looking lazy. They carried his body—Nissim did, then Lev—and put it down like schoolbooks when they finally located the roadblock and moved in on it.

The roadblock was not so bad at first; it was stationary and quiet, they came in behind it and they were in and out fast, but there was the explosion and fire and the pieces of bodies, and the smell of scorching, and his own rifle that knocked him back and threw the Syrian boy forward, both at once like twins, and the Syrian coming inside out on the ground and screaming, eyes open, so that you got confused and wanted to help him; and then there was Am-Shalom's body, waiting for them, blue now, mouth open and puckered in, wrinkled and astounded and monstrous.

Nissim shouldered the body again and they made their way to the rendezvous, a little grove off the road, and after two hours even Zadok understood that it was all turned around. The helicopter wasn't coming. They were cut off behind the lines, or in the middle of a circle of lines, they and Am-Shalom, and no one was coming for them.

Dani had been out with Lev, getting a fix on their position, and when he came back to the grove and saw what Shemmy was doing he crouched down to look.

"Kid took a bullet? Don't cut it out; we'll get him to a medic in a couple of hours."

"No bullet."

"Then—?"

"*Alfesht*," Nissim said sardonically. "Another quaint custom of Merhavi's. Watch this, Dani. You don't see too many witch doctors in modern combat." Shemmy went on cutting the white flesh of Zadok's back with a razor blade, tenderly, crooning to the boy. Zadok sat rigid and white. His fingers were digging into his thighs.

"*What*? Shemmy—"

"No, okay, that's all now, see the blood is running black. That'll take care of it, you'll see. Let it run, let it come red. Nothing to worry, Dani. Just getting at the black spot."

"You crazy son of a bitch—"

The boy was hunched over now, sitting bonelessly, blood running in a thin line down his back. His breathing had become loud and even.

"The kid was panicked, he was about to start yelling. This helps, Dani, believe me. You don't know everything. When you have terrible fear, the blood turns black. If the black blood goes all through you, you get crazy with fear, paralyzed. You can die. So you cut until you reach the black spot, then you purge it, see? See how red?"

"If that gets infected, you medieval jerkoff . . . Zadok? You okay? Put your shirt on. Wait. Nissim, wrap something around that cut, something clean. Shit, you ought to have known better, at least—"

". . . but dead."

"What? Put your shirt on."

The boy didn't say anything else. He kept his head down while Nissim tore up an undershirt and wrapped it clumsily around his chest.

"We digging in?" asked Bloch.

"We're moving. We'll meet up with them. Let's go."

It was midmorning before they met up with the decimated infiltration force, and another half day before they got through to Kuneitra. It was night—Monday night; they'd been awake since Sunday morning—before they could sleep. They wound down, smoking and rehashing the two days. Dani was cleaning out the cut on Zadok's back and bandaging it.

"It's no big thing, you know," Lev said kindly to Zadok. "Am-Shalom's only going to be six feet away from the rest of us."

"But dead!" Zadok said.

"What dead? What do you mean, dead?"

"Tchhh. Dead. Not moving, not thinking: *Dead.*"

"Not thinking . . . you don't know that. Maybe you think like crazy, after. Like dreams. And not moving . . . you never stop moving. There's the rate of galactic fall through space. Then the earth moves at four-point-seven kilometers per second and you move with it, right? And how about the shifting of the earth layers? And evaporation and freeze and thaw? What's so special about walking a few meters? All the time Am-Shalom is going to be falling, rotating, shifting, freezing, thawing, evaporating, drying, flaking, settling, merging, loam, topsoil, pressure, more pressure, rock, rock core, faulting, crazing, cracking, sliding—what dead? Never."

Absolute silence.

"He's right," Bloch said then, grinding out his cigarette and flopping over on his side. "Lev, you son of a bitch, you'll never die. Your luck you'll be a hundred and ten and still weird."

That was right, as it turned out. Even when Lev hurled himself into the path of the Syrian's fire at the mouth of the cave on the eighteenth of October, he was unscathed. It was no more unbelievable than the rest of what happened.

The cave was high in the Golan, in rocky terrain outside the town of Um Butne. The Golan Plateau is volcanic. It was ancient lava flows, sudden reminders from the hot molten core, that sheeted over the plateau with basalt and hardened into abrupt tels, volcanic cones, cold now and seemingly permanent, and of the right size to interrupt visibility.

The two Syrians in the tank couldn't see out and they had no radio set. All the radio sets had been removed on Friday before the invasion to prevent the Israelis from receiving early warnings. Anyway, the Syrians were well trained for the maneuver: artillery leads, infantry bridges the antitank ditches, then tanks roll forward, wave after wave, regardless of what happens to the waves preceding. Any Syrian soldier who withdraws under fire or fails to obey a command will be shot. By Monday morning, October 8, about forty hours after invasion, the forces of IDF will be destroyed and the Golan will be in Syrian hands.

Late on Tuesday, October 9, the two Syrians were in their tank on the Hermonit-Booster line, desperately entangled with the Israeli 7th Brigade. There were no orders for this situation: tanks and artillery in a melee, no one able to move, everyone surrounded and surrounding, pounded from everywhere. They'd been grinding away for a day and a half, eating dust and breathing cordite, undirected—unable even to identify the surrounding tanks in some cases, Syrian or Israeli—when their tank was hit. They tumbled out. Suddenly it became clear that the others were falling away; Syrian artillery and tanks were breaking and withdrawing. Their officer took to his feet, commandeered a half-track and was gone.

The two Syrians withdrew under fire. It was some time later, maybe a day, before they found the cave outside of Um Butne and crawled into it and slept.

"Look." Shemmy held out the Torah for them to see, small army-issue scroll dressed in khaki. He brushed some of the debris and ash off it, kissed it because it had been dropped and dirtied. They were picking their way in the night into Syria ahead of the infiltration force, looking for breaks in the minefields.

"Put it down, Shemmy. We can't drag that along."

"We can't leave it." Flat, a man's authority. "We carried Am-Shalom, we can carry the Torah. It's forbidden to let it fall into their hands to be destroyed."

"Shemmy—"

"What are we fighting for, Dani?"

Dani looked at Shemtov, stunned. There was suddenly no language they could use together. Anyway, Shemmy was pulling off his belt and strapping the Torah to his back with it.

Sunday, October 14, first light

They were hitched up with the Golani Brigade again. Raful had been sending them on night raids against positions and supply lines. Dani ran into a guy from officers' training. "You hear anything about Atsmon?" he asked the guy.

"He's up here with the Thirty-first Parachute; they took out Tel Shams last night, up along the Damascus road. Sagger missiles on both sides— you know, in there behind the rocks?—the Thirty-first took it right out from under their noses, only four wounded. Some job."

All right, Atsmon. One for you.

Which may have been another reason why Dani didn't simply throw a grenade into the cave in the first place.

Sunday, October 14, midday

"Listen—listen to this." Oded had the Torah open on the seat of the jeep—a book, not the scroll. Dani had made Shemmy leave the scroll at command post; now he insisted on carrying the book everywhere, an amulet. "Listen to yesterday's portion."

"Now you, Oded?"

"*Listen*, it's a good sign. It's about Gog attacking Israel. God says, '. . . and I will cause thee to come up from the uttermost parts of the north; and I will bring thee upon the mountains of Israel; and I will smite thy bow out of thy left hand, and will cause thine arrows to fall out of thy right hand.'"

"Oh, good," Bloch commented. "Now as long as they're using bows and arrows we're in great shape."

"Shut up, will you? Listen: 'Thou shalt fall upon the mountains of Israel, thou and all thy bands, and the peoples that are with thee; I will give thee unto the ravenous birds of every sort and to the beasts of the field, to be devoured. Thou shalt fall upon the open field, for I have spoken it, saith the Lord God.'"

"Great. So why don't we go home now?"

"Check your magazines, all of you. Where's your canteen, Zadok? Put it on."

Thursday, October 18, before first light

Heavy artillery. They're pushing at the lines again, widening the wedge into Syria. There's been heavy fighting in Um Butne and Dani's unit is going to be put down behind the lines in the high ground to disrupt the Syrian firing pattern. Shemmy and Bloch are huddled with Zadok, going over it all again, a cram course in guerrilla choreography. "Surprise, speed," Dani hears. "From here . . . off balance." They're tracing patterns on the window with their fingers; Lev and Oded and Nissim are adding comments. The boy is nodding. They've closed around him to teach him how to get through the engagements. They don't seem to need Dani for much.

The pilot is talking to Dani. "It'll take you how long to get to the position after I drop you, you figure?"

"Half an hour. Then . . . give us . . . let's say pick us up at the position at seven."

"If you're delayed—"

"Half an hour after sundown. Same place, or look for us; we'll flash you. What's the code now?"

"Here, look."
"Okay."
Thumbs up.
Thumbs up.

It's dark. Their fighter cover has been suddenly engaged; they're dumped in haste and the 'copter is up and gone. Dani looks around fast. They're intact. The kid is sitting ridiculously sprawled, dusting himself off, grinning widely. Dani jumps up first and stands crisp and alert, a focus for the boy, as their eyes get used to the dark.

7:30 A.M.

It was easy. The Syrians are strung thin, and this time for once there was a discernible "line" and the Syrians were facing down at it. They never saw them coming. They were sparsely manned, sluggish in reaction, easy targets. But the helicopter hasn't come.

"Again. They got it in for us."

"It's bad in Um Butne, lots of artillery. He probably couldn't get up. Come on, we'll wait it out."

"Where?"

"Not here. Nissim, come on; we'll scout."

They find it right away. Quiet cave, minefields out to the side but a couple of escape routes around it, out of the Syrian line of defense. They collect the others, bring them back to the cave. It's full daylight now, no time to waste. Shemmy has an arm around Zadok, congratulating him on the fighting. Zadok is beaming. Lev stumbles over a root; Shemmy and Zadok laugh at him together, a pair. Zadok is stuck to Shemmy like glue, in idiotic hero worship. So that when they approach the cave and Shemmy whispers, "Better throw a grenade, Dani, make sure it's empty," Dani rejects it testily. "Want me to wake up the whole Syrian ninth division? Buck up once, Merhavi. I'm going in; you follow after a minute." And then he does the thing he knows, has been trained, not to do. Hands empty, unhesitating—*Watch this, Zadok. Watch it, Atsmon*—he walks into the cave, widening his eyes to see in the dim light, and what he sees, he and his men behind him, is the Syrian and the Syrian's gun.

Behind the Syrian is another Syrian holding another pistol. "Weapons," the first one says. He's unshaven; his voice is high and harsh. "Lay them down at once." Lev unstraps his Uzi, then abruptly hurls it at the first one, yelling, "Go!" But his aim is off, the Uzi only glances the Syrian's arm. The Syrian doesn't move. They freeze, waiting for the shot, but the Syrian only steps over to Lev and cracks the butt of his pistol across Lev's face. Zadok cries out. The Syrian whips around and waves his pistol at them all. "Now," he says. "Lay them down. Who is officer here?"

"No officers," Oded says quickly. "All privates."

"We shall see." He gestures, the other picks up the weapons and piles them along the side wall. The cave is deep and damp, glistening with water. "Names now, step forward. You first, you came in first. Tags." He holds out his hand. "Say name and rank."

Dani pulls the chain off his neck. "Daniel ben Avraham," he says. Two-one-four-one-zero-five-three. I am the officer. Lieutenant. You want a hostage? You're deserters, right? So take me; you don't need all of us."

"Undress, Jew."

He hears them pull in their breath behind him. Don't let him see you're afraid, he thinks. Don't let them see. He smiles evenly at the Syrian and pulls his clothes off matter-of-factly, stands easily in his shorts and T-shirt.

"My mother always said wear clean underwear," Bloch murmurs. A tight little laugh from someone.

"Shut up. Silence! I said undress."

Someone grunts in surprise. "Don't worry," Dani says to his men, pulling off his underwear and tossing it down. "They're not going to shoot so fast. They're more afraid of bringing their own guys down on—" The Syrian moves in, slaps Dani's face hard. Dani, naked, slapped before his men, holds his easy stance.

"Now you." The Syrian points at Nissim.

"Nissim, when he sees how you're hung he'll never get it up again," Dani says quickly. The Syrian slaps him again but it's all right; Nissim's been defused so he doesn't have to attack the Syrian and get himself killed, and Dani has demonstrated that he is unbroken. While the others undress, Dani looks for exits and finds none. No light coming in from anywhere but the front. No weapons, not even their clothes. Maybe two, three days before the fighting reaches here, maybe never. The war's turning, though; the Syrians can't hold out much longer. So the worst is that they use us as hostages, trade us for their own hides and some of their prisoners.

No, the worst is they cut off our balls and stuff them in our mouths and leave us to bleed to death.

They won't. They're deserters, it's obvious. They've been hiding out in here. They need us; they won't shoot because someone will hear—their guys or ours. Their guys would shoot them or throw them back into the fighting to get killed; our guys would take them prisoner. But if they can wait it out and keep us alive here, they'll make up some story about capturing us in battle; they'll be heroes, and they'll get to go home.

What are they likely to do?

Kill one of us—knife him, mutilate him, terrify the rest of us into obedience.

His mind went white.

The Syrians were going through their things, pulling out chocolate and biscuits and dried food packets, lining up canteens, pocketing their prisoner cards—three for one, four for the other—and conferring.

Atsmon would have thrown the grenade.

Atsmon wouldn't have tossed an untrained kid into a war, big fucking gesture, to get him killed by some Syrian in a cave.

Atsmon wouldn't have led his men into ambush.

Come on, you useless bastard, find a way.

Even nightmares develop a kind of logic, if you're patient, and all through the rest of that first day and night he waited for the logic to show itself: either they were going to be safe—guarded, tended like a herd until market day—or there was going to be violence. But the Syrians didn't seem to have any clear plan themselves.

One of the Syrians spoke no Hebrew, and that heightened the uncertainty. There was a dreamlike doubling of every interchange: they to the one Syrian, the one Syrian to the other and back again. What was lost in translation? What lies they couldn't hear, what harmless meaning made sinister? Then they couldn't tell which of the Syrians was dominant. The two of them disagreed, that was clear, but since it was only the Hebrew-speaking Syrian who spoke to them, they couldn't be sure whose decision he was mouthing. They feared being trapped between the languages: what if the one who spoke no Hebrew relayed an order to them through the other one and, for his own crazy reasons, the Hebrew-speaking one decided to change the order in translation? They could be shot for failing to obey an order they'd never heard.

Because the one who did speak Hebrew was a madman; that became very clear. When they were all naked, he made them sit against the cold, wet wall of the cave, well back, where they could barely make him out until their eyes became accustomed to the darkness, and he addressed them. "Now," he said in that high-pitched voice, "I am going to tell you something. Allah, He has sent you into our hands to ransom our brothers when we shall have finished our work and wiped out the whore Israel. Your spider state is finished, that is clear. Finished: even now your State of Donations whimpers for peace. There is no doubt that when the mongrel collapses—and it shall, Allah promises and we carry out His will—there is no doubt that some of our brothers will have been spirited away, prisoners scattered among the Jew brothels of United States and so on. Every Syrian child of God who has in his keeping a piece of garbage from that garbage heap of garbage heaps will force the world to ransom out one of our brothers for one of you. Then let them do what they will, with you. We shall cleanse the land and the Foundling State shall be a brief, putrid memory."

They could see him now all right. He was looking fierce, glazed over with his own rhetoric. They waited. He'd lost the thread. "Meshugeh," Bloch breathed. The other Syrian came up and said something to the first one. The first one nodded impatiently, waved him aside. "Now," he said. "Therefore you are our prisoners, therefore I shall tell you how it shall be. We have a rendezvous in a few short days, all arranged, when we shall reunite with our forces. At that time you will have your use. Until that time," he trained a finger on them, "you shall and will be still. You shall and will tell us what we need to know. You shall and will do our bidding exactly, and you may save your skins. Do not try any foolish thing. You are in danger here. You are in great danger, garbage, Jews, believe me, because we shall prevail; we have already prevailed. We are lions of valor, lions." He was lost again. They waited for him to finish, or for the other one to prod him again, but he turned his back abruptly, and the two of them walked off. He was apparently satisfied he had delivered a message. They waited but the Syrians were devouring something from a packet stashed in a dry spot, and searching the packet for crumbs. They'd been dismissed.

"I thought we were going to die of pneumonia, but there seems to be a lot of hot air here," Lev said.

"He's a lion," Bloch snorted.

"Smells like one," Oded said.

So they called the first one Lion and the other, because of his expression, they called Smolder.

"Quiet; don't waste words," Dani said. "Do you understand? They're deserters. They're afraid for their skins if their army finds them, worse than that they're scared of being taken by our side. We're their ticket out, if they can lie low until there's a truce. Let them blow off steam and don't provoke them and either we'll figure a way out or they'll trade us in. They aren't going to hurt us."

He said it to calm them, and actually by then it seemed as though they were going to be safe. As a matter of fact, they were pretty much left alone until the night. Lion tossed them their heap of underwear and socks and tags without a word and, covered, they began to complain. A good sign, Dani thought. Oded was hungry. He was tall and lanky, still growing, and he was in misery when he missed a meal. He'd missed two now.

The Syrians had run out of rations, apparently, because they were looking over the food they'd taken from the Israelis and conferring. Lion stood up and called to Dani. "You," he said, and pointed to a spot before him. Dani went over to where he stood.

"Some of your rations are edible, some are poisoned," Lion pronounced.

"What?"

"A trick in case of capture. You will show us which are the edible ones, or you will eat nothing."

"There's no trick. The food is okay."

A moment passed. Lion's expression went from stern to enraged; suddenly he slapped Dani backhanded across the face. "You will starve, then!" he thundered. He returned to where Smolder squatted hunched over the packets of food and kicked the packets violently. They scattered. A canteen rolled into the darkness.

"What the hell?" Dani said to the others.

"He didn't believe you," Shemmy said. It was the first time he'd spoken since they'd entered the cave.

"Why not? Why the hell not?"

"It was the way you said it. You only said it once. To them, it was a weak reply. They figure you're lying."

"Are you kidding?"

"No, it's how they are."

"How many times makes it true? Three? Seven?"

"No, it's how you say it." Shemmy gestured rolling amplitudes with his hands. "You have to . . . you can't be so—"

"You talk to him, Shemmy. I can't do that bullshit."

Shemmy froze, blanching. Bloch spoke up. "It's better if you do it, Dani. You don't want it to look—"

"All right." He walked over to Lion and Smolder. "I want to assure you," he said in the evenest tone he could muster, "that the food is fine to eat. It's pure and perfectly edible. None of it is poisoned. We couldn't carry all that extra, poisoned food just in case we got captured. We carried the food to eat and our weapons to attack with. The food is fine and the water is fine. It's up to you what you want to do with it now." He walked away.

"How the hell do they say 'Aim, fire?'" he muttered when he sat down.

"Backward." They laughed, except for Shemmy and Nissim.

The Syrians tossed them a packet of dried food and a canteen and watched them eat. They'd found the brandy and were sharing it, eating nothing.

"Some Moslems," Shemmy said. Nissim still sat grim and silent.

"How long do you figure they've been in this cave?" Zadok asked.

"Since the day before Yom Kippur," Bloch said.

"If they were out of the fighting," Zadok said in a tight voice, "then they've got lots of ammunition."

"They have ours."

"Right, oh right. Of course." Zadok was afraid.

"Anyone got a plan?" Oded asked. "We could overpower them, of course. There's seven of us. But someone would buy it."

Silence.

"No alternative exists."

"No."

"No fire in here."

"No."

"No. Hey, how about this? It's dark in here. We could dazzle them, shine a flashlight in their eyes, jump them—"

"They have the flashlights. And anyway, someone would die in the first scuffle."

"No. The thing is to stay alive until our people get up this way. It won't be long," Dani said.

Silence.

"This would be a good time for a little magic, Dani."

"Yeah, hey, no kidding—you could convince them you were a wizard. Scare 'em."

"Not here, Zadok; that will get us killed. I can't do any big magic, you know that—only little tricks. Little tricks are going to get us killed here. What we have to do is outlast these sons of bitches." He put an arm around the boy, briefly, to bolster him.

There was a murky rivulet running in a shallow crevice of the rock wall at the back of the cave, and the Syrians seemed to have established that as a latrine. First Lev, then Oded and then the rest of them used it unhindered by the Syrians, who had finished off the brandy by nightfall. Lion slept now; Smolder kept watch, pistol in hand. "We'll have to run watches," Dani said. "I'll take the first one."

"No, let me," Zadok said. "I'm not even tired."

"Want someone with you?"

"No, why?"

"Wake me, then, if anything comes up. Wake me anyhow, in two hours; I'll relieve you. No heroics, understand?"

"Sure, don't worry."

So Zadok and Smolder sat on opposite sides of the cave and scanned the darkness while the others slept.

Half an hour into the watch, Zadok got up cautiously and pointed to the back of the cave; he had to pee. Smolder nodded slowly, smiling a little. The brandy cheered him up, Zadok thought. He was peeing with his head twisted around to keep an eye on things when Smolder came up to him, pistol raised. He was undoing his pants and still smiling. He's got to pee, too, Zadok thought, and smiled back a little and then the pistol was in his back and the Syrian's hand was on his butt.

They woke up to the sounds of a scuffle. Lion was running toward the back of the cave. His IDF flashlight played over the walls and caught Smolder, pistol raised and cock erect, trying to force Zadok to the ground. The light went out, there was a short, ferocious argument between the Syrians, and Smolder retreated, pulling his pants up. Lion ordered Zadok back to the others, then came over himself and stood over them, shining the flashlight in their faces.

"If you try that filth again, you will be shot," he said. "We know Israeli army is a brothel. They provide you with women, boys, anything you want. The whole world knows what Jewish women are. Animals. It is why you lose this war. But we have control; it does not work over us. Next time someone dies."

Zadok lay turned away from them, shaking visibly. No one could touch him; they looked helplessly at each other. Across the cave they heard a low argument, sounds of anger and denial, then conciliation. Then they saw Smolder hold up a rifle by its wooden stock and heard the rhythmic chant:

> "Wa hayet hal'oud,
> Wa rabb el ma'bud.
> Wa sleyman bin daud,
> Wa mat ul'Yahud."

Lion nodded, satisfied, and took up the watch.

"What'd he say?" whispered Bloch.

"An oath: 'By the life of this sliver, and the Lord the adored, and Solomon the son of David, and the Jew's death,'" Nissim translated in a hollow voice. "I've heard it before. When they swear by the Jews' death, it's a holy oath."

He glanced at Shemmy; Shemmy knew it, too. From the moment they saw the Syrian in the dim light of the cave, gun trained on them, he and Shemmy had known what it would come to. Standing naked on the cold damp floor of the cave, exposed before two uniformed Syrians, his cock in their gunsight, his life in their rotted teeth, Nissim had known. It was all happening. Their death would be the least of it. Everyone knew that the Syrians were of all of them the most vicious, the most perverse and sadistic. He was going to be raped in front of everybody. As his father had made him pull down his pants and had beaten him while his whole family watched, these uniformed men were going to pull their cocks out of their uniforms and make him bend over, naked, and they were going to force him before everyone. First they would cut him, beat him, make him crawl and scream. Death would be nothing.

"Merhavi," he whispered. Shemtov looked up. Yes, there it was in his eyes: he knew. "We have to get them," Nissim told him. "Even if we die; we can't just wait."

Shemtov nodded, but there was weakness in the gesture. Fear. Nissim went to Dani. "They mean it," he told him.

"What?" Dani was preoccupied. Blood and rage were stampeding in him. He had put an arm around the boy, inviting the Syrian to think—

"That oath of theirs. 'By the death of the Jew.' They mean it, Dani; they're going to destroy us."

"No, they're not. They can't afford to."

"What do you think that oath was about?" Nissim whispered furiously.

"It seems obvious. Lion made Smolder swear not to pull any more of that stuff."

"You don't know them, Dani. Once they get . . . once they have the upper hand, there's no limit. We have to do something now. I'll do it; I don't care what—"

Dani put a hand out but stopped short of touching him. They both glanced at the Syrians, then warily at each other. "Wait a minute. They're not so stupid, Nissim," Dani said. "If they . . . hurt one of us, the rest of us will have no choice but to rush them. There are seven of us and two of them. They know that. It's been a whole day and they haven't made a move. They have no plan, except to keep us alive as hostages. We're going to outwait them, and none of us is going to endanger the others. There's no danger unless one of us gets crazy." He looked steadily into Nissim's eyes. "All right?"

"If they start—"

"If they make a move, we'll have no choice. They haven't made a move. Now let me think a minute."

Nissim went back to the others. He squatted and fixed his eyes on Lion, a penetrating stare. Let him know that a man was facing him.

"It could have been any one of us," Lev was saying matter-of-factly to Zadok. "Whichever one passed by him at the moment. He's drunk, and anyway that's the Arab national sport."

"Come on, Zadok, man, forget the crazy bugger."

"Too bad he didn't try it on Nissim. Nissim's so tight-assed the son of a bitch would have broken his cock."

"Sit up, Zadok," Dani said suddenly. "You've got an hour to go on your watch. Hey," he called across to Lion. "Pass us some biscuits and water here."

343

"Get them yourself, Jew. One packet and the small canteen, that's all."

They passed the canteen around and shared the biscuits. Dani made Zadok take a drink, watched him down the piece of biscuit. "Now finish your watch," he said. "Wake me in an hour," and lay unconcernedly down. The others followed his lead.

Through the hour, Dani lay watching the boy and the Syrians through the crook of his arm. No one moved. Even then, even with all the things that passed through his mind in the hour, he didn't put it together.

But the next day Lion tried working on Oded, and then it came so easily clear. It was hours after they'd awakened, and the Syrians hadn't allowed them anything to eat. Lion strode over and pointed at Oded. "You," he said. "You will report for interrogation." Dani started up to his feet. Lion put up a hand. "Standard interrogation, Red Cross," he said absurdly. He gestured Oded over to the Arab side of the cave, where he placed him ostentatiously at a little distance from himself. They couldn't make out what the Syrian and Oded were saying. Lion made a long speech. Oded listened. He shook his head once or twice, then nodded slowly. Then he was released, and he came back to the Israeli side.

"What did they want?"

"They're nuts. They wanted to know our troop positions, emplacements, flight plans."

"Maybe they're running the war from in here."

"They want to buy insurance for themselves if they're caught here by their people before there's a truce. What did you say?"

"Nothing. I said I was a foot soldier, had no idea what the plans were. I said the fighting looked pretty ragged to me out there, and both sides looked pretty tired."

"Good man."

"You shook your head a couple of times, and then you nodded. Then he let you go," Dani said evenly. "What was all that?"

"I was coming to that. He wanted me to spy for them. He said was I hungry. I said we were all hungry, but we were trained to survive. It all took so long, you know? Because first Lion would ask, then Smolder had to hear what I said and—"

"So he offered you food."

"He said if I would be their eyes and ears with you, they'd take care of me."

"You nodded."

"Of course." Oded was indignant. "What the fuck should I have done? This way they'll think—"

His voice, held low, wound on in defense and it was all suddenly clear to Dani—rape, blood oath, and all.

"There'll be no kapos in this outfit," he said clearly, his voice riding right over Oded's. "No accommodations here, no separate deals. You all understand that? We eat the same, we drink and sleep the same, and we let them know it."

"But maybe—"

"Look at me, Oded. I'll decide what's true here, and I'll tell you what to believe. If there's anything I know it's bullshit, and these guys are one-hundred percent bullshit. Forget them, man; fear me, not them, because if I catch any of you even smelling of selling out, you'll first have trouble. You understand what they're up to? Play on us, get us to make little choices, buy time, buy food. Pretty soon we'll forget—"

He stood up. "Get up." They sat, confused. "Come on, come on, get up. What day is this?" he asked Shemmy. "Friday, right? So it's the regular weekday prayers. You'll have to lead us."

Shemmy was pleased and surprised. "Yes, we should pray. God will—"

"Forget it. There's going to be no saving hand for us, Shemmy. We're on our own here. What we do to save ourselves in this shithole, that's all there is."

"Then why the hell *pray*?" Lev asked.

"Because it says we're not them, we're us. We stand up together like men and we make a noise here. *Our* noise. It says 'fuck you' to the whole thing."

Shemmy gasped.

"And it makes some of us feel better, so all of us will do it. Get up."

"I don't know any prayers."

"Me neither."

"Fake it."

"We don't have ten men."

"You going to quibble or pray? Stand up, dammit." They stood up cautiously, one by one. "We're getting up now," Dani called across to Lion. "We're going to pray."

Lion laughed. "Good idea. Pray to your banker God to save you."

"Just saying our prayers. Jews do, you know, every day. Together." He looked his men over. "Cover your heads. Let's go, Shemmy, begin."

345

He thought it through in the night. He had heard it all before, over the radio in Chava's apartment and in the auditorium in Jerusalem, looking up at the image of the man in the glass cage: starvation, humiliation, rape and sexual abuse, fear of torture, threats of death, all of it random. It dehumanizes people, keeps them between terror and hope, off guard. Then they pick one out to favor, you get people doubting each other, making choices, you destroy the group, and no one gets out whole. That's what they're up to.

So there's going to have to be a confrontation here. You either go up against it or you give in. Someone will have to go up against it.

It has to be someone with nothing to lose.

He almost laughed aloud in the dark, hollow, dripping cave.

Who else?

Look, I fouled it up, I should make it right. I led them right into this. I dragged Zadok along on a whim—big shot, going to waltz him through the war in glory—I get him shot at and cut up and nearly raped by an Arab, and what next? Who next? Beaten, one by one, or worse? Knives, belts, humiliation . . .

Smolder sat watch, yawning and scratching. Lion slept with one hand in his crotch.

I'm perfect for the job, best man in the world for it. Dead end anyway, right? Who has less to lose than me?

(She had laid one palm open against his cheek, sealing his old army fantasy of single-handed victory: *yes, I see you that way*. In the dark, in captivity, on the hard, cold, damp floor of the cave he gave in for only a minute to her. He was going to die, so it didn't matter now; he could let himself think of her. You had to surprise a smile out of her. She was so solemn, but then sometimes just after she came, flushed and easy, the smile would begin in her eyes and catch his. Caught, he would echo the smile of a shy child and a woman opened.)

Watch this, Ronit:

He choreographed the face-off: a single spotlit circle in the dark cave. He finds the right moment and he goads them; the Syrians are caught off guard and respond. Then they leap to it, he and his men, one powerful unit, himself in the front, bullet-catcher. The Syrians collapse, drop their guns, plead mercy. They emerge from the cave with the Syrians tied, splendid booty, in time to meet the advancing IDF. Zadok, bonded to him forever, walks out at his side.

And if they kill you?

All right: he falls, glorious sacrifice. The killing gives his men in the momentary confusion the chance to jump the Syrians, overpower them. He has redeemed them and there will be six men to tell his story. Ladies and gentlemen, the bastard who died for his people. Cut off, read out, he was freed to be a man for all men.

Ronit would grieve and he would feel nothing. Finally having made an end of it, he would feel nothing at all.

The next morning, as though they had divined his thoughts, the Syrians put a ban on conversation. Nissim had last watch and before the rest of them were awake, Lion was standing over them.

"You run with words like a urinal, you Jews. There will be no more of it. From now on silence, absolute, total, and complete. He who speaks will be shot. I myself will kill him, run him through and feed his putrid body to the animals." He waved a hand grandly at the silent morning showing dimly at the mouth of the cave. "One word and you shall die and rot and decay at my hand." He turned and strode back to Smolder, who offered him a piece of chocolate.

Dani had awakened remembering his night plans. Now he watched the Syrian striding away. He'd been going to give his men a plan of action this morning. Now what? Think, you bastard.

Shemmy got up and walked over to the Arab side. He stood there until Smolder poked Lion and Lion looked up.

"What is it, Jew?"

Smolder said something, laughing. Lion laughed too. "Speak, Jew coward. I grant you leave to speak."

"There is a book in there with our uniforms." Shemmy spoke quietly, his voice tense but unwavering. He pointed to the tangle of uniforms on the wet cave floor. "It's our Torah. We need it for our prayers today. This is our Sabbath."

"No and no. No speaking."

"You are men of God, I know. In your righteousness you will not deny us the obligation of our prayers."

The Arabs consulted.

"We are men of the true God," Lion declared. "And by His hand we have struggled, and we shall and will prevail. Your prayers are a fraud and a blasphemy."

"In your abode we are guests. As guests we seek the comfort of our service."

Nettled, Lion got up himself and thrust his hand into the pile of uniforms. He held up the boo' and tossed it onto the ground at Shemmy's feet. Shemmy picked it up and kissed it.

"I warn you that I have excellent Hebrew and I know your Torah. You will speak clearly and say no word that is not written there, or you will die."

Smolder was restless. He paced the cave, pistol in hand; he stood near the mouth of the cave and peered out, squinting against the daylight. It was perfectly quiet outside. He went to pee. He turned the pile of uni- · forms over again, looking for something they'd missed. Dani was keeping half an eye on him and half an eye on Lion, who stood stiffly on the Israeli side of the cave, monitoring the service, and he was weighing the possibilities: when was he most likely to have a chance to provoke the Syrians, and how was he going to alert his men? So Shemmy was all the way up to the prophetic reading before Dani picked it up.

"'I have called thee,'" Shemmy was chanting, "'. . . taken hold of thy hand . . . covenant of the people . . . light of the nations . . .'"

Dani began to listen.

> "To open the blind eyes,
> To bring out the prisoners from the dungeon,
> And them that sit in darkness out of the prison-house."

Dani's first thought was that Shemmy had picked this passage purposely, and that there was just a chance that Lion did know the yearly cycle of readings and would call them on it. He wasn't ready for trouble now, so he held his hand out for the book. Shemmy passed it to him.

It seemed right, though. This was the week they would begin the annual cycle of reading, and Shemmy had been reading the year's first prophetic passage. He scanned the passage and nearly smiled and gave it all away. Oh, Isaiah, you prophetic son of a bitch, I couldn't have said it better myself. He looked up and fixed Shemmy with a warning look: *Not a word from you. Not a peep.*

"Behold," Dani read; *Listen,* his voice said. "The former things are come to pass,

> "And new things do I declare;
> Before they spring forth I tell you of them."

He was improvising the melody to cover the fact that he was skipping lines and weaving together a new message from scraps of the prophet.

Shemmy held his tongue and paid close attention. They were all paying close attention.

> "I have long time held My peace,
> I have been still and refrained Myself;
> Now I will cry out . . .
> . . . And I will bring the blind by a way that they knew not,
> In paths that they knew not will I lead them;
> *I will make darkness bright before them*;
> . . . *They shall be turned back.*"

He risked a quick survey. Their faces showed cautious comprehension. *Okay.*

> "Hear me . . . they are for a prey . . .
> Who among you will give ear to this?
> Who will hearken and hear for the time to come?
> . . . Fear not, for I am with thee;
> I will . . . gather thee from the west
> . . . And let you hear and say: 'It is truth.'"

"It is truth," they chanted, repeating his invented melody. They had it. He slammed the book closed and handed it back to Shemmy. It was going to work. He had only to wait for his chance.

It looked, late in the day, as though Lion was going to give him his chance. The Syrians had become increasingly restive. Smolder peered out a hundred times, but it remained absolutely silent outside the cave; the daylight came and dwindled away and brought no news. Inside, the sounds of breathing were amplified, and everyone attended the sporadic dripping and the occasional stream of piss as music, or messages. Smolder and Lion observed their own ban, seemingly, and barely spoke.

At dusk Dani and his men stood for their brief service, pitching their voices low. Even the quiet singing seemed to fill the cave. *Now*, Dani thought, and he urged their voices up with his hands, like a conductor.

"Too loud," Lion barked. Dani conducted a swell of sound—their voices rang in the cave, shockingly loud—and stepped away from his men, only a pace or two. Lion bounded over. *Now*.

But Lion stopped a few paces short of Dani. The voices swelled. "Silence!" Lion hissed. He drew his pistol. Dani gestured to his men and their voices stopped but he chanted on, bellowing the lines of prayer that Shlomo had taught him. He stepped forward another step, daring Lion, to draw the attack.

Still Lion only held his ground and spoke. "Lieutenant Daniel ben Avraham of IDF," he drawled. "This is the limit of your courage?" He smiled down at the pistol, and then at Dani, standing a pace away.

"Try me," Dani said. He felt his men tense behind him. They were ready. Electric, poised, he held himself motionless, waiting. Lion's eyes widened, took in the moment, closed sleepily. *"Bondouk,"* he said pleasantly from behind his pistol. "Bastard son of a whoring mother."

Because it was true, only for that reason, because the Syrian had chosen the one thing to say that Shemmy knew to be true and unspeakable—because Shemmy knew Dani's mother to be in fact a whore and Dani to be a bastard—there was all at once no choice and no time. Shemmy hurtled, leapt, hands out for the Syrian's throat; the Syrian fired into Shemmy's face and Shemmy died in suspension, midair, taking Dani's moment for his own last.

No one moved. They listened: nothing. They watched each other.

Lion bent over and pulled the identity disk off Shemmy's neck and dropped it around his own neck. Then he picked up the body and carried it to the mouth of the cave and heaved it, tossed it out so that it landed in the minefield. They flinched, waited, but there was still only silence; no mines exploded. Smolder and Lion stood together near the mouth of the cave, out of reach, pistols drawn. Smolder played the flashlight over the minefield. Shemmy lay alone in the dark in his white underwear, oddly bent.

So that when Dani finally announced himself to the Syrians, his moment had passed; it was in the shapeless time that followed the right moment. He'd missed the timing and he had no plan. Unrehearsed, dully, he simply went to take care of a task.

"I'm going out," he told Lion. Lion, grim and shaken, raised his pistol. Someone said, "Don't."

He explained it to the foreigners. "There's no choice now," he told Lion. "I have to get the body. He's married, he has a wife. She's maybe twenty. The body is out there—"

"It's a fucking minefield, Dani! You'll be killed! You don't have to risk—"

"The body is out there unidentified, you see?" he went on, reasonably explaining it to Lion. "If we don't bring it back there'll be no proof that he died. She'll never be able to remarry."

"Dani, don't—"

"She'll be tied forever to an unidentified body. I'm not leaving him out there so that girl can be alone the rest of her life, or so she can remarry and have a kid anyway and the kid is a bastard. There'll be no more bastards. It's enough."

Smolder said something. Lion flipped the safety. "You can kill me," Dani said evenly. "But then every one of these men is going to go out there after me and you'll have no choice but to let them go or try to kill them all, and either way you lose your hostages. I give you my word I'll come back. I give my *men* my word. Think about it, man. If you lose us, what happens? Your guys find you here alone, they'll shoot you for deserters. They find you with bodies, they'll ask why you're hiding out and *then* they'll shoot you for deserters. *Our* guys find you here alone with our dead bodies out there . . . well, this is war, right?"

He waited for Lion to explain it to Smolder. Smolder expostulated. There was a brief exchange. No one actually said anything to Dani; both men trained their pistols on Dani's men and Dani stepped out of the cave.

Just like that he was outside in the night. The open space, the air in motion, the random outdoor night sounds held him still a moment. Free. Except for the wavering circle of light from Smolder's flashlight that pinned him, and the bent white figure waiting twenty-five paces from where he stood. All right, Shemmy, here I come.

You couldn't see the mines, of course. The ground was scrubby, flat and innocent, and beyond the faint spill of Smolder's flashlight, it was black. He felt himself poised, straight and whole. He put one light foot out, lent it weight, found solid ground unmined, gave it his whole weight, one step forward. He had a pace to keep; people were watching. One more foot, easy in the dark, Shemmy, go lightly, pull your weight up into yourself and away from the unpredictable ground; just touch, just touch, use the darkness, move easy in the dark—

They see him move easy as daylight over the treacherous layer, hopscotch lightly from spot to spot and never break his easy rhythm, two steps, three, and then the flash blinds them, they hear the ragged crack and boom, and through white dazzle they see Dani flung up by the seat, earth fragments following him, Dani dropped, earth raining down, Dani lying still in sudden dark like a curtain overlaid by phantom eyeflashes of light.

Quick crack, flash and dazzle, Lion and Smolder are blinking, caught blind in the explosion. Zadok hurls himself at Smolder, who clings to the pistol, but it isn't the pistol Zadok's after, it's the flashlight dangling from a slack hand. Zadok's going by Dani's coded instructions: "I will make the darkness bright before them." Zadok understood: *use the flashlight, dazzle them,* so now he plays it into their faces.

Lion and Smolder paw the air, shouting; before they can charge, Bloch tackles Smolder, there's a scuffle, Lion turns, firing, hits Oded and is caught sideways by Lev, who leaps at him and for once lands right. Lion falls. Nissim dives for Lion's pistol, wrenches it from his hand, and fires once, missing. Lion is on his knees, rising, and Nissim, on his feet, fires again coldly downward into Lion and turns to Smolder, tangled with Bloch on the ground—

"No, don't," Lev says.

—and shoots, coldly, missing Bloch and stilling Smolder. He shoots again into Lion's body and again into Smolder's, and again.

Zadok plays the flashlight around the cave, picking up Smolder, dead; Bloch staggering to his feet; Lev; Oded clutching his bloodied arm; Nissim still coiled, pistol cocked; Lion, blood flowing from his mouth. He clicks off the flashlight and they listen to Lion die.

Tel Aviv, Friday morning, October 19

"What does this mean, *missing?*"

"Missing in action, Mrs. Kovner, in the Golan."

"Captured? Lost communication? Unidentified body? What?"

"Simply missing. We have no reports from the Syrians; they haven't released names of prisoners, but he was with an advance force, and when the helicopter got free to pick them up, there was no sign of them. We've checked the rendezvous over and over; we'll keep checking. There's a lot of action in the area. Just as soon as we know—"

Simply missing. Dead somewhere or someone had him, *they* had him. The codes coming through the office were useless, no information was coming in at all about prisoners; it was all troop movements and supply lines. Still she prowled the office all day, saying nothing but scanning copy for word from the Syrians. "Everything all right?" someone asked her. Wartime discretion.

"Fine," she said. "Everything's fine."

When they had all left for the day and the nighttime skeleton crew were engrossed on the other side of the room, she phoned Degania. It took an endless time for them to get Rivka to the phone, then additional fumbling moments before she heard her mother's voice. She felt herself ready to cry, release. "Dani's missing," she said. "In the Golan. In Syria, actually, I think."

There was a moment, then a little strangled sound, then a whispered, high-pitched "No" and breath after breath assaulted Rachaeli. Her mother was crying. "Alik is fallen in Suez, and Gidi and Ran, also in Golan," Rivka was saying brokenly. "And now this. It's too much, too much."

Also in Golan. All the children belong to you, Rachaeli thought, stilled by rage. You grieve for all the children, don't you; they all belong to you.

"Don't cry for Dani, Rivka. He isn't dead. I'll call when I hear."

She hardly thought where she was going, so that when she got to the concert hall she had to organize her thoughts. Yes, the woman told her, they were in town, in fact there was a concert tonight, tickets still available, the Bruckner . . . no, not until eight . . . well, perhaps in the dressing room or backstage.

In fact he was on stage when she found him, tuning up. He has a right to know, she prodded herself, and she stood in front of him until he looked up.

Yossi looked up, thinking it was Karin. Rachaeli Kovner stood looking down at him, waiting. His first thought was that she looked old. There were lines pulling downward from her nostrils to the corners of her mouth, and her hair was shot through with gray. Still good-looking, though, still in there. His second thought was that she had a message for him, she was vibrating with it. His third thought was that he didn't want to hear it.

"How are you," she said briskly. "I have to tell you something."

"Sit down. I'm as you see me, aging but fine. They've left me out of this one."

"This . . . ?"

"War." He smiled ruefully. "Too old."

"Mmm. You're not exactly out of it. Yossi—" She put a hand on his knee. Her face assumed a look of . . . tenderness? Pity? What the hell, was she going to cry? "Remember the boy? Dani?"

"Of course. How—"

He heard talk in the back of the hall. People were beginning to filter in. She was having trouble delivering her message. "He—you were right, you know." That was significant, obviously; she waited.

"About what?"

"You said he was yours, you knew it as soon as I was pregnant, and you were right. Dani is your son. You really knew it."

"No, you told me he was—"

"But you saw—"

"No."

"He's just like you. Beautiful. Black, curly hair—remember?—and the same grin." She blinked over a fixed smile. She was going to cry. He put a hand on her arm, to turn them both away from the people who were settling in around them, talking and tuning up.

"Yossi, he's missing in action. In the Golan, since Wednesday."

"Oh, Rachaeli, I'm sorry. Tch. It must be . . . but listen, there'll be a cease-fire today or tomorrow; it's a question of hours now. You'll have him back. Don't cry. Are you crying?"

"No. I'm sorry to do this just before a concert, but you had a right to know. Will you be all right?"

What? Will he be . . . he didn't understand the question, and Karin was coming toward them. Rachaeli was sitting in her chair. He stood and held out a hand, so she had to get up. "Sure, don't worry about it," he said. "Will you stay for the concert?"

"Want me to?"

"Sure, it always helps to have a friendly audience." He grinned, then remembered. "Listen, don't worry about your boy. He's tough, like you; he'll be okay. Anything I can do . . ."

She looked at him, shaking her head with theatrical bitter amusement. "Nothing you can do. See you."

What did she expect? He remembered the boy. Cute, showoff; they'd played the crab duet; he'd had a pretty good ear, sloppy fingering. Yossi smiled. He'd fathered a kid; that kid with the magic tricks and the violin was his son. He couldn't connect, though, with a grown man missing in the Golan. How was he supposed to do that?

Later. He cleared his mind and laid a loving hand on his cello. It was only rough tuned and he'd have to hurry, now, with the fine tuning. He closed his eyes to listen for the minute discrepancies.

Rachaeli covered ground, her high heels biting pavement, long strides putting it behind her. She held her hair off her neck with one hand, held the useless coin tightly in the other. She wasn't going to take any bus; she couldn't sit in a bus. It hurt to breathe; she could feel the rawness in her chest and there was no place to fit the air, because of the fear and the rage, but she drank great gulps of air anyway, forcing it past rage, past fear: *get out of my way*. Sweat rolled down her temples, along her sides and down her legs; she rubbed at it impatiently. People stared. Let them. Let them see how it looks.

In Chava's darkened hallway she was suddenly stilled, grounded. She wiped her face and closed her eyes and gave up on taking in air. Everything slowed. She pulled herself up the stairs and rang the bell and waited.

Shlomo opened the door, putting her off stride. She stood blinking in the white light, but Chava came up behind him and she delivered herself to Chava. "Dani is missing," she said.

Chava said nothing at all, put strong arms around her and held firm and then it was easy, Rachaeli cried.

Sunday, October 21, early morning

"Morphine!"

  . . . .

  . . . .

  . . . .

"Now pick him up. Easy! *Easy*, will you—"

He feels something grip his ankles, his armpits. Searing pain shoots his leg and he slides sideways, fast into darkness.

———————

They were overflying the area and they saw the light, wrong spot and wrong flashlight code but near enough. They came in close and saw the bizarre group, chanced a landing.

What they saw first was four men standing sentry in a ragged square outside a cave in their underwear. One had the flashlight. Two bloody bodies in Syrian uniforms lay nearby and another body in underwear lay out in the field. Then, within the square the four standing sentries made, they saw a fifth who sat on the ground and cradled a sixth in his arms, both in their underwear. The sixth man was wounded, losing blood from his leg, unconscious or dead. Maybe dead because the boy who held him was crying.

"He's bad," one of the four standing men said, gesturing toward the bleeding one. They were Israeli. The one doing the talking was a Sephardi, dark. "You got a medic?" he demanded. "His leg, he's lost a lot of blood, shock. And he's burned. We've got another one hurt— Oded?—see, his arm, not so bad, and then you'll have to hover over the field so we can get Shemmy"—he pointed—"it's a minefield, we'll have to get him from above. I can do that . . ."

He went on, babbling orders in his underwear, but he was a good man; he saw to it that the men were settled in the 'copter and the medic got onto the wounded, then he hung down off the ladder by one arm and dangled out over the minefield, fishing for his friend's body. It took three passes before he got it and then he was too exhausted to carry it up; they had to take it from him. When he got back up into the 'copter, he pulled one set of tags off his neck, extras, leaving one on, and hung them gently around the dead man's neck. Everyone watched him do it, tense, and then relaxed. It was like a ceremony.

———

Noise, clatter, rumbling his bones. His muscles shriek against pressure.

Sliding—

Hands grab him. "We're up." The pressure eases.

He has skin but no insides. A tongue and teeth, no lips. There is a pain somewhere.

Light slants onto his face, flashlight on cunning closed lids. Her skin is apricot in the light, her hair is like ruined leaves, she's crying.

Dying, maybe? Sliding out, me, getting out easy, easy ending.

End of the line. Dead end.

Maybe—he chuckles behind still cheeks and closed eyes, getting away with the secret thought, making no noise in the noisy clatter—maybe I could shoot it from here, last sperm message shooting from me through the sky down into

between those sweet thighs, a stream to fill her, don't cry

beam into her another black-haired curly-haired boy, under his prayer shawl, in the bend of her arm, blessing hand on his black curls, mouth on her hard little nipple, breast pillows his cheek.

Ronit. Me. Ronit.

Take it, Ronit, save me. Save him alive.

Sweet apricot thighs. Whirlpool eyes   I'm coming   hold me   there'll be nothing left of me—

Saturday, October 20

"Do you know where Ronit is?" Chava asks Rachaeli.

"I heard she was here. She flew back with everyone else, the first week. Where she's stationed, I don't know."

"Find out," Chava says. "Call her."

"What for? She's done with him."

"It's not so simple," Chava says with the strange half smile and the gentle tone of a mother hinting to her daughter about love. "It isn't done with so easily. Call her. You don't know what she feels."

She means that having Dani snatched away, imperiled, is different from leaving him or being sent away by him. She means that this brutal pillage might open Ronit to other feelings. She knows something about that.

Rachaeli thinks about what Chava said: It isn't done with so easily. For her it is; a man takes something from you—the one thing you can't let him take, whatever it is—and there is a chill and a turning in you and that's the end of it. But Chava is another kind of woman, Rachaeli knows that; maybe Ronit is, too. There are women who will go on compromising forever.

Dani is missing, it's been three days now. Whenever Rachaeli is alone panic seizes her. She has gone to Chava, and Chava has done what she could—went out shopping with Rachaeli, made her stay for dinner. This morning Rachaeli napped at Chava's because she's had trouble sleeping, and somehow when Chava was there, she could sleep. But Chava can't be there all the time—she has Shlomo and her mother and the cronies—and besides, Chava doesn't really share it; Dani wasn't hers, and she has her own grief. No one shares this with Rachaeli.

If Ronit still loves Dani, then she'll be afraid, too, with Rachaeli. They can be afraid together.

Ronit has a right to know, Chava says. That doesn't register with Rachaeli at all. But she makes a call to someone she knows in Deployment and finds Ronit easily.

No woman loved Aaron, Chava is thinking, watching Rachaeli make her phone call. She'll never be able to unthink it now; she'll have to grieve for that, too, another unfinished piece of Aaron.

It is one day between the time Ronit gets the first call from Rachaeli and the time that Chava calls to tell her that he's found, he's wounded, they've brought him home to Rambam Hospital in Haifa. As it turns out, she can't be with Rachaeli at all during that one day of waiting; she's helping out at the hospital in Tel Aviv and they're receiving the stabilized wounded from the border hospitals for special surgery. One after another, the stiff white packages arrive—boys and men wrapped, splinted, taped, and doped. Only the blood oozing through the bandages and the sounds that escape them seem alive.

All that long day she pictures Dani dead. She sees him lying crumpled. His beard has grown in a little as she imagines it, and he's filthy and his body lies uneasy at the strange angle, but he looks very young and simply asleep, not like the grotesque bodies she sees around her. She keeps seeing that image of him crumpled and still, though, and she wants urgently to move him, straighten his body so that he lies comfortably. She wants to pass a hand over his face and touch his lips. She wants to lie right up next to him and pull his arm around her so he can warm her. No, so she can warm him. She can't think of him dead.

Damn him, she doesn't care, dead or missing. She presumes that he went dancing out into the limelight and drew someone's fire, couldn't bear to be unnoticed. She remembers his army fantasy—bright lights, flash and dazzle, savior of his men—and she can see him doing it. He would, he'd do it, and he'd write the headline himself: BASTARD LEGITI- MATED IN DEATH. Damn him, God damn him, he would do it to make the point.

But missing. Missing means captured, held by the Syrians. She presses her eyes closed, shutting out the pictures of torture, and she sings a popular song in her mind, verse by verse, to keep from thinking and to make a rhythm to breathe by. There are too many things she can't think about, and the worst of them is loving him. She's going to have to sing every song she ever knew, to keep it all out.

He opens his eyes a little and he sees Rachaeli sitting at the end of the bed. He's somewhere . . . a hospital? It's quiet, no artillery. Everything is momentarily very sharp and clear: the pain, Rachaeli, the quiet, the door beyond Rachaeli. He isn't interested in anything except the pain. Rachaeli has taken a clipboard off the end of the bed and she's reading what's on it. She looks drawn and tired, old. Someone comes in—a nurse—and remonstrates with her for reading the chart.

Rachaeli stands up. For a moment across the pain he feels the old danger of her, the charge and spark, and he focuses warily.

"I'm all he has in the world," he hears her saying. "You think I'm going to leave it to chance, what happens to him? If I don't see that he's taken care of, who will?"

The nurse takes the clipboard out of Rachaeli's hand. "I will," she says, kindly enough. "And the surgeon and the O.R. team."

"Well, where the hell are they?"

"In surgery, working on other boys who have mothers waiting." She puts a hand on Rachaeli's shoulder. "There are boys out there blinded, legs blown off. This one is going to be fine. They'll get to him as fast as they can."

"The fever—"

"They all have fever. It's the trauma." She replaces the clipboard and walks out.

He drifts off, then is recalled by a strange noise. It's Rachaeli, crying in a thin little whine that sounds as though it comes from behind clenched teeth. She looks small, she sounds small. She's just somebody's mother. He tucks the thought into a fold of the fever, keeping it for later.

An unfinished vagrant thought teases him awake. He hunts for it, worries it out of the fog. *I'm all he has. I'm all he has.* He loses it, finds it again, comes at last to the other part of the thought: *Whose fault is that, Mother? You wanted it that way.* But it's pale, it's just words. He waits for the feeling, but it doesn't come. He isn't angry. She's just somebody's mother. He lets go and spirals back into the fever, easy release.

———

It's Chava, not Rachaeli, who calls to tell Ronit that Dani is found, he's wounded and burned, they've brought him to Rambam Hospital, he's waiting for surgery on his leg.

"Is he conscious?"

"Feverish, but he can talk to you."

Talk to her. Suddenly, because it's all possible—he's alive, he's here

and not in a Syrian camp, she could go to see him, he could talk to her—
she is enraged. "Thank you for letting me know," she says crisply. "Tell
him I'm glad he's all right."

"You tell him yourself. His mother told him you were here and he's
asking to see you," Chava lies boldly, knowing that it's unlikely that
Rachaeli has mentioned Ronit to Dani. That it's a lie is incidental. She
woke up knowing she had to take care of it. She lays a hand lightly on her
stomach now, and thinks of her dream. Last night, for the first time since
they came bringing word of Aaron's death, she didn't dream of him
trapped and burning. She dreamed of him alive—just briefly, just a
snapshot, Aaron whole and alive—and of a baby at her breast. In her
dream the baby was Dani and he was hot and squirmy, crying penetrating, broken screams until she put him to her breast. She was cool and she
cooled him, soothed him, and then she realized that it was Aaron she was
soothing and she was so glad; she willed the heat into her own body and
cooled him so that he stopped screaming and lay easy; and her relief then,
her dream gladness, felt as though it would stretch forward into time a
long, long way. When she woke up she cradled the dream in her consciousness, fixing it there, and she remembered the first day of Dani's life
when she got him by mistake and she did nurse him, and she decided to
call Ronit. Dani is burned, too, and his leg is badly hurt and it's foolish to
think that the girl will make any difference in the pain. That's one of
those things you dream. But she doesn't want him to be alone. It's
important to her that Dani not be alone.

Ronit hangs up and pulls at her hair with both hands. Alive. Wants to
see her. Feverish. Hurt. Alive. Calls her in like a hat check. Oh God
damn him, alive and hurt. It could be anger or fear or relief she feels. She
calls it anger and rides it all the way to the hospital in Haifa.

In the early morning, Shlomo arrives at the hospital. Rachaeli takes
the opportunity to go downstairs for a cup of coffee. "He won't say much;
he's barely conscious," she tells Shlomo. "They tell me they're just about
ready to take him upstairs. Finally."

Dani is worn and light-headed; they've given him Demerol. The pain
hovers just above his leg and circles the burns on his chest and neck, but
doesn't connect. Shlomo pulls a chair up beside the bed and sits close to
Dani.

"How are you?" he asks softly, leaning in.

"Okay." The answer seems to come a long time after the question. He thinks he could speed it up, make the effort to answer more quickly, but he knows he doesn't have to, with Shlomo. Shlomo will wait. In the long interval the thought he has been trying to catch comes up to the surface. It's a bad thought.

"I couldn't do it," he tells Shlomo. "I got them into a mess. I left them—"

"Your men? They said you kept them alive. They said you made them stick together and that got them through it."

"No, I—"

"They said you figured the plan to get them out, created a diversion so they could—"

"No." He waves his hand. "I just got blown up and I left them to . . ." He sees Shemmy suddenly, faceless on the scruffy earth. He pushes the picture away and it drifts off, not far. "Is anyone alive?"

"All of them."

"Not Shemmy."

"No, all the others."

"Zadok?"

"Fine. He carried you out of the minefield."

He thinks about it. He doesn't understand. "But then didn't he . . . is he hurt?"

"No. You'd already tripped the mine; he followed your path in and out. He's very pleased with himself. He feels like a hero."

"I should have saved them."

"They saved themselves. You should be proud."

There is a long interval, humming with silence. Shlomo doesn't understand, Dani thinks in the silence. Shemmy bobs back, still dead, still bent. His face is blown away, there's a black pulp where— Dani makes a little sound in his throat, trying to blot out the picture: not now. Not yet.

Shlomo stands up and leans over him. "I have to go," he says. "They told me only a minute." He puts a hand on either side of Dani's face and kisses his forehead. The boy is burning. "You did the right thing," he says. "I'm proud of you."

Moving with dreamy slowness, Dani puts a hand over Shlomo's hand, secures it against his cheek. Tethered, he closes his eyes and lets the Demerol float him. The pain floats with him, suspended. He lets his hand drop and some time later Shlomo leaves.

He's heavy. Something is sitting on him, pressing him down into the ground with enormous weight. It hurts. He opens his eyes to protest. "Hey," he begins.

"Hey." She's standing between him and the light.

"Will you get it off? It hurts."

She looms over him. Ronit, it's Ronit. He lurches awake.

"The cast? I can't get it off," she says. "Is it bad? I'll get the nurse."

"Ronit."

"Yes. Hi."

"Did I . . . are you pregnant?" He tries to sit up.

"No. Shh."

He thinks about it. "I dreamed it," he says. "Are you going away?"

"I went away. I'm back because of the war. You had surgery; they fixed your leg. Do you remember?"

The war. The cave. Shemmy. Zadok and all of them. Shemmy, my God. It all falls into place, heavy gray pieces. But bright and alive in the front of his mind is his morphine dream and he has to tell it to her, get it clearly to her. He tugs her arm so she has to sit down on the edge of the bed, but he lingers deliberately in half-sleep, a satellite beaming her the picture from the place of the dream. His eyes are hooded, his voice throaty with sleep. "Listen," he says.

"I was on the thing . . . stretcher . . . helicopter, coming home, and I was dying." He sneaks a look at her. She's listening. "I felt myself going, slipping across, and it felt like, you know, like making love. Like the end when I would let it go, freefall, let it all go into you. And I thought . . . I saw myself way up there and you way down, floating along way below, and I saw myself coming." His hand describes a long, dreamy arc downward from his groin. "I wanted to come; I thought the come would find you, shoot into you, I could ride it into you and be safe."

It has the easy flow of a dream; he's telling her everything, like a child or like someone in a dream. At the same time he knows that he's taking liberties and taking chances. He remembers that she left him, and he's talking as though he didn't. He has to, or she'll move away.

She is very still. She doesn't say anything.

There's nothing between him and the heavy gray pieces, now that he's told it to her. He remembers what he thought about in the lucid hours before surgery. It's urgent, suddenly: he has to tell Ronit.

"Shemmy's dead," he tells her.

"I know."

"For nothing." He looks at her. "Because of me."

"Don't say that."

"No, it is. It's only because of me. I had to go charging into that cave, great hero—took Zadok, threw him into the war, almost got him killed—and Shemmy did get himself killed and it was because of me. Because I made such a goddamned issue of it."

"Of what?"

"Of being a bastard. Shemmy knew—he was the only one who did for a long time—and he never told anyone because he was so horrified. I made sure that he was horrified; I made sure that he pitied me. He could never forget that my mother was . . . that she made me illegitimate."

"But—"

"I was going to take on the Syrian, I was ready, but then he said this thing to me." Dani says it quietly, just like the Syrian: "'*Bondouk*. Bastard son of a whoring mother.' And it was true and Shemmy knew it. So he . . . I'd been shamed, so he had to jump the guy. And the Syrian shot—it was supposed to be me, I planned it—but Shemmy jumped him and the Syrian shot his face off. Right into his face. He was dead in a second and thrown away because the Syrian said 'Bastard.' The biggest thing about me was that I *was* a bastard. Right? Rub everyone's face in it, never let them forget the innocent victim. *How do you do, I'm Dani Kovner, the bastard; no one is outcast like I'm outcast.* For that he died. For nothing."

"You fool."

"That's what I'm telling you—"

"You're a *fool*. You missed the point, as usual. Shemmy didn't die because you're a bastard. They all knew that by now, didn't they—you never let anyone forget it—but it was only Shemmy who jumped the Syrian. He died because you were family. You were his brother, part of his kin, and the Syrian attacked you, so he went to get him back. He loved you." She looks defiantly at him. "You take a terrified Yemenite, he's ashamed in front of everyone because he's afraid of the dark, right? Right?"

"Yes." He doesn't know what to do with the anger. It was turned on Rachaeli first, and then on the system, and then on the Syrians, but the Syrians are gone now. Finally he turned it on himself and now she's going to tear it away, peel it off and leave bloody, burning flesh. She can't. She can't. He turns it on her. *You left me,* he hurls silently at her.

"—and you buck him up, give him courage. More than that, you give him face. They respect him. Everyone—Sephardim, Ashkenazim, everyone. He respects himself. You help him to stay in the paratroopers and he makes a man of himself and he isn't ashamed. He *loves* you."

You left me. So stay away, shut up, shut up—

"So he's in the cave. It's *dark,* right? And he's in the hands of the Syrians—all his worst fears: armed Arabs, himself helpless again, darkness—and they attack his brother and he jumps. He doesn't even think or stop to be afraid. He—"

Dani is crying.

"He loved you."

After a minute she leans over and touches her cheek to his face and cradles his head with her hand. Her hair blocks out the light and her cheek and her hand and her body blanket him lightly, not moving. It's all torn away now, a fearful loss, and he cries—at first hard, racketing cries and then freely like a child, and then slowing, easing.

She sits up, her hair sliding across his face. She's watching him, waiting. She knows there's more.

"He's out there in Syria in a minefield, in his underwear," he says brokenly. "No face, no tags. I couldn't even get him out. His wife will never—"

"They got him out."

"Who?"

"Nissim, all of them. The funeral was today. I went. He had his tags. And the Syrians are dead. They killed them both."

"Who did?"

"I don't know. All of them, I guess."

"I should have done it. I got them into it; I didn't want anyone else getting hurt."

"Limelighter."

"What?"

"Nothing, I'm sorry."

"'Limelighter,' you said?"

"Playing for the audience, making the big gesture. I'm sorry, I shouldn't have—"

"No, you're right. You're right. But never again, Ronit; I'll never do it again."

Yes you will, she thinks, loving him. You always will. She wants to touch him but instead she hands him a tissue.

He turns his head as far as the dressing on his neck will allow and closes his eyes behind the tissue. He calls up the picture of Shemmy bent carelessly in the minefield in his white underwear. He concentrates, lifts Shemmy out, transports him to a coffin, one of those pine boxes for the war dead. He lays him out straight and clean in the coffin, wrapped in his prayer shawl, and he gives him his tags. Tears seep hot onto his cheeks, different tears now, easier.

"How are you doing? I've got to check a few things."

It's the nurse. He wipes his face and blows his nose.

"You'll have to go out for a while," the nurse tells Ronit.

She stands up. The bed resettles around him, heavy center. "Don't go away," he says.

"No, all right."

But when she walks back in, he's wary, collected. She went away, then she suddenly appeared and he spilled it all. More than likely she'll leave again. "How was New York?" he asks quickly, brightly, to hold her off.

She gets it right away; her eyes widen briefly, but she answers in kind. "All right. Good food. A lot of variety. A hundred varieties of everything."

"A nice life."

"No. I was afraid all the time. It's not a safe place, you know."

They both glance at the huge cast on his leg at the same moment, and they laugh.

"You know what I mean."

"Yes. This *is* a safe place. Safe enough. It has to be; there's nowhere else to go if it isn't. I thought about it in the cave: if we don't hold this country together, there is no place. You know? You might like living in America, but you can only do it if we keep this place for you to run to when there's trouble."

"I don't want to live in America. I never wanted to."

"You went."

"You wanted me to go."

It's all said too fast, shocking them both. They stare at each other.

"You wanted to prove something, make a point," she says. "To spite them or yourself, or something. You pushed me away."

"So did you replace me?"

"You pushed me away," she repeats.

368

"Did you?"

"No." And then, defying him: "Not yet."

She hasn't sat down or moved toward him. She stands at the foot of the bed, out of reach and angry now. The anger is more intimate and more trustworthy than her touch on his face or her body blanketing him while he cried. He knows, old certainty, that if he kissed her now she would tense her body against him, but her lips would be hot. The whole length of his body lies between them, the cast blocking her midsection. He doesn't feel the bad leg, but the stitches on the other leg are drawing, and the burns on his chest and neck are beginning to prick through the painkiller haze. He is alive.

"Come over here," he says. "I can't reach you."

She just stares.

"Please."

She comes to stand over him.

"Please sit; I can't see you."

She sits.

"You want to know what I really thought about, in the helicopter?"

"What?"

"I thought everything I told you—but what I was shooting into you was a baby. I thought—I can still see it so clearly—I thought, *Save me, Ronit, save a part of me.* I could see him at your breast."

She's listening hard.

"It looked so . . . you should have seen him. You were naked, his eyes were closed, he was curled there at your breast—"

"What did he look like?"

"Like me." He looks away from her for a moment, to see it again. "He *was* me," he says then.

She closes her eyes.

"We're never going to have that, Ronit."

"I know."

"I'm never leaving this country."

"I know."

"And I can't keep you from having it."

"Yes you can."

"No, I—"

"Ask me," she whispers. "Ask me not to go." Her eyes, whirlpool eyes, are fixed on his. The skin on his chest prickles and burns, the cast presses hard against his leg and between them, life stirs in his body. It's hot. The skin of him is burning, blistering, lifting off. Pulsing too fast in his throat

369

and behind his eyes, in his mouth and belly and thighs, is Ronit. He silently pulls in deep, inflating draughts of air to feed the pulse until it steadies, a regular, thudding beat. It's making great demands on him. He can't stop now.

"Live with me," he says. "Don't go anywhere."

She nods slowly, half-time to his breathing.

Rachaeli comes in after work. He's at the end of the hall, in his walker for the first time, and he watches her swing down toward him, flowered skirt furling against one leg and then the other, blouse open and white against her skin. She's holding a bunch of flowers from a street vendor.

He is irritated at her flamboyance. Why doesn't she cut her hair? She's too old, her hair's half gray and still she wears it loose, maidenlike. Her feet, bare in the sandals, are knotted with raised veins and the painted toenails are ridiculous, but she walks—covers ground swinging—like a girl.

"You're up!" She thrusts the flowers at him.

He tightens his grip on the walker and takes a step. "I have no hands free," he says. It's true; he's holding on to his cage fiercely, afraid to put any weight on the leg, reluctant even to straighten it.

Two men walk out of a room across the hall, a doctor and a civilian. He feels it come alive in her: she's onstage. She reaches up and tugs at the back of his hair, smiling. "You need a haircut," she says, playing to the men. The doctor's eye is caught. He watches them. Dani looks down, hitches along, one more step.

"You've got to come down on the leg," the doctor says. "That's a walker, not crutches. *Walk* in it." He strides over. "You'll have to move," he says briskly to Rachaeli. "Come on, boy, let's see a step."

He puts the foot down and rests his weight on it for a second, steps heavily down on the other.

"More."

Another step.

"*Weight* on it, let's *go*."

Another. The pain shoots through his leg right up into his teeth but he goes on, the walker clanking on the linoleum. They pass by Rachaeli, who is standing against the wall, flowers dangling frm her hand, watching the two of them. He feels sorry for her, fleetingly, but he has no time to think about it because it's time to bear down on the hurt leg again and that takes all his concentration.

"Shrapnel?" the doctor asks, distracting him.

"Minefield. My own stupid fault."

"You didn't plant the mine, did you?"

"No." Rachaeli is out of sight.

"Then it isn't your fault, is it? Forget that crap. It's a waste of time, blame. Want to turn around?"

"Okay."

They turn and head back down the hall. He aims toward Rachaeli, a place to stop and let up.

Potasnik goes to the hospital to see Dani. Dani is walking slowly up and down the halls, therapy. Potasnik walks with him.

"It hurts?"

"Yeah."

"It'll heal up, you'll be running around with the notebook in no time. Have a look at me—this is my *regular* walk."

They laugh. "How's Anni?" Dani asks.

"She has her days. A lot of times she doesn't know anybody."

"Does she know about the war?"

"Sometimes. She forgets. She goes traveling around in time, we don't have the itinerary." He shrugs. "Sometimes she talks to the husband— you know, in Hungary? Poor guy, how she talks to him he's better off dead. Some woman she is. Some woman."

Dani stops walking. "I want to tell you something, Potasnik. Remember the time of the Eichmann trial, we listened to the radio all the time?"

"Sure I remember. She was all right then."

Potasnik is only half listening; he is reminding himself not to let it slip to Dani about Aaron—two boys raised together like brothers, Potasnik thinks mournfully. Let Dani get well, then they'll tell him—so he misses the drift of what Dani is telling him. Something about a cave.

"—when it clicked. They were just two asshole Syrians, you know? But there we were, isolated—no one knew where we were—and they had the guns. At first they didn't do anything too bad, I thought—took our clothes, cut the food rations way back. But then one of them almost raped a kid and they really started threatening us, and they began to separate us—no talking, they offered food to one of us if he'd be their ears, you know?"

"Yah. I know."

"*Right*, see? So I'm lying on the ground and it clicks; I see it clearly all of a sudden. *This is how it happens*, I think. First they strip you, take away your dignity and your identity, then they abuse and humiliate you, then they terrorize you, and finally they use some of you against the others. Suddenly I thought, This is a pattern. I've heard all this before. Two more days of this and we'll be destroyed, dehumanized, and then they'll think nothing of killing us off. Just like the Nazis. You see, Potasnik?"

Potasnik makes a sound.

"So I thought, There's more of us than them; we've got to stand up together right away, or we're going to die." He's all fired up. He stands leaning on the walker with one hand and gesticulating with the other.

Potasnik never thinks about Auschwitz any more. It's over, let it be over. Now he flinches at the absurdity of the boy's comparison. But listen, at least they learned something from it, he thinks. At least the boy came out alive.

"You taught me, Potasnik."

"Some lousy lesson," Potasnik says.

Ramat Gan, early December 1973

Chava looks around the apartment, agitated, waiting for Dani. There's clear, bright daylight coming in and she spots a white blur on the mirror over the couch. Soap, probably, left from the mourning week when they soaped over all the mirrors. She takes off her shoes and stands on the couch, leaning over Anni to reach to the edge of the mirror; might as well polish the whole thing. Anni doesn't stir. Chava is careful about how she reaches, because she is pregnant.

No one knows it, not even Shlomo. She's going to tell him very soon; anyway, he'd ask because she's just missed her second period. He'll be glad of that—no periods for the next seven months. She smiles. Forty-one years old; it's ridiculous, really, except that this one is special. There can be no question of aborting; it's all caught up with Aaron, somehow, and with the night Shlomo told her the story.

He's never told her another story—probably he never will—but it doesn't matter. And now encoded in the tiny organism in her womb is the linkage of stories his cells told hers in the single instant: one about enduring color of iris; one about gender; one about height and handspan; one about a certain quirk of mind, even one about potential length of days. In July there will be a new set of givens in the random world. She knows exactly when, she thinks, because she knows the moment of its conception.

She has never flung herself at Shlomo again, either, but she waits some nights, conscious of waiting, conscious of her swelling breasts and of him growing restless beside her; and when they make love, something is different. It's not possible for them to mention it and there are no out-landish innovations, but there is the way she encloses him and the linger-ing, the slowness of it, and the way they lie together in the quiet before they disentangle. She never conjures up the cave any more. In fact she doesn't think of Anni at those times at all, or of Aaron or of anything. She thinks it's the same for Shlomo and that perhaps he has turned to her especially on the days he's been to see Dani at the hospital, for example.

She hasn't seen Dani. They didn't tell him about Aaron until he was ready to leave the hospital, and she couldn't face him until he knew.

Chava doesn't understand, will never understand how near a thing it was with Shlomo. Rachaeli knows it. She saw it for herself.

Rachaeli went to Haifa alone to see Dani when they brought him there; she didn't even tell anyone he was found and returned to the hospital until she'd seen him for herself, but then she called and left a message at Degania for Rivka, and she called Chava. Early in the morning, before it was even light, Shlomo arrived at the hospital. She was glad enough to see him, actually; she needed a break and they were understaffed at the damned hospital, so that she was unwilling to leave Dani alone. It wouldn't matter who was there with him; he'd been intermittently unconscious and the rest of the time he was dazed and uncommunicative. But then as she left and Shlomo approached the bed, she caught on his face the stunned agony one sees in hospital corridors and at military funerals—the look of one whose beloved has been snatched away or hovers suddenly over the abyss—and in a flash she knew that that look had nothing to do with Aaron. She understood, finally, that it was Shlomo she should have been wary of. She and Chava had been deceived; the man bore a secret, father's love for Dani. Chava would never have seen it—she hadn't Rachaeli's sixth sense of the waxing and waning of loyalty—and Rachaeli had no intention of telling her. It was between Shlomo and herself.

Rachaeli couldn't know that it was already a dead issue; Chava without understanding had done the one possible redemptive thing. She had closed around Shlomo, demanded, claimed his manhood when both of them were raw and open. He would still love Dani, even with a father's love, but his focus had shifted to Chava, a subtle, undiscussed, irreversible shift.

And then Dani would open his eyes just before surgery and take in the room and feel for his body and ask for Ronit. So there it was: a dead issue; there was no holding him after all.

He's outside in the amazing world, alive, and this afternoon he's going to go to Ronit's where they'll close the door and he'll take her to lie down on a bed he's never seen. There have been days in the hospital when he was wild to make love, restless and hot, but today all he can think about is

---

bringing her back to him. He knows her; she's smiling and soft, and she seems to be her old self, but something in her is afraid and still closed to him. She doesn't even know it, but then she doesn't remember how her face looks when she's really open to him. He does remember. She says, jokingly, that she'll have to go easy with him because he's still healing. He knows that she's still healing, too. She's keeping him away from the raw places. He doesn't know what he'll have to do to bring her back, but he knows that he'll have to go to dangerous lengths himself to do it, and he's afraid. He's more afraid of being without her, though, so he has no choice.

But first he has this to do: he has to see Chava.

Haim walks to Chava's with him. The boy's pace is too fast for Dani, but Dani keeps up until, pressed to his limit, he barks at the boy, who then contritely slows his pace to a maddening, deliberate invalid's-side processional. He chatters on about Franklin's Still-Water trick. Dani has trouble attending; he's lost interest in magic. He has no patience for timing, distraction, plastic devices, hidden strings, when everything he sees on this walk is so intense, things come up so wonderfully unexpectedly. That's probably just an invalid's re-entry, though.

And Aaron is dead, who was always there. What will he say to Chava? Does she hate him because he's alive? It was Aaron who had the future. They hadn't much to say to each other recently, he and Aaron. Will she expect him to cry? Will she cry, and what can he say to her?

But Chava is holding out her arms, even smiling. There's a big sign on the front door—WELCOME HOME DANI—and inside over the couch the mirror is festooned with a chain of colored paper links. Anni sits formally under the mirror, looking out of place, a dignitary in a rowdy scene. One end of the paper chain has come loose and dangles down, and she is absently playing with it.

". . . Aaron," Dani says, cheek to cheek with Chava. It's easier not looking at her.

"Poor Dani," she says. "I know. Do you know you were born minutes apart?"

Of course he knows. He can't remember a time when he didn't know.

Chava says how well he looks, how well he's walking, then casts around for something else to say. She could tell him that she's pregnant, but she remembers not to flaunt that before him, a man doomed to childlessness. If they talk about Aaron she'll cry, and Dani has had

enough; he shouldn't have to go through any more. "Come in. Come, Haim, have a cookie," she says finally.

Anni saves the day. She spots Haim. "Come over here," she orders. "What's that you're wearing? Where is your tie?"

He stands before her so she can look him over.

"Get your tie, please. You're not going out like that." She's switched to Hungarian. She beckons commandingly. He bends over. She pulls at his shirt, tries to push it into his pants with her knobby, bent fingers. He looks at Dani.

"It's not Jacob, Mother. It's Dani's boy, Haim. Speak Hebrew."

"Stand up straight. Stay with me. You hear? Stay with me."

The boy doesn't understand the Hungarian.

"Say you'll get your tie," Dani prompts him.

The boy backs away a little. "Want to see me make a tie appear, Anni?"

Anni doesn't answer. Haim goes to his satchel anyway, and pulls out some colored paraphernalia. He shrugs into his windjacket, hunches over, comes up smiling. "Ladies and gentlemen," he says, "your attention please. Pay close attention; things are not always what they seem. The lady wants a tie, I shall produce a tie, a green one." He goes through the trick, pulling out a yellow one, then a blue, finally with a flourish producing the green one tied between the yellow and the blue.

"I know that trick," Anni says in Hebrew. "You had it in your sleeve." She picks up the end of the paper chain again, tears off a link, and begins to make intricate folds in it. Dani sits down beside her and takes her hand.

"Hey, Anni. How are you? It's me, Dani."

"Dani. Dani? Who are your parents?"

"You know my mother, Rachaeli."

He wants to tell her what he learned from her and how it helped him to understand things in the cave, but she is nodding politely, glazed over, lost. She's flickering from time zone to time zone; he can't catch her. What did you expect of her? he thinks ruefully. Suddenly he feels her hand, surprisingly firm, on his head.

"Be a good boy."

He starts at the benediction.

"Be a good boy and take me to my room," she says clearly. "I want to lie down." She drops the folded paper.

"Wait, don't, Dani—you mustn't—"

"She can't weigh anything. Don't worry."

"Haim, help him."

Dani and Haim make a cradle of their hands, and they lift the old woman, stagger a little, adjust. Chava can't help—Anni is out of her hands—but she rushes to straighten her mother's blouse, which is gaping open. The afternoon light catches the diamond on Chava's right hand and throws a prism, a wiry rainbow, back into the mirror which beams it out again, white light to be caught again and refracted. There is no end to it.